ONE KISS IN TOKYO...

BY
SCARLET WILSON

THE COURAGE TO LOVE HER ARMY DOC

BY
KARIN BAINE

D0988450

MILLS
BOON

Scarlet Wilson wrote her first story aged eight and has never stopped. She's worked in the health service for twenty years, trained as a nurse and a health visitor. Scarlet now works in public health and lives on the West Coast of Scotland with her fiancé and their two sons. Writing medical romances and contemporary romances is a dream come true for her.

Karin Baine lives in Northern Ireland with her husband, two sons, and her out-of-control notebook collection. Her mother's and her grandmother's vast collections of books inspired her love of reading and her dream of becoming a Mills & Boon author. Now she can tell people she has a *proper* job! You can follow Karin on Twitter, @karinbaine1, or visit her website for the latest news—karinbaine.com.

ONE KISS IN TOKYO…

BY
SCARLET WILSON

Published in Great Britain 2016
By Mills & Boon, an imprint of HarperCollins*Publishers*
1 London Bridge Street, London, SE1 9GF

© 2016 Scarlet Wilson

ISBN: 978-0-263-91516-7

Our policy is to use papers that are natural, renewable and recyclable products and made from wood grown in sustainable forests. The logging and manufacturing processes conform to the legal environmental regulations of the country of origin.

Printed and bound in Spain
by CPI, Barcelona

Dear Reader,

I absolutely *loved* writing this story set in Tokyo. It gave me a chance to learn about a new country and culture, and also gave me the opportunity to look at the point of view of foreign personnel based there.

My US Air Force base is fictional, but there *are* a number of real US Air Force bases in Japan. I might have stolen a little bit of information from them all!

My heroine, Katsuko, is of mixed race: half-Japanese and half-African-American. Her nickname in Japanese is 'firecracker', and although professionally it might suit her, on a personal level she's a lot less confident than she seems.

It takes a good man like my hero, newcomer Captain Avery Flynn, to recognise the signs and help build my heroine's confidence. He has issues of his own, but spending time with Katsuko helps him realise that he's met someone worth taking a chance on.

I love to hear from readers. Please feel free to contact me via my website, scarlet-wilson.com, or via Facebook or Twitter.

Happy reading!

Love,

Scarlet x

This book is dedicated with thanks to Kay Thomas—
a fellow author—and her son,
who was good enough to help me with my Japanese!

Praise for
Scarlet Wilson

'The book is filled with high-strung emotions,
engaging dialogue, breathtaking descriptions and
characters you just cannot help but love. With
the magic of Christmas as a bonus, you won't be
disappointed with this story!'

—*Goodreads* on
A Touch of Christmas Magic

'*200 Harley Street: Girl from the Red Carpet* is a
fast-paced and feel-good medical romance that
sparkles with red-hot sensuality, mesmerising emotion
and intense passion.'

—*Goodreads*

'I am totally addicted to this author's books. Not once
have I picked up a book by her and felt disappointed or
let down. She creates intense, perfect characters with
so many amazing levels of emotion it blows my mind
time and time again.'

—*Contemporary Romance Reviews* on
Tempted by Her Boss

CHAPTER ONE

THE NOISE HAD CHANGED. The steady drone of the engines had taken on a new pitch. Avery lifted his hat from over his eyes and sat up a little. Every bone in his body ached; muscles he hadn't even known he had were protesting. Three plane journeys over twelve hours would do that to a man. It didn't help that he'd been on duty for twenty-four hours before that.

He'd expected to have a few days' rest before shipping out to Italy from Utah. But plans in the US Air Force often came unstuck.

His orders had changed overnight. A fellow physician who'd been scheduled to come to Japan had been struck down with a mystery illness. So, instead of flying over the boot-shaped coast of Italy, he found himself looking at the emerging coastline of Japan. The change of noise was due to the flaps moving and wheels coming down on the aircraft. His stomach growled loudly and the serviceman sitting next to him gave him a smile and passed over a packet of crisps. They weren't flying on a commercial jet—there were no air hostesses, no bar and no food. They were flying on a military jet and it wasn't exactly built for comfort. Avery couldn't wait to find his accommodation and get his head down for a few hours. Sleep was all he cared about right now.

The plane landed with a bump. He pulled open the packet of crisps and started eating—the quicker he ate the sooner he would get to sleep. The jet took a few minutes to taxi to a halt. The rest of the servicemen were grabbing their packs, ready to disembark.

Avery kept looking outside, trying to get a better feel for the base. It housed nineteen thousand servicemen and servicewomen and contained one of the biggest military hospitals. Set in the outskirts of Tokyo, the base was a home away from home. Most of the staff stayed on-site. There were stores, cafés, schools for the kids, places of worship and even a golf course. The base had been here since the end of the Second World War.

He waited until the rest of the servicemen disembarked before finally grabbing his backpack and walking down the steps of the plane.

The warm air hit him straight away. The base was situated on the coast, and the air was muggy. He could see the metropolis of Tokyo stretching in front of him. He smiled. A whole world he'd never experienced.

He was kind of excited. He'd been stationed in a range of bases all around the world. Normally, he spent a little time finding about where he'd be stationed. Europe. The Middle East. And numerous places around the US. This time around he hadn't had a chance. He'd no idea what he'd find at Okatu.

He followed the rest of the servicemen into the main hangar. Transfer between bases always took a little paperwork. A few were already heading towards the housing department.

Avery sighed and completed his obligatory paperwork and picked up the information sheet on the base. His stomach growled again. There was no way he could sleep until he'd eaten. It made more sense to find something to eat first, then come back and speak to the housing officer to find out where he'd be staying.

He walked out of the building, glanced at his sheet and turned left. He took things slowly, trying to shake off all the aches and pains of travel. The base was huge and during the stroll he passed an elementary school, a middle school, a gymnasium, the officers' club, a travel centre, a few shops and a library. It was a fifteen-minute walk before the ten-year-old hospital appeared before him.

There it was. The buzz. The tickle. That crazy little sensation he felt whenever he saw somewhere new. The William Bates Memorial Hospital was named after an aviator hero from the First World War. It had one hundred and fifty beds, an ER, four theatres, an ICU, a mother-and-infant care centre, a neonatal intensive care unit, a medical ward, a surgical ward and a mental health inpatient facility. He loved hospitals like this. Most surgeons liked to specialise in one area. The military gave surgeons that opportunity too—there were a few specialists already here. But Avery had never just wanted to work in one area. He liked variety—and here he would get it.

He started to walk towards the main entrance to the hospital, then changed his mind, turning right and heading towards the ER. He may as well get a look around the place.

The glass doors slid open just as a siren started to sound. He looked around. The main reception area was empty. Where was everyone?

It didn't take long to find out. Someone came running towards him, making the doors ahead slide open. He took a quick glance and kept walking down the corridor.

The ER was set up like many he'd worked in before. Cubicles with curtains, some side rooms, a treatment room and a room with around ten people standing outside. Resus, the most important room in the ER.

A Japanese orderly rushed past, pushing a wheelchair. He threw Avery a second glance, looking him up and down. 'You work here?'

He nodded and waved his ID. 'From tomorrow. Captain Avery Flynn. I'm a doctor.' He was relieved the man had spoken to him in English. He didn't know a word of Japanese and he wasn't sure if it was going to be a problem. Most military bases didn't just serve their own personnel. Often they took cases from the surrounding areas. Having no grasp of the language could prove a problem.

The man gave him a nod. 'No time for introductions. We're expecting seven.'

He disappeared quicker than a cartoon character. Seven what? wondered Avery. 'Oof!'

A force hit him from behind, knocking him clean off his feet and onto the floor. He barely had time to put out his hands to break his fall.

'Get out of the way' came the sharp voice.

All he could see was feet. Lots of feet, crammed into the resus room. He pushed himself up and shrugged off his backpack. If he was needed, he was needed.

A hand grabbed him from behind and a male nurse grinned at him. 'Hey, you must be new. Falling for the nurses already?'

Avery blinked as he dumped his jacket next to his backpack and flashed his ID. 'What...? Who was that?'

The guy hadn't stopped smiling. *'Faiyakuraka.'*

'What?' Avery couldn't quite make sense of the word.

The guy tapped him on the shoulder. 'It's Japanese for firecracker. But you can only call her that once you know her well. For you, it'll be Katsuko.' Then he shook his head. 'Actually, let's try to keep you safe. Just call her First Lieutenant Williams.' He moved forward. 'Now, let's see if you're any good or not.' And with that, he disappeared into the scrum in front of them.

It was difficult to tell who was who. These people weren't in regular military uniforms. The majority of them wore the usual garb for an ER—pale green scrubs. He had no idea who was a nurse, a doctor or an aerospace medical technician.

'I need an airway. I need an airway now!' came the shout.

Avery shouldered his way in.

It brought everything into focus. That, he could do.

He put up his hand. 'I'll do it.' A few heads turned at the unfamiliar voice and a little space appeared in the crowd.

The woman who had sent him flying had her short dark hair leaning over the patient. Her head shot up and her eyes narrowed. She had the darkest brown eyes he'd ever seen.

'Who are you?'

Blood. Everywhere. All over the chest of a young child. His reactions were instant. Now he understood the clamour around the bed. Hands were everywhere, pressing on the little chest, trying to stem the flow.

The woman was right. This young patient needed an airway now.

The large penetrating wound—a spear of some kind through the chest—told him everything he needed to know.

He moved to the top of the bed and nudged her out of his way. Or, at least, he tried to.

Her hips stayed firmly in place. 'Who are you?' She was practically growling at him.

He glanced at the nearby trolley, opening the first few drawers until he found what he needed. 'Do we have IV access?' he asked a nurse to his left.

'Just,' she said promptly.

A small, firm hand closed over his. He turned around.

The woman who'd sent him flying was just about in his face. Her dark brown eyes could have swallowed him up. She spoke so quietly he was sure no one else could hear. 'I'm not going to ask you again.' She gave a squeeze over his hand—and this time her grip was like iron. 'I'm just going to break your hand.'

He lifted his ID and slid it between both their faces. 'Let me do my job. We've got six months to fight with each other.'

She was small, obviously of Japanese descent but her skin was slightly darker than he would have expected. Her hair was poker straight, cut very short at the nape of her neck but becoming longer down past her ears. From straight on it looked like a bob. A smart cut for a nurse, short enough to be off her collar but not long enough to need tying up every day.

There seemed to be something about her. A presence. She was like a cannonball. People paid attention to her even though she couldn't be the highest-ranking person in the room. Far from it, in fact. She only looked in her mid-twenties.

Firecracker? He couldn't remember what the Japanese word was but somehow the nickname suited her. It seemed to sum her up perfectly.

It was obvious that in this room people respected her. He liked that. He liked that she was direct and efficient at her job.

Her eyes shifted and focused on the ID. She turned without a word and started shouting orders at others in the room. 'Get an IV run through.' She glanced at the endotracheal tube in the hand of her colleague. 'I think we'll need something smaller.'

Perfect. A nurse he could work with. All air force and military nurses and personnel were efficient and well trained. But he always worked best with those who could think ahead and weren't afraid to voice their opinion. He had a sneaky suspicion that Katsuko—was that her name?—would never be afraid to voice her opinion.

Avery tried to ignore the bedlam around him. He tried to cut out the noise. There were two trolleys in the resus room and another team was working on another patient. They were moving like clockwork, performing cardiac massage.

He moved swiftly. 'Any other doctors in here?'

'Two are up on the helipad. They haven't even managed to get the patient down yet.' She pressed her lips together. 'Blake won't give up on the other kid. Not until he's tried everything.'

The doctor attending to the little boy on the other trolley. Blake Anderson. The guy he was supposed to report to tomorrow. The scene on the other trolley was disheartening and he didn't feel the urge to introduce himself right now. If he didn't pay attention to the kid directly in front of him, he might end up resuscitating him too.

Avery took a breath and held out his hand. The area around this little boy's neck and chest was swelling, a reaction to the severe injury that could compromise his airway. His sallow skin was losing its natural colour rapidly. A nurse was poised next to the IV meds, awaiting his instructions. He gave them quickly. Something for pain control. Something to sedate the boy and steroids to reduce the swelling and allow him to intubate. Airway first. Everything else later.

The nurse nodded and inserted the drugs into the IV cannula on the inside of the kid's elbow.

'ET tube.' Avery held out his hand, bending down at the top of the trolley and tilting the little boy's head. 'Do we have his name?'

'Mahito. His name is Mahito.' The firecracker nurse was watching his every move.

'Mahito, I've given you something for the pain and something to relax you. I'm going to have to slide a tube down your throat. Don't panic. We'll take good care of you.' It didn't matter that the little Japanese boy might not understand a word of English, or his Ohio accent.

He'd done this a hundred times before and he'd do it a hundred times again.

He gave Katsuko a few seconds as she translated his words rapidly. The little boy was barely conscious. He probably had no awareness of what was going on right now and that wasn't a bad thing.

He tilted the little boy's head back, lifting his jaw and sliding the silver laryngoscope into place. He could barely visualise the cords—if he waited any longer he'd probably have to do an emergency tracheotomy—but thankfully he had time to slide the thin blue ET tube into place and inflate the cuff. It took less than four seconds to secure the airway. He attached the bag to the end of the tube and let the nurse take over.

With the airway secure he could now take a few minutes to assess the situation properly. 'We're going to need to take him to Theatre. Can I get a portable chest X-ray?'

A woman in a blue tunic stepped forward, pushing the machine towards them. She'd been waiting for his signal. Like in most military hospitals, radiographers were always available in the ER.

A heavy lead-lined apron was dropped over his head. He didn't even question where it had come from. A few people stepped from the room for a second.

'Done,' said the radiographer.

She glanced back at Avery. He could see the question on her face. 'Avery Flynn. I officially start tomorrow.'

Satisfied with his answer, she gave a nod. 'Dr Flynn, I'll have your X-ray in a few minutes.'

Avery nodded. 'Can anyone tell me what actually happened?' He could see his counterparts still working on the kid on the other trolley, the flat line on the monitor almost mocking them.

'Some kind of explosion. Lots of penetrating injuries. It was outside a local factory. The kids were playing, waiting for their parents to finish their shifts.'

'Major Anderson,' a voice boomed through the resus room doors. Everyone froze for a second then immediately resumed what they'd been doing. Eyes glanced at each other and the noise level in the room plummeted.

Avery frowned at the uniformed figure in the doorway. He had three people standing nervously behind him. The rank was instantly recognisable—as was the glint of the two silver stars—and he could hardly hide his surprise. He'd never seen a major general in an ER before.

He looked to be in his fifties and had a mid-Western accent. He was well over six feet tall with broad shoulders and what looked like thick dark hair under his hat. There was something about him. An aura. An air. And it wasn't all about the rank. What had brought him to the ER? He could understand any major general in charge of a base this size wanting to be informed about incidents. He just wouldn't have expected him to attend personally.

Blake glanced upwards but didn't stop what he was doing. 'General Williams.'

The Major General was watching Blake carefully as he continued his resus attempts. 'I heard there was an explosion. Does your team require assistance?'

Blake kept working steadily. He glanced in Avery's direction but the Major General didn't follow his glance. He was focused on Blake.

'I have all the assistance I need. If anything changes, I'll let you know.'

'I'll expect an update in a few hours.'

'General.' Blake gave a nod in acknowledgement. He

was attaching defibrillator pads to the young boy's chest. 'All clear.'

There was a short ping.

Avery was holding his breath and bent to pick up an oxygen mask that had landed on the floor. Major General Williams turned to leave, his eyes lingering for a second on Avery.

Was he looking at him?

Two seconds later the major general disappeared down the corridor.

Avery straightened up, his gaze shifting around the people in the room. The noise level increased instantly. Katsuko was still bagging but her gaze was fixed on the door.

That was who he'd been looking at. What was going on there?

The male nurse he'd met earlier shouted towards the door, 'Two emergency theatres are open. The guy from the helipad is in the first one. We can take our kid to the other.'

There was a tiny second of silence, then it was broken with a little beep. Every head in the room turned. The monitor for the other patient. They finally had an output.

Avery paused as the doctor he hadn't even had a chance to meet yet raised his head from the bed. The look of pure relief on his face made him catch his breath. 'Do you need the theatre?' Avery asked.

He had to. This was another doctor's ER. He might be treating a patient but this was the military. He had to follow the chain of command.

Blake shook his head. 'No. I'm heading to paediatric ICU.' He frowned for a second. 'Do you need assistance?'

Avery shook his head. 'Is there a surgeon?'

Blake nodded.

'Then I'm good.' He turned back to the team. 'Right,

get the IV fast-flowing, monitor his blood pressure.' He turned back at the nurse who'd threatened to break his hand. 'Are you good to bag?' He could see the determined tic in her jaw. There was no way she was leaving this patient.

Another nurse appeared at the door. 'We've another four trauma cases—two paediatric, two adult and about twelve walking wounded.'

Avery glanced down at his now blood-splattered shirt. At some point he should really change. The radiographer walked back in and stuck the X-ray straight up on the light box, flicking the switch.

It didn't take a genius to see what was wrong. Both of Mahito's lungs were deflated. Oxygen wasn't circulating properly because of the penetrating chest injury. If there was no other choice, he could try to insert chest drains but it was unlikely the lungs could reinflate with the spear still in place. It would be foolish to attempt anything like that now—particularly when he had a theatre and surgeon at his disposal. Avery shook his head. 'Let's go, folks. We're never going to get these lungs to reinflate until we get this spear out of his chest. Someone point me in the direction of the theatre.'

'Let's go, people!' shouted Katsuko. For someone small and perfectly formed her voice had a real air of command. Everyone moved. Monitors were detached from the wall, oxygen canisters pushed under the trolley, a space blanket placed over the patient. Avery kept his eyes on the patient but after a second he looked up. They were all watching him expectantly.

There was something so reassuring about this. And he'd experienced it time and time again in the military. These people didn't know him. He'd walked into an emergency situation with only a wave of his ID. That was all he'd needed.

From that point on—early or not—he'd been expected to do his job. At first he'd been a bit concerned about the chaos. Now he realised everyone had known what to do, but the rush of blood and age of the child had fazed them all.

'Everyone ready?'

Eight heads nodded at him. 'Then, let's go.'

Hands remained pressed to a variety of areas on the little body. The move along the corridor was rapid. The theatre was on the same floor. The porter at the front of the procession swiped his card and held the doors open. A surgeon strode over and nodded at Avery, not even blinking that they didn't know each other.

Avery handed over the X-ray. 'Explosion at a local factory. This is Mahito. I don't have an age. Penetrating wound to the chest, two collapsed lungs, intubated but sats are poor.' He nodded at the monitor. 'Two IV lines, tachycardic at one-sixty and hypotensive. BP seventy over forty-five.'

He frowned. 'Sorry, didn't have time to catheterise.'

The surgeon shook his head. 'My staff will get to that. We'll take it from here.'

Theatre staff dressed in scrubs surrounded them, one set of hands replacing the others and a stern-looking woman taking over bagging duties from Katsuko. She moved away swiftly. It was the first time he'd actually seen her relinquish control to someone else.

The trolley moved forward, being pushed through another set of swing doors as the surgeon shouted orders.

Just like that.

Mahito was someone else's responsibility.

Avery looked down at his hands, smeared with blood. The rest of the staff turned and headed back out of the doors.

Katsuko folded her arms and glared at his hands.

'If you ever come into my ER again and touch a patient without washing your hands and putting on gloves, I will make sure you live to regret it.'

Her accent was odd. It had a lilt. A twang. Part Japanese, part American. Her English was completely and utterly fluent.

'And as for this…' She lifted her hand and picked his fedora off his head. He'd completely forgotten about it. 'Who do you think you are, Indiana Jones?'

He let out a laugh. 'It's a pleasure to meet you too. And who said this was your ER?' He glanced over his shoulder. 'I was planning on making it mine.'

A spark flashed across her eyes. It was almost as if he'd issued a challenge.

There was a potent silence for a few seconds. Things had been chaotic before. Mahito had been the priority. Now the only noise around them was that of the swinging doors.

She was looking at him. Sizing him up. Did he meet the grade? His curiosity was sparked. What was the grade for the firecracker?

He couldn't help but start to smile. The air around them had a distinct sense of sizzle.

Despite the chaos of earlier her poker-straight hair had fallen back into place, framing her face perfectly. Those brown eyes could get him into a whole load of trouble. They hadn't even had a proper introduction yet, but Katsuko was one of the most gorgeous women he'd ever set eyes on. She might be small but she had curves in all the right places. One thing was for sure—if she was only six inches taller she would be on the catwalk.

It was odd. Avery had always gone for blondes— usually leggy. But all of a sudden leggy blondes had flown straight out of his mind.

She crossed her arms over her chest and met his inquisitive gaze. From the determined tilt of her chin it was clear she knew he'd been checking her out.

She plonked his hat back on his head, then turned and walked away, giving him a clear view of her tight, perfectly formed ass. The pale green scrubs looked good on her.

He couldn't help but laugh.

Shaking his head, he walked after her, stopping at the nearest sink to wash his hands. He didn't even have time to catch his breath. The siren sounded again and another trolley crashed through the doors from an ambulance outside. This time the patient was an adult. His colour was poor and he was rasping.

The ambulance crew spoke rapidly in Japanese. Katsuko didn't even blink, she just translated. 'Thirty-five-year-old also injured in the factory explosion. Bruising across his torso already visible. No penetration wounds. They suspect broken ribs. Poor oxygen saturation. He's complained of chest pain and he's tachycardic. Probably tension pneumothorax.' She bit her lip. 'First the kid, now the adult.'

She was mirroring his exact thoughts. Two cases of pneuomothorax, each requiring different management.

In their absence, someone had cleared the resus room. Both bays were empty again. Avery grabbed the pink stethoscope that was hanging around Katsuko's neck. 'Hey!' she shouted.

'Needs must. Haven't been able to find mine yet.'

As the trolley eased to a halt he listened carefully to both sides of the man's chest. He waved his hand. 'Sit him forward so I can check his back.' Two nursing assistants responded instantly, helping to sit the man forward. The back was clear. No sign of any wounds. The patient was eased back. The shift in the trachea was evident. There was no need for anything else. A pneumothorax was air in the chest cavity. This had probably resulted from a fractured rib puncturing his lung and releasing air into the pleural space. A pneumothorax wasn't usually life-threatening unless it progressed to a tension pneumothorax, causing compression of the vena cava, reducing cardiac blood flow to the heart and decreasing cardiac output—and that was exactly what had happened here.

A tension pneumothorax could be life-threatening and needed prompt action. The military had collected vast amounts of data regarding tension pneumothorax and subsequent treatment. In a combat setting, tension pneumothorax was the second leading cause of death, and was often preventable. Today Avery was going to make sure it was preventable.

'Tension pneumothorax.'

Two words were all it took. Packs opened around him. Surgical gloves appeared. He pulled them on and swabbed the skin. Katsuko was speaking into the man's ear in a low voice. She waved Avery on with a nod of her head.

'Let's get some oxygen on the patient.'

The staff responded instantly.

'Do we have a name?'

His body was already starved of oxygen. They had to supplement as much as possible.

One of the physician's assistants put his hand in the man's pocket and pulled out a wallet. 'Akio Yamada.' He frowned as he calculated in his head. 'I make him forty-four.'

Avery leaned over the man. His eyes were tightly closed and he was wincing, obviously in pain. He put his hand gently on his shoulder. 'Akio, I'm a doctor. I'm going to do something that will help your breathing. It might be a little uncomfortable.'

This wasn't a pleasant procedure but the effect would be almost instant relief. Air was trapped and had caused the man's lung to collapse. As soon as the pressure was relieved and the lung reinflated he'd be able to breathe more easily again. Katsuko gave a nod that she'd finished translating.

There were specially manufactured needles designed just for a tension pneumothorax. Avery held out his hand. 'Fourteen-gauge needle and catheter.' He'd done this on numerous occasions in the past. It only took a few seconds to feel with his fingers for the second intercostal space, at the midclavicular line. It was vital that the needle be inserted at a ninety-degree angle to the chest wall so it would be positioned directly into the pleural space. Any mistake could result in a chance of hitting other structures—even the heart. But Avery was experienced.

The room was silent during the procedure. In a few seconds there was an audible release as the trapped air rushed out and the tension was released from his chest. Avery removed the needle and disposed of it, leaving the catheter in place. He secured it with some tape as he watched the man's chest. Sometimes the lung inflated again immediately, sometimes it took a little time. The patient would need to be monitored.

He pulled off his gloves. 'Can we keep an eye on his sats for the next few hours and get a portable chest X-ray?' The man's eyes flickered open.

Avery put a hand on his shoulder. It didn't matter that the patient couldn't understand him. 'You should feel easier now. Just relax. We'll keep a close eye on you.'

Katsuko's gaze met his and she translated again. At least, he hoped she was translating. The truth was she could be saying anything at all and he'd never know. In a way it frustrated him. When he'd thought he was being shipped out to Portugal and Italy he'd learned a few words and phrases that he could use in clinical situations to reassure patients. He'd need to try and learn some basic Japanese.

'Doctor?'

A clerk was standing at the door. 'Yes?'

She waved an electronic tablet at him. 'I'll need you to write some notes on the two patients you've seen and fill some orders.' She hesitated for a second. 'Because you're not officially on duty yet I'll need to get another doctor to sign off on your cases.'

He met her worried gaze with a smile. 'No problem.' He could almost hear her inaudible sigh. Was she really worried he'd be offended? Of course he wasn't.

He turned back to the patient. The male African-American nurse he'd met earlier had appeared back in the room. This time he held out his large hand towards Avery. 'Frank Kelly, pleased to meet you.' Avery had thought he was big at six feet two, but this guy was a giant. With his regular runs and gym workouts he normally felt pretty fit, but Frank would make a professional wrestler shrink away.

'I'll take over, Katsuko,' Frank said confidently. 'The other two majors are fractures, one a femur, the other a humerus and shoulder displacement. Do you want to check them over? Katia is triaging the walking wounded.'

Katsuko paused. He could see her hesitation to hand another patient over. Didn't she let anyone else take charge?

He tried to hide his smile and he turned back to the patient. The colour in his cheeks was gradually improving.

He scribbled some instructions on a chart for Frank. 'I'll write him up for some pain relief and order a chest X-ray. Can you monitor his obs every ten minutes for the next hour?'

Frank nodded. The smile seemed to remain permanently on his face. Avery's gaze followed Katsuko as she washed her hands and left the room. He turned back to Frank, whose knowing smile had got even wider.

'Watch out, new boy, she bites.'

The professional thing to do was to pretend he had no idea what Frank was talking about but somehow he knew that wouldn't wash. Besides, he was curious.

'What's that supposed to mean?'

Frank shrugged and pushed the button on the machine to inflate the blood-pressure cuff. He was laughing away to himself.

'Frank?'

Frank shook his head. 'Just remember who her father is.'

Now he was really curious. 'Why? Who is her father?'

Frank raised his eyebrows. 'That would be Donald Williams.' He paused for a second. '*Major General* Donald Williams. Our commander.'

Avery couldn't help his head flicking sideways. It didn't matter that Katsuko's retreating back was nowhere in sight.

Of course. That was why the Major General had been looking at her. A giant of a man, notoriously strict, he'd commanded this base for over ten years. He also had pale skin.

There was no family resemblance at all.

'Donald Williams is Katsuko's father?'

Frank nodded. 'Sure is.' His eyes gleamed. 'And watch out because he bites too, especially anyone who looks at his daughter the way you do.'

CHAPTER TWO

A TEN-HOUR SHIFT had turned into a fourteen-hour shift. There was no way she was going back home when the ER waiting room was so full that patients couldn't find seats.

After a few hours some of the local police arrived to collect statements and details of injuries. 'Any idea what happened?'

The first one nodded. 'Delivery mistake. Chemicals for the printing factory had been mislabelled. They got mixed together as they normally do and...*boom*.'

Katsuko sucked in a breath. It all seemed so matter-of-fact. She'd seen exactly the damage those mislabelled chemicals had caused. The man who had been brought in by helicopter had died. Mahito was currently in their paediatric ICU. It would be a few days before they'd even attempt to wake him up from his induced coma.

Her paperwork was finally finished. The next shift had come on duty and all patients were currently being seen.

There was a nudge at her shoulder. 'How about you show the new guy where he can get some food?'

Avery. That was his name. These US doctors rolled in, dated their way around every department and rolled back out without a second glance. Did he really think he was the first new doctor to show a spark of interest in her?

He leaned against the wall next to her, folding his arms, his Indiana Jones style hat back on his head.

'I can't believe you actually walk about like that.'

He tipped his hat at her. 'What can I say? It's a precious family heirloom. I don't leave home without it.'

At some point he'd changed into a set of obligatory pale green scrubs. They suited him, matched his pale green eyes. There was a borrowed stethoscope around his neck and his military boots were still in place. His feet must be aching.

His blond hair was longer than normal for the military—most of the men had buzz cuts around here. She resisted the temptation to smile. Her father would have a fit. As soon as that tiny bit of forward-flopping hair touched his eyebrow there would be memos flying about the base.

He was still smiling at her. A lazy, sexy grin. This guy was movie-star material and he knew it. That rankled.

Now that he was dressed in thin scrubs she could see practically every outlined and defined muscle on his chest and arms. The scrubs were cutting into the muscle around the top of his arm. It was clear he worked out.

Another one. Cheeky. Sassy. Following her about the place. Most scattered when they found out who her father was. Well, not really her father, but as good as. The odd newcomer had thought it a challenge to try and date the Major General's daughter. But she'd learned quickly.

It had only taken overhearing one conversation. A few sentences from one airman to another—that dating the General's daughter would be a fast track to promotion—to make her stomach turn over and her blood boil.

She was immune. Immune to the too-long hair, twinkling eyes and defined muscles. She was immune to the cheeky innuendo and admiring glances.

No matter how cute the overall package.

'I'm sure you can find someone else to show you where to eat.'

'But what if I want you to show me?'

She shot him a beaming smile. 'I'm busy.'

He lifted her stethoscope off her neck. 'No. You're not. Your duty shift finished four hours ago.'

She raised her eyebrows. 'And yours doesn't even start until tomorrow.'

He placed his hand across his heart. 'Just shows you what kind of guy I am. Dedicated. Hard-working. Self-less.'

She grabbed her stethoscope back and started to walk down the corridor towards the changing rooms. 'Big-headed.'

'Ouch.' He gave a little stagger against a wall. He was still smiling at her. 'First Lieutenant Williams, is that how you treat a fellow airman?' He'd raised his voice a little and she could see heads turning in their direction. He opened his arms. 'I've travelled halfway around the world. Billeted here at short notice. Walked in and worked a fourteen-hour shift.' He shrugged his shoulders at two other amused staff members walking towards them. 'I didn't have time to check in with the housing officer and find out where I'm staying, let alone have something to eat.' He gave them a conspiratorial smile. 'Is this the kind of welcome Okatu gives new staff members?'

Katsuko felt the rush of heat into her cheeks. This guy was actually getting to her a little.

Caleb, one of the nurses, shook his head as he moved past and tutted. 'Shocking.' It was obvious he was trying not to laugh.

'Not so much as a cup of coffee,' added Seiko, one of the aerospace medical technicians.

It was odd. Avery's grin was almost infectious. She could feel the edges of her mouth turning upwards even though she was willing them not to. She might not have paid enough attention before, but he did look tired. Who knew how many hours he'd travelled before he'd done an unexpected shift? And she couldn't remember him taking a break at any point. The guy must be starving.

Avery shrugged. 'Or maybe you have someone waiting for you at home?'

The flush in her cheeks warmed even more. Nothing like asking if she was single. What was worse was that she could see the exchange of glances between her colleagues.

Katsuko threw up her hands. 'Fine. Fine.' She glanced at her watch. 'I'll phone Barney, the housing officer, and we can pick up your keys before I show you where to eat.'

'Food!' exclaimed Avery. 'It's been so long I don't even remember what it tastes like.'

He was walking right alongside her, so close their arms were almost brushing together. She bumped him with her hip and laughed as he lost his balance. 'Cut it out, drama king. I'll give you ten minutes to shower and get back into your dress uniform. If you're not outside in ten I'm leaving you behind.'

He gave her a wink as he backed into the changing room. 'Not a chance. I'm all yours.'

She gulped. The new guy was too smart for his own good. Too sassy. And a whole lot too sexy.

One of her colleagues gave her a nudge. 'Hmm... Dr Flynn? Is he single? Because if he is, I'll fight you for him.'

Ten minutes later she emerged from the changing room and walked straight into the chest of Avery Flynn.

'Oof!'

He grinned. 'I got you back. And at least I didn't leave you sprawling on the floor.'

She straightened her blue jacket. She'd spent longer

than she usually did getting changed. For some strange reason she'd felt the urge to check her make-up and spray on some perfume.

'Maybe next time you won't get in the way.'

If he'd looked good in the scrubs he looked even better in the dress uniform. The pale blue shirt and dark jacket fitted his frame perfectly. His eyes swept up and down her quickly, taking in the regulation skirt, her legs no longer hidden in scrubs. She resisted the temptation to clear her throat.

He waved his arm in front of him. 'Lead on, then, First Lieutenant. I'd hate to get in the way.'

She rolled her eyes and started walking. 'Are you always going to be this annoying?'

His backpack was slung over his shoulder and his darned fedora was in his other hand. At least he wasn't trying to wear it while he was in uniform. He fell into step alongside her. 'Believe me, I've got annoying down to a fine art.'

He pushed open the door and held it for her. She swept through in front of him. 'I bet you have.'

She pointed in one direction. 'Let's go this way. We'll pick up your keys from the housing officer. I gave him a call and he told me where he'd leave things for you.'

Avery frowned and looked at his watch. 'Is that the time? I'd no idea it was so late.' He nudged her with his elbow. 'Just as well I'm with you. The housing office would be closed at ten o'clock at night.'

She started crossing the road. 'It might surprise you but we have lots of night-time deployment flights. The housing officer has a page. He wouldn't have minded if you'd called him out.'

He gave her a curious glance. 'Lived here long?'

'Almost all my life.'

His footsteps faltered a little but she didn't halt. She

knew exactly what would happen next. He lengthened his stride and walked a little in front of her, turning around to catch sight of her face. 'I didn't think that was possible.'

'It's not.'

He wasn't going to be put off with her short answers. By this point, he was almost walking backwards, keeping his gaze on her the whole time.

'So how have you managed it?'

He was so busy watching her face that he wasn't paying attention to the road. She reached out and grabbed him just as his foot hit a small rut.

His reaction was automatic. As his balance tipped he grabbed her hand that was clutching the front of his jacket. The warm skin of the palm of his hand wrapped firmly around her wrist. It was like slow motion. A flood of electricity shot up her arm towards her chest. If she could have snatched her hand back she would have.

But he hadn't let go. His pale green eyes fixed on hers. Nothing was said. Neither of them moved again. Her breath caught some way in her throat and all of a sudden she felt the desperate urge to find something to drink. Preferably alcohol.

'Can't have you falling for me twice in one day.'

It was meant to come out as a quip—a joke. But the intensity of his gaze made her normally firm voice turn into a whisper.

He responded instantly. 'Oh, I think we can.' There was an edge to his voice, a raspiness she hadn't noticed before, that sent a shiver straight down her spine.

Her fingers slowly let go of his jacket. Avery stared at his hand for a few seconds before finally letting go of her wrist.

There was a tiny shake of his head, as if he was trying to process what had just happened.

'Over here.' She spoke quickly, pointing to an office

block. 'That's where we'll get your keys.' She strode ahead. It was crazy. But this guy was unsettling her. Touching her. Giving her glimpses of a whole other world out there.

She buzzed them into the block and picked up his keys and a map of the base from the reception desk. She glanced at the key fob and circled a place on the map with a pen.

'Look, we're here. And we'll probably go and eat in this street here. Your house is over here. It's about ten minutes from where we'll eat.'

She was conscious of him leaning over the map beside her. Even though they'd been close up earlier in the ER she hadn't noticed the woody smell of his aftershave. Maybe he'd just put some on? Just like she had...

And that darned bit of hair at the front fell over his forehead. Her fingers itched to push it back.

He picked up the map and turned towards her, their noses almost touching. As it was night-time the reception area wasn't brightly lit. There was no one else around. It was almost...intimate.

She stepped back and sucked in a breath. His head tilted to the side a little, as if he was surprised by her sudden movement. What was he used to? Women falling at his feet?

'There's a courtyard five minutes away.' She moved over towards the door again. 'What is that you want to eat?'

As if on cue his stomach gave a loud growl and he put his hand over his belly and laughed. 'Something that no doctor would approve of.'

She pushed open the door. 'Like what? You've just arrived in Japan. Don't you want to try some local cuisine?'

He shook his head. 'Not tonight. Tonight I'm ravenous.

If I'm sampling genuine Japanese food I want to savour every mouthful. Think of me as a horse.'

She turned to face him. 'Are you crazy?'

'Yes, I am. It's called low blood sugar. I just want to stick my head in a bucket and eat and eat until I'm ready to collapse in a corner. I want calorie-laden carbs. Can you find me some?'

She wagged her finger at him. 'Sure I can. But I'm warning you, this is blackmail material.'

His eyes twinkled. 'Well, I can't think of anyone I'd rather have blackmail me.'

Five minutes later they reached a pizza place and slid into a booth. The smell was enough to make him keel over. Food. He needed food.

He clocked a buffet in the corner. 'Let's not wait. How about we just go to the buffet?'

He could see the ready-cooked pizzas under the heat lamps. They were practically calling out his name. His hand was poised on the table, ready to get back up again.

Katsuko laughed and shook her head. 'What do you want to drink?'

He looked around. 'A beer. I'll have a beer. I'll probably sleep for a week.'

She gestured to one of the waitresses. 'Just make sure you're ready for your shift tomorrow. If you don't appear on time, remember—' she pointed to the key that was still in his hand '—I know where you live.'

He couldn't help the instant grin that appeared. He paused for a second and stared at the key dangling from his hand. 'Yeah, you do, don't you?'

He hadn't quite meant to say it like that. But it had just naturally come out that way. He locked gazes with those dark brown eyes. He wanted to get closer. He wanted to see if they were flecked with gold, or if the dark brown was as intense as it looked from here.

She licked her lips and his feet instantly shifted. The waitress appeared next to them, talking rapidly in Japanese. Avery pulled down his jacket and moved over to the buffet. He couldn't help but shake his head. He hadn't slept and had barely eaten in nearly two days. He was flirting with a colleague. No, he was getting fresh with the base commander's daughter. He was clearly losing his mind.

He picked up a heated plate and put two slices on it.

Katsuko appeared at his side. 'Did you even look?' She was smiling and had a glass of wine in her hand.

She picked up a plate and put two slices of pizza and some salad on it. 'Remember your five a day,' she whispered, then added a spoonful of salad to his plate.

Avery stared down at his plate. 'Sorry,' he murmured. 'At last count it was around forty-eight hours since I had some proper food.'

She gave a knowing nod. 'Is it the joys of being an ER doctor, or the joys of being in the air force?'

They returned to the booth and he spent the next few minutes eating. It appeared he'd picked two slices of pepperoni and mushroom pizza and they hit all the right spots. After a few minutes he rested back in the booth and picked up his bottle of beer.

The cold liquid felt like nectar sliding down his throat.

Katsuko was sipping her wine and eating her pizza with a knife and fork. She raised her eyebrows at him. 'Finally feeling human again?'

He nodded. The horrible churning feeling in his stomach had abated. After the long travel, the working hours and the fast eating, he should be ready to lie down and go straight to sleep.

But there was no way he wanted to sleep when he had the sparkiest woman he'd ever met in front of him.

'You know, we haven't even been properly introduced.'

She frowned for a second. 'Yes, we have.'

He shook his head. 'Oh, no, we haven't. You threatened to break my hand.'

The expression on her face softened a little. 'Yes, I did.' It was as if she were reliving the memory.

He held out his hand towards her. 'Captain Avery Flynn, doctor. I'm from Ohio but have been stationed in just about every air force base that's ever existed. Joined as soon as I qualified. Been in the service now for eight years.'

He held his breath. She waited a few seconds, then wiped her hands on her napkin and reached out her hand for his.

There it was again. That tiny little buzz. He hadn't been imagining it.

Her hand was cooler than his. But it seemed to fit in his grasp.

'First Lieutenant Katsuko Williams. I joined when I was eighteen and did my nurse training. I did a few months in Georgia to complete my nurse training. The rest of the time I've been based here.'

She gently withdrew her hand from his and took another sip of her wine.

He looked at her carefully. In the brighter lights of the pizza place he could see just how flawless her skin was and just how dark her eyes were. No gold flecks. No trace of another colour. Just pure, deep, dark brown.

'Katsuko's a nice name. What does it mean?'

'You think my name means something?'

He shrugged. 'Everyone's name means something. Mine is French—it means wise.'

She let out a laugh and he raised his eyebrows. 'Or, if you're a fan of *Lord of the Rings*, it means ruling with elf wisdom in English.'

She spluttered. 'You're joking!'

He shook his head. 'I'm not.' He waved his phone at her. 'Want to check it?'

'No.' She waved over the waitress and spoke quickly. The waitress gave him a knowing smile and walked away.

'What did you say to her?'

'I ordered more drinks.'

'Trying to get me drunk?'

'As if.' She leaned across the table towards him.

He hesitated. What was she doing? Was she actually flirting with him? No one could deny the electricity in the air around them or the occasional little gleam in her eye. But Katsuko Williams didn't strike him as a woman to mess with. And that just made him like her all the more. So he couldn't resist. He leaned forward too.

She looked him straight in the eye. 'Victorious child.'

'What?' He was confused. So *not* what he'd thought she might say.

She sat back, looking pleased with herself. 'You asked me what my name meant.'

He blinked. She pulled her shirt a little straighter over the curves of her breasts. From the expression on her face it was clear she knew *exactly* what she was doing. She was playing him.

He pushed his plate away and pressed his forehead on the table with a sigh.

'What are you doing?'

He turned his head to the side. 'I'm done. I've travelled too far. I've eaten too much. Worked for too long. And now my local tour guide is being mean to me.'

She gave a snort. 'Mean to you?'

He looked up through the floppy part of his hair—he really needed to get that cut. 'Yes, mean to me.'

She folded her arms across her chest and he sat back up.

He liked her. She was smart. And direct. Maybe even

a little bit quirky. This flirting could lead somewhere. He didn't do long-term. But he could be here for up to six months. She could make those six months fun. 'Victorious child. I like it. But it doesn't quite have an elf-like ring to it. What was the other name they called you?'

She rolled her eyes and picked up her wine glass again. 'Nothing.'

She didn't like her nickname? Interesting. 'It wasn't nothing. It was *faya*-something.'

She sipped at her wine. 'Only close friends get to call me that.'

He was curious. Could he get to be in that category?

'Say it for me again?'

She sighed. *'Faiyakuraka.'*

He scrunched up his face and tried to concentrate on the sounds. *'Fay-acure-aka.'* He leaned back, feeling pleased with himself. 'Firecracker.'

'Not even close. You need to work on your accent.'

He took a drink from his beer bottle. 'Will you help me with that?'

This time Katsuko dropped her head on the table. 'Give me strength. Do you ever stop?'

'Not if I don't have to.'

He pushed her head back up. 'Hey, it's my first time in Japan. I'm learning. Why shouldn't I learn with a beautiful colleague?'

Something flashed across her face and he instantly knew it had been the wrong thing to say. Great. He tried to cover his tracks quickly.

'Talking of accents, I thought you said you'd stayed here most of your life. Your accent is distinctly American.'

She gave a little nod. 'And when I speak Japanese, my accent is distinctly Japanese.'

He was confused. 'What do you mean?'

Her eyes fixed on the corner of the room. 'Let's just say I'm kind of caught between two worlds.'

It was a strange thing to say. And it wasn't just the words. It was the delivery of them. As if she wasn't entirely happy.

It felt too personal to pry. He barely knew her. He was brand new around here and he didn't want to do anything that would upset a colleague.

He gave a smile. 'So, what's it like being the daughter of the commander?'

The unsettled feeling on her face vanished. She gave a little shake of her head. 'Oh, you have no idea.' She lifted her wine glass again and took a careful sip. 'Let's just say that the man you saw today is not the man that I live with.'

Avery set his beer bottle down. This conversation was getting more curious by the minute. The man he'd seen today had been like most other major generals he'd met in his career—someone not to be messed with.

Katsuko was biting her bottom lip as her fingers ran up the stem of her wine glass. It was as if she were contemplating what to say.

'So he's a different man behind closed doors? I just can't imagine that.' Avery leaned back against the booth.

She met his gaze. 'He's not really my father.'

'He's not?' He couldn't help it. The words just came out. 'But Frank said...' His voice tailed off.

'I know. Everyone says that. Because that's what everyone really knows. Don was a pilot—my dad was his RIO. They had to eject from a plane during a combat mission and my father hit his head on the cockpit. He died instantly.'

Avery felt his mouth instantly dry. 'Wow. I'm sorry.'

She held up her hands. 'Didn't you spot the family resemblance?' When he didn't answer she shrugged. 'My dad was African-American, my mother Japanese.'

'What happened to your mom?'

'She became unwell just after my dad died. Everyone thought she was grieving—maybe they even thought she was depressed. It turned out she had leukaemia.'

Avery shook his head. This story was getting worse and worse.

Katsuko flicked open her wallet. 'Here they are.' She turned her wallet around. Behind the plastic inset was an old photo. Even though it was behind the plastic it was a little weathered around the edges—as if it was pulled out frequently—and the colours were a little faded.

He leaned forward to get a better view. It was a close-up of a couple laughing together. The woman had her arms wrapped around the man's neck. She was a petite, beautiful Japanese woman with long straight dark hair wearing a bright red top. The African-American man was much taller and dressed in his uniform. He was laughing too, staring straight at his wife. It was obvious they were in love. Even though the photo was old it was like a little moment captured in time. The love emanated from it.

He looked up. Katsuko was staring at the photo, lost in the memory. It was like a fist grasping inside his chest and squeezing his heart. He'd never experienced anything so intense. Her finger traced over the photo and she gave a sad smile. 'They look really happy together,' he said.

She looked up. 'They were. My dad said that he had to court my mom. She pretended to be very traditional to begin with, even though she was secretly more like a rebel. He even learned some Japanese to try and win her round.'

'What did he learn?' He'd struggled to get his tongue around even a few words today. He'd have to learn the basics for working in the ER. No matter where he worked, he always tried to learn a few words of the language. Japanese just seemed a little trickier than most. Maybe Katsuko could help him?

She shook her head and met his gaze. 'Oh, I don't want to give away any of my dad's secrets. Before I know it you'll be using them on all the women in the base.'

'Maybe not all the women.' The words came out naturally. He couldn't help but flirt with her. He'd be crazy not to.

She laughed at him. 'You think you're good at this, don't you?'

He laughed back. 'Only when I'm jet-lagged or drunk.' He stared at his bottle. 'I'm not sure which one I am right now.'

She gave a nod and glanced back at the photo, touching it with her index finger. *'Kokoro no sokokara aishiteru.'* It was almost a whisper.

He bent forward. 'What did you say?'

She shook her head. *'Kokoro no sokokara aishiteru.* It's just something my dad used to say to me as a little girl.'

Now he was really curious. 'What does it mean?'

She made a face. 'I guess the literal translation would be, "I love you from the bottom of my heart." But when my father used to say it he pressed his hand to my face and then to his chest. It was more like, "You have my heart."'

'That's lovely.' It wasn't really an expression he used much. Most guys in the world didn't describe things as lovely. But it seemed right. 'You must miss them so much.'

She closed her wallet and pressed her lips together. 'I do—just like any kid would. In a way, I was lucky, even though it didn't feel like that. I didn't lose them both together. That would have been worse. My mother helped me through the death of my father, and she helped prepare me for her own death. She, and Don.'

'So, the General adopted you?'

'He had to. It was the only way I could stay on the base. He wasn't a major general then. And he'd never married.' She toyed with her glass. 'Apparently long before anything happened to my parents they'd named him as my guardian in their will. I guess they just never really expected him to have to act as it.'

'Didn't your mother have other family?'

Katsuko shifted in her seat. 'My grandmother lives in Tokyo. She wasn't well enough to cope with a ten-year-old. She has rheumatoid arthritis. She's in a wheelchair now. I visit—I've always visited—but she hates Don with a passion. And she didn't like the fact that my mother had married an American. It seems I can't really do anything to please her.' There was a wistful tone to her voice.

The edges of her lips turned upwards in a forced smile. 'Don's great. He's always treated me as if I was his own. He tells me I'm the daughter he never had. But sometimes I feel like him adopting me might have ruined his chances of ever meeting anyone else. He and Dad were best friends. I was so used to being around him that when both my parents died I never even thought I could end up anywhere else.' She licked her lips and stared at the table for a second. 'I remember when my mother was really ill he came and sat with her. My mother held my hand and told me that when she went to sleep I'd go and stay with Don.'

Avery reached over and squeezed her hand. He'd been in the air force for years. He'd worked on servicemen who had been injured in action and sometimes even killed. He'd dealt with sick family members. But he'd never met a kid who'd been orphaned. He couldn't even imagine what that felt like.

Katsuko's gaze fixed on their joined hands for a few moments. Then she pulled her hand back against her chest.

Avery licked his lips. 'Frank says the Major General bites.'

There was a millisecond of confusion on her face before the comment obviously fell into context.

'Frank should learn to mind his own business.'

Avery drummed his fingers on the table. 'Just as a matter of curiosity, how often has he bitten?'

The words hung in the air between them. It was ridiculous and he knew that. He'd only just met her.

He'd been stationed on air force bases before. There were always people you clicked with straight away—hospitals were like that. But he had always been a little cautious. He liked to get know a woman before he decided if wanted to date them. And he didn't do long-term—not with the kind of family he had. His relationships only lasted as long as his posting at the base.

He didn't generally do things on impulse. Not like this.

He might as well have painted on the table between them, *I like you*.

It made him feel a little odd. He had no idea what was normal for Katusko. Maybe she did date servicemen that she knew weren't there permanently? Maybe that suited her as much as it suited him. But somehow the curl in his stomach was telling him not to count on it.

'I can look after myself,' she said sharply as she waved to the waitress. 'Can we have the check, please?'

The waitress nodded and pulled the prepared check from her uniform.

Avery reached over and grabbed it. On the air base you could pay in dollars or yen. Luckily he had both. It was the one thing he had been able to organise.

Katsuko pulled some notes from her pocket but he shook his head. 'Let me. You found me my keys, somewhere to eat and hopefully you'll point me in the direction of my house.'

He could tell she secretly wanted to argue but he handed the money straight to the waitress and slid out from the booth. 'Shall we?'

She picked up her jacket and followed him out into

the balmy night air. She nodded her head to the side. 'This way.'

He swung his bag over his shoulder and fell into step alongside her. She pointed to places as they walked along. 'Down that street is the high school. At the bottom of that road is the swimming pool. And there's a golf course if you're interested.'

He was watching her carefully. She seemed so comfortable in her own skin. He liked that in a woman. She was confident at work and confident in her personal life. She'd only revealed a tiny part of herself to him tonight but he definitely wanted to find out more. He stopped walking and looked at her. 'Aren't we doing this the wrong way? Shouldn't I be walking you home?'

'That would only work if this was a date. And this definitely *isn't* a date.'

'It's not? Darn it.' He couldn't help but smile.

She stopped under a streetlight and turned towards him. She had a smile on her face too. 'Are you always this infuriating?'

He leaned forward a little, stopping just a few inches from her face.

It was ridiculous. He wanted to kiss her. He really wanted to kiss her. But she was difficult to read and the last thing he could afford to do was upset a work colleague by making an unwanted move.

She was staring right at him with those dark, dark eyes.

There was no one else around them. The street was completely empty. But he still whispered. 'Why don't you hang around and find out?'

Katsuko blinked. The smile stayed on her face and her eyebrows rose just a little.

She spun away, leaving her scent trailing around him, a mixture of jasmine and amber. He had to resist the temptation to inhale the scent completely.

She glanced over her shoulder as she kept walking. 'Come on, lazy boy. Your house is just around the corner.' She had an easiness about her, a casualness that he could easily misconstrue. His brain might be addled from the long journey, the travel, and not helped by the two beers but he was finding her pretty mesmerising.

She stopped in front of a standard air force house and pointed to the number on the door. He swung his pack from his shoulder and pulled out the key. 'Let me dump my bag and I'll walk you back to yours.'

He put his key in the lock and opened the front door. Her amber and jasmine scents were swept away by a musty odour. Katsuko let out a laugh. 'Uh-oh. Remind me to buy you some air freshener.'

He winced, reaching inside the front door to flick on the light. 'Do you think the whole place smells like this?'

She wrinkled her nose. 'All I know is, if you report for duty tomorrow smelling like that, no one will work with you. It's damp. Like a men's locker room.'

'And how do you know what a men's locker room smells like?'

She gave him a wink.

A wink. An actual wink.

'We all have our secrets.' She walked past him down the hall and opened a cupboard.

For around half a second earlier tonight he'd thought of backing off. Once she'd shared about her mum and dad and her painful past he'd wondered if Katsuko would really be the kind of girl who would be up for a fling.

But he'd kept flirting with her and she was flirting right back. Katsuko Williams was proving hard to resist, no matter how many red flags were flying in the back of his head.

'I'll let you find your own way around your new home. All I need to show you is this.' She held up a bag.

'What's that?'

'Earthquake emergency kit. Dry rations, drinking water, basic medical supplies. There's a hard hat and gloves too. Oh, and a flashlight.'

'Will I need it?' He didn't really like the sound of that.

She put the kit back down and held up her hands. 'You're in Japan now, Avery. This is earthquake central. We average a thousand a year and have more drills than you could ever know. Just be sure to keep your shoes and flashlight next to your bed. They'll send you on training in the next few days.' She stepped right up under his nose and tapped a finger on his chest. 'You'll soon be saying "Drop, cover, hold" in your sleep.'

She turned to walk away and waved her hand. 'Nice to meet you, Captain Flynn. Go on now, get to bed and try and get rid of those huge bags under your eyes. Don't worry about me. I can find my own way home.'

She'd already started to walk slowly back down the path and he felt an unexpected pang of disappointment.

'I can walk you. I will. Let me lock up.'

She stopped walking and turned around, illuminated by the streetlight behind her outlining her figure and framing her face perfectly. 'No. It's best you don't.'

Whoa. He sucked in a breath. *Was he watching a scene from a movie? That was what this looked like.*

His hand was already on the key but he stopped. She'd said no. The chivalrous part of him wanted to argue, but his rational head told him that Katsuko had lived here since she was a child. She knew this base like the back of her hand. She could find her way home safely without his help.

He paused in the doorway. 'Katsuko?'

She looked up.

'Thank you. Thank you for tonight.'

She gave a little nod.

He leaned against the doorjamb. It would be so easy to go on inside but he wanted to watch her walk away. Her outline was silhouetted as she strolled down the street. Her uniform hugged her curves well and there was a sass to her step. His head leaned against the doorpost. Fatigue was washing over him now. At the bottom of the street she turned again and shouted, 'Hey! Avery?'

His head shot back up. 'Yeah?'

'The answer to your earlier question—'

His earlier question?

'—is only when I tell him.' She was grinning broadly as she rounded the corner.

His brain tried to kick into gear. He closed the door behind him and tried not to inhale the smell. It would be windows open tonight. It didn't really matter anyway. He never stayed anywhere for too long.

A spark went off. And he smiled. The question. It had been about the Major General. *How often has he bitten?*

He couldn't wipe the smile off his face as he went to find the bedroom.

CHAPTER THREE

HE WAS ALREADY there when she arrived for duty the next morning.

And yep. She liked him just as much in his scrubs as she did in his dress uniform. Darn it.

'How did you get on last night?' Frank nudged her at the front desk.

'What do you mean?'

The old rogue's eyes were twinkling and she felt herself start to bristle. She had a horrible feeling she knew where this would go. Nothing on this base was a secret. 'I heard you took the new boy out for something to eat, then showed him back to his place. Get back late last night?' He nudged her again. Twice.

There was a giggle behind her. Seiko. The aerospace medical technician who had seen her with Avery outside the changing rooms.

'Don't be ridiculous. Nothing happened.' She glared at Seiko and turned back to Frank. 'And if I find out you're saying anything else…'

Frank held up his hands and laughed as he walked away. 'He's a good-looking guy. Got to get in there quick. Who knows who else might decide to get friendly with him?'

Something uncomfortable crept down her spine. She

didn't even want to think about that. And that was even more ridiculous because she hadn't even thought to ask him last night about his family. Or any attachments. Or any children.

She felt sick. For a few seconds last night she'd thought he might actually kiss her. Even more ridiculous. You couldn't just meet a guy and let him kiss you. News like that would sweep around the base quicker than a new karaoke song. She'd no intention of being the subject of anyone's gossip. Her father would flip.

He'd intervened twice that she knew of. And even though she'd joked with Avery last night, she'd never asked him to intervene. One guy had been boasting about dating the General's daughter—and boasting about a bit more than that. He'd ended up at a different base in Japan. Another guy who'd told her he was single had been mysteriously transferred after a few months of heavy dating. She'd heard later through the grapevine that he'd had a pregnant fiancée back in the US who was also in the service.

Neither guy had ever been mentioned but the General didn't take kindly to anyone making a fool of her.

Trouble was, Avery was kind of fun. And fun was what she needed right now. She might even have to warn the General off.

She'd heard Blake mention earlier that they weren't even sure how long his posting would be as he was covering for someone else. Her brain was telling her to back off. But she couldn't get over how comfortable she'd been around him—or how one look had given her a tiny buzz she'd never experienced before.

Even if it was only for a few weeks or months, what was the harm in seeing Avery Flynn?

She stalked down the corridor and checked the board

to see how many patients were in the ER. A little voice drifted down the corridor towards her. 'You smell funny.'

'Do I?'

She almost laughed out loud. She peeked around into the cubicle. Avery was talking to a little girl with blonde curly hair. She was sitting on her father's knee as Avery bent in front of her. The father, First Lieutenant Bruce, caught Katsuko's eye and cringed.

'Hi, Abigail. What is it today?'

She walked behind the curtain and knelt down next to Avery. The tidal wave of fresh aftershave swept over her. She tried to keep her face straight as she mumbled under her breath. 'Wow. You've overdone that a bit.'

His eyes darted towards her and she thought he might actually blush, but he kept his cool and his brow furrowed. 'You've met Abigail before?'

Katsuko nodded solemnly. 'Abigail seems to like us here.' She counted off on her fingers. 'We've had fingers glued together, an allergic reaction to the permanent marker she tried on her lips, a broken wrist from her trampoline and an X-ray for a dime she swallowed.'

Abigail's father continued to cringe. He shook his head. 'I know. I'm sorry. We can't seem to stay away.'

Avery opened up his hand. 'Well, today is something different. Today we have beads.'

Katsuko stared at the small multicoloured wooden beads in Avery's palm. She dreaded to ask.

'Can I have a set of alligator forceps, a set of bayonet forceps, a curved hook and a cerumen loop?' Katsuko gave a nod. It was the standard equipment that could be used to try and retrieve the variety of items that kids could stuff up their noses.

He pulled out a small pocket torch and spoke to Abigail. 'I'm just going to tilt your head back and see if I can see anything up there.'

Abigail gave a giggle. 'Red and purple,' she said happily.

Avery's eyes widened. 'You stuck a red and a purple bead up your nose?'

Her father rolled his eyes. 'This is what I'm up against.'

Katsuko had collected the equipment on the trolley and added a sterile dressing pack and gloves. She opened a nearby cupboard. 'Some phenylephrine?'

Avery gave a nod. She prepared the equipment and waited until he'd explained what he was going to do.

'Okay, Abigail. We can't leave those nasty beads up your nose. They could cause lots of trouble. So we need to try and get them back out.' He picked up some tissues. 'We'll start easy. I'm going to get you to blow your nose while I hold one side closed. It might feel a bit strange, but just try and blow as best you can.'

Katsuko watched patiently. He had a nice manner with Abigail. Her dad looked exasperated and she couldn't blame him—their ER was becoming a second home to the little girl.

Avery examined the contents of the tissues and shook his head. 'Okay, then, no beads. Let me have another look.'

He dropped to his knees again and checked with the torch. 'I can definitely see one of them. It shouldn't be too hard to reach. Let's try a little phenylephrine first—this helps stop any swelling,' he explained to Abigail's father.

Katsuko handed over the medicine and waited until he'd applied it. She gave him a little wink and nodded to the father. 'I expect First Lieutenant Bruce might want you to have a chat with Abigail while the medicine is working.'

Avery picked up on things quickly. 'You're absolutely right, Nurse. I'll do that.'

He knelt back down and held up the bayonet forceps. 'Abigail, I'm going to have to very gently put these inside your nose to pull out the beads. It won't hurt. You can stay on your dad's knee but I'll need you to stay very still. Can you do that for me?'

Abigail eyed the forceps suspiciously. They could be intimidating for kids, but Avery obviously believed in being straightforward.

Avery sat them back down. 'You've been here a few times now. Everyone can have an accident, but sticking things up your nose isn't really an accident. Neither is sticking your fingers together or deciding to put pen on your lips. You had an allergic reaction that time. That could have been dangerous.'

'I like it here,' Abigail said simply.

Avery straightened a little and glanced over at Katsuko.

He positioned Abigail back against her father's chest and got him to put one arm across her chest and the other on her forehead. 'Are you okay holding her?'

He gave a nod. 'I've had to do it before and I'm sure I'll have to do it again.'

Avery handed the torch to Katsuko, washed his hands and put on the gloves. 'I'm going to stick with the bayonet forceps. I think they will be best.'

He positioned himself in front of Abigail and her father and tilted Abigail's head back gently, letting Katsuko shine the torch. He spoke quietly and calmly. 'This will be over in a few seconds, just hold still.'

There was barely time to suck in a breath. Avery moved swiftly. The forceps were inserted, he grasped a bead and pulled steadily. There was a tinkle of the purple bead hitting the metal trolley. Abigail's eyes widened. 'You got it.'

Avery nodded. 'I got it. I'll give you a second then we'll have a look with the torch to see if I can see the red bead.'

'He got it, Daddy, he got it.'

Her father sighed and looked relieved. 'So he did.' He positioned Abigail back against his chest. 'Now, hold still and let's see if he can get the other one.'

Katsuko bent down and shone the torch for him again. Avery didn't hesitate. He saw the bead and had the forceps in swiftly. The red bead landed on the metal trolley with a satisfactory ping.

Avery set the forceps down, pulled the gloves from his hands and walked back over to the sink.

He signalled to Katsuko and she understood instantly. 'Lieutenant Bruce, can you come with me to fill in some paperwork?'

'Oh, okay.' He lifted Abigail from his knee and sat her up on the ER trolley, following Katsuko from the cubicle. She knew that Avery wanted a chance to talk to Abigail alone. It wasn't that she had any child protection concerns. She didn't get that vibe at all. But it was obvious that something was going on in the little girl's head and if Avery could get to the bottom of it, maybe it would stop the frequent ER visits.

She took him over to the desk. 'Chari, can Lieutenant Bruce get the paperwork he needs to fill in for his daughter, Abigail? And could you get him a coffee?'

Chari looked up from the desk and stood up, her telepathic powers working instantly. All of the staff in the ER were good at this kind of thing. Chari would know that Katsuko was stalling for time. She shot Katsuko a beaming smile. 'Absolutely, no problem. Come with me, Lieutenant Bruce.'

Katsuko nodded and headed back to the cubicle. She could hear Avery talking to Abigail and she paused outside to listen.

He was joking with her. 'So, you've been here quite a lot. What is it you like so much about this place?' He slapped his hand on his chest. 'It's me, isn't it?'

The little girl shook her head, looking from side to side. 'Don't be silly, it's not you. You just got here.'

Avery had moved her from the trolley to the chair but she jumped down and looked underneath the trolley.

'Is it the candy? Did you hear that some of the nurses carry candy for kids?'

Abigail frowned. 'Not all of them.' Then she smiled. 'But Frank does. He has Jelly Bears.' She'd moved over to the curtains separating the cubicles and was trying to peer around them.

Avery walked over the pulled the curtain back. There was no one in the next cubicle. 'Did you want to see something?'

Abigail walked over and bent down, looking under the other trolley, then shook her head and stood back up.

Katsuko couldn't help but grin. While her actions were curious, she was acting more like a little old lady than a kid.

Abigail pressed her lips together and looked carefully at Avery. 'Can I go over there?'

She was pointing to the cubicles at the other side of the bay. Now Katsuko was definitely intrigued.

Avery spoke gently to her. 'What are you looking for, Abigail?'

There was a long pause. It was clear she wasn't sure about replying. She looked around as if she was checking who was listening. 'I'm looking for my caterpillar,' she whispered.

'Your caterpillar?' Avery looked as confused as it was humanly possible to look.

'I had it with me when I fell off the trampoline. I lost it. I didn't remember until I got home.'

Katsuko smiled. Now things were starting to make sense.

'So why didn't you just ask someone to find it for you?'

The little girl pressed her lips together. 'It matched a book that Nanna bought me.'

'What was the book?'

'It was about a caterpillar. You could stick your finger through the pages.' Katsuko nodded. She'd had the same book as a child. Most kids had probably had the same book.

Abigail's eyes filled with tears. 'Nanna's gone now. I can't tell Daddy I've lost her caterpillar. He'd be angry.'

Katsuko caught her breath. Things were becoming crystal clear. This was why Abigail had created a range of reasons to come back to the ER.

Avery shook his head and pulled Abigail up onto his knee. 'I don't think he would be, sweetheart. I think he's more worried about the fact you keep coming back here. Is that why you do it? You want to come and try to find your caterpillar?'

She nodded and he sighed. 'What say I speak to my favourite nurse and see if we can try and find your caterpillar?'

'Will she tell?' whispered Abigail.

'I can promise you she won't tell. She's very good at keeping secrets.'

Katsuko leaned back against the wall for a second. She could still just see them. He had a good way with kids. He knew how to engage with them and he knew the right questions to ask. Not all military docs could do that. Most of them were used to dealing with adults instead of kids. There was something so sexy about seeing a guy who was good around children.

Avery stood up and put Abigail back on the chair. 'Lieutenant Williams, are you around?'

She felt her chest swell a little. A tiny little part of her had hoped that he had been talking about her. But she hadn't really been sure.

She pulled back the curtain. 'Yes, Captain Flynn.'

He smiled at her. 'Do we have a lost property box here?'

She frowned. 'I think we might have. But I'm not sure if there's much in it. Do you want me to look for something?'

He glanced over at Abigail. 'Would you be able to check it for a caterpillar?'

Katsuko tried not to smile. She kept her face as straight as possible. 'And what does this caterpillar look like, Captain Flynn?'

He knelt down next to Abigail. 'Can you tell Katsuko what your caterpillar looks like?'

She nodded. 'It's green and yellow. And squishy. With a red face and purple...things.'

Katsuko touched Abigail's shoulder. 'Give me a second and I'll go and check.'

Avery shot her a grateful smile and it sent a little buzz right through her system as she walked down the corridor. It only took a few seconds to find the lost property box. Katsuko had a quick rummage through it. Umbrellas, hats, books and kids' jacket. There was even a single shoe. But no squishy caterpillars.

She sighed and bit her lip. There had to be a solution. She pulled out her phone and did a quick search. It didn't take long to find what she needed.

She smiled and stuck her phone back in her pocket, walking back to the cubicle. She ducked in behind the curtain, glancing between Avery and Abigail. The little girl was clutching her arms to her chest, waiting for the news.

Katsuko knelt down next to her and spoke carefully. 'I couldn't find the caterpillar, Abigail. I'm sorry.'

The little girl looked as though she might cry, and Katsuko put her hand over Abigail's. 'But I think I might know where I can get one.'

Abigail's eyes widened. 'You do?'

'You do?' Avery knelt down beside her and Katsuko almost laughed as she was hit by the overkill of his aftershave again. She pulled her phone out and turned it around.

'Does your caterpillar look like this, Abigail?'

The little girl let out a squeal. 'Yes! That's it. Where is it?'

Avery closed his hand over hers to take the phone. Tingles shot up her arm.

She met his gaze. Those pale green eyes fixed on her and she swallowed. It was almost as if the person who'd chosen their obligatory green scrubs had picked the exact shade of his eyes. She'd never seen green eyes quite that pale before. It was making her think a whole lot of thoughts she shouldn't about a guy she hardly knew. A guy who seemed to flirt for fun.

Thing was, flirting back was kind of fun. And when was the last time she'd done that?

'There's a bookshop nearby that sells a boxed set with the book and toy together. I'm sure we'll be able to find one.'

Abigail gasped. 'There's another caterpillar?'

Avery smiled and leaned forward. He whispered, 'What if I promise that I'll buy you another caterpillar? If I can get you one and Katsuko brings it around, would you stop finding reasons to come to the ER?'

Abigail nodded solemnly, her eyes wide.

'Is everything okay?' They both turned towards the voice. Abigail's father was standing at the curtains. 'Can I take her home?'

Avery nodded. 'Of course you can. We've had a little chat about Abigail's visits to the ER. Here's hoping we won't see you again for quite a while.'

Abigail's dad looked a bit confused but he nodded and picked up Abigail. 'Come on, mischief. Let's get you home.'

Avery leaned against the wall and watched father and

daughter go down the hall. He was smiling that dopey smile again.

She'd need to watch out. He was beginning to do strange things to her normally rational mind. The last thing she wanted to do was let her guard down. Not with an American. Not with someone who would disappear in a few months when he was reassigned. Fitting in around here was hard enough, without becoming the talk of the base by dating a co-worker.

A gentle nudge at her waist brought her out of her thoughts. He was looking very pleased with himself. 'You know what this means, don't you?'

She shook her head. Her stomach was starting to rumble and it was definitely time for coffee. 'No. What does it mean?'

'It means we have a date.' He glanced at his watch. 'And it starts in five hours.'

CHAPTER FOUR

SHE APPEARED AT his door within an hour of them finishing their shifts. She wrinkled her nose as she walked inside. 'What did you do?'

He shook his head. 'What didn't I do? I've used every air freshener on the base, I've tried industrial-strength cleaner… This place was borderline cold last night because of the amount of windows I had to open.'

He lifted his T-shirt from his chest and smelled it. 'I'm just worried that the smell will start to permeate me. If I start to smell like this place you need to tell me.'

She laughed. 'Believe me, if you start to smell like this place I'll be nowhere near you.'

He picked up his fedora and stuck it on his head. 'Well, we can't have that, can we?'

'Are you really going to wear that?'

'I told you. It's a family heirloom. Can't leave home without it.'

She'd thought he'd been joking before, but now it seemed he was serious.

'There has to be a story there.'

He shrugged. 'There might be.'

He opened his front door and picked up his keys. 'This will be my first time off base. My first time in Japan—

my first experience of Tokyo. What do you have planned for me?'

She felt a mild sense of panic. She hadn't even thought about anything like that. Normally, if she had friends visiting from abroad she'd plan a whole host of things for them to do. When new people started at the base she'd sometimes take them on a city tour, or at least sit down with them and make some recommendations.

'I'd only planned on taking you to a book store. What do you have in mind?' She walked out the door ahead of him.

He closed the door behind them and fell into step beside her. She was conscious of the fact that anyone who saw them would realise they were going off base together. It was no big deal. None. So why did it bother her?

'How about you try some sushi this time? Or some karaoke?' She let out a laugh. 'Or maybe I'll introduce you to a *sento* or an *onsen*.'

He looked at her curiously. 'What do you mean?'

She waved her hand. 'No. I'll save that for another day.' A breeze swept by them, giving her another dose of his aftershave.

She stopped walking. 'That's what we'll do.'

'What?'

'We'll go somewhere you can find some new aftershave. You smell like all the teenage boys around here when they've stolen some of their father's aftershave for the first time.'

He lifted an eyebrow at her. 'That bad, eh?' She almost laughed out loud. The move, and the line delivery was almost like something from a movie.

There was something about this guy that was so infectious. Most of the staff had been talking about him today. They were impressed by his quick actions the day before and his clinical skills. There had been the inevitable discussion about his good looks and whether he was attached or not. Then there had been a few comments about the fact that he seemed to have homed in on the Major General's daughter already.

Those comments had made her distinctly uncomfortable. She was almost sure that he hadn't known initially— no one did. But by the time he'd asked her to show him where to eat he *had* known.

Part of that made her skin prickle. She'd like to think that who her father was didn't matter to him, but she really didn't know him that well yet.

It didn't help that the first thing she'd noticed had been how well his dark blue jeans fitted around his backside, or that the thin designer T-shirt showed the definition of his pecs.

She almost jumped when he slung his arm around her shoulders and pulled her closer. 'Hey? Where are you?'

She stopped walking. 'What?'

'You looked a million miles away. You had a strange expression on your face. Everything okay?'

She stepped out from under his arm. He'd already got too close.

'I'm fine.' She gave herself a shake as they approached the base exit and held out her arm. 'Here we are, the prefecture of Tokyo.'

'Don't you mean city?'

She shook her head. 'Tokyo isn't a city. It's a prefecture. It has twenty-three wards, twenty-six cities, five towns and eight villages. Not to mention the two island chains. It's the most populous metropolis in the world.' She laughed and said, 'We could stand here all day and argue about the size of the population.'

His eyes widened. 'Wow.'

She nodded as they left the base. 'Let's head to the subway. It's the quickest way to get to where we want to go.'

'You've still not told me where we're going or what we're doing.'

She gave a little shudder. 'Feel free to pile the pressure on. There's a million things to do in Tokyo. But most of them have to be planned. I could take you to Shibuya's shopping district and the famous Hachiko crossing.'

This time he gave a shudder. 'Not tonight.'

She smiled as they bought tickets for the subway. 'What about the Imperial Palace? Or the Meiji Shrine? Do you like the outdoors? We could visit the Japanese Gardens. Or plan for another day and go on the bullet train or visit Mount Fuji.'

The subway was fast and efficient and only took a few minutes to appear. 'Sounds like there's too much to do in Tokyo.'

She nodded. 'There is. Whatever it is you want to find, I'm pretty sure I'll be able to find it. You just need to plan. Tokyo and its districts are a big place. It would take around two and a half hours to get to Mount Fuji from here.'

Avery fixed his eyes on the snow-topped peak in the distance. 'It looks fantastic. I'd love to go there one day.' He met her gaze and smiled as the subway rolled along. The shudder of the subway echoed the shudder in her body. The smile seemed genuine. He seemed a warm and friendly guy. But did she really want to get involved with someone she worked with?

Wow. Where had that thought come from?

He reached up and put his hand on her shoulder. Touch. He seemed to be big on touch.

'But from the list you gave me there's a whole lot of Tokyo out there. Seems like I'll be spending most of my time off exploring the place.'

Someone jostled her from behind and she stumbled

forward a little, pressing right up against Avery's chest. She looked up. 'Sorry.'

He put his hand on her hip. 'It's fine. It seems really busy around here. I guess we should just get used to being up close and personal.'

It was the way he'd said it. Half joking, half serious. She wasn't quite sure which. And she wasn't quite sure which one she wanted.

She pressed her lips together and gave him a nudge. 'Get ready to wrestle your way out of here. The next stop is ours.'

Three minutes later they were standing in front of the multi-storey bookshop. 'I thought these places had gone out of fashion. Doesn't everyone read on phones these days?'

She gave him a shocked glance. 'Shame on you. There's nothing nicer than the smell of a brand-new book. Don't you just love the way they feel in your hands? Can't you remember the excitement of being a kid and been taken to a bookstore and told to pick what you wanted?'

He had an amused expression on his face, with tiny crinkles around his eyes. He glanced upwards at the huge store, which had windows lined with books. 'I can't say that I did. I was more a racing-track and cars kind of kid.'

They walked through the main entrance and she shot him a curious glance. 'You mean you didn't have a mini-stethoscope and medical kit?'

He shook his head as she pointed at the escalator towards the kids' books. 'No way. I didn't want to be a doctor then.'

She turned to face him as they rode up the escalator. 'Really? What did you want to be?'

He tipped his hat at her. 'Can't you tell?'

'No way. You wanted to be Indiana Jones?'

'Doesn't every small boy?'

She reached up and touched his hat. 'I thought you said it was a family heirloom? Oops!'

He grabbed her arm as she fell backwards. She'd been so engrossed in quizzing Avery that she'd forgotten the escalator would reach the top quickly. But his timing wasn't so good. As she fell back she pulled him with her and they both landed on the floor at the top of the elevator, Avery flat on top of her.

A teenage boy with wide eyes stepped over them as Avery rolled her to the side.

'We've got to stop meeting like this,' he groaned.

He was squished right up against her. She'd thought they'd been close on the subway. But now she could feel every one of his tight muscles pressed against her. She could actually feel the beat of his heart against her chest. She didn't even want to think too hard about anything else she could feel.

She pushed back and scrambled to her feet. 'Sorry, I should have been paying attention. I got distracted. It's just that—'

He stood up next to her and shook his head. 'We're fine, Katsuko. You're babbling.'

Her reaction was instant. She wrinkled her nose and put her hands on her hips. 'I am not.'

Her cheeks started to flush. Maybe she had been babbling just a little. He grabbed her hand. 'Come on. Let's find the kids' books. There has to be a caterpillar in here somewhere.'

She was trying not to focus on the fact that his hand was encircling hers. She was trying to completely ignore the tiny sparks that were shooting up her arm directly into her chest.

The kids' section had huge signs hanging above it—some in Japanese and some in English. It didn't take long to find the children's picture books. They had a number of little sets and the caterpillar book was among them. Avery smiled as he picked it up. 'She was right, you know. Mainly green and yellow with a red face and purple… things.'

Katsuko laughed. 'That would be antennae, Captain Flynn.'

'Yeah, yeah. Well, I'm a doctor, not a vet.'

She frowned for a second. 'So how come you're so good with kids? You said you don't have any of your own—does someone in your family have kids? Are you really Avery, the fun uncle?' She was curious.

He gave a visible shudder.

'What?'

He gave his head a shake. 'Thankfully, my sister doesn't have kids.' He put his hand on his chest. 'I do however, have a number of good friends who have children. In fact, two of my friends seem to be having a competition of fitting in the most number of kids under the age of five.' He raised his eyebrows. 'It's currently a draw.'

'How many kids do they actually have?' She was leaving the sister comment, even though she was still curious. It was clear that was for another day.

'Tess and Ray have four—a set of twins of eight months, a son of two and a son of four. Jamal and Aiysha have four too. They're like stepping stones. Four, three, two and one.'

'And what are you, chief babysitter?'

He gave her a beaming smile and nodded. 'Of course I am. It helps that I'm a big kid myself. Letting any of them get a few hours for dinner, or an evening to themselves, is no big deal. It might take me a few days to recover but it's worth it.'

He pulled some money from his pocket. 'How are you going to get this to Abigail?'

She thought for a few seconds. 'It should be easy

enough. I'll just take it out of the box and pretend I found it in the ER and wondered if it was hers. It's almost true.'

He paid for the boxed set and they walked back to the escalators. He gave her a wicked smile and gestured towards the moving stairs. 'After you. Don't want to land on you again.'

She stepped onto the escalator and turned to face him again. 'What if I like living dangerously?' She leaned back a little and held her hands up as they travelled downwards. 'Hey, look at me, I'm going to fall. Woo…!' She gave him a cheeky wink. 'Don't worry, you're safe. I knocked you down and now you did the same to me. I think we're even.' She spun around just as they reached the bottom and stepped off sharply.

'I'm not sure we're even,' murmured Avery. 'I'm sure both times it was your fault.' He had a mischievous gleam in his eye that she'd no intention of falling for.

She planted her hands on her hips as they walked back out into the crowds. Darkness had fallen and Tokyo was lit up with a whole array of coloured lights. 'What kind of gratitude is that? You drag me out after a busy shift to take you shopping and introduce you to life in Tokyo, then you hit me with the guilt trip?'

He kept going. 'I'm just pointing out that you seem to like me flat on my back.' For a second she was mesmerised. Those pale green eyes were quite startling under the brown fedora and bathed by neon lights. The noise and bustle around her seemed to dull. All she could feel right now was the electricity in the air between them. It didn't matter that he was teasing. It didn't matter that his blatant flirting was ridiculous.

She liked it. She could feel herself start to react it. To flirt back. She was comfortable around him. Already, in the space of two days.

She bit the inside of her cheek. She could tell that shopping wasn't really his thing. But she wasn't ready to go home yet. Her phone buzzed and she pulled it out of her pocket, glanced at the message and quickly pushed it back in her jeans. Her grandmother. Not what she needed right now. 'How about I promise you somewhere really cool to go and eat genuine Japanese sushi?'

'Now, that does sound tempting. Do you promise not to get me flat on my back again?'

'Not unless you want me to.' It came out before she thought about it. Like a lightning flash in her brain that reached her lips before the mute part of her brain started to function.

He raised his eyebrows. 'Oh, touché, First Lieutenant Williams.'

'Touché? What's that?'

He waved his hand. 'Never mind. Tell me more about where we're going to get some food.'

She gave him a knowing smile. 'Well, strangely enough, it's right next to one of the main tourist attractions.'

'Which one?'

'The one you're most excited about seeing. Come on, it's just a quick jump on the subway.'

Ten minutes later Avery found himself in the middle of a film set. At least, that was what it looked like and felt like.

He'd never seen so many people before. The sun had set quickly and darkness had fallen across Tokyo. The whole street was lit up by the biggest array of neon lights he'd ever seen. It reminded him partly of Times Square and partly of a futuristic film.

But the thing that was most noticeable was the number of people in one area. He'd never seen a busier place in his life.

Yes, he'd realised that Tokyo was busy. It was the most populated place in the world—of course it would be busy.

But as they exited Shibuya station he had a sudden realisation that he'd never truly understood the definition of busy before. He spent every second step stopping to avoid crashing into someone.

Katsuko, on the other hand, moved nimbly and ably through the throngs of people. His eyes were repeatedly drawn to her neat bum in the bright red skinny jeans. She pointed to the crossing before them. 'Watch out because when the lights turn red they turn red everywhere. People just surge forward onto the road. Keep close or you'll get lost.'

He resisted the temptation to reach out and grab her hand. He'd made a few close moves around her and got the distinct impression she wasn't quite sure what to make of them. Truth was, neither was he.

It felt natural to touch Katsuko—even though he'd no right to, or had any invitation to. If he'd been challenged about it, he'd claim he touched all his female friends. It was casual. It was friendly. But the buzz that flooded his body every time he came into contact with her skin was telling him a whole other story.

Would it be fine to date the General's daughter? Or would it be frowned upon? Because in the space of two days those thoughts were definitely starting to float around his mind.

She seemed fun. She was good at her job. And she knew the area like the back of her hand. She bordered on flirtatious without being forward.

It didn't matter that he never settled anywhere. It didn't matter that his longest relationship had only lasted the length of time of his posting.

His family was the best ever example of things not lasting for ever. With a father who'd married four times, and was about to move on to number five, a mother who latched onto the nearest guy with money until she'd spent it all, and a sister who was learning from her mother's example, it was no wonder he didn't do any kind of family gatherings.

His last stepmother had been a woman only a few years older than him and she had insisted on inviting him around at New Year. The last New Year's dinner had been a complete disaster. His father had got horribly drunk, insulted just about everyone sitting around the dinner table, then passed out on the sofa.

Never. Ever. Again.

He hadn't even told any of them his orders had changed and he was in Japan now. They probably wouldn't care.

The only person he'd really respected in the family had been the owner of the fedora—his uncle Stu. He'd been a real life Indiana Jones, disappearing into parts of the continents that no one had heard of and coming back with artefacts for the museum he'd worked for and a whole host of fantastic stories.

Because he'd been a kid, Avery hadn't really understood the politics of it all—or the danger. All he'd known was that Uncle Stu had been shot at a few times, been threatened on occasion and had had to run from a bunch of robbers in more than one set of circumstances.

It had been very exciting for a young boy. Right up until the point an official-looking letter had been delivered to the door and his father had disappeared for a few days, returning with only the fedora. 'It seemed Uncle Stuey took the wrong artefact' was all he'd said before he'd dumped the fedora onto Avery's head and disappeared into his study.

Avery had been lost. Uncle Stu—crazy as he'd been—had been the most normal person in the family. They'd joked about working together when he was old enough to join his uncle on the expeditions. It had never occurred to him that might never happen.

Nothing else in the world had seemed certain after that.

Joining the air force had been the steadiest part of his life. Stu had left him a little money that he'd used to part pay for college and medical school. With no family or home to support back in the US he was now almost debt free. A great position to be in.

Why shouldn't he date the woman he wanted to?

As they darted among the crowds, recognition dawned in his brain. This time he did reach for her hand and tugged it. 'Hey, this is that place, isn't it?'

She gave him her most innocent expression. 'What place?'

He wrinkled his nose. 'I can't remember what you called it. *Ha*-something—the crazy crossing?'

People all around them had their phones in the air, ready to capture the moment that the lights changed. A few seconds later it happened. And it seemed like the whole world moved.

'Watch out!' said Katsuko as she pulled him back against the wall of a building.

It would be so easy to get swept along with the momentum of the crowd. He climbed up a few steps to get a better view. 'Wow.' It was almost like a form of dancing or synchronised swimming. And it wasn't slow—it was fast. People dodged around each other instantly, heading in all directions. Some moved in straight lines, some diagonally.

'How do they do that?' he wondered out loud.

Katsuko smiled at him and shrugged. 'What can I say? We're naturals. Welcome to Hachiko crossing—the busiest crossing in the world.'

As the throng of people disappeared quickly the lights changed again. Within a few seconds people started to accumulate at the sidewalks all over again.

He folded his arms and faced her. 'You mentioned this place and I said not tonight.' He was still gazing in wonder. 'I didn't expect it to be quite like this.'

'Well, get used to it. The place we're going for dinner is diagonal to us.' She pointed to a silver and blue highrise building. 'Are you chicken?'

'What?'

He finally dragged his eyes off the crossing to face her. There was no doubt about it. There was a definite smirk on her face. She was baiting him. Again.

'You think I'm chicken?'

She leaned forward, as if their conversation could be heard by others. 'I think you're a Hachiko virgin. Let's just call it survival of the fittest here.' Her voice was low and he had to move closer to hear. Somehow he knew it was a deliberate act. And the choice of words?

He didn't have a single doubt that over the next few months Katsuko Williams was going to drive him crazy. Good crazy.

'Do you want to take a bet on this?'

She looked at him curiously. 'And what exactly would that bet be?'

He liked it. She'd take the bet, whatever it was.

'Who can get across quicker?'

She laughed out loud. 'Are you crazy? You, the slow-moving, never-been-here-before American, against me, the agile local girl?'

Every word made his skin prickle. He loved her feistiness. He loved the challenge in her eyes. He glanced over at the throng with his chin held high. He could hardly see any gaps between all the bodies. 'I played American football. That's not a crowd. That's just a smooth path to home.'

She shook her head. He could tell from her expression

that she thought she'd already won. She waved her hand. 'I guess it doesn't matter, but what do I win?'

A group of rowdy workers passed by, singing at the tops of their voices. 'A kiss,' he said suddenly.

He'd touched her. He could smell her. But he wanted to taste her. Taste those lips.

Her brow furrowed and she pulled back a little. 'Not a chance.' She was surprised but she didn't seem repelled. Although she might flirt with him and taunt him a little, there was still a whole host of invisible barriers surrounding her. She put her hands back on her hips. 'Loser has to buy dinner. That seems fair.'

She gave a flick of her shiny geometric-styled hair. It seemed to all move together. There was never a hair out of place. What would she look like if it was all mussed up? He was beginning to realise that that move seemed to indicate she'd made up her mind. 'I still plan on collecting that kiss,' he murmured under his breath.

She took a few steps in front of him and he grabbed the back of her black fitted jacket before she disappeared into the crowd completely. By the time they reached the edge of the crossing people were packed around them. He tucked his head on her shoulder and stood right up close. He had the perfect excuse. There was no space around them at all.

He pointed diagonally across the street. 'That building over there? That's where we're headed?'

She nodded. 'Twenty-second floor has one of the best sushi restaurants around. We can sit and watch the madness of the crossing.'

'Sounds good.' He glanced upwards. He could sense the people around him leaning forward a little, ready to move the second the lights changed. He lowered his mouth to her ear. 'See you at the front doors.'

He couldn't wipe the smile from his face as he darted

out from behind her, making a beeline for the building. Once he was in the middle of the thing it wasn't quite so daunting. The Japanese people were endearingly polite. They seemed to have a sixth sense for stepping out of the way—in the right direction. The only blips on the horizon were the number of crazy tourists who were standing in the middle of the crossing, holding their phones above their heads and filming. Didn't they realise as soon as the traffic lights changed colour they could be squashed by oncoming traffic?

He couldn't see Katsuko anywhere. But how on earth would he in this crowd? He kept his eyes on the prize, the glass doors, now just in front of him. If the crossing had been empty, it would probably have taken around twenty seconds to run from where they'd started to their final destination. But the sea of people made that impossible. How long would the lights actually stay on red?

He dodged out of the way of a few more people. Any second now he would be dizzy with the amount of zigzagging he was doing. But the prize would be worth it. He would pay for dinner no matter what. What he really wanted was the kiss.

The crowd thinned a little as he approached the faraway sidewalk. There, standing with an amused expression on her face and her arms crossed, was Katsuko. She looked as if she'd been there for a while.

'What?' He glanced behind him and back to her again. Yep, it was definitely her. Red skinny jeans, black T-shirt embellished with sparkling sequins in the neon lights and a cropped black leather jacket. She was laughing now.

He thudded in front of her, pretending not to be breathless. 'How on earth did you do that? Where did you come from?'

She kept laughing as she spun around and the automatic doors slid open in front of them. 'You'll have to be here twenty-five years to keep up with me.'

He still couldn't believe it. The lights had changed behind them and the crossing was instantly filled with traffic. She walked over and pressed the button at the elevators. 'I'm going to have the most expensive thing on the menu.' She glanced at him sideways as they stepped inside. 'And I might even have some wine.'

'You can have as much wine as you like. I still want to know how you did that. Is it a trick?'

'What? Like you trying to get a quick getaway?'

The elevator slid smoothly upwards. He was smarting. He was thinking about that kiss a lot more than he should. It might have sounded like a joke. But it wasn't really. A bet had seemed simple. A way to get permission to kiss her. And right now he wanted that way more than he should.

The doors slid open at the twenty-second floor and they stepped out to a restaurant that had glass panels all around. There was a perfect view of the Shibuya shopping district with all its chaos.

Avery checked the queue of people ahead of them. 'I take it this is a popular place, then?'

She nodded. 'Once you've been you'll want to come back. Guaranteed.'

He looked at the queue ahead. Even though the restaurant had gorgeous views—particularly of the crossing below—people didn't seem to stay long. Their orders were taken, then they slid along a bench in front of the chefs as their meal was prepared. Once they reached the end they picked up their plate and took it to one of the tables to eat. Most of the sushi dishes were prepared within a few minutes so the queue moved along swiftly. He was kind of amused that the people seemed to eat their dishes equally quickly then leave. There was no lingering over a meal like most Europeans and Americans did. The Japanese didn't seem to waste any time anywhere.

Katsuko turned to face him. 'What do you want to eat?'

He made a face. 'To be honest, I'm not really sure. Although I've eaten in Japanese restaurants all over the world, I've never been in one in Japan before. What do you recommend?'

'Is there anything you don't like?'

He gave her a taunting smile. 'I'm pretty much a guy who'll try anything.'

She rolled her eyes. 'You never stop, do you?' She gave a shake of her head and stuck her hands on her hips. 'It's going to get old, you know.'

She pointed at a nearby menu. 'I'd recommend starting with some *nigiri* and some miso soup.' He smiled. *Nigiri* was one of the basics. A slice of raw fish pressed over some vinegared rice. 'Then my favourite from here are the fatty *chu-toro*—that's tuna—super-soft *aori ika*—that's squid—and fresh, local *aji*—that's mackerel with ginger and *negi*.'

Avery nodded. 'All sounds good to me. You're the expert here. I'm just happy to watch the cooking and get eating.' They ordered drinks at the bar and Katsuko sipped her wine as she spoke rapid Japanese to the chefs. They slid along the cream leather bench and watched in fascination as the chefs expertly sliced, chopped and prepared food. The preparation time was minimal. These guys were complete and utter professionals. Avery pointed to one small plate of food with a few *nigiri*. 'That would probably take me hours to prepare,' he said to Katsuko as he took a drink from his beer. 'I think I could watch them all day.'

'I couldn't,' she said quickly. 'I just want to eat.'

As they slid along the bench, following their food being finished, Avery was fascinated with the whole experience. When the food was plated they carried it over to a table overlooking the Hachiko crossing. He had used chopsticks before but just wasn't very good with them. Katsuko laughed at his efforts and leaned over to reposition them in his hands, her warm skin touching his.

'Watch out, Katsuko,' he warned with a smile. 'I'll think you're trying to deliberately touch me.'

'I'm trying to stop your food landing in your lap,' she said smartly.

He ate for a few minutes, looking down in awe at the still crowded crossing. It was teeming with people and after a few minutes they started pointing out the people they thought would never reach the other side in time. It was almost like a kids' game.

'This food is delicious. You're right. I will come here again.'

She nodded. 'It helps to eat it just after it's prepared. Sushi should be eaten at the optimal fish and rice temperature. It tastes best then.'

He noticed a few of the other men around glancing in her direction. Katsuko was bright and lively. It didn't hurt that she was the prettiest woman in the room with a whole lot of sexy thrown in there too.

'Who texted you earlier? Was it an admirer? I bet you've got a few on base.'

She didn't flinch at all. 'Nope. No admirer. It was my grandmother.'

'Your grandmother? You mentioned her before. How is she?'

'Still here.'

He was surprised by her blunt answer. 'What does that mean?'

She took a deep breath. 'Let's just say I've always had the distinct impression that my mother and subsequently me are the biggest embarrassments of her life. In fact, it's not really an impression at all. It's fact. She's said it.'

'She what?' It seemed like such a harsh thing to say. And even though Katsuko said it so matter-of-factly there was no hiding the glimmer of hurt in her dark brown eyes. His insides automatically coiled upwards.

Katsuko took a sip of her wine. She was trying so hard to appear indifferent. Did she know she couldn't look indifferent no matter how hard she tried?

He reached over and touched her hand. 'Tell me more about your grandmother.'

He was definitely curious. There was a story there. But he was more curious at Katsuko's reaction to her grandmother's text.

She shrugged. 'What's to tell? I see her when I have to, which isn't often as she doesn't particularly like me. She wants the whole world to jump for her. I've learned the hard way not to do it. The more I get involved the more I get hurt. Adulthood has taught me to move into self-protect mode.'

He didn't know quite what to say. Lots of families were fractured, lots of families were broken. His own wasn't ideal. But this? This was a whole other story. Was her grandmother her only living relative?

'Do you have other family in Japan? Aunts, uncles, cousins?'

She shook her head. There was an air of sadness about her. 'No. My mother was an only child. I think my grandmother had some cousins once, but I'm sure she treated them the same way she treats everyone else.'

'And how is that?'

She met his gaze square on. 'With disdain. With disapproval.'

He released her hand and leaned back in his chair a little. 'Those are harsh words.'

'She's a harsh woman.'

He signalled to the waiter.

'What are you doing?'

He gave a rueful smile. 'I'm ordering us more drinks. I don't care if we're supposed to eat and run in here. I want to know more.'

She bit her lip and he wondered if he was pushing her more than he should. But she'd been the one to mention it, and he wanted to know more about her. He gave her a moment as she pulled something from her bag. Her lips were still perfectly red but she slicked something over them that gave a waft of strawberries. He could sense delaying tactics easily.

He tapped his fingers on the table. 'Your grandmother must be quite modern.'

Katsuko let out something resembling a snort, then covered her face in embarrassment. 'I don't think anyone would describe my grandmother as modern.'

He held up his hands. 'She's texting. She must own a mobile phone. What age is she?'

'She's just over eighty. My mother was a late baby. She thought she couldn't have any children.'

'Then she must have been delighted when your mother came along.'

Katsuko sighed. 'You'd think so. But I think she'd got used to having no children. She'd accepted her fate. My mother was a shock. I don't think she ever really adjusted to having to replan her life.'

Avery pried a little further. 'You said she was unwell—she's in a wheelchair?'

Katsuko nodded. 'Her rheumatoid arthritis has been severe for as long as I've known her. She's been in a wheelchair since I was tiny. Her muscles are wasted. She has fibrosis of her lungs and kidney problems too. Every joint is affected. Her fingers are all disfigured. She doesn't use a phone. She uses a tablet.'

'Who takes care of her?'

Katsuko swallowed and glanced out of the window towards the busy crossing. A classic avoidance technique if ever he'd seen one.

'She has help.' Katsuko bit her lip again. She seemed annoyed.

'What kind of help does she need?'

Her gaze was fierce. She was obviously regretting this conversation. 'Every kind of help. Someone washes her, dresses her, prepares her food and amuses her for the day until they have to do it all again in reverse.'

Avery's brain was spinning. He wasn't quite sure of the healthcare system in Japan. Who helped when someone needed care at home?

But Katsuko didn't even let him ask the question. 'I pay for it. Don pays for it. She wouldn't let us help her. She told us in no uncertain terms.'

There it was again. That flicker of hurt. That deep-seated resentment.

'Why on earth does your grandmother treat you that way?'

Katsuko rested her elbows on the table and ran her hand through her shiny hair. She glanced around the restaurant, looking at the other people around them. She straightened in her seat and looked at him. 'Do you see anyone who looks like me?'

He frowned and looked around. Was it a trick question? 'Of course. There are lots of Japanese people in here.'

She shook her head. 'Look again. Look hard. Do you see anyone who looks like me?'

If this was test, he was going to fail.

'I don't know what you mean.'

She sighed and held up her hands. 'In Japan, I'm known as *hafu*—it's the term we use for biracial.' She glanced over her shoulder. 'I can't see anyone else in here that looks like me. Japan is one of the least ethnically diverse countries in the world. Some people think that people like me—*hafu*—aren't fully Japanese. My grandmother has always felt that.'

He was more than a little stunned. All he could see when he looked at Katsuko was her beauty. He hadn't thought much deeper than that. Oh, sure, when he'd first seen her he'd been a little curious. But that was all.

Working in the air force all around the world meant that race had never really been an issue for him to consider. His life had been full of people with varied nationalities and more mixed genetics than he could ever imagine.

He chose his words carefully. 'What does Don say about this?'

She sucked in her cheeks. 'Oh, Don is mad. Don has always been mad about the way she treats me. He was mad long before my mother and father died. When I was younger, he took me to visit her every two weeks. But he sat outside in the car for two hours, then knocked on the door to pick me up again. I gather they exchanged words during the custody issues—but neither of them has ever spoken about it.' She glanced out at the street again. 'When I turned eighteen, he told me it was up to me if I wanted to visit. I could drive by then. He just let me know he wouldn't force me to go.'

Avery tilted his head to the side. 'Was he trying to stop you going?'

'I don't think so. I think he'd just felt some sort of duty up until then. In Japan, you're not officially an adult until you're twenty. But I think Don's patience had worn thin by that point. I'd already been accepted for nursing. He told me it was up to me to decide what I wanted to do.'

Avery was watching her closely. She liked to keep things guarded, as if she held them close to her chest. Oh, she was talking. But years of being in the medical profession had frequently taught him that it wasn't what was said that was important—it was what *wasn't* said.

'What did you do?'

Her eyes fixed on the table. 'I visit when I can.'

'And you don't want to?'

Her fingers slid up and down the stem of the wine glass. 'Not really.' Her voice was barely a whisper.

He reached over. This time he didn't squeeze her hand. This time his fingers interlocked with hers. 'She doesn't know how lucky she is to have you.'

Her deep brown eyes met his and he could see her swallow. It was odd how he understood the awkwardness of family. The not-quite-fitting-in part. Their circumstances were completely different. But strangely similar. She'd lived here her whole life. He'd spent most of his adult life flitting around.

But the connection between them was real.

He hated the fact that she looked unhappy. 'Surely there must be lots of people on the base who are *hafu*?'

She nodded. 'On the base there are quite a few. I don't think there's anyone else that's Japanese and African-American, though. I guess I stand out a little because of the colour of my skin.'

'And that causes problems?'

She shrugged. 'It depends entirely on where you are. My mother wanted me to attend the same Japanese school that she did instead of a school on the base. But after a year of my being bullied for being "different" she changed her mind. I had some interviews at universities before I decided on becoming a nurse. Some of them were awkward. They asked me outright where I fitted. A lot of Japanese companies are very traditional. In a way, I think they were trying to prepare me for the adult working world. The truth is, even with a university degree, I might have found it difficult to find a job. The base is really the only place that makes me feel comfortable.'

Avery's brain was spinning. She looked so sad when she spoke that it was clear these experiences had really affected her. Who did she have to talk to about them?

The city he'd lived in as a child had people of every nationality—as did most of the bases he'd worked on. What he really wanted to do right now was hug her. She looked like she needed one. Instead, he leaned forward. 'Just for the record, I think you're pretty much perfect just the way you are.'

She rolled her eyes. 'You're flirting again.'

'Of course I am. I'm with the prettiest woman in the room. I'd be a fool not to.'

He couldn't help it. Katsuko could give blasé and smart answers. She was good at that. He'd thought before she was just sparky. Now he was realising it was part of the barriers she erected around herself. Self-protection.

He recognised them. He just wasn't ready to tell her why.

In his head, part of him was already walking away. No matter how much bravado she had, Katsuko wasn't the kind of woman he wanted to toy with.

He wasn't planning on being around her. He couldn't give her what she really needed. Someone to stand by her side. Someone to tell her how beautiful she was, and how good she was. He wasn't sure he could ever be that person.

The thing was, it didn't stop him wanting her.

In fact, it just magnified it.

No matter how wrong it was, he knew exactly what he'd do next.

He stood up. 'Let's go. There's something I want to do before we go back to the base.'

She gave a little start and made a grab for her jacket as he signalled to the waiter and settled the bill.

'No. Wait. Let me pay for part of that.'

He waved his hand. 'You can buy dessert.' He waited until she'd slid her arms into her jacket, then took her hand, leading her towards the elevator. There was already a crowd waiting and space was tight.

He smiled all the way down in the elevator, keeping her hand in his.

'What are we doing?'

He bent his head. 'Let's just say I'm still a tourist and I'm living the dream. Hachiko Crossing just made my bucket list.'

Outside it was even busier than before. The streets looked even more magical with their bright neon lights and flashing signs. They joined the crowd waiting to cross.

His thumb brushed against the inside of her palm. She gave him a curious smile. The lights changed and he shouted, 'Run!'

The shocked expression on her face was priceless. He wasn't quite sure how he managed it, but they darted in and out of the crowd without any injuries to either of them. As they approached the midway point of the crossing he stopped dead. Katsuko barrelled straight into the back of him. 'What?'

He spun around. They were dead centre. Exactly where he wanted to be.

A few eyebrows rose from people who sidestepped around them.

'What are you doing? Are you crazy? We need to cross before the lights change.'

Katsuko's head was darting from side to side. Time was running out.

But not for Avery.

He caught her head between both his hands. Her hair shone in the neon lights and her eyes sparkled. 'This is what I'm doing,' he said as he bent down and caught her perfect strawberry lips in his.

He felt her breath catch. But she was only rigid for the tiniest moment. One second later her body relaxed against his. Her lips were soft, pliable and seemed like they were moulded just for his.

His hands moved from her cheeks and tangled through her silky-soft hair. He could smell her. He could smell the perfume she was wearing, the shampoo from her hair and the strawberry from her lip gloss. He'd be happy if he could just stay here all night, inhaling her essence.

Her hands moved up to his shoulders, her fingers brushing against the skin at the side of his neck.

Reactions. That was just what he needed. Right in the middle of the busiest crossing in the world.

But somehow he knew Katsuko could cause this reaction in him anywhere.

There was a shout near them. She jumped back, pulling her lips from his.

The crowd had virtually disappeared around them, the last few stragglers reaching the far sidewalk. 'Come on!' she shouted with a flash of panic.

For a second he wanted to object. To tell the world that his only priority right now was to get his lips back on hers.

But any second now they would resemble two squashed bugs.

He grabbed her hand and ran, sprinting as fast as they could towards the further sidewalk. He was laughing now. He couldn't help it. The whole thing was so ridiculous. It had flashed into his head in the restaurant, an overwhelming urge to have their first kiss in the middle of the monumental crossing.

People parted around them, amused expressions on their faces.

Avery and Katsuko bent over, both gasping for breath.

She was laughing now too. 'What on earth were you thinking? Are you completely crazy?'

He shook his head as he caught his breath. There was something else in her eyes now. A sparkle that hadn't been there before. The sadness that had been there in the restaurant had vanished and he didn't ever want to see it again.

For a few minutes he pushed away his doubts about whether he could give her what she needed. This was all about the here and now.

He was still laughing. He straightened up and grabbed hold of her wrist again, pulling her over to the side of the street and into a doorway. 'I must be completely crazy.' He couldn't wipe the smile from his face. 'Because I'm going to do this again.'

And he did.

CHAPTER FIVE

HER SKIN FELT ITCHY, as if it prickled when she walked down the corridor at work.

She'd never felt self-conscious at work before. She could see her colleagues standing at one of the desks, talking in low voices. Were they talking about her? Did they know?

Then she saw who was standing among them. He was telling them some kind of story and his arms were waving around just like he did when he was excited.

A little shiver ran down her spine. She knew. She knew what he did when he was excited. Was that a good shiver or a bad shiver?

He leaned back and laughed and caught her eye. No. *That* was a shiver. One that sent electric pulses around her body.

She fixed her eyes on the floor and kept walking towards the treatment room. Her cheeks were warm and she wasn't normally the kind of girl who blushed. She wasn't normally the type of girl to lose sleep after a few kisses. Her lips had tingled for most of the night and when she'd taken her jacket off she'd caught a whiff of his aftershave. Just how close had they got?

She'd pulled back, laughing again, after the second kiss. Her stomach was doing backward flips and, with a mixture of alarm bells going off in her head and imaginary white unicorns charging around before her eyes, she wasn't quite sure what to think.

He'd looked thoughtful when she'd stepped back and hadn't pressed things any further. He'd slipped his hand into hers and they'd taken the subway back to the base.

Her skin had trembled as he'd walked her to the door of her house. She had felt like a teenager again, waiting for Don to throw the front door open and demand an introduction. But Avery was much cooler than she'd expected, he'd squeezed her hand and dropped a kiss on her head before walking away.

Don had been engrossed in his computer but had stood up when she'd appeared. 'Coffee?' he asked as he walked to the kitchen. 'I think I've missed dinner.'

No explanations were asked for. She was an adult. He didn't generally ask for a list of her activities. But once he realised she might be seeing a colleague he was quite sure Avery's file would fall across his desk.

Lily, one of the other nurses, looked up as she walked in. 'Katsuko—great. Can you check some diamorph with me? I've got a patient with a fractured femur and the Entonox gas is wearing off fast.'

Katsuko nodded, pleased to have something—anything—to do that would distract her. Checking controlled medicines was an everyday part of the job. She counted the vials, drew up the prescribed amount and locked up the cupboard. The patient in cubicle three was wincing as he moved. They double-checked his name and date of birth before administering the injection. 'Who are you on shift with today?' asked Lily.

Katsuko shook her head. 'Not sure. Haven't had the handover yet.'

They rounded the corner. Lily beamed. 'Oh, lucky you.

It's our very own superhero, Avery. I kind of like him. He's fitting in well.'

The words were easy for Lily and she threw them out without a second thought. She was happily married, with her first baby on the way, and was currently seeing the world through a pink or blue hazy glow.

She'd been put onto night shift for the last part of her pregnancy as she hadn't been sleeping well and the night shifts were generally a little quieter.

Katsuko kept her gaze somewhere else. 'Yeah, he seems fine.'

Lily gave her a nudge. 'More than fine.'

'What's that supposed to mean?' It must have come out sharper than she'd meant because Lily looked surprised.

'Nothing.' She picked up her bag and stretched her back. 'Time for me to go. Keep an eye on my patient, will you? They'll be here to collect him soon for Theatre.'

Katsuko nodded and headed over to the desk for the handover report. It was swift. Twelve patients in the department. One for theatre, three kids with minor ailments, four elderly patients with a variety of chest conditions, one guy with an anaphylactic reaction to something and three other adults with minor ailments. The staff shared the patients out between them and got to work.

She was trying her absolute best to be cool. She was always calm and collected at work—nothing usually fazed her. So why did she feel like a bumbling wreck?

She messed up a sterile trolley while doing a simple dressing, then tripped over her own feet while walking to the treatment room.

The whole time she was working she was constantly looking over her shoulder, wondering where Avery was, and if anyone would notice something between them.

It was a couple of hours before he finally spoke to her.

'Katsuko, there's an ambulance bringing in one of the servicemen's teenagers. Can you give me a hand?'

Her response was automatic. She walked over to the sink to wash her hands. Avery walked up behind her, his hand brushing against her bum.

'Don't!' she snapped.

They were at work. She was a professional. She wasn't the kind of girl to be caught in a compromising position in the treatment room or in the store.

At least that was the excuse she was letting bump around in her head.

It was nothing to do with the fact his kiss had driven her crazy. It was nothing to do with the things she'd shared with him—things she would never normally tell people. She'd worked with some of the people here for years and had never really shared about her grandmother. She could almost feel herself retreating a little. Trying to take back some of what she'd said.

Avery raised his eyebrows at her but didn't say a single word. He gave her a little hip-bump and washed his hands at the sink too. Katsuko grabbed an apron and some gloves and walked out to the receiving door. 'Do you know what's wrong?'

He frowned. 'Not clear. No accident. Sleepy and agitated.'

Katsuko joined in his frown. It wasn't exactly anything to go on. 'Age?' she asked. It could be anything. Alcohol, drugs, infection—the list was endless.

The ambulance appeared in the distance with the siren blaring. 'Nineteen.'

As it pulled up, Avery moved quickly to open the doors and pull the trolley towards him. The wheels automatically snapped down and allowed them to pull the trolley straight inside. The ambulance technician was talking rapidly in Japanese.

Katsuko walked alongside, translating as best she could. 'This is Jay Lim. He's nineteen. Came home last night and told his mother he wasn't feeling too well and went to bed. When she tried to wake him for breakfast this morning she realised something was wrong and called an ambulance.'

'Let's take him into Resus.'

She wasn't surprised at those words. Although the report seemed bland—the condition of the patient wasn't. The technician shot out another round of words.

'Respirations high, forty, heart rate one-forty, and blood pressure one hundred over fifty-five. He's been aggressive and extremely tired. They haven't understood all of what he's saying.'

As soon as they hit the resus room Katsuko started hooking up the monitors for Jay. She turned to the technician and asked a quick question.

Her eyes met Avery's as she glanced at the oxygen saturation. 'No history of asthma so we can put him on oxygen.'

Frank Kelly hurried into the room. 'What do you need?'

'I need bloods—lots of them—and set up an IV.'

Avery turned back to Katsuko. 'Can they give us anything else?'

She looked over at the technician, asking swiftly in Japanese. A few seconds later she turned back to Avery. 'He's a keen windsurfer and was away for the last two nights at a competition.'

'Any chance he used drugs or alcohol?'

'The technician said they've had no report of that.'

He was the ultimate professional. She was starting to cringe at snapping at him a few minutes ago. A quiet word was all it would have taken. It was hard enough to fit in. The last thing she wanted was to give her colleagues anything to talk about.

Avery moved around the teenager quickly, pulling out his stethoscope and listening to his chest. He lifted his hand. 'Ask the technician to hang around for another few minutes.'

He carefully examined Jay's head and checked his pupils as Jay tried to bat him away. Then he checked his ears, which nearly earned him a punch.

'No chance he could have an undiagnosed head injury from the surfing?'

She asked again. 'Nothing reported.'

This was baffling her just as much as Avery.

He looked up. 'What's his temperature?'

She lifted a tympanic thermometer as she asked the technician. It was unusual he hadn't mentioned it in the handover. The technician shook his head. 'They couldn't get near his ears to get a temperature. He does feel warm to touch.'

Avery nodded to the technician to come back over and help hold Jay. 'Jay, we're just checking your temperature. Can you tell me how you're feeling?'

Katsuko was quick. The tympanic thermometer only took five seconds to register. Thank goodness. Because by six seconds, Jay was thrashing around again. He made a loud noise and then retched. Katsuko grabbed a nearby sick bowl, but it seemed that Jay didn't have much to bring up.

'Thirty-nine point five,' she said swiftly to Avery.

She could almost see his brain calculating everything. He watched as Frank nodded to another colleague who held Jay's arm firmly in place. Frank inserted a cannula and withdrew blood quickly, filling five different tubes.

Jay started to try and thrash again. 'It'll be enough,' said Avery. He walked over to the medicine cupboard in Resus. 'With a temperature like that there's likely to be an infection somewhere. His chest sounds clear, but call for an X-ray. The agitation is the thing that's worrying me most.'

Katsuko was watching him closely. Jay had been in the room around two minutes and she could already tell Avery was close to making a decision. At work he was decisive and trusted his instincts. She was learning to trust them too.

He caught her gaze. 'Can you ask the technician what the sleeping arrangements were for the surfing competition?'

She frowned. It was an odd question, but easily asked. She listened to the technician and turned back. 'It was university-style dorms.'

Avery nodded. 'I'm going down the meningitis route. There's no visible rash but we all know that seeing the rash is bad news. In an ideal world we'd do a lumbar puncture and get some CSF. But he's just too agitated right now. I'm going to have to make an executive decision. Let's start with some IV penicillin.' He looked around the room. 'Is there a relative? Can we ask about allergies?'

Katsuko held up the technician's paperwork. 'Mum was following the ambulance in the car. She told the technician Jay had no allergies. Do you want me to find her and double-check?'

Avery shook his head. 'If it's already recorded that's good enough for me. Let's not waste another second for this kid.' He mixed up the preparation and drew it up into a syringe. 'Frank, can you hold his arm while I administer this?'

Frank nodded and held Jay's arm firmly. Avery slotted the syringe into the cannula. IV antibiotics had to be administered over a few minutes and Avery watched the clock while he completed the process.

He met her gaze again. 'I'll talk to his mother as soon as she arrives. Jay needs one-to-one nursing care. Fifteen-minute obs. IV fluids. I'd love to monitor fluid intake and output but I'm not sure that inserting a catheter is feasible right now. I want his breathing watched carefully and also his oxygen saturation. I'll write up some other meds for temperature control, nausea and agitation if required, along with the rest of his IV antibiotics. We need to watch this boy carefully.' He gave a little shake of his head. 'I'd still prefer to have got some CSF.'

She could see the worry lines on his forehead. Meningitis could be a killer. If this was the correct diagnosis they had to hope they'd administered antibiotics quickly enough to have an impact and halt the progression of the disease. Frank disappeared with the blood bottles and forms and she walked over next to Avery. She knew that testing cerebrospinal fluid could be a crucial part of the diagnosis. But the procedure for a lumbar puncture meant the patient had to lie very still in a certain position. Jay just wasn't able to do that right now.

'You okay?'

She watched as he licked his lips and took a few seconds to answer. He looked up. All she could see was the pale green of his eyes. She was closer than she meant to be. But it was natural for her. The skin on their arms was touching and it felt like that was meant to happen.

It was the first time she'd actually seen Avery look a little vulnerable. Something inside her squeezed tight. She reached up and touched the side of his face. 'You've got this, Avery.'

Her voice was low and his head inched a little closer to hers. Their noses almost touched. 'Do you need to tell me something?'

He shook his head. 'I'm just not good with waiting games. I want to know right now if meningitis is the correct diagnosis. The penicillin won't do any harm. But I want to know right now if it's doing any good.'

She gave a little smile. 'Avery Flynn, do you have no patience?'

He smiled too. 'Not a single bit.'

She licked her lips. 'Then let's get logical.' She tilted her head to one side. 'Tell me why meningitis.'

Avery nodded. 'Teenage boy, quick onset, he's probably immunised against some strains of meningitis but not every type. Neisseria meningitis is most common in teenagers, particularly if they've been in a communal environment. It could be serotype C, Y or W.'

She put her hand on his arm. 'And you could have just saved his life.'

It was the oddest feeling. But since her palm was in contact with his warm skin she didn't feel the urge at all to pull it away. It was pathetic. Look at how she'd acted when he'd brushed against her behind. Why did this feel like exactly what she should be doing?

Avery glanced over at Jay. 'Let's hope so. The next few hours will be crucial.' He straightened up. 'Is his mother here yet? I'll need to speak to her.'

Katsuko pulled back her hand. 'I'll go and check.' She stepped back and hurried down the corridor.

Avery stared at his arm for a few seconds. He could almost feel her imprinted on his skin. There was a distinct feeling of unease. It had only been a few short days but he'd made a real connection with Katsuko and he wasn't quite sure what to do next.

The initial harmless flirting had quickly turned into something else. Every relationship he'd ever been involved in had been cool on his part. He'd been happy for the companionship. Enjoyed the friendships and physical connection. But the emotional connection? On his part, it had never really been there.

But Katsuko felt different. He wanted to be around her.

He wanted to know so much about her. It would be easier if she weren't the General's daughter. It would be *so* much easier if she weren't the Major General's daughter.

But no matter how much he was feeling the first real pull at his heartstrings, the little twist inside was still there. Japan? He hardly knew anything about it. He wasn't even entirely sure how long this assignment would last. Apparently his sick colleague had requested this posting to Okatu. It was likely that once he'd made a full recovery he'd want to pick this assignment up again.

Part of those thoughts felt like relief. He wouldn't want to settle down. He wouldn't want to put down roots anywhere. He wouldn't be in the difficult position of having that kind of a conversation with a woman because he always had a get-out clause.

It didn't matter that he'd known lots of fellow colleagues who had found love, married and happily combined their family lives with working in the air force. Sure, it was difficult. Sure, there were sacrifices to make.

The whole thing had just never computed for him because of his example of family life back home. He'd loved the freedom of the air force. It gave him a safe haven. It had become his family. Could he even contemplate something else?

A dark hand appeared on his arm. Frank. 'Avery? Jay's mother has arrived. I've put her in the relatives' room. Katsuko is with her.'

'Thanks very much. You'll keep an eye on him while I'm gone?'

Frank gave him a resolute nod.

The relatives' room was bland. It didn't matter how hard the staff tried to make it warm and friendly, it was always a place where difficult news was delivered, and it seemed to have that atmosphere around it permanently.

As soon as he walked in, Jay's mother jumped to her feet. 'Where is he? Where is Jay? Why can't I see him?'

Katsuko had her lips pressed together and Avery could sense the tension in her body.

He reached out and touched the woman. She had the broadest Texan accent he'd ever heard. It was such a surprise. In the last few days he'd become accustomed to the quieter tones of Japanese voices or Japanese accents when colleagues were speaking in English to him.

'You can see Jay, but I need to make a few things clear.' He spoke calmly and honestly. 'Where is Jay's dad?'

The colour faded from the woman's face. 'Why?'

Avery shook his head. 'Jay's sick. I think he might have meningitis. The next few hours are crucial. It would be best if his dad could be here too.'

Jay's mum took a little step backwards. 'He's...a pilot. He's flying to Kadena Air Base, then onto Okinawa. He won't be home until tomorrow.'

Katsuko looked at him. 'Do you want me to deal with that?'

Avery nodded. He didn't know what she'd do—he was just sure that as the General's daughter she could sort whatever she needed to.

She turned to Jay's mother. 'Can you give me your husband's name and rank?'

'Captain Rizalino Lim.'

Something flashed across Katsuko's face for the briefest of seconds before she disappeared out of the door.

Avery wasn't sure but the name sounded Filipino. The mother was distinctly American. A huge percentage of US Air Force families were from different nationalities. Had Katsuko just had a flash of familiarity with this family?

The call to her father took moments. His secretary answered straight away. 'It's Katsuko. There's a medical

issue. A parent is required to be located. We have a teenager with a suspected diagnosis of meningitis. He's being
treated but the next few hours are crucial.'

'Details?'

'Pilot. Captain Rizalino Lim. He's flying to Kadena,
then Okinawa today.'

'I'll find the details while I put you through to the
General.'

Katsuko could almost hear her fingers fly across the
keyboard. Her father had always been great when families had medical emergencies on the base. He would do
everything he could to find the relative and get them back
to their family. On occasion, it couldn't happen. But nine
times out of ten her father would make sure it did.

'Something wrong?'

She smiled. He was all business. She quickly explained.
If she closed her eyes for a second she could picture him.
With one hand he'd be playing with a pencil, making little notes on the pad in front of him. He'd be nodding his
head slowly too.

There was a loud creaking noise. His door.

'Ah, that's Leah with the details. Give me a second.
Hmm…yes. Yes, that should be fine. Katsuko, tell Mrs
Lim that arrangements are being made for her husband
to be with her and Jay as soon as possible. Leah will also
arrange for one of our welfare officers to come and wait
with her until her husband arrives. Everything else okay?'

She was surprised. When she phoned him about air
force business he didn't tend to talk about anything else.
'Yes, why shouldn't it be?'

'I haven't seen much of you these last few days.'

Her skin prickled a little. 'Don, I'm twenty-five. I have
a social life.'

'Any kind of social life I should know about?'

Now her whole body prickled. Someone had told

him—told him that she was spending time with Avery. There was nothing surer.

She looked instantly over her shoulder. If her father knew, there was no point pretending her colleagues hadn't noticed things too. She might as well have a neon sign flashing above her head.

She gave a silent shake of her head. Don would soon get around to asking her outright. She'd just need to figure out what kind of answer she was going to give him.

'Nothing you should know, Don. Don't worry.'

She put down the phone and sucked in a deep breath. Her head didn't know what to do with this information. She spun around and saw Avery's outline behind the darkened window of the relatives' room.

Darn it. She even liked his reflection. And as for the unexpected feel and taste of his lips on hers the other night… She squeezed her eyes shut. Thinking about it pushed every other thought from her brain. Not something she could do at work—ever.

She straightened her shoulders and walked back down the corridor, entering the relatives' room and giving Mrs Lim a reassuring smile. 'General Williams wants to assure you he's making arrangements to get your husband back to be with you both.' She held out her hand. 'Will we take Mrs Lim along to sit with her son?'

He put a gentle arm around Mrs Lim and led her down towards the resus room. Mrs Lim put her hand up to her mouth when she saw Jay. Frank came over to join her and waited patiently while Avery explained what he could. 'At this point we have to look at why Jay's having these symptoms. Meningitis is a likely cause and it's something that has to be treated straight away. Because of that we've got Jay on some intravenous antibiotics. We also have him on some other drugs for some of the other symptoms he's having. He's agitated, has been vomiting and has a high temperature. We need to monitor Jay very carefully for the next few hours. You're welcome to stay and sit with him.'

She turned around. 'But he's had injections for meningitis. It can't be that.'

Avery nodded and pointed towards the computer. 'We're lucky. I have access to Jay's medical records. He has had some vaccinations for Hib, a strain of meningitis, and Men C, another strain. But there are many different types of meningitis and we don't have vaccines for them all.'

'So this is a different kind?'

Avery nodded. 'We think so. We've taken some blood from him for testing—the results will show if there are bacteria in his blood. Unfortunately, the other test we need to do is called a lumbar puncture. We'd have to curl Jay on his side and put a needle into a specific part of his spine to collect some fluid. Jay is just too agitated to do that test.'

'Will it matter?' Her eyes were wide.

He took a deep breath. 'We might not be able to specify the exact type of meningitis, but we would still be able to identify it as a bacterial meningitis.'

'Would his treatment change?'

Avery shook his head. 'It would still be intravenous antibiotics. We just need to wait and see how he is over the next few hours.'

Frank came over to show Mrs Lim to a seat. He gave a nod to Avery and Katsuko. 'I'll give you a shout if I need you.'

Katsuko gave Avery a little smile. Both of them could recognise the signs of being told unofficially to take a break. They were lucky. The ER had its own coffee room. Staff here frequently didn't have time to make it to the hospital canteen or other facilities.

Katsuko flicked the switch on the kettle and opened the huge tin that sat in the middle of the coffee table.

Avery looked over her shoulder and pulled something out. 'What are these things? I see them everywhere.'

She gave a laugh as she spooned some coffee into the mugs. 'I think you'd call them…' she pointed to the first packet '…chocolate pretzel sticks, and those ones…' she pointed to the other '…are strawberry rice cakes.'

Avery was still staring at the pictures on the packaging.

She poured some water into the cups. 'They are two of most popular snacks in Japan. Think of it as an initiation of fire.'

He pulled open the first packet and sagged down onto a chair as Katsuko tipped some milk into the mugs, stirred the coffee and brought them over. She hesitated for a second, then sat down next to him. There wasn't much point in worrying if someone saw them sitting together.

Avery settled back, letting his shoulder come into contact with hers. 'Okay, introduce me to your strange snacks. I wanted potato chips and a candy bar.'

She raised her eyebrows. 'What? No apples or bananas?'

'Usually yes. But today? After that diagnosis? Definitely something sweet and nasty.'

She handed him the chocolate pretzel sticks. He took a few and started eating. After a few minutes he smiled, picking up his coffee and relaxing a little. 'Hey, these are actually okay. I could get used to these.'

'You'll have to. There isn't much else in the tin.'

He turned his head towards her. 'So, you're off in a few days. Where are we going?'

She was trying so hard to appear like the coolest woman on the planet as she felt all the blood starting to rush to her cheeks and ruin her disguise.

And, for some strange reason, *What makes you think we're going anywhere?* turned into, 'Where do you want to go?' She wasn't entirely sure how that had happened.

What had happened to the walls she'd wanted to build around herself earlier? The fact she didn't really want to give her colleagues anything to talk about? It seemed a few hours in the company of Avery Flynn made her go against all the things she'd planned in her head.

He gave a little nod. 'You took me to the busiest place on the planet the last time. This time I'd like to go somewhere a little quieter.'

Uh-oh. Those pale green eyes were staring at her. And there was a definite twinkle in them. She didn't want her brain to start imagining what he was hinting at. If that was what he'd done in the busiest place on the planet, what could he do somewhere quieter?

She gave a little nod. 'Tokyo is huge. I'm sure I can find us somewhere more scenic to go.'

He grinned. 'And definitely quieter?'

There he went again, teasing her. She could play him at his own game.

'I have the perfect place in mind.'

CHAPTER SIX

HE'D TOLD KATSUKO he would pick her up at home but she'd suggested they meet in the base coffee shop. Part of him was relieved and part of him was a little put out. Was she trying to hide him from her father? And did he really want to be under the General's interrogating gaze anyway?

He blinked as she walked in. Katsuko was wearing a bright red dress patterned with dark flowers. He'd never seen her in a dress before—he'd never even seen her in a casual skirt before and he was surprised by how much it suited her. The dress was decorated with black flowers that matched her sharp dark hair.

She had a red leather bag slung across her body, black shoes with a cork sole and bright red lipstick.

She shot him a smile and joined him in the queue. 'What are you having?'

You. On this base that response would probably get him jail time.

'Just a cappuccino. You're looking gorgeous. I feel distinctly underdressed.' He tugged at his polo shirt.

She waved her hand with a smile that made him curious. 'You don't need to worry.' She nodded to the cashier. 'I'll have a skinny latte to go.' While they waited for their drinks he tried to tease out of her what their plans were for the day.

'I heard Jay is out of ICU and on the road to recovery.'

'Yeah, I went up to see him last night. He was tetchy. I think people forget that even though antibiotics fight off meningitis, the recovery process can be slow. At least he's a teenager. He can tell us how he feels. Think of all the poor babies and toddlers who can't put into words how they feel for the next few months.'

He'd noticed something else. The whole time he'd been around Jay's mother she'd seemed quite rigid. But as soon as her husband had appeared she'd just crumpled. It was like she had been holding herself together until he'd been there to catch her. Their devotion to each other and their son had shone through. Their relief at having each other there had been almost palpable. It was a connection that he'd never seen between his parents—or their future partners. Another reminder of how little his family actually functioned.

She was looking at him a little strangely. 'What?'

She shrugged. 'You're quite sentimental. I didn't take you for that.'

He gave her a crafty look. 'I have lots of hidden qualities. You just have to find them.' He waved his hand. 'Anyway, you didn't tell me what to bring. Should I change?'

This time she laughed. 'Believe me, you don't need to change. You'll be fine just as you are.' She leaned forward to pick up their coffees. 'At least I think you are.'

'What does that mean?'

She shot him a cheeky wink. 'All will be revealed. Let's go.'

They headed to the subway and Katsuko bought them tickets to a station he'd never heard of. The gleam in her eye was unmistakeable.

It felt like payback. He'd hinted at something the other

day. And he was still waiting for a response. She was hard to read. At work, it seemed like she only focused on the job. That was good. But it meant that there was only the occasional glimpse of what lay beneath the surface. She hadn't objected when he'd suggested they see each other again. In fact, she'd responded almost immediately. But what was normal for Katsuko? He had no idea.

The subway wasn't quite as busy as it had been the last time and he sat down next to her. 'Tell me about your assignments.'

'Why do you want to know about them?'

She shrugged. 'Because you've been on lots of overseas assignments. I've only ever gone to Georgia to complete my nurse training.'

'I spent some time in Georgia. It's a pity we missed each other.' Did she even realise how gorgeous she looked today?

'Where else have you been?'

He settled back into the seat. 'Ohio, Florida, Arizona, Texas, Afghanistan, Germany and Italy.'

'What was your favourite?'

'They all had something good. I probably learned the most in Afghanistan. It's a combat zone—nothing else compares to that. You never know what is going to happen next. Florida had fantastic surf and weather. Texas was good for me as doctor. I got to shadow one of the doctors at NASA for a few weeks and learn a little about the qualifications I'd need to go into that field.'

Her smile was broad. 'That sounds fabulous. Will you do it?'

'I might. Competition is tough. I'd need to go back to Dayton, Ohio, and study aerospace medicine for a couple of years.' He gave her a nudge. 'Fancy being a nurse out there?'

She gave a little sigh and stared off into space. 'A world

of possibilities. I'm just not sure. I love being in Japan, but I'm a member of the US Air Force. I think it might be good for me to try someplace else.'

'Because of your grandmother?'

'Yes. And no. I'd hate to leave and something happen to her. I'm all the family she's got left—even if she doesn't want me. But sometimes I wonder just how long I should wait.'

'What does the General say?'

She bit her lip. It took her a few moments to answer. 'We don't really talk about it much. Apparently he was a bit of a bear for the few months I was away in Georgia— even though he's never said anything about it to me. We've never really discussed the fact that I should probably be based somewhere else. A few other colleagues have been and gone in the space of time that I've been here.' She rubbed her hands on her thighs. 'I kind of wonder if he feels like me?'

'What do you mean?'

'He's practically put his life on hold to raise me. Don's a good-looking guy. And he's fun. I'm quite sure there are a whole host of women out there that he could have made a connection with and didn't.'

It was instant. He could tell there was something else. 'So why didn't he?'

She shook her head and lowered her gaze, so he reached over and put his hand on hers. 'Why do *you* think he didn't?'

'Sometimes I wonder if he was a little in love with my mother. He's never said anything that led me to believe that, but he talks about her with real respect and affection.'

'And how does he talk about your dad?'

She gave a little smile. 'Much the same.' The subway trundled to a stop and she looked up. 'It's the next station.' Her fingers reached up and twiddled with her hair.

'Then maybe the women that he's met didn't want to be lumbered with someone else's child.'

Avery shook his head. 'Please tell me you don't actually think that?'

Her brown eyes met his. 'Why not? There are lots of women in this life who wouldn't want to take on someone else's child. What if the love of Don's life came along and he let her slip through his fingers because of me?' There was a little wobble in her voice. He was struggling with this—probably because he could see her emotions bubbling underneath the surface.

'You're an adult, Katsuko. Not a child. Let me put it this way. Do you honestly think Don would have a serious relationship with the kind of woman who would make him choose between you and her? He doesn't strike me as that kind of guy.'

She gave a sad kind of smile. 'Probably not. I just hate to think that I'm the reason he's stayed all these years and now I'm thinking about leaving.'

He grabbed her hand as the subway pulled into the next station. 'All kids grow up and leave home. You've just left it a little later than normal.'

They exited the subway and she led him up a flight of steps. This part of Tokyo wasn't quite as built up. It was lighter, with areas of green around them. The station was part way up a mountain that gave a good view over the city.

'Where on earth are we?'

'It's all part of my master plan. Have you heard of a *sento*?'

'A what?'

She held out her hands. 'They're all around here. A *sento* is a bathhouse.'

He looked stunned. 'A bathhouse?'

'Yes. The other alternative is an *onsen*, which is built

around a hot spring. There is a whole variety around here. Some are completely modern, some more traditionally built.'

She could see him look around the area. Some of the buildings were sleek, rising out of the mountainside and sheeted in glass. Others were constructed from wood, painted white, with their large, dark, gently curved roofs being the most visually impressive component. She pointed to the one straight in front of them. 'This one is my favourite. It's a super-*sento*.'

Avery stopped walking. 'So, what actually happens in a super-*sento*?'

She was trying very hard not to grin. Avery had hinted about getting her alone. He had no idea what he was about to get into.

She smiled sweetly. 'It's a traditional bathhouse.' She gave him a wink. 'And it's communal.' She walked swiftly ahead.

'What?' Avery's voice shouted after her. Then his footsteps pounded along and he pulled at her shoulder. 'What did you just say?'

She'd reached the door of the *sento* and pulled it open. 'Bathhouses in Japan are communal.'

He paused at the door, his mouth hanging open. 'But I didn't bring my swimmers.'

'Who says you need swimmers?' She couldn't help but laugh—he looked rooted to the spot. She pulled out her bag and paid at Reception. It only took a few seconds for Avery to appear at her shoulder.

From the expression on his face he'd collected his thoughts in a whole different direction. His smile reached from one side of his face to the other. Everything was going perfectly to plan.

She pointed off to the right and handed him a key. 'You go that way—I go to the left. Take off your clothes in the changing room. There will be pyjamas or a loose kimono inside for you to change into. Leave all your other things in the locker, then head inside.'

He was still smiling. 'I'll see you inside, then.' He walked towards the door—no, he swaggered towards the door and Katsuko almost burst out laughing.

The receptionist was smiling at her broadly. She'd seen it all before.

The next hour or so would be interesting.

Avery just about flung his clothes into the locker and pulled on the pyjamas. They were thin and light—almost like a pair of surgical scrubs. He moved outside and looked up. It was a bright corridor, sealed off from the outside world but clearly outdoors. Ahead was another door.

He couldn't stop smiling. He pushed the door open and stopped walking promptly.

The room was filled with naked men and steam. Lots of steam. An assistant gestured for him to take off his clothes. He paused, he couldn't help it. Avery had never been embarrassed by his body and it was apparent that every single man in this room felt the same way. He was a doctor—there was nothing he hadn't seen before. Men of all shapes and sizes stood in front of him. Most of them were chatting to each other as if they were fully clothed. Nakedness didn't seem to be an issue.

Avery pulled off his pyjamas and sat on the stool that the smiling assistant pointed to—it was obvious he was used to visitors. Two seconds later he was hit by a warm shower spray and handed what looked like a kind of loofah.

He gave a nod and scrubbed at his skin while the warm shower buzzed over him. When he was finished the assistant gestured for him to walk further on. Ahead, was the biggest array of large tubs he'd ever seen. Some were empty, some had a few men in them, and others were busy. To the side were rooms with a range of glass doors that looked like saunas.

He stuck his toe in the nearest tub and pulled it out sharply. The water was near scalding. The doctor in him wanted to tell everyone not to go near it. But a few seconds later a man who resembled a sumo wrestler stepped into the tub with no trepidation whatsoever.

For a minute Avery forgot all about his nakedness. Any second now the guy would have a heart attack in water at that temperature. Instead, the man spread his arms out around the side of the tub and leaned back, as if it was his favourite place in the world.

Avery gave his head a little shake and moved forward. He dipped his toe in a variety of tubs. They ranged from scalding to very hot to hot. The next tub had only one man in it and the water temperature was warm and pleasant. The man gave him a gracious nod that made Avery feel it was impossible to walk away.

He gave a nod too and climbed in. The water was soothing. It instantly relaxed his tense muscles. He kept glancing around. First of all, at the other tub where he kept expecting the large man to faint, then around the whole bathing area.

It took him a few seconds to realise that Katsuko was nowhere in sight. In fact, no women were anywhere in sight.

The man in his tub nodded towards him again. 'Visitor?'

Avery smiled. He really did need to learn some Japanese. 'Yes.'

The man smiled politely. 'Okatu base?'

Avery laughed and nodded. He might as well have a sign on his forehead that said he was American.

'Pilot?'

He shook his head. 'No, doctor.'

'Ah. Doctor. Good.' He gave him a thoughtful glance and pointed to the tub. 'First time?'

Yes, it seemed he did have a sign on his head.

'It is, yes.'

The man pointed further down the bathhouse. 'Try bath with tea.'

'Tea?'

He gave a knowing nod. 'Yes.'

Avery was surprised. He'd never heard of a bath with tea. When Katsuko had told him not to bring anything she hadn't been joking. Towels were everywhere. Along with soap, shampoo, moisturising lotion and cotton swabs. But no one actually used these products in the water. They only used them in the showers.

He rested his head back for a moment and closed his eyes. Katsuko had surprised him. When she'd brought him into a bathhouse and hinted they'd be naked his mind had naturally gone into overdrive—just as she'd intended.

He almost laughed out loud. She'd got him. Fair and square. She'd led him right up the proverbial path.

He couldn't wipe away the grin as he opened his eyes again and stared around the vast bathhouse at the wide variety of naked men. Of all the places in the world to come...

He nodded to the other man and climbed back out, walking along—not particularly conscious of his nakedness—past the variety of other tubs. Some were bubbling with jets. One definitely looked like green tea. Another had a very odd aroma. No one was in it and he bent down to have a closer smell. He almost spluttered. Red wine? In a bathhouse?

He looked around to see if anyone was watching. Everyone was going about their daily business, so he dipped his finger into the water and brought it up to his nose. Definitely red wine. He'd seen everything now.

He had a half a mind to climb into it. Cleopatra had apparently bathed in red wine. If it was good enough for the Egyptians...

Five seconds later he was in the wine.

It was the oddest feeling. The smell was so strong and the feeling exuberant. And it was hot. Very hot. Was it possible to boil in a tub of wine? He'd never seen this much wine before and he was pretty sure people could get drunk on the fumes alone.

A few minutes was long enough, then he headed back to the showers and tried to scrub the smell of wine from his skin. He could just imagine the look on Blake Anderson's face tomorrow morning if he turned up smelling of wine.

Curiosity was killing him. There had to be a women-only section in here too. He could only imagine it was completely hidden from view, otherwise it would be every teenage boy's dream.

As he headed to the changing room he was surprised by the time. He'd been in here for more than an hour and a half. One of the assistants signalled for him to put back on the scrubs-like pyjamas and head through another door.

He should have guessed. Katsuko had the widest grin he'd ever seen and was sprawled across a chaise longue.

'How do you like a Japanese bathhouse?' she teased.

He pushed her legs over and sat down beside her. 'I can think of a few improvements.'

'I wonder what they might be. Did you enjoy the experience?'

He raised his eyebrows. 'What's not to enjoy? If I didn't know enough about body shapes before, I certainly do now. Once I got over the shock of being naked among complete strangers I was kind of hoping there might have been naked females around too.'

'I bet you were.' She shook her head. 'But the bathing is always completely separate. Some super-*sento*s are more equipped for families. They have mixed bathing and everyone wears swimsuits. But I thought I should show you the genuine Japanese experience.' She looked around. 'It's usually busier when I come. Most people come to the bathhouses in the evening rather than during the day. I just wanted to give you a gentle introduction.'

'You think I needed it?'

She swung her legs to the floor. 'What do you want to do next? There's a bar upstairs and there's a restaurant. There are also some rooftop footbaths or there's a low-temperature sauna—you keep your clothes on in there.'

A few teenage girls walked past, their wet hair tied up in ponytails. They were looking at him and Katsuko and whispering together.

He shifted in the chair. They must have been in the bathhouse at the same time as Katsuko. It was clear she'd noticed their actions. She waved her hand. 'Pay no notice, they're just silly schoolgirls. One of them was talking about me while she was sitting next to me. She nearly died when I turned around and answered her in perfect Japanese.' She raised her eyebrows. 'I even corrected her grammar for her.'

Was this the kind of thing Katsuko experienced regularly? He tried to temper the little flame burning inside him. He glared at the teenagers. 'Silly schoolgirls who should know better,' he said.

He turned back towards her. It was clear that Katsuko didn't want to take this any further. He could see her biting her lip.

He shook his head and bent down. 'What's wrong? You're better than this. You're stronger than this.'

She closed her eyes for the briefest of seconds. When she opened them again he saw a whole host of vulnerability in the tiniest of flashes. 'Welcome to my life, Avery. Just as well you don't plan on being around too long. You'd have to get used to it, just like I have.' Her voice was barely a whisper. The most fleeting of glances was taking the whole shine off their day.

He didn't know where the words came from. They were just on his lips and out there before his brain had processed them. 'And I would. Every. Single. Day.'

Both of them froze. He hadn't meant to say them. Of course he would be leaving soon. He didn't even know what *this* was.

Those deep brown eyes of hers were like a bottomless pool. They'd sparkled earlier. He liked them best like that. He wanted to bring that back. That was all this really was. That was all this could ever really be.

Her eyes blinked shut again for a second. *He knew.*

He knew she wasn't really taking him seriously.

But when she opened them again it was as if she were giving herself a mental shake. She was putting it all behind her.

Part of his heart twanged as her mask slipped back into place and she smiled up at him.

He took a deep breath. It was time to get things back on track. 'What do you have in store for me this afternoon?'

She stood up, arching her back and stretching. His eyes were instantly drawn to one place. Underwear didn't appear to be required under the pyjamas. Any more thoughts like that and he'd need to find his jeans again.

She put her hands on her hips and looked at him. 'Today is all about culture. I'm introducing you to some of the most famous Japanese pastimes.'

'Do any of these pastimes involve food?'

She laughed. 'You should know me by now. They all

involve food. We've got a bit of a journey next. Why don't we grab a drink and something to eat before we head out?'

She headed for the stairs and he followed close behind. He'd just spent ninety minutes in one of the hottest places he'd ever been, yet Katsuko still looked immaculate.

'Did you even go into the bathhouse? How come your hair hasn't frizzed in the steam? You don't have a hair out of place.'

She turned in the stairwell and put a hand on his shoulder. Because of their position on the stairs her breasts were directly in his line of vision. Some things just couldn't be complained about.

'I told you. I've been coming here for years. It only takes me five minutes to fix my hair as they have hair-dryers and straighteners in the changing room.'

'You straighten your hair?'

She gave him an astonished look. '*Every* girl straightens her hair.'

He shrugged. 'Good to know. Must have missed that one.'

They walked into the bar and sat at one of the tables. Avery went to pick up the menu but she put her hand on his. 'Can I give you a recommendation?'

'If I let you, can I claim a reward?' The words came out instantly. He could feel the connection again. Feel the buzz between them. The truth was, it never seemed to go away. He couldn't remember ever feeling like this.

But he could remember someone talking about it. His father. He'd always talked about feeling electricity between him and whatever number wife he was on. The trouble was, the electricity always shorted out. His father lost interest quickly and moved on.

Katsuko leaned across the glass-topped table towards him. He couldn't imagine ever losing interest in her and he'd barely even scratched the surface. There was just that tiny little gnawing feeling that he didn't want to end up like his father.

'Has anyone ever told you that you can be quite cheeky?'

'Has anyone ever told you that you bring out the best and the worst in them?'

She sat back a little, the smile dropping from her face. 'I bring out the worst in you?'

His stomach churned. Wrong, wrong thing to say. He'd been thinking too much. Drawing comparisons with a man he'd never had anything in common with. He covered quickly, leaning across the table again and whispering, 'You bring out lots of bad thoughts in me.'

There was a second of silence, then she smiled again as the waiter appeared. She spoke rapidly in Japanese to him and he nodded and disappeared.

'What did you order?'

'Two beers and two portions of prawn and pork pancake with caramelised onions and crispy noodles. Trust me, it's delicious.'

He groaned. 'I trust you already. It sounds delicious. How long will it take them to bring it out?'

'Ten minutes.' She tilted her head to one side. 'This is the first time I've seen you out of work without your hat.'

His hand went automatically to his head. 'I know. I had no idea where we might go. I know there are a lot of theme parks in Tokyo. I didn't want to lose my hat on the first ride.'

'You thought I might take you to a theme park?'

He held up one hand. 'I had no idea. I thought you might be a bit of an adrenaline junkie.'

She frowned. It was obviously an expression she wasn't familiar with.

He waved his hands. 'You know, someone who likes motor racing, bungee jumping and parachuting.'

She shuddered. She actually shuddered. 'Not a chance.'

He was amazed. 'But at work you seem fearless—you don't like theme parks?'

She counted off on her fingers. 'I don't like roller-coasters, I don't like things that make you go upside down, things that shoot you into the air. I definitely don't like ghost trains.' She held out her hand and gave it a little shake. 'I don't mind simulator rides because I know they're not real, and I *might* go on a water ride depending on how big the drop is.'

'You're really a big scaredy-cat. I'm so surprised.'

She shrugged as the waiter brought over their drinks. She took a sip from her beer bottle and gave him a wink. 'Maybe I just like to surprise you.'

Was she joking? Pulling his leg because she wasn't really scared of anything?

A gorgeous smell wafted towards them as the kitchen door swung open. He waited until the plates had been put down and the waiter had walked away. He picked up the chopsticks and wondered how on earth he could do this without getting into a mess.

Katsuko was staring at him as if she had something else on her mind. 'You already surprised me,' he said as he tried to grab some of the pork.

'I did?'

'You got me naked on our third date.'

This guy was going to drive her plain crazy. She hated to admit that she loved being in his company. But one minute he seemed to flirt like crazy and the next he seemed to back off. Yet if he did anything else as well as he kissed...

She had to keep reminding herself he'd been gentlemanly earlier. He hadn't really meant what he'd said. He had been protective of her. And that was nice. It was kind. But she had to remember it wasn't more than that.

She took him to the train station and listened to him

talk about his favourite places in America for most of the journey. He was reluctant at first but she was glad that she'd asked. After a few questions his answers grew more passionate and she could see the love for the place reflected in his eyes. By the time they reached Komagome Station she knew that he loved the Lincoln Memorial, the Smithsonian and an original nineteen-fifties diner back in Ohio. The one thing she did notice was that his memories all seemed attached to his uncle—none of them were about his mother or father. It seemed odd. Her favourite places were always associated with the people she'd been there with, a few with her parents and a few with Don. None with her grandmother.

'Your family must miss you,' she said as they rode on the train.

He blinked. 'What do you mean?'

'You've been to lots of overseas bases. You've moved around a lot. Don't they get tired of it all and ask when you'll come home?'

It seemed a natural question. She knew it was one that Don would ask her if she moved base.

He hesitated. And in that second her insides curled up a little.

'My family aren't the most…traditional.'

'And mine is?'

She could see him thinking about what to say. He met her gaze. 'The picture you carry, of your mum and dad? I think it's safe to say my mum and dad have never looked at each other like that. They weren't a match made in heaven. In fact, both of them seem to have made it their life's ambition to get married as many times as possible. My sister seems to be learning from their examples.'

She was stunned. The way he'd delivered the words made it clear this topic wasn't really open for discussion.

She licked her lips and said quietly, 'People can make mistakes.' They were pulling into the station.

Avery must have recognised the English signs as he stood up. 'But wouldn't it be nice if they learned from them?' he muttered.

They walked out of the train station into the clean, fresh air.

'Where are we?' Avery looked around.

She pointed forward. She'd just glimpsed a tiny part of the man that was Avery Flynn. She was curious to know more. But not curious enough to press where she shouldn't.

'This is Rikugien. It's my favourite Japanese garden in Tokyo. It is so peaceful you can easily forget that you are in the city.' She held out her arms as they walked towards the entrance. 'And we've come at the perfect time of year. It's gorgeous in autumn when the maple trees turn a stunning blend of red and yellow. The only time of year it looks better is spring when all the pink cherry blossom is out.'

She turned and he was watching her carefully. 'First a bathhouse and now a Japanese garden? You're like a different person today, much more chill.'

She stepped up right under his nose and whispered, 'Say the word, Avery, and I'll take you shopping. I can guarantee complete and utter chaos.'

He slid his hand into hers. 'I think I'll stick with the Japanese garden.'

They wandered around the gardens for nearly an hour. The main part of the gardens had a large central pond surrounded by hills and trees. Katsuko led him to a bridge and stopped halfway. 'Look over there. That's *garyu-seki*.'

He wrinkled his nose as he stared at the half-submerged rock in the water surrounded by a whole array of turtles. 'What does that mean?'

'It's called the sleeping dragon rock.' She gave him a nudge. 'If you close your eyes and squint a little it looks like a dragon.' She couldn't hide the hint of laughter in her voice.

He tilted his head from one side to the other, obviously trying to picture the rocks as a dragon. 'It might have helped if they'd painted it.'

She laughed. 'You're supposed to use your imagination.'

He pointed to the widely dispersed small buildings surrounding the pond. 'What are those?'

Something inside her fluttered. She'd had lots of different colleagues from all parts of the world. It wasn't the first time she'd taken someone sightseeing around Tokyo, but sightseeing with Avery felt different than normal.

No one else had kissed her at the Hachiko Crossing. Most people wanted to go to sumo wrestling or one of the theme parks. She'd never really shown a colleague the things that she loved in Tokyo. The things that she would miss most if she ever left.

She stepped a little closer. 'If I tell you, will you promise to behave?'

He put his hand on her hip, pulling her closer to him. 'Me? Behave? After you've already gotten me naked?'

She shook her head. He was going to bring this up for ever. A little breeze blew between them, sweeping her hair across her face. His fingers reached up and stroked her face, catching the hair and tucking it behind her ear.

For a second she was lost. It was like an instant flash forward to something that would never exist. She'd kind of like to feel like this for ever. She could picture him in fifty years' time, telling their family that Katsuko had got him naked on their third date.

She sucked in her breath sharply. Where had that come from?

'You okay?' He must have seen her moment of panic. His stubble brushed against her ear and she caught her breath again. Time to focus.

She nodded. 'Those are Japanese tea houses. I thought you might like to visit one and see a traditional Japanese tea ceremony.' She held up her hand. 'But be warned. It takes just under an hour. You'll have to learn some patience.'

He caught her unawares, leaning forward and brushing his lips against hers. 'You're teaching me everything I need to know about patience.'

If he hadn't stepped back when he did she would have responded instantly, wrapping her arms around his neck and demanding to be kissed like before. Instead, he slipped his hand into hers again and gave it a little tug.

She pointed to the nearest tea house. 'This is the one we'll go to. It's built from wood from the Meiji period. It survived the war.'

'What's the Meiji period?'

'It was the late eighteen hundreds right up until the First World War.'

The free-standing tea house had a good view of the sleeping dragon, built in an arbour on a stream that ran through a gorge. The water fell down through the rocks, sending a light spray into the air, and a large collection of koi circled nearby. There was a tranquillity about the place—even though it was in the open air. Quiet noises of the lapping water, rustling leaves and forest wildlife echoed around them.

'It's beautiful,' he whispered.

She smiled. 'Yes. Yes, it is.' She gestured towards the tea house. 'We call them *chashitsu*.' She pointed to a variety of exquisitely dressed women in traditional kimonos with their hair in intricate styles decorated with combs and ornaments. 'And these are the *teishu*, the host and teachers of the tea ceremony.'

He looked amazed. 'Are we going in there?'

'We are. Now, take your shoes off and…' she put her finger to her lips '…don't speak.'

The *teishu* met them at the door and gave a little bow. The floor was covered with tatami mats. She invited them to sit down and Katsuko sat cross-legged on the floor and Avery joined her.

She loved the tea ceremony but she enjoyed it even more as she watched Avery's face. She could see him itching to ask questions at every part of the ceremony. Even though it was called a ceremony it was more like a carefully choreographed dance.

The host ritually cleansed each item for the ceremony— the tea bowl, whisk and tea scoop, using prescribed motions, and then placed them in a precise order. The whisk was used to create a thin paste from water and a special type of powdered green Japanese tea called matcha. The paste was then whisked into a thick liquid.

This was the part of the ceremony that Katsuko loved. It was rhythmical, almost hypnotic, watching the liquid being whisked. Avery hardly moved. He was even breathing quietly as he watched everything intently. She slid her hand over next to his. He didn't even blink but must have sensed it was there because his warm hand covered hers. His thumb found its way under her palm where he stroked softly, sending a whole host of tingles up her arm. No. She'd never felt like this at a tea ceremony before.

When the tea was ready it was served in the tea bowl—the same tea bowl used by everyone. Bows were exchanged and Avery followed her lead. She raised the bowl as a gesture of respect to the host. Katsuko rotated the bowl, took a sip, complimented the host then wiped the rim of the bowl clean and passed it to Avery.

He mimicked her actions perfectly. He never even grimaced when he tasted the bitter tea.

When the ceremony was complete the *teisha* invited Avery to ask questions. And he did. More than Katsuko could ever have imagined. He'd paid attention to everything.

Every day this guy did something else to make her like him more.

An hour after the ceremony started it was finally complete. They emerged back out into the afternoon sun and had only taken a few steps when Katsuko's phone buzzed.

She pulled it from her pocket and sucked in a breath. 'Not again.'

Avery turned towards her. 'What? What is it?'

She paused, well aware that she was about to ruin a perfectly good day. 'I'm really sorry, but I'm going to have to go. It's my grandmother.'

'Is she sick?' There was instant concern on his face.

She gritted her teeth. If she were sick, things would be more straightforward. She gave a wry smile. 'Not sick, just cantankerous. She's flung her carers out. She does this on a regular basis.'

He half smiled. 'She what?'

Katsuko turned on the path to head back to the train station. 'It's like dealing with a toddler. At least I think it's like dealing with a toddler. Every now and then she throws her carers out and texts me to complain. What it means for tonight is that there's no one to make her dinner or get her ready for bed. I'll need to go and help.' She shook her head. 'Then I'll need to phone whoever she's insulted this time and apologise.'

Avery kept pace beside her. 'She does this a lot?'

'Oh, yes.' Katsuko was trying to calculate in her head the simplest way for Avery to get back to base. She pulled their tickets from her pocket.

'I'll tell you which line to get and where to change.'

He shook his head. 'No, you won't.'

She stopped walking. 'Why?'

He stuck his hands in his pockets and kept walking. 'Because I'm coming with you.'

She couldn't hide her surprise. 'What? No, you can't. I mean, you don't want to do that. You go back to base. I don't know how long I'll be. It's not fair.'

He slung his arm around her shoulder and pulled her closer. 'Life's not fair. Anyway, I want to meet your cantankerous old grandmother.'

Now she felt horrified. 'Why would you want to do that?'

He smiled down at her. 'I want to see if you've inherited any of her traits.'

CHAPTER SEVEN

As a DOCTOR, Avery Flynn had met a lot of cantankerous patients in his time. But he'd never met anyone like Hiroko Satou. She definitely won the prize.

From the second they left their shoes at the entranceway and entered her single-storey home he could sense the tension in the air. Not that he could understand a word of what was going on.

She didn't shout, but her tone spoke a thousand words. Katsuko tried to introduce him but he was instantly dismissed with one look. Then the tirade clearly aimed at Katsuko started.

Avery had never been rude, but as the staccato words flowed freely he started to get annoyed. It was clear Katsuko was doing everything she could to placate her grandmother, who clearly wasn't listening.

After about fifteen minutes Katsuko threw her hands in the air, walked through to the kitchen and started banging things around. She'd already warned him she'd need to make something for her grandmother's dinner.

He folded his arms and leaned against the wall. It could appear impertinent. But he was a twenty-eight-year-old man—not a boy—and now he could understand clearly why Katsuko had looked nervous on the way over.

The smell of food cooking quickly wafted from the kitchen. 'Can I do anything to help?' he asked.

There was a tiny rise of the old woman's eyebrows. Interesting. Katsuko had said she didn't speak or understand a word of English. Avery wasn't so sure.

'No, thanks' came the reply from the kitchen. 'She wouldn't like it.'

Avery caught the sharp gaze of the woman in the wheelchair currently scowling at him and gave her a knowing smile.

He started to walk slowly around the room. As expected, it was clutter-free with everything in easy reach. She had a giant modern television on the wall and her tablet sitting on the table next to her. It seemed she wasn't entirely steeped in tradition.

He stopped as he caught sight of a photograph in a frame on the wall. A beautiful young Japanese woman, around Katsuko's age, dressed in a traditional red kimono smiled back at him. The photo had aged a little around the edges. It had obviously been there for a while. He glanced around the rest of the room, looking for any photos of Katsuko. There were none.

'Your daughter was beautiful,' he said quietly. 'You must miss her.'

She blinked and her scowl deepened.

He kept walking. Her eyes occasionally darted towards the kitchen. She could hear Katsuko making dinner. Avery kept walking slowly, aware that the old lady's eyes were following his every move.

'Katsuko's a great nurse. A real credit to you.' He pointed to the photo. 'I can see she gets her beauty from her mother.' He paused. The old woman really did have an unwavering glare.

He faced her square on. 'You must be very proud of her.'

Finally, she drew her eyes off him, giving him a look of disgust. She understood a whole lot more than she admitted to.

Katsuko stuck her head back through the doorway. 'Dinner will be ready soon. I'll just go and get her bed ready for later.' She crossed through the main room.

Avery leaned against the wall again. Hiroko Satou watched her granddaughter leave the room, then turned to glare at Avery again. He crossed one leg over the other and folded his arms. It was like a Mexican stand-off. But he wasn't afraid.

He could see the fury emanating from the old woman. In a lot of ways he felt sorry for her. Her gnarled hands were sitting on her lap. Her bare feet were visible under her blanket. The toe joints looked swollen and distended. Every bone in her body must ache. How many years must she have felt like this?

Had she been frustrated when she'd been unable to look after her granddaughter? Was that why she had such a poor relationship with the General?

But what was her excuse for the way she made Katsuko feel? There was no excuse for that.

He opened his mouth to speak again just as Katsuko came back into the room. Her grandmother started talking instantly, her eyes darting between Avery and Katsuko, her words low and fierce.

It took around ten seconds to realise that the latest rant was about him. Katsuko looked uncomfortable and she kept trying to answer, but her grandmother cut her off at every turn. It appeared that all her venom was now aimed at Avery.

He hated this. He had no clue what the words were, and he didn't care in the least that they were about him—all he cared about was the fact that Katsuko looked as though she was about to burst into tears.

If they were in the emergency department and a patient or relative spoke to her like this, she wouldn't be long in putting them in their place. But here, in her grandmother's home, she looked the most vulnerable he'd ever seen her.

He straightened up and walked over to her, putting his arm around her waist. Every muscle in her body stiffened but he pretended he didn't notice. He was sending a clear message to the woman who was upsetting the woman he cared about.

'Let me help. What can I do?'

The words were simple but he hoped the look in his eyes told her a whole lot more. She stared up at him for a few seconds. Her brown eyes fixed on his and he could see her swallow nervously. 'Let me help you,' he urged.

Her grandmother spat out some more words and Katsuko blinked back tears before turning and going back into the kitchen. Two minutes later she appeared with a bowl of food for her grandmother.

Avery went into autopilot. He wheeled the chair over to the nearby table and positioned her carefully. Katsuko brought some chopsticks and a napkin for her grandmother and gestured for Avery to sit down at the other side of the room. A few seconds later she joined him. 'She doesn't like people watching her eat. She struggles to hold the chopsticks now.'

She stared down at her hands and he put his arm around her again, staring across at her grandmother defiantly. It was ridiculous. It made him feel like a teenager again, but he wasn't intimidated by the woman and he could see the affect she had on Katsuko. It was almost poisonous.

'Why do you come when she texts?'

Her eyes were wet. 'Who else would come?'

He pressed his lips together. 'I get that she's in pain. I get that she's from a different generation. But I'm struggling to see what you get from this relationship.'

She blinked in surprise. 'What does that mean? She's my grandmother.'

'She is. But you don't have to like her. And you don't have to jump when she texts.'

She shook her head in bewilderment. 'But then she'd have no one.' She sighed. 'I try not to. Sometimes I text back and tell her I'm at work. One time she threw her carers out seven days in a row.'

'Did she treat your mother like this?'

Her lips trembled. 'I remember lots of arguments. My father used to refuse to visit. He didn't want my mother to bring me here.'

'But here you are.'

He left the statement hanging between them.

There was so much he could say here. So much he wanted to say. But he wasn't sure how appropriate it was. It certainly wasn't appropriate to say it in her grandmother's house.

He took a deep breath and spoke quietly. 'As I've grown older I've realised the old adage that blood is thicker than water means nothing. You should surround yourself with people who love you—or no people at all. People who have a positive impact on your life.'

Her brow furrowed. 'Does that mean you don't see your family?'

A wave of sadness flooded over him. 'My parents aren't the best example of family. And my sister seems to have learned from their examples. The air force helps me keep a distance. It's my family now.'

Katsuko glanced over towards her grandmother. She'd finished her food, her slightly trembling hands were back in her lap and her eyes were closed. Katsuko reached over and laced her fingers through Avery's. 'That's sad,' she whispered.

'So is this,' he replied.

CHAPTER EIGHT

THE CATCALLING STARTED as soon he walked in.

'Woo-hoo, Captain Flynn, how are those kissable lips?'

'Hey, Avery, do you have a death wish or something?'

Frank walked past, shaking his head and tutting. 'The things some people will do to try and get a transfer out of here.'

Avery looked about, catching a few raised eyebrows. He walked down to the desk where the majority of the staff were standing.

'Well, if it isn't our very own Romeo,' said one of the nurses. The rest of the staff were laughing and looked at him in expectation. He felt a weird prickle go down his spine.

For the last few weeks he'd continued to see Katsuko on a regular basis. They weren't entirely keeping it a secret, he just hadn't discussed it with anyone he was working with.

And things had been a little awkward. After the visit to her grandmother's house Katsuko had pulled back. She hadn't said the words, but she'd been distant.

It should have dented his confidence but it hadn't. It wasn't his confidence he was worried about. It was hers. The visit to her grandmother's had taken the sparkle from her eyes and the shine from her confidence. He hated that—probably more than he should for a guy that was a temporary arrangement and only looking for some kind of fling.

Because he liked her. He liked her more and more. Their connection felt so real. She was feisty. She was good company. And she was sexy as hell. The perfect woman in every way. So why wasn't he telling the world they were dating? And why wasn't she?

He frowned at the faces around him. 'What on earth are you guys talking about?'

Glances were exchanged but no one spoke. Blake Anderson walked up behind him and gave him a slap on the back. 'Come with me, Captain Flynn. We need to have a chat about your risk-taking behaviour.'

He was smiling but there was seriousness behind his eyes. The rest of the staff found their voices again.

'You're in trouble now.'

'The plane leaves for Ohio in an hour.'

Avery had no idea what they were talking about. Risk-taking behaviour? Maybe in the past, but not recently. He followed Blake into his office and closed the door behind him.

'Are you going to tell me what all this is about?'

Blake looked at him carefully. 'No one has told you?'

'Told me what?' Avery looked over his shoulder. 'Is there a camera in here? Is this some kind of game show?'

Blake pulled his phone from his pocket. 'There isn't a camera in here, but there sure was one where you were a few weeks ago.' He touched the screen and turned the phone around. 'You really haven't seen this?'

Avery took the phone and tilted it to get a better view of the screen. It was like a movie. A film clip.

The view was high, as if taken from one of the street cameras. It was Hachiko Crossing at night, lit up by all the neon lights. One second the crossing was swarming with people, the next the camera zoomed in on a couple. A couple kissing in the middle of the crossing, just as it emptied and the lights were about to change.

Avery's breath caught somewhere in his throat.

There was no mistaking the couple. There was no mistaking his fedora.

And there was no mistaking the heat of the kiss.

He looked up at Blake. 'What on earth…?'

Blake still looked faintly amused. He folded his arms across his chest. 'Look at the caption.'

Avery scrolled back above the video clip. The words were written in English and—he presumed—Japanese: *Can you identify the mystery couple?*

He shook his head. 'But this was weeks ago. Who filmed it? I never saw anyone.'

He felt distinctly uncomfortable. Had Katsuko seen this? What would she say? Would she be happy or upset that people knew their relationship had developed? He played the clip again and tried to ignore the instant dryness in his throat. There was absolutely no mistaking his intentions with that kiss. He had one hand in her hair and the other firmly on her backside, pressing her against him.

Blake sighed. 'Check out the comments.'

Avery glanced underneath the video and blinked. More than a thousand comments. Then he looked at the views. *'What?'*

Blake held up his hands. 'It seems you're a bit of a slow burner. It appears that one of the street camera operators caught sight of your liaison and decided to post it, asking if anyone knows the couple. It's gone viral. People have been posting it all over. And if you scroll through the comments you'll see that some people have identified exactly who you both are…' he paused '…and which air force base you're from.'

Avery groaned. 'Oh, no.'

'Oh, yes.'

'I need to speak to Katsuko.'

'I think someone else is speaking to her—at least that's the impression I got when the General phoned me an hour ago.'

Avery cringed and closed his eyes for a second. 'What did he say?'

'You really want to know?' From Blake's tone it was apparent that, no, he really didn't want to know. 'Consider yourself spoken to about being a captain in the US Air Force and being caught on camera undertaking risky behaviour. You made it off that crossing with less than a second to spare.'

'I was kind of caught up.'

Blake smiled. 'I could see that.'

Something shot through Avery's mind. 'You only saw this an hour ago? How did everyone else see it?'

Blake shrugged. 'Coincidences, I imagine. I've got to assume you haven't been online this morning. I imagine you have a few messages waiting. Once you'd both been identified and tagged, the video clip circulated like wildfire among the staff.'

Avery groaned again. 'Great, just great.'

Blake gave him a serious stare. 'Avery, do me a favour, don't get caught on camera in future—I can't afford to be down one doctor.' He pressed his lips together for a second. 'And just so you know, she might be called firecracker but she's not as confident as you think. She's popular around here. Treat her badly and it won't just be the General you need to worry about.'

Something was wrong. It was her day off but she could hear the front door opening. Seconds later there was a shout. 'Katsuko?'

What on earth was Don doing home? He should be at

work. She rubbed her eyes and climbed out of bed, walking slowly out into the corridor and standing at the top of the stairs. He didn't look particularly happy.

'I'm off today.' She sighed. She'd never fall asleep again now. 'What's wrong?'

He gestured towards her. 'I need to speak to you. Come downstairs.'

She frowned. 'What? Can't this wait until later?'

He shook his head. 'No. It can't.'

By the time she got down the stairs Don had flipped open his laptop and had a video clip showing. Now she was really confused. She'd thought he wanted to talk to her.

'Watch' was all he said.

Two minutes later she had her head on the table. Shock. Embarrassment. And definitely cringeing.

'I think just about everyone on the base has seen this.'

'They have?' She didn't even ask where it had come from. She could find that out later.

'You were standing in the middle of the crossing. You barely made it off the street.'

She tried not to smile as memories of the kiss flooded through her.

'How do you think it reflects on this air base—on me—if members of our medical staff are seen behaving in a way that could put people at risk? What happens if the next big thing is people mimicking what you did? How long do you think it will be before one of those couples ends up the ER?'

She sat back in the chair. She wasn't normally a morning person and her patience was always short. Don was saying everything except what he really wanted to.

'It was only a kiss.'

'I'm not talking about the kiss.'

She stood up. 'Yes. Yes, you are. I'm twenty-five. I

could be living in another country somewhere by now. I probably should be. It might surprise you exactly how many kisses I've had.'

He held up his hand. 'Too much information.'

She licked her lips and tried to let her befuddled brain make sense of things. 'I get it that you're not entirely happy about two members of base staff kissing in the middle of the busiest junction in the world. Believe me, it wasn't pre-planned. At least, not by me. I also get it that you might ask their supervisors to speak to them. But this isn't a big deal, Don. This isn't something you get reprimanded over.' She ran her fingers through her hair. 'So, if you want to ask me something about Avery, ask me.'

He raised his eyebrows and remained silent. It was difficult not to try and immediately fill the silence. Don had always been extremely good at this. It was one of his 'techniques'. He'd told her once he used it often—particularly when trying to get to the truth of an incident. People tended to panic and fill the silence with babble—babble that probably gave more away than they intended.

It might be first thing in the morning but Katsuko was far too smart for that. She raised her eyebrows back at him.

The corners of his mouth started to turn upwards. 'What do you know about Avery Flynn?'

She stepped forward and gave him a knowing nod. 'I guess that's the question I should be asking you. At this point, I imagine, you know his file off by heart.'

He blinked. Once.

'I like him.' There. She'd said it out loud.

Her stomach instantly churned. It wasn't entirely true. But only she knew that. She more than liked him. She just didn't know if she was ready to admit that.

Don was staring at her. She didn't move, didn't flinch— no matter how uncomfortable she felt. Sometimes it felt like those eyes could feel about in her brain and find the truth that she kept hidden. Like the time she'd sworn at a neighbour's kid, then said she hadn't. Or the time as a teenager she might have gone somewhere she shouldn't have. Don seemed to know everything.

'Only like him?'

Yep. He could see right into her brain. She thought for a second. 'I don't know. He makes me smile. I enjoy spending time with him. I intend to keep spending time with him.' She sucked in a deep breath. 'I took him to meet Hiroko.'

One eyebrow rose. 'Were you trying to determine his staying power?'

She smiled. 'Nothing like a cantankerous grandmother to scare a man off.'

'And has she?'

Katsuko paused, then shook her head as little pieces of the puzzle of Avery Flynn started to fall into place in her brain. 'Actually, not at all.'

Don gave a silent nod. 'What did you mean earlier?'

She was surprised at the subject change. She'd expected to be grilled on Avery—or at the very least asked for an introduction. She cringed as she realised he'd met her grandmother before he'd met Don. In hindsight that didn't seem quite right.

'Which part?'

Don looked serious. 'The part about living somewhere else?'

Had she said that out loud? Oh, no. That wasn't how she wanted to have this conversation. She wasn't even sure she was ready to have it yet. It had just been floating around inside her.

'I've been thinking. If I want to do well in the air force, if I want to get a promotion, I should probably think about serving on another base.'

Don moved around the table and picked up a pile of papers. Distraction technique. Thinking time.

He didn't meet her gaze. Just nodded as his eyes fixed on the table. 'Yes, you probably should.' There was the tiniest waver in his voice and that broke her heart. Don wasn't her biological father, but she'd come to think of him that way. After a few years of staying with him she'd just started calling him Dad. It had seemed natural. It might be by default, but he'd become every bit as important to her as her own father had been. It had only been in the last few years, as an adult, that she'd occasionally called him Don again. He didn't seem to mind what she called him. Their relationship was that good, that steady, and she'd just hurt him.

Tears filled her eyes.

Don looked up. 'Where do you want to go?'

She shook her head and tried to blink back the tears. 'I haven't thought about it enough yet. I'd like to work somewhere I can get some different nursing experience.'

'You're bored with the ER?'

'I'll never be bored with the ER, but I need to grow as a nurse. Maybe I need to think about Theatres or ICU.'

Don opened his mouth to say something, then closed it again. Whatever it was, he must have reconsidered. 'Why don't we sit down sometime and look at the options?'

He was so matter-of-fact. So supportive. She walked over and put her hands around his neck and hugged him. She didn't do that much now. But she could tell he needed it. The man who'd practically given up his own life for her, manoeuvred a way to let them both remain in Japan, and supported her every step of the way was doing what every parent did at some stage—letting their child move on without them.

And after a few seconds Don hugged her back.

* * *

It was a weird kind of day. Some people were still shooting him strange glances. Some were cracking jokes to his face. There was even an occasional warning glance.

Katsuko had been a little strange when she'd come to see him last night. After six weeks his house was finally starting to smell like something resembling normal. He'd bought around a hundred candles at a local market, all smelling of Japanese maple and jasmine, and had nearly burned them all. Katsuko hadn't even wrinkled her nose when she'd walked through his door last night.

But things had been a bit strained. Something was on her mind and she didn't seem to want to talk about it. She said the General had spoken to her but was fine.

Fine. What did that mean?

Tonight's night shift was slow. Which was unusual.

But it was a Tuesday. Did anything happen on a Tuesday? The other doctor on duty was due to sit exams so Avery had told him to hide out in the office with his books. Lily, the pregnant nurse, had looked a bit tired, so he'd sent her off to the staffroom to put her feet up for a while.

Katsuko had chatted casually, but had seemed very conscious that people were watching their every move so had managed to keep herself busy.

His stomach gave a little grumble so he stood up and stretched his back. 'Back in five, folks. I'm going to grab a sandwich.'

He strolled down the corridor, glancing from side to side. Katsuko was around here somewhere, maybe she'd join him for a coffee.

He pushed the door open.

And stopped thinking about food.

Lily was on the floor, having a seizure. Her arms and legs were jerking heavily.

'Help! I need help in here!' he shouted. Avery had never been a doctor who panicked. But a sudden wave swept over him.

What on earth...?

He was next to her in a second, turning her on to her side into the recovery position. She'd vomited, so he wiped at her mouth trying to maintain her airway. How long had she been doing this?

He glanced at his watch. It was important to time any seizure. He could only time it from the moment he'd found her, so that was where he'd start.

'Help!' he shouted again. Katsuko and Frank burst through the doors, complete confusion on their faces.

Katsuko's eyes were wide. 'Lily!' She ran over and dropped to her knees beside Avery. Frank turned on his heel and left.

'What on earth's wrong? She's been fine.'

Avery shook his head. Now he felt sick. He'd told her to come and rest earlier. She'd looked tired and had complained about her sore back. A pregnant woman nearing the end of her pregnancy. He hadn't thought any more than that.

'I have no idea. Has she complained about anything to you?'

Frank burst back through the doors, carrying a patient slide and pulling a trolley behind him. Two other members of staff were pale-faced behind him.

'We'll need to lift her onto the trolley, put this under her,' said Frank.

No one cared they were about to break all the health and safety rules about lifting patients from the floor. There wasn't time to go and find a proper patient hoist.

Avery was still trying to maintain Lily's airway. 'Anyone know anything about this? I thought Lily was well.'

'So did I,' said Katsuko quietly.

'Hold on.' Avery lifted his hand and everyone froze. The seizure seemed to be coming to an end, the jerking slowing.

'Wait until it's finished before we move her. I have no idea if she fell to the floor or slid from the chair. The last thing we need to do is drop her and cause any harm to her baby.'

When the jerking stopped he gave the signal and they pulled her further onto her side and slid the patient slide underneath her. They had her on the trolley with the safety sides in place in only a few seconds.

Avery didn't even need to give the command. They took her straight to the resus room.

All the staff moved instantly. A blood-pressure cuff was put in place, her airway checked and an oxygen mask put on her face.

'I'll pull up her medical records,' said one of the admin staff. Avery gave her a grateful nod. She didn't normally come near the resus room but these were exceptional circumstances.

'I need to know what her last BP reading was. I need her last set of blood results and her last urine test. Shout them out when you find them, along with special notes from her obstetrician.'

'I'll contact her husband,' shouted someone else.

Katsuko took less than a minute to draw some bloods and insert a cannula. They'd need access to a vein if she started to fit again.

Now her airway was secure he walked around the bed and pulled off her shoes. Lily was wearing scrubs, the same as everyone else. He pulled up one trouser leg. And blinked.

Oedema. Lots of it. He pressed hard against her skin, trying to reach her ankle bone, and watched as the impression of his finger slowly filled again. Pitting oedema.

He pulled up her scrub top to get a look at her belly. 'Someone find me a foetal monitor—I need to check the baby.' He pressed his hands against her stomach. Oedema too.

'Why did we never notice any oedema?' he said out loud. He looked back at Lily's face. Did it look any different from normal? He didn't think so.

He reached for one of Lily's hands. She only wore her wedding ring. It was a little tight but not excessively so. Her face and hands weren't obviously swollen like her abdomen and legs.

'What's the BP?' His eyes glanced at the monitor.

'One-eighty over one-fifteen.'

There were anxious glances around the room. Avery turned to Katsuko and spoke in a low voice. 'Find me her obstetrician. I don't care what time of the night it is.'

He turned to the rest of the staff. 'We have to treat this as eclampsia. I need a magnesium sulphate infusion to help prevent more seizures and some IV hydralazine for her blood pressure. Let's get Lily stabilised.'

Hardly anyone spoke. All the staff were too shocked. Everyone kept their heads down and moved on automatic pilot. Avery felt a bit like that himself. He'd only been here six weeks, some of the staff here would have worked with Lily for years. He couldn't even imagine how they were feeling.

Katsuko walked back in, her expression serious. She handed him the phone. 'Her obstetrician, Dr Tanaka, is on the other side of Tokyo. He's more than an hour away. Can you talk to him?'

Avery looked around the room again. This time it was

a shout of pure frustration. 'Did someone find me a foetal monitor?'

Someone scurried from the room. He grabbed the phone from Katsuko's hand and walked to the doorway, out of earshot of the rest of the staff. Luan, the doctor who'd been studying earlier, appeared wide-eyed in front of him. Avery gestured over his shoulder. 'I need to speak to Lily's obstetrician. Keep an eye on her.'

He waited until Luan was inside the room, then pressed the phone to his ear and leaned back against the wall. He kept his voice low. 'Dr Tanaka? You'll need to help me out here. I'm an emergency physician. I've delivered two babies in the last seven years and both of them virtually fell into my hands.'

He didn't have time to be coy. He knew basic obstetrics but he was by no means an expert. Some doctors didn't like to admit that they didn't know everything. Avery wasn't that foolish. A staff member's—and her baby's— life could be on the line here.

Even Dr Tanaka sounded panicked while he spoke. 'Tell me what you've done.'

'Lily was seizing when I found her. She'd previously said she was getting tired and her back was sore. She has widespread oedema on her legs and abdomen but not her hands and face. She's hypertensive, one-eighty over one-fifteen. I've started her on magnesium sulphate and given her a bolus of hydralazine.'

He heard Dr Tanaka suck in a sharp breath. 'Give me a second. I'm pulling up her notes. Okay. There have been no problems with this pregnancy. It's been straightforward. Lily had two miscarriages before this, but no other history of note. I saw her around ten days ago. BP normal, urine clear. I examined her—there was no oedema.' He took another breath. 'Lily's a nurse. She's an intelligent woman. This has to have been sudden onset.

A little lower leg oedema in late pregnancy wouldn't be alarming. She's currently just over thirty-five weeks and was due to see me again in a couple of days. I think, at this stage, we have to consider HELLP syndrome. Tell me about the baby.'

Avery let out the breath he'd been holding. HELLP syndrome. Not what he wanted to hear. Haemolysis, elevated liver enzymes and low platelet count. It could be life threatening for both mother and baby.

There was a hand on his shoulder. Katsuko held up the foetal monitor. 'Do you want me to do this?'

He could hear the waver in her voice. She was scared. Scared that something bad was about to happen to her colleague. He shook his head. 'Give me a minute,' he said into the phone as he handed it to Katsuko. 'Talk to Dr Tanaka.'

As he strode back into the room he felt like all eyes were on him. The foetal monitor wasn't the most modern he'd ever seen but then again this wasn't an obstetrician's office. All he needed to do right now was find a heartbeat.

He switched on the monitor and put his hands on Lily's abdomen again, trying to establish the lie of the baby. He turned the sound up on the monitor. The room instantly quietened.

He pressed the monitor to Lily's swollen stomach and held his breath.

Nothing.

He adjusted the position and pushed back the horrible little surge of panic. Doctors didn't panic. They just didn't.

Still nothing. Did this thing even work?

'Dr Tanaka says he's found a family history of eclampsia in Lily's notes. Both her mother and aunt suffered from it.'

Perfect. Just perfect.

He pressed harder.

Finally. A heartbeat. The wave of relief only lasted a few seconds. He checked the reading on the monitor. One-eighteen.

He walked back to the doorway and took the phone from Katsuko. He kept his voice low. 'Foetal bradycardia. One hundred and eighteen beats per minute.'

'That's not unexpected with eclampsia and HELLP syndrome, particularly after a seizure,' said Dr Tanaka. 'It could also be due to the magnesium sulphate. You'll need to keep monitoring closely. Have you taken bloods?'

'Yes, they're done.'

'Good, in that case find an anaesthetist to assess Lily. I'm leaving now. If this is HELLP syndrome we'll need to deliver the baby as soon as possible. Keep monitoring her blood pressure and the baby.'

Avery listened to a few more instructions before finally hanging up. Katsuko was at his side in an instant. 'Are you okay?'

'Are you?'

She closed her eyes for just a second, then opened them again, pushing her shoulders down and meeting his gaze. 'I have to be. *We* have to be.'

We.

He knew what she was saying. He knew that she didn't really mean *that*. And while he'd always been an attentive and caring boyfriend, as soon as any ex had started referring to them as *we* it had sent uncomfortable prickles down his spine and he'd looked forward to shipping out.

He'd never made promises of for ever because he just didn't believe in them. They didn't exist. Oh, the start of every relationship was good. The honeymoon period when you wanted to see someone as much as possible and just the fact they walked in the room could make you smile.

But it never lasted. At least it hadn't for his mother, father or sister. Why should he be any different?

But this time he didn't have uncomfortable prickles. He didn't have that horrible worry of letting someone down.

Even though the resus room was the busiest room in the ER, no one was looking at them. Everyone was focusing on Lily—just the way they should.

He reached forward and threaded his fingers through Katsuko's. Something about touching her felt completely natural. Felt like the thing that he was supposed to do. 'Let's get through this,' he said quietly. 'We're not leaving until Lily and her baby are safe.'

Katsuko nodded. 'Let's do this.'

Lily's husband was distraught. Avery had spoken to him calmly and with an assurance Katsuko knew he didn't really have. 'I told her to stop work,' he said, shaking his head. 'I told her it was time to rest and forget about work.'

'Did she complain of anything except being tired and having a sore back?'

Lily's husband nodded. 'She's felt sick the last two days. She was joking about the morning sickness being back. And she was uncomfortable. She had a weird kind of pain around her right side. And she had a bit of a headache last night that wouldn't shift.'

Katsuko shot a glance at Avery. Everything fitted with the guidelines she'd pulled up for HELLP syndrome. It wasn't something she'd seen in the ER before. Last time she'd encountered this she'd been doing a student placement in a labour ward. She held out her hand towards Lily's husband. She'd known them both for a few years. 'Come on, Luke. Let me take you to see her. The obstetrician will be here any minute and I suspect you're going to meet your baby soon after that.'

She led him down the corridor to the resus room and put her arm around him when he seemed to crumple. Frank found a chair and said lots of reassuring words.

There had been no more seizures and Lily's blood pressure had started to drop just a little.

Two hours later Lily and her husband had a baby son. Protocols stated that because a member of staff had become unwell on duty, Blake Anderson had to be called. He took the decision to call in the next shift early and send everyone else home.

'We'll debrief tomorrow, folks. It's always hard when it's one of our own. Let's give Lily and her husband some time and space to recover. Then we can all celebrate the new arrival.'

They were carefully optimistic words. Lily had been transferred to the ICU. There was still a chance she could go into organ failure. They just had to hope and pray that she didn't.

Katsuko gave a grateful nod and headed to the changing room. Five minutes later she was searching for Avery.

Fifteen minutes later she was still searching. One of the cleaners finally gave her some hope. 'I think I saw him heading towards the vending machines.'

She headed down the corridor. It was in darkness, and only the dim lights from the machines let her notice a pair of white runners sticking out.

'Avery? Is that you?'

She hurried down the corridor.

It was definitely Avery. He was slumped halfway against the back wall and the side of one of the machines. His eyes looked half-glazed. She crouched down. 'Avery? Are you okay?'

She reached forward and touched his hand. He looked up.

Those eyes. Those pale green eyes that had mesmerised her right from the beginning. Those confident, cocky pale green eyes that seemed to both taunt her and flirt with her at the same time. They didn't look like that tonight.

She flung her bag to the side and knelt on the floor. 'Avery? What's wrong?' She shuffled a little towards him. His permanently too-long hair was ruffled in every direction but the right one. 'Honey?'

His eyes connected with hers. He looked exhausted. Completely exhausted.

She grabbed his hand and pulled him forward. 'What's wrong?'

He shook his head. 'Nothing.' Then gave her a dopey smile as he lifted up his other hand and shrugged. 'Everything. I was hungry. I just came in here to find some food. That's what I was doing when I found Lily.'

She froze. It was the way he'd said her name. She got it. She really got it.

'Come on, Avery. You're exhausted. It's been a horrible shift for us all. But you were the doctor in charge. Everything was on your shoulders.' She reached forward and ran her fingers through his hair. 'You need to get some sleep.'

She pulled at his arm a little more, bringing him closer to her.

He gave his head a shake. 'I just sat down for a second.'

She smiled. 'I know. I get it. I've been there. But let's go. This isn't the best place to hang out.'

He pushed himself up and she grabbed hold of him. 'Do you have any food in the house?'

He frowned and then nodded, giving her a curious look. 'Why?'

She touched his cheek. 'Because I'm going to make you something to eat.'

He paused and let out the longest breath. 'Kat—'

She held up her hand. 'Whatever it is, it can wait. You did good today. We all did good.'

He shook his head, then spun around unexpectedly

and took a kick at one of the vending machines. It rocked backwards and forwards for a few seconds.

He didn't shout but the voice that came out was one of pure and utter frustration. 'I didn't! Why didn't I notice something was wrong with Lily? What if I hadn't walked into the coffee room when I did? She'd vomited. She could have choked. Anything could have happened.' The worry lines on his forehead were so deep and she could practically see the thoughts churning around his head. Both hands pushed against the glass of the machine, then his head sagged down against it.

She was stunned. She'd never seen him like this. The whole time she'd been in that resus room she'd been giving silent prayers of thanks that Avery was the doctor on duty. She trusted him. She had faith in him.

She reached out and touched his shoulder.

'Well, if you missed it, so did her obstetrician. So did I. So did Frank. So did Samuru. So did everyone on duty tonight. And so did Lily. You heard Dr Tanaka. He thinks it was very rapid onset. It can happen.' She pulled him around to face her and clasped his hand. 'I heard you. I heard you tell Dr Tanaka that you'd only delivered two babies in the last seven years. You were totally out of your comfort zone tonight and I think I was the only one that noticed.'

He shook his head and ran his fingers through his hair. 'You have no idea how much I was out of my comfort zone. And it's ridiculous. I've treated bomb injuries. Even though I'm not a surgeon I've ended up in Theatre more times than I care to remember. I've seen hundreds of kids even though I'm not a paediatrician. If I had a dollar for every MI or chest infection I've diagnosed, I'd be a millionaire. But obstetrics?' He shook his head. 'I've hardly seen any cases.' He paused for a moment. 'Lily spoke to me last week about how happy she was and how much she was looking forward to this baby. She couldn't wait to be a mother. When I thought that might slip away today and it was all in my hands…'

He stared off into the distance. Katsuko put her arms around his neck, staring up into his eyes. She kept her voice low. 'When you shouted me through to the coffee room and I saw Lily fitting on the floor I thought I was going to be sick. When you didn't find a heartbeat straight away I thought I was going to be sick again. When Dr Tanaka said he was over an hour away I wanted to cry.'

His gaze met hers. There it was. The flash of recognition in his eyes. He nodded in appreciation, then said slowly, 'But this is our job, Katsuko. This is the life that we've chosen. I just hate it that I didn't know everything in there.'

He looked so racked with guilt that her heart squeezed. She leaned forward and kissed his cheek, her lips coming into contact with his stubbled jaw. 'Avery, I'm sure I've heard of HELLP syndrome but I could barely remember what to do. I heard you. You spoke to the obstetrician straight away and were completely honest with him. The treatment you'd started was correct. You did nothing wrong. Lily was in good hands. Lily was in safe hands. That first hour was crucial.'

He ran his fingers through his hair again. 'But what if she ends up in organ failure? It's still a possibility. She isn't out of the woods yet.'

Katsuko nodded. 'I know she isn't, but if we go upstairs now we'll just get in the way. Blake told us all to go home. That's what we need to do.'

His stomach growled loudly in protest and she let out a laugh and threaded her fingers through his. She was a nurse. She was used to taking care of people. But she wasn't on air force time now. She was on her own. And this was the first time she'd been absolutely sure about her next step.

Avery wasn't dating her because she was the General's daughter. Avery wasn't looking for promotion. Avery wasn't trying to win friends and influence people. Avery was just a guy, trying to do the best job that he could.

And it was quite possible she loved him for it.

'How about a little company?'

He blinked. Then his gaze narrowed a little as if he was trying to work out what she was saying. 'What kind of company?'

She licked her lips and met his gaze. She wasn't embarrassed. It didn't feel awkward. It felt completely natural.

'Overnight company.' Her words were assured.

He put his hands on her hips and leaned back a little. 'Katsuko, did you just proposition me?'

He was teasing her again. He was starting to get back to normal.

She stood on tiptoe. 'So, what if I did?'

He grinned. 'What if you get seen leaving the Captain's house first thing in the morning?'

She placed her hands on his chest. 'I've no intention of being seen leaving the Captain's house first thing in the morning. I'm planning on sleeping late and having breakfast in bed.'

He slipped his arm around her waist as they started walking back along the corridor. 'What do you eat for breakfast?'

She slapped his arm. 'Eggs. You'd better have some.'

He stopped walking and pulled a face. 'Oops.'

'And obviously I'll want my favourite coffee.'

'I don't think I can whip up a skinny vanilla latte with my poor kitchen supplies.'

'What exactly do you have in your cupboards and fridge?'

He smiled. 'I have some sushi, a can of beans and some beer.'

She shook her head and wagged her finger at him. 'Watch out. I expect to get exactly what I want.'

He picked her up and twirled her round. The twinkle in his eye that she was used to was back. 'I'm sure I'll be able to give you exactly what you want.'

'Promises, promises.' She pushed open the door. 'How about a wager?'

He raised his eyebrow. 'I like the sound of that. What's the wager?'

She looked around. 'Oh, I've left my jacket by the vending machine. Can you grab it?'

'Sure,' he said. He walked back down the corridor quickly and she didn't even try to hide her smile.

'Avery, the wager?'

He bent to pick up her jacket. 'Yes?'

'Last one back to your place has to do the coffee run in the morning.'

And with that she winked and raced out into the dark night.

CHAPTER NINE

'CAPTAIN FLYNN, WILL you report to the Major General's office, please?'

Avery nearly choked on the cup of coffee that he'd just taken a drink from.

'Of course. I'll be there directly.'

He stood up and looked around. He was dressed in scrubs so he'd need to change into his uniform.

He stuck his head around the door of Blake's office. 'Blake, I've been told to go to the General's office.'

Blake looked up. It was obvious he was trying not to grimace. 'Any idea what about?'

Avery shook his head. 'Not a clue.'

Except for the fact I've been seeing his daughter ever since I got here.

Everyone knew. They didn't even try to hide it. Katsuko had stayed over at his house on more than one occasion. The last month had been a steep learning curve. He'd learned how to make her the coffee she liked. He'd learned not to wash her delicate underwear with his uniforms. He'd learned that she mumbled in her sleep. But most of all he'd learned just how much he enjoyed being around her. She was feisty. She was smart. And loved to laugh. And sometimes she was vulnerable.

If he was working a shift and she wasn't on duty he'd

started to look at the clock and count the minutes until he could see her again. Part of him wanted to tread warily—he'd never really been like this before. But the other part of him just wanted to enjoy it.

'Better hurry along, then,' quipped Blake. 'I'll cover your patients.'

It only took five minutes to change, then another ten to walk across the base to the General's office. He was a grown man having an adult relationship with a grown woman. So why did he feel like a teenage boy?

He'd never actually met the General. Katsuko had made a few vague noises about them meeting at some point but it hadn't been an issue he'd laboured. He just hadn't expected to get called to the General's office.

There was no way he was going to act nervous. He pushed his shoulders back and held his head high as he entered.

The General's secretary looked up and smiled. 'Captain Flynn? Good. I have something for you.'

She stood up and walked to a table behind her and picked up a large envelope.

Avery glanced at the General's door. It was closed. No sounds. Maybe he wasn't even in?

The secretary held out a log book for him to sign. She handed the envelope over with a rueful look. 'It seems like this has taken a while to get to you. It seems to have been halfway around the world.'

She wasn't kidding. His name and rank, along with various base addresses, had been crossed out and rewritten on the front of the ragged envelope.

He looked at the return address. An attorney firm in New York. He'd never heard of them. There was an uneasy pang in his stomach. Was he being sued for something? Doctors did get sued for malpractice, but he'd never had any complaints raised.

He held up the envelope. 'Is this it?'

The secretary smiled and nodded. 'That's it, Captain.' She sat back down in her chair and carried on working.

Part of him was relieved. The General didn't want to see him at all. It was nothing to do with the General.

He walked outside and tore open the envelope, pulling out the papers inside.

As executors of the estate of the late Stuart Elijah Flynn, we are acting on behalf of our client, previously undeclared dependant Mary Elizabeth Flynn...

Who?

It was like a blast from the past. No one brought up Uncle Stuey's name any more—only him. His eyes scanned the rest of the letter. There. A date of birth. A daughter? Uncle Stuey had had a daughter? Since when?

He kept reading. According to this letter—which had taken nearly a year to reach him—Uncle Stuey had fathered a child twenty years ago in Brazil. It appeared that the daughter had only found out who her father was when her mother had become unwell and had since put in a claim on the estate.

What estate?

There was also a request for a DNA sample from himself to assist verification of the familial links.

He couldn't believe it. He couldn't believe a single word of it. The one person in his family he'd actually respected. The one person he'd actually looked up to had refused to acknowledge the birth of his daughter.

He could feel fury build inside him as he stalked back towards the ER.

'Avery! Avery! What are you doing? I thought you were on duty?'

Katsuko came running up behind him, her hair pulled back from her face and her swimming bag on her shoulder.

'I am.' He kept walking.

'Hey,' she said, tugging at his arm. 'What's wrong?'

He paused and thrust the letter towards her. 'It seems that Uncle Stuey had a daughter he'd never acknowledged. She's put a claim on his estate.'

'What?' Katsuko looked horrified. She started to scan the letter but couldn't stop the barrage of questions. 'How do you know he never acknowledged her?'

'Well, I've never actually heard of her.'

Katsuko screwed up her face. 'When was she born? Twenty years ago? How long is it since your uncle died?'

Avery stopped walking. 'Just short of twenty years ago.'

'Then did he even know about her?'

Avery took a breath. That hadn't even occurred to him—probably because he hadn't been thinking straight.

'Brazil? Was that one of the places your uncle visited? And how do you even know she's your uncle's daughter?' Her voice climbed in pitch and she stopped walking. 'They want you to do a DNA test?'

She shook her head. 'Avery, this is crazy.'

He pulled his hat off his head. 'I know. I can't believe it. Uncle Stuey was the one person I thought had got life right.'

Katsuko wrinkled her nose. 'Even though he "acquired" artefacts he probably shouldn't have?'

It was a valid question. And one that he'd spent most of his life ignoring. He waved his hand. 'I've never really looked into all that. I was young at the time. And my father has never wanted to discuss the details of what Uncle Stuart really did. I only have what I can remember.'

'Then let me ask the key question.'

'What's that?'

'The estate. This is all about inheritance. Did your uncle leave you anything and if he did, is there anything left?'

The realisation hit Avery like a bolt of lightning. Money. Of course. These were attorneys. This was actually about money.

He let out a laugh. 'After all these years someone wants money from Uncle Stuart? Well, it's long gone. He left me some money to help pay for college and medical school. All I've got left now is his fedora.' He shook his head. 'And I'm not handing that over to anyone.'

'I don't get it. Isn't she far too late anyway? Doesn't the statute of limitations apply?'

Avery pointed to the bottom paragraph of the letter. 'I have no idea. They're talking about a discovery rule and something about probate. It doesn't matter anyway. There's nothing to claim.'

Katsuko reached over and put her hand on his arm. 'Then why are you getting so worked up over this?'

The tension that had been building inside him bubbled over. 'Because of that!' He pointed at the letter. 'The implication in it. It destroys the memory of the man that I knew. The only good memories I have of my family are the ones of Uncle Stuart. He was my one hope that I wouldn't grow up to be like my father or my mother. You know that old nature versus nurture debate?'

She nodded.

'Well, I don't win on any count. Uncle Stuart was the last chance that the family genes might actually be okay.'

Katsuko took a deep breath and looked away. He hadn't meant to shout but he hated everything about this. He hated to be blindsided and this had been totally unexpected. No one had ever mentioned that Uncle Stuey had had any love interests. Avery couldn't ever remember his uncle talking about a girlfriend or anything like it. Everything had always been about the excitement of his job.

He frowned. But why would a grown man talk about adult relationships with a nine-year-old?

'You know what?'

Katsuko's words snapped him away from his thoughts.

Her brown eyes were flashing. She looked mad. 'I get it that you're annoyed about someone slighting your uncle. And I know that lots of families have issues. But you still have your parents—both of them. You still have a family that you could choose to fit into if you want to.'

Were those words supposed to make him feel guilty?

'And you have the General. And your grandmother. But you don't want to visit her, do you?'

She stepped back as if she'd been stung.

He shook his head. 'You have no idea what they're like, Katsuko. After ten minutes my father would probably be trying to date you, my mother would probably be trying to date Don, and my sister would be trying to con you into giving her a credit card.'

He threw up his hands. 'I mean, what am I even doing here—with you? No one in my family has ever had a relationship that worked out. My father has been married four times—each marriage more ridiculous than the one before. Any day now he'll reach number five. My mother just looks for the next rich, eligible bachelor and my sister is going exactly the same way. Uncle Stuey was the only person who gave me hope—and now I wonder why. He didn't even have any relationships with anyone that I knew about.' He stopped dead and looked her straight in the eye. 'I can't give you what you want, Katsuko. I can't give you what you need, or what you deserve. My family track record says it all. I'll be gone soon and you have a career to build. You can do better. You can do better than me. Go and find him.'

The words were out. He didn't want to mean any of them. But he had to be honest with her. He had to tell her what he was. What type of family he was a part of. What could he really offer her?

He wanted to be so much more than the sum of what he thought he was. Did genes really play a part in who you were? Could he ever hope to have any kind of loving, normal relationship?

She worried so much about fitting in. The truth was, it was the other way round. His family would never fit with the beliefs and ideals she had in her head.

He wasn't good enough for her. His family wasn't good enough for her.

Katsuko looked away. It was clear she was still upset. Her hands were shaking.

He hated himself right now. He wanted to put his arms around her and promise her that he would do his best for her. But would that ever be good enough? Right now, he wasn't sure.

She stared at the ground for a few seconds, then spoke quietly. 'I guess you'd better get back to work.'

Silence filled the air between them. He'd been too blunt. He hadn't meant to hurt her. His mind flew back to that first night when she'd run her finger over the picture of her mother and father.

He ran his fingers through his hair. 'Look, I'm sorry.'

She gave a nod. 'So am I.' And turned and strode away.

The words played on his mind for the rest of the day. He was mad with himself. It was almost as if he was trying to push her away. Why would he do that?

No matter what he did, he couldn't get Katsuko out of his head.

She was there. She was there to stay.

He'd met her grandmother. She was impossible. It

didn't matter that he couldn't speak Japanese. The language she spoke was pretty universal.

There was no love or compassion in her eyes for her granddaughter. And Katsuko certainly hadn't acted like the *faiyakuraka* she was nicknamed after at work. In her grandmother's presence she was meek.

Some people might call it respectful, and in a way it was. But she shouldn't need to hide her personality and nature from her grandmother. He'd hated the expression in her eyes as she'd run after her grandmother. She was a nurse, caring was in her nature, being downtrodden was not.

He wondered if he'd experienced a little of what Katsuko's father and then Don had. It lit a little fire inside him.

His fists clenched as he sat at the computer screen at work. He shouldn't be wearing green scrubs, he should be dressed as a Neanderthal. That was how he felt. He wanted to protect her. Let her know how much she was valued. Let her know how much she was loved.

His hands sprang apart—the fists lost. His skin prickled and he looked down. This was the first time he wasn't looking forward to the end of a posting. In fact, he was secretly dreading the fact he didn't even know how long he'd be here. The commander of the medical service had already let him know that because of his willingness to step in at the last minute with no fuss or complaint, his next posting was his call. But did he really want to leave at all?

Katsuko had already spoken about looking at other postings. He should be excited for her—some of the places she was considering he'd already worked in. Now he was doing something he'd never done before. Instead of thinking about facilities and new experiences all the different bases had to offer, he was thinking about miles. And the distance that could be between them. And that was brand new for him.

He'd never tried a long-distance relationship. He'd never wanted to. But now, all of a sudden, it was definitely on his mind. Lots of colleagues in the forces had long-distance relationships. They had to. Families couldn't go to some bases. If husbands, wives or children had certain medical conditions it could mean they were deemed unsuitable to live in some bases with restricted facilities. Husbands, wives and families could be apart for months—and with his family history, what made him think he could even be cut out for that?

He hated these doubts. He hated feeling like this. He hadn't even sat down and had this conversation with Katsuko yet—the *What about the future?* conversation. It terrified him.

He'd proved that earlier when he'd blurted out the most stupid words he could possibly have said.

He thought about the expression on her face, the foolish words he'd said to hurt her. Why do that to someone that you loved?

Love. The thing that his father claimed to be permanently in or out of. Love. What he'd seen in the eyes of Jay Lim's parents when they'd seen each other again. Love. It practically emanated from the photo that Katsuko had of her parents.

He'd always assumed it would never work for him. He'd never really had a reason to think differently.

But now he did. And that reason was Katsuko.

He leaned forward and put his head in his hands and groaned. How on earth could he make things right?

He had to make a phone call. He had to deal with things back home—things in the past—if he could ever hope to build a future.

He stood up quickly, making his wheeled chair skid

across the floor. He had to try and take some control back. And he knew where to start.

Seiko, one of the aerospace medical technicians, was restocking the emergency trolley. He walked over. 'Seiko? Have you got a minute?'

She looked up and nodded. 'Do you need help with a patient?'

He shook his head. It didn't matter that this news would probably spread like some crazy infectious disease around the department. 'I need some help with some Japanese words. If I tell you what I want to say, would you write it down for me and help me with the pronunciation?'

She gave a nod. 'No problem.'

Wait until I tell you what I want translated.

It was time to make a start—and the sooner, the better.

He dialled the number and waited impatiently for the phone to ring.

After the longest time his father picked up. 'Dad, it's Avery.'

There was a silence. 'To what do I owe this honour?'

He winced but wasn't really surprised. After the last visit he'd kept contact to a minimum. There was no point in trying to make small talk. 'I've been contacted by a firm of attorneys.'

'What have you done?'

Avery sighed. '*I* haven't done anything. Have you heard of a Mary Elizabeth Flynn?'

'Who?'

Avery hesitated. He wasn't quite sure how to say this. 'She claims to be Uncle Stuey's kid.'

His father let out a raucous laugh. 'Another one? Well, they're all coming out of the woodwork now.'

Avery shifted uncomfortably. 'What's that supposed to mean?'

'So where's this one from, then?'

'She's from Brazil. But the attorney letter was sent nearly a year ago. It seems to have ping-ponged around every air force base trying to find me.'

'A year ago? She'll long since have given up. Bet she's changed her name to something else by now.'

'Dad, what are you talking about? What did you mean, they're all coming out of the woodwork?'

His father made a strange slurping noise. Great, he was drinking again. Avery glanced at his watch and tried to work out what time it was back in the US.

'How long has it been since you were home?' his father asked.

That didn't require much thought. Even though his father's reference to home and Avery's reference to home were two different things. 'More than a year ago. More like sixteen months.'

'Ah, you missed all the fun, then.'

'What fun?'

'One of the crazy cable TV stations made a documentary about Stu. It was one of those hunt-the-artefact kind of things. Some of what they said was true and some of what they said was complete and utter rubbish. They interviewed me. I think they wanted to interview you too at the time but you weren't around.'

Avery was getting impatient. 'Dad, what happened?'

His father laughed. 'You know television. They made it all mysterious. Lots of mist and references to lost treasure. They made out that Stuey had stolen a whole host of artefacts from all around the world and had been a secret billionaire. About two weeks later the letters started pouring in.'

'What letters?'

'Like the one you got. Lost children, some of whom

had mysteriously changed their names by deed poll two days after the show. It was all a lot of hocus pocus.'

'So none of this is true?'

'Of course it's not true.'

He should feel reassured but he couldn't be. He'd never heard of this TV show. Plus his father was obviously drinking. 'How can you be sure? Uncle Stuey spent his life wandering the globe. There is a chance he could have children he didn't know about.'

His father's tone changed. It was almost as if he was looking over his shoulder to see who was listening. 'I know there's no possibility that Uncle Stuey could have kids. He had mumps as a child. There was no chance of children. Why do you think he left your mother and went halfway around the globe? He couldn't stand the fact that she married me instead. You were the son he always wanted.'

An arctic breeze swept over Avery. 'Uncle Stuey went out with Mom?'

'Of course he did. But your mom wanted a family and after he had mumps there was no chance of that. He decided that exploration and archaeology were his new profession—got a job with the museum and never looked back. He only ever really came back to see you.'

Avery's head was swimming. He'd never heard any of this. He'd never noticed anything weird between his mother and uncle. How could he have missed this?

'Why didn't you ever tell me any of this?'

'What did it matter? Your mother and I were never really suited.'

Avery leaned back against the wall. Part of him felt relieved that his Uncle Stuey wasn't some old-fashioned kind of cad and part of him felt sorry for the man who'd had to watch the woman he loved marry his brother.

'So, none of this is true? I can just destroy the letter?'

'That's what we did with all the rest. We did have one persistent attorney who decided we must have secretly hidden all of Uncle Stuey's artefacts. He tried to serve us with something or other.'

Avery shook his head. 'What was it?'

'Who knows? Who cares?' His father kept talking but Avery stopped listening. Other thoughts were flooding through his mind. How must his uncle have felt?

It was bad enough that mom had married his father. But when their marriage had failed and she'd immediately zoned in on any man with money it must have made him feel even worse. First she'd wanted kids. Then she'd wanted money.

His parents had ping-ponged from one bad relationship to another. And for the first time in his life he could finally understand why.

But that was them.

That wasn't him.

His sister might be following their example, but he didn't have to.

Uncle Stuey was still exactly the person he'd thought he was. In fact, he was more. He'd loved someone and walked away to let her have the life she'd thought she'd wanted.

And he'd stayed away to ensure he didn't influence the relationship any more than he should. Avery's heart gave a squeeze. His memories of his uncle were even more precious than before.

'I have to go, Dad,' he said quickly. 'I'll call you some other time.'

He sat down for a second, the battered envelope still in his hands.

It was amazing what some people would do for money. He was mad. He wanted to ring the legal firm and tell them exactly what he thought of them and their client. But that would achieve nothing.

He had too much else to think about.

He pulled another piece of paper from his pocket. The scribbled words that Seiko had written for him. She'd only slightly raised her eyebrows when Avery had asked her to translate a few things for him.

The question was—what would he do with them?

Katsuko was sitting at the table with a whole host of print-outs in front of her. Every base. Every hospital. Every facility.

There was a whole world of opportunity out there. She just hadn't had the chance to explore it. She'd made herself a checklist, narrowing down what specialities were listed.

Then she pulled up a blog site for air force personnel. This way she could find out the more informal things. Where did other staff recommend? Were there places that had difficult reputations? What were the chances of having her request accepted at particular bases?

She put down her pen. Avery. He'd told her to go ahead. To make plans without him. The words had been awful, but the pain in his eyes had been worse. Did he really think he wasn't good enough for her?

She wasn't even sure if she should be thinking this way. But Avery Flynn had managed to creep under every defence system that she had. She'd known his position here was temporary. They'd never really discussed anything long-term. But she'd never really wanted to discuss anything long-term before.

She stared down at the papers. If she could just live her life in the bubble that was Okatu base, that would be fine. She'd still have Don. She'd still have the place she'd grown up in and she'd still have her friends.

But life was changing around her. She wanted more. She wanted to sit down and look at her career and see what should come next. She wanted to think about the future.

What had hurt most were his words today. They'd affected her in a way she hadn't expected. How could so few words make her feel like her feet had just been swept away from her?

It had been a simple squabble. She knew that. She just hadn't been ready for the impact.

It had been their first argument—and it hadn't even really been that. All couples argued. That was normal. And it didn't matter that he'd apologised by text a little while later, telling her he wanted to see her. He wanted to talk to her. The topsy-turvy feeling in her stomach hadn't shifted.

And it wouldn't shift until she saw him again and he put his arms around her.

She kind of hated the fact that another person had the ability to affect her feelings and emotions. Her grandmother had done it on a regular basis since she'd been a child. But never had a man.

Her grandmother. She gulped and stared at the papers again. She could only imagine what her grandmother would say if she told her she was being posted elsewhere. What would happen if her grandmother messaged her while she was on another continent, telling her that something was wrong? Who would help her?

She could hardly ask Don. He couldn't bear to be in her grandmother's presence. Was this really the right time to go?

Wine. She needed wine right now.

The doorbell rang and her heart gave a little leap. Was it that time already?

Avery opened the door with a bottle of white wine in one hand and the biggest bunch of flowers she'd ever seen in the other. 'I'm so sorry.'

He didn't wait for her to speak. He just stepped forward and put his arms around her. 'I should never have said anything. I'm sorry. I didn't mean any of it.'

She pushed him back a little. 'What? I've not to go and conquer the world? I've not to look at my career options and decide the best place I should be?'

He cringed. 'Well, yes. Yes, of course you should.' He held up the flowers and the wine again. 'But could we maybe discuss how we can still be friends, even if we're on different continents?'

She folded her arms across her chest. She didn't plan on making this too easy. 'I thought you couldn't do that. I thought you weren't cut out for that?'

He held up the wine again. 'I'm hoping that maybe you could teach me. Maybe we could teach each other?'

There was a long silence. The clock ticked loudly in the distance.

She licked her lips. 'How about we go back a little? How about we drink the wine and let's take it from there?'

His sigh of relief was audible. She was prepared to give him a little leeway. But just a little. She still had to sort out in her head what she actually wanted to do.

He glanced at the table. 'Wow. Did you kill a tree?'

She groaned. 'I know. But I like to spread everything out in front of me. It makes it easier to compare.'

'Next you'll tell me you have a spreadsheet.'

Heat rushed into her cheeks and she turned the laptop around. 'Maybe.'

He held up the bottle. 'Should I open the wine?'

'I think you'll have to.'

She brought two glasses down from the cupboard while he uncorked the bottle. 'You don't mind doing this with me?'

He shook his head. 'What else am I going to do?'

She didn't know whether to be grateful or upset. His background knowledge of some of the bases would be invaluable. But she couldn't help but wonder how he felt about her considering going somewhere else.

It was the conversation that neither of them seemed able to have.

For the next hour he sat patiently next to her, filling her in on some of the details about the different bases she'd highlighted. It was mind-boggling. He could tell her about housing, facilities, airports. And if he didn't know something, he knew someone who did.

After an hour and a glass and a half of wine, Katsuko sat back and sighed. Avery had an arm wrapped around her and she put her head on his shoulder. 'It's a lot to think about. I'll need to have a talk with Blake about making a base of preference request.'

Avery shifted in the seat beside her. 'When do you think you might do that?' His tone was a little strained.

She shuffled the papers in front of her. 'Whenever I've made up my mind. I'll need to give a few options. I want to make sure I choose carefully.'

He lifted his arm from her shoulder and leaned on the table. 'Have you spoken to Don?'

She pressed her lips together. It was a natural question. Her fingers slid up and down the stem of the wine glass. 'I spoke to him last week.'

'And?'

'He seemed to take it okay.'

'What about your grandmother?'

Her grip tightened on the glass. 'What about her?'

'Have you told her yet?'

She shook her head. 'I won't tell her until everything is final. She won't be happy. I know she won't. I'll need to try and make some other arrangements in case she argues with her carers again. I think I'll need to leave a deposit with another agency in case she refuses to let her carers in.'

'I thought she'd already worked her way around most of the local agencies?'

Katsuko sighed. Even though she knew it was true she was trying to push those thoughts from her head right now. Everywhere she looked it felt like there were barriers to her going. The guilt she felt about her grandmother. The guilt she felt about leaving Don after everything he'd done for her. The blossoming relationship she had with Avery. Was she really ready to give everything up?

The lump in her throat that had appeared a few seconds ago started to seem larger.

'Are you sure about this?'

Her reply was instantaneous. 'Don't you want me to go?'

There. She'd said it. The elephant in the room. She was finally calling him on this relationship. Finally asking what it meant.

Avery had a one-second look of panic. She could recognise it from a mile away. 'Of course I don't want you to go,' he replied. 'But if this is about your career, then I'd be a hypocrite not to support you. I've spent the last few years moving around in order to get the best experience that I could.'

She blinked. That didn't quite sound the way she wanted. 'What do you mean, *if this is about your career*? What else could it be about?'

He turned to face her. Darn it. Those pale green eyes were deadly serious. It made her stomach churn. She much preferred it when they had a wicked gleam in them, the one that usually led to...

'It could be about running away.'

'Running away from what?'

He bit his lip. He was obviously trying to find the right words. 'From the way your grandmother makes you feel. From the way other people make you feel.'

Her mouth instantly dried. 'My grandmother is just an old woman with old-fashioned views.'

'Your grandmother has never accepted you for who you are. Don't make excuses for her behaviour. By all accounts, she made your father uncomfortable, she's made Don uncomfortable and she's spent the last twenty-five years treating you as if you're not good enough. I actually think you're right to get away from her.'

She was stunned. And she hated the way those words made her feel.

'Then why are you saying anything?'

'Because I think you need to be clear about why you want to go.'

'What right do you have to comment? You're a fine one to talk about running away from family. You've spent the last few years doing it too.'

He nodded and pressed his hand against his chest. 'But I know why I distance myself from them. I don't want to be like them. I don't want to be like them at all.' He held up his hands. 'I see people in relationships here who look as if they'll stay together for ever. I have no examples of that in my family. I don't know what that is. I don't know if I'm even cut out for that.'

She held her breath. For a few seconds she'd been so annoyed about his words that she'd almost missed what he was telling her.

'And that's part of why you've moved so much?'

His eyes lowered. 'I've never really tried to find out. When it's time to leave a base I'm generally happy to. All relationships come to a natural end. I've never considered trying to maintain one when I've left.'

Her heart twisted in her chest. 'And that's what's going to happen to us?'

Was this his idea of letting her down gently? Because it felt like an elephant had just trampled across her chest. 'You're not prepared to even try?' She picked up the papers in front of her. 'So, if I decide to put in for a transfer, that's it? Goodbye, Katsuko?'

He opened his mouth to speak but nothing came out. He closed it again and swallowed. He looked at her steadily. 'What I think is that as soon as you tell your grandmother you're going, she'll make you feel guilty. I think you're making a really brave decision. And the best thing I can do is back you. I want you to feel happy and confident about where you decide to apply. I want you to know that you're a great nurse who'll probably get promoted six months after you leave here. I want you to know that you're good enough to go to any of these bases and they would be lucky to have you. You're making decisions about your life and your career, Katsuko. The last thing you want is for someone to stand in your way.'

She pressed her lips together. There was so much she wanted to say but she didn't want to make a fool of herself. What was the point of putting yourself out there, only to have it thrown back in your face?

She stared at the printouts for a minute. She was taking charge of her life. She'd thought she'd found something special. But maybe the connection she felt was all in her head?

I don't want you to stand in my way, Avery. I want you to stand by my side.

Those were the words she wanted to say—she just didn't have the courage to say them out loud.

She dug under the pile of papers and pulled out the one she'd left till last. 'We didn't talk about this one. What about this one? They put out a special call on Friday. There's only three weeks left if I want to request it.'

He paled visibly and reached for the paper. It was almost as if he was trying to choose his words carefully. 'Afghanistan. Why Afghanistan?'

She'd researched it until her brain had almost died

from overload. 'The combat support hospital is more advanced that some modern inner-city ERs. They've devised more patented technology there than anywhere else in the world. The joint theatre hospital at one of the bases is renowned the world over. You should know. You've been there.'

It was almost like a challenge. He'd talked about nearly everywhere he'd been and even though he'd told her initially that he'd probably learned most in Afghanistan, he hadn't gone into the finer details.

He looked at her carefully. 'Why there? Why now?'

What was he asking her?

She couldn't have timed things any worse. It had taken her twenty-five years to find someone she could consider a future with, and as soon as she'd discovered that, she'd realised she had to spread her wings and fly if she wanted her career to develop. Apt for an air force nurse.

She licked her lips. None of the words she wanted to say seemed right. And some of the things he'd already said prickled more than they should. Was he right? Was she running away from things? And was she running away from him too?

'I think it will be good for me. I think it will give me the experience I need if I want my career to flourish.' It was the kind of answer you'd give to an interview question.

His face was unreadable. She had no idea what he was thinking. Her insides felt like they were dying. She wanted to tell him how much he meant to her. She wanted to tell him that she spent all day counting down the minutes until she could see him again. Wanted to tell him that she didn't even want to consider a future without him in it.

Her phone beeped and he picked it up from the table, frowned and handed it to her. It was her grandmother.

Her fingers immediately started to punch out a reply but his hand closed over hers. 'Don't.'

The warmth of his hand sent pulses shooting up her arm. He was right there, right there in front of her but he didn't have his arms around her. He didn't have his lips on hers. The emptiness she felt right now was almost an ache.

'Why not?'

He squeezed his eyes closed for a second. 'How many times has she messaged you since she met me?'

The question took her by surprise but it didn't take much thought to answer. 'Every day.'

'And before that? Before that, how often did she message you?'

It hadn't even occurred to her. 'Maybe...once a week?'

He shook his head. 'She senses things, Katsuko. She senses the changes in you. She's still trying to control you. Once you tell her you want to leave she'll do everything she can to stand in your way.'

His clear green eyes were so intense, so sincere. And in a horrible way she knew he was right. She'd just been pushing things away, trying not to think about them too much.

'How much control you let her have over your life is up to you, Katsuko.'

His gaze was so intense, so penetrating that she had to look away.

All the words that couldn't be said.

She got that. She got that now.

This could be about them. Her grandmother was sensing change. She recognised the signs. She'd seen them in her daughter—and now she could see them in her granddaughter. Two women who had fallen in love. And in her grandmother's eyes with two totally unsuitable men.

She put her hand down on the table to steady her legs. Now she got why Avery wouldn't say the words.

If he felt the same way she did, he didn't want to make her choose. He wouldn't ask her to.

And he was right. As soon as she told her grandmother she'd requested to move base she'd be faced with a whole host of problems. Her phone would probably go non-stop.

She could almost see words forming on his lips. Avery—the confident, intelligent doctor she knew—was racked with self-doubt. His family history preyed on him in a way that it shouldn't. In a life without different bases, different career pathways, no grandmothers and no multi-married parents, she could see them sitting on a porch, growing old together.

Nothing in her head felt straight. How her grandmother continually made her feel. The fact that she hadn't spoken to Don about Afghanistan. How she would feel about being away from her family and friends for months at a time.

And the fact that right now she just wanted to love and be loved.

She felt herself start to tremble. This so wasn't like her. But she just didn't know what to say. She just didn't know what to think.

His gaze was fixed on her. It was like he was looking for a sign. Looking for a prompt so he could say what he really wanted to.

Tears pooled in her eyes. 'But she's my grandmother' was all that came out.

Avery looked at her for the longest time. Then he gave a little nod of his head. 'Yes. She is.' He brushed a kiss to the side of her cheek and walked out.

CHAPTER TEN

THE ALARM SHOT through the ER. A few newer members of staff frowned, trying to decipher why the cardiac arrest call sounded different.

The rest of the staff didn't hesitate. Katsuko lifted her small patient from the trolley and dropped to her knees. Blake's voice echoed on the Tannoy system.

'Drop! Cover! Hold!'

The shaking started a few seconds later.

Most of the staff here were old pros. They'd trained for this and had to use their training on a regular basis throughout the year. For the light quakes the alarm didn't sound. It only sounded for the moderate and strong quakes—anything above five on the Richter scale.

There was no space to get beneath the trolley so Katsuko pulled the little girl she'd been treating close to her chest and spoke quietly to her as the ground and walls shook around them.

There were inevitable noises. A few shrieks. A few crashes. The hospital was well prepared. Heavy items weren't stored on high shelves where they could fall and do harm. Larger pieces of furniture were bolted to walls—no one wanted a hospital wardrobe or filing cabinet to land on them.

The little girl didn't seem at all bothered. She'd just

had her hand stitched after lacerating it on a piece of glass during a fall. Her mother had gone to the front desk to sign a few forms. Katsuko hoped that she had taken cover somewhere too.

Frank was in the room across the hall. He had an elderly patient next to him on the ground. 'You two okay?' he shouted.

She nodded, just as the trolley in his room managed to release its brake and roll towards them. 'Watch out!' she shouted.

Frank barely blinked as the shaking continued. He caught the trolley with one hand and one foot, protecting both himself and the patient.

He squinted up the clock in the hall. 'This one is lasting a bit longer than normal, isn't it?'

Katsuko nodded. 'Let's hope there's no damage.'

A phone cut through the shaking. It had a different tone from normal.

Frank mouthed a silent expletive at her as the force of the shaking started to diminish. They both knew exactly what phone that was. It meant there was a problem somewhere else in the hospital.

When the shaking finally stopped Katsuko jumped to her feet. Everything in her surrounding area seemed fine. She put her charge back on the trolley and pulled up the sides just as the mother reappeared. 'Is she okay?'

Katsuko nodded. 'We're both fine. How about you?'

The woman nodded, her trembling lip betraying her fear. 'Thank you.'

Katsuko glanced across the corridor. 'Need a hand, Frank?'

He shook his head as he snapped the brake back on the trolley and lifted his elderly patient easily on his own. She hid her smile. Health and Safety would have a fit.

Blake appeared at her side. 'Kat, ICU. Now. Two of

the ventilators are down and they need help bagging. The emergency generator hasn't kicked in.'

She took off at a run. Blake's voice carried behind her. 'Seiko, implement the phone muster. Frank, injury and patient reports. Lei, structural damage.'

They'd hear just how big the earthquake had been in a while, but in the meantime they had systems and processes in place to try and ensure the safety of all the staff and patients.

ICU was silently chaotic. She burst through the doors and was given an immediate wave by a member of staff in the corner. She ran straight over and took over bagging the patient. It wasn't a hard job—it was just essential to maintain the patient's breathing. The emergency generators usually kicked in straight away. This had never happened before.

Staff from other areas arrived too, all moving wherever needed. After a short while maintenance staff arrived, covered in dust, wheeling a portable generator alongside them.

'The line to the emergency generator has fractured. Repairs will take an hour. There's a gas leak somewhere else, so the main power can't be turned back on.'

The maintenance staff set up the portable generator and the staff from ICU connected the two ventilators. After a few minutes everything seemed to be working again. Katsuko was just putting down the bag and mask when Blake walked through the doors and waved her over.

The senior nurse shot her a glance. 'Thanks for your help.'

Katsuko gave her a nod and walked to the door. 'What's wrong?'

Blake looked anxious. He held open the door and started walking back along the corridor with her. 'Avery was due on duty. He isn't answering his house phone, his mobile or his page. Do you know where he could be?'

Katsuko shook her head. They'd parted on such bad terms last night that she no idea what his plans were for today. 'Are there reports of any problems?'

Blake nodded as they reached the ER front desk. 'Some reports are telling us already it was five point nine on the Richter scale. They also think we were only thirty miles away from the epicentre.'

'Are we expecting casualties?' She was asking the questions she should be asking. But not the questions she *wanted* to ask. She was on duty. She was a nurse. The military were expected to be able to react in the event of emergencies. All staff were supposed to respond.

Avery knew that. He'd been in emergency situations before. She couldn't understand why he wasn't here.

The emergency radio was on behind the desk, the Japanese voice speaking steadily. It sounded like there was some damage across the city. All of the modern buildings had been constructed to withstand earthquakes but some of the older buildings hadn't fared so well. It seemed that years of being shaken by earthquakes had caused some older foundations to finally crumble.

The emergency phone rang again and Blake answered. His brow furrowed as he listened intently. 'Yes, yes, no problem.'

He looked at the staff who had automatically collected around him—the emergency phone was almost like a homing beacon to ER staff. 'We're expecting between fifteen and twenty casualties, mainly broken bones and lacerations. There have been a number of wall collapses around us.' He replaced the receiver and glanced at Katsuko, muttering under his breath, 'Where on earth can he be? We could use him right now.'

The deep voice came from behind her. 'Who could you use?'

Katsuko jumped and spun around. She hadn't expected to see Don here. She thought he'd be coordinating everything from the control centre.

Blake gave him a nod. 'General Williams. We're missing Dr Flynn from the staff muster. Can't raise him at all. We don't know where he is.'

'I know where he is.' He touched Katsuko's elbow and pulled her to the side.

'What? How do you know where Avery is?'

She didn't understand. Don and Avery hadn't even had an official introduction yet. She hadn't meant to keep him away from Don, it had just worked out that way.

Don spoke in a low voice. 'Avery came to see me earlier.'

'What? Why would he do that?' Now she was totally confused. Why on earth would he go to see Don?

Don sighed. 'He wanted to meet me. He wanted to tell me that he might have upset my daughter by not telling her how he felt about her. He also told me that he didn't want to stand in the way of your career plans.'

'Why on earth would he tell you any of that?' She didn't get it. She really didn't get it. Last night all she'd wanted him to do was tell her how he felt about her—to be honest with her. He hadn't seemed able to do it, but he could tell Don instead?

Don laid a hand on her arm. 'He went to see Hiroko.'

'What? Why?' This was just getting crazier by the minute.

'He felt as if she might try and ruin your plans. He didn't want her to do that. He told me he was going to see her and tell her how great a nurse you were, how great your career prospects could be, and…' he paused '…how proud she should be of you.'

Katsuko gulped. That didn't sound like the actions of a man who didn't care about her. 'Why would he do that?' she whispered.

Don looked at her with the patient eyes of a father. 'He also wanted to tell her that at some point he intended to propose to you. And that as your husband he wouldn't allow his wife—or your future children—to be treated as if they weren't good enough.' Don gave a little smile. 'It seems he's got the size of your grandmother.'

Katsuko looked around. 'Then where is he?'

Don took a deep breath. 'That's why I'm here. I can't raise Hiroko on the phone. I've heard reports that some of the houses in the area have collapsed.'

'What?' She stepped backwards, reaching out for the wall behind her to steady herself.

Don nodded. 'There's a military car and driver outside.' He glanced over at Blake, who was hovering around, pretending he wasn't listening. 'We've called in all the extra staff. I'm sure you can be spared.'

Blake walked over to a nearby cupboard and pulled out an emergency pack and hard hat. 'Here. Take these with you. And bring Avery back. I need him. I need you both.'

Katsuko flung her hands around Don's neck. 'Thank you,' she whispered.

'Stay safe,' he replied as he handed her a radio. 'Let me know how you are.'

It took more than an hour to reach her grandmother's street. Some roads had wide fractures in them, meaning traffic couldn't go the normal routes. Potholes had opened in some places, with a whole variety of police cordons around trees or buildings affected by the earthquake.

Her grandmother lived in a more rural part of Tokyo. The houses were older single-storey wooden constructions with thatched roofs.

At least they used to be.

Two out of the four houses on the street were still standing.

The other two had collapsed completely, leaving their thatched roofs on what resembled piles of firewood.

'That one!' said Katsuko, and the driver ground to a halt.

She jumped from the car and ran towards the rubble. A few people were at the other collapsed house in the street, picking up strewn belongings.

Katsuko felt a wave of panic wash over her. Where did she even start? Was her grandmother in there? Was Avery?

She tried to be logical, tried to think with her head instead of her heart.

She crouched down and looked at the pile in front of her. The driver appeared at her side, bent down and unwound her tightly gripped fingers from the radio.

The radio. Of course. So much for thinking with her head. She heard him talking rapidly. All she could think right now was whether anyone could be alive in there.

'Avery! Avery,' she started shouting. Apart from the noise of distant sirens, the street was strangely quiet.

'*Sobo! Sobo!*' The Japanese word for grandmother was usually an affectionate term. It had never really fitted her grandmother—even now it felt strange to use it.

She shuddered. The house looked so alien to her—as if a giant had walked along the street and flattened it with his foot. It was odd, though, parts of the thatched roof looked strangely intact—as if a crane could come along and lift it back up on top of a newly constructed house.

She started to pull at some of the shattered wood, throwing it behind her as she tried to see anything she recognised amongst the debris.

The driver joined her. 'What did they say?' she asked.

His face was serious. 'I've got to radio back if there are any sign of survivors. Emergency services are only reacting to reports of trapped survivors right now.'

Of course they were. What he wasn't saying out loud was that the emergency services didn't have the resources right now to recover bodies. That would come later.

She started to work more frantically, her muscles burning as she tossed pieces of wood behind her.

After ten minutes the driver touched her elbow, almost earning himself a piece of wood in the face. 'Listen.'

She froze, her ears pricking up instantly.

There it was. A kind of moan.

She dropped to her knees. 'Avery! *Sobo!* Hiroko!' she shouted at the pile of rubble.

There it was again. A faint noise in the debris.

The driver knelt beside her. They practically had their ears to the ground.

'Avery!' she shouted again.

'Kat.' It wasn't a shout. It was more like a hoarse whisper.

She started pulling at the wood again, trying to get closer to the source of his voice. After a few minutes she realised it was useless. The edge of the roof stopped her going any further.

She leaned in, pressing her face right up against the thatch of the roof. She didn't care about the fact it was scratching her face. She didn't care about anything other than finding out that the people she loved were actually in there.

'Avery, are you there? Are you okay?'

There was a bit of a groan. Then a quip, 'Oh, so you're talking to me now.'

A tear slid down her cheek. He was alive. He was definitely alive.

She tried to find some words. 'Are you okay?' she repeated. 'What about my grandmother?'

It took a few seconds to get a reply. Was he going in and out of consciousness? Could he have a head injury?

'Give me a minute.'

The driver pressed on her shoulder. He was back on the phone, obviously trying to get them some assistance in the midst of chaos.

It was too quiet. She could hardly bear it. 'Avery?'

She adjusted her position, trying to figure out exactly where he was. It wasn't easy and she ended up crawling over part of the roof. 'Avery?'

'I've got her.'

'You have?' A second wave of relief washed over her. 'Is she okay?'

'I think so.' He made another strange noise. 'I'm trapped next to her. Give me a second.'

The waiting game. The thing she really wasn't good at.

'She's breathing. I'm just trying to wake her up.'

Katsuko was conscious of the driver talking next to her in rapid Japanese. He took off down the road towards some of the bewildered-looking neighbours who were standing in the middle of the street, staring at the road.

'Oh, now she's awake. She's glaring at me again.'

Katsuko started babbling in Japanese, telling her grandmother that she was here and she would get her out. Telling her to be strong.

She heard a rapid string of Japanese but it was so quietly spoken she couldn't make out a word.

'Avery, what's she saying?'

Avery could hardly move. His legs and chest were pinned. The only thing he could really move was his head and one of his arms.

One minute he'd been standing in the doorway, having an almost argument with Katsuko's grandmother, the next minute the ground had rumbled all around them and the house had started to shake. His brain had screamed at them to get out of there.

But Hiroko had been in her wheelchair and the handles hadn't been facing him. As he'd tried to jump inside to get her out something had crashed into his back and knocked them both to the ground. He didn't remember much after that.

He tried to take a deep breath. Impossible. Breathing was a struggle. He was guessing that one of his lungs might have collapsed. He only hoped it was a pneumothorax and not a haemothorax. It wouldn't do it have a medical emergency right now. He didn't want to think where he could be bleeding from.

Katsuko kept talking. Nervous energy. He could only imagine how frustrated she was right now.

Hiroko started another tirade and he aimed the pen torch at her. One of his legs was pinned under her wheelchair, the other caught between part of the roof and the floor. She had a large wound on her head, but her temperament and voice remained unchanged. It was amazing. It was almost as if he could understand every word she was spitting at him. Hatred was a pretty universal language.

'Avery, what's she saying? I can't hear her.'

'I think she's telling me she doesn't like me much.'

Silence for a second. It was clear Katsuko was trying to make sense of what was going on. 'Why on earth were you visiting my grandmother?'

He let his head rest back on the floor. This was so not how he wanted to do this.

He'd spoken to the General. Or, he should say, he'd been interrogated by the General. Don Williams was an impressive man. It was clear that for him, without any question, Katsuko was his daughter. Genes didn't matter. Blood didn't matter.

By the time Avery had told him how he felt about his daughter and what he intended to do, he'd felt lucky to finally leave with the General's blessing.

He reached over and touched Hiroko's shoulder. It was all he could do. His pen torch was the only light they had—thank goodness he'd had it in his back pocket. 'Hiroko, I don't know how long we will be here. Katsuko's outside, she knows we're trapped, she'll get help.' He tried to wriggle a little bit to ease the pressure on his right hip.

In theory, Hiroko shouldn't be able to understand a word he was saying. But he saw something flash across her eyes—just like he had the first time he'd met her—and just like he had when he'd arrived today and told her how much he loved her granddaughter. He turned the pen torch to look at the time on his watch. Really? How long had he been unconscious?

Then something else occurred to him. How long had Hiroko lain trapped in the dark, wondering if anyone would come to rescue her? She must have been terrified.

He wriggled some more and lifted his hand from Hiroko's shoulder and moved it down, taking her gnarled hand in his.

She made a little noise of displeasure but she didn't let go.

'Avery?' Katsuko's voice was just to his right. It didn't seem so far away now. There was only this roof separating them. How long before he could look into those dark brown eyes again?

He took a deep breath. 'I came to tell your grandmother how special I thought you were. I came to tell her that you might have to move base. You're in the air force, it's expected of you.'

There was a sniff beside him. And he knew instantly

what it was. A silent tear slid down Hiroko's face and he gently squeezed her gnarled hand.

Katsuko hadn't answered. She'd realised that he hadn't told her grandmother that she was choosing to go away, choosing to find a new life. He'd made it sound like it was part of her air force medical corps service.

He heard some discussion through the thatch, but it was all in Japanese, he couldn't understand a word.

'Avery? I've got an axe.'

'What?' He couldn't help but shout his reply.

'I have to do something. It will be hours before we can get help. There's been a few older buildings that have collapsed across the city. But most of the damage is to the streets. We're going to try and get through the thatch. We need to get some air to you. Even if we can't get you out, we can maybe get some water to you both.'

Air. He hadn't really thought about air. Wouldn't some just come through the densely packed thatch? In truth, he had no idea. 'I'm not sure about this. I don't really want an axe in the head.'

'We'll do it to the side. I can't stand here and do nothing. We have to try and reach you.'

'Have you any idea how thick this thatch is?'

'I guess we're about to find out.'

She shouted some more instructions, asking questions and trying to find out their positions under the thatch.

Eventually, after a lot more discussion outside, he heard the noise of the axe. It took a long, long time. At first the noise seemed far away. It took quite a time before the actual vibrations of the axe started to reach them. Their judgement was good. It sounded close enough but not so close as to do them any harm. The light started to filter through as some of the thatch was dragged away. Eventually, a metre away from his head they finally broke through.

For a few seconds all he could see were hands, pulling and pulling at the thatch to try and make a gap. It wasn't large, certainly not big enough to get through, but the light and warm air that flooded in was welcome.

A few seconds later somebody shone a torch inside. Katsuko started shouting first in Japanese, then in English. 'Avery! Avery! I can see you.' Her hand reached in, her fingertips barely touching the top of his hair.

It didn't matter. It was enough.

The torch light swung slightly past him and she spoke rapidly to her grandmother, obviously trying to reassure her. He waited for the venom, the disapproving answer, but it didn't come. Her hand was still in his, and he gave it a little squeeze again. This time she squeezed back.

'You have no idea how glad I am to see you. I was so scared. So worried about you both.' Katsuko took a deep breath. 'I'm so glad you were here with my grandmother.'

It didn't matter how long they'd been here. It didn't matter how uncomfortable they were. It didn't matter that his breathing was awkward. All he cared about was the fact that she'd come. The fact that she was here.

She pushed in a bottle of water, it was tied to a stick this time and his hand could reach it. It took a minute to open the top with one hand, then hold it towards Hiroko to let her have a drink. Of course he spilled it half over her. But she didn't complain. She just closed her eyes in grateful silence.

Katsuko's face pressed up to the space again. Her cheek was smeared with dust and her normally smooth hair was sticking up in all directions. He'd never seen anyone quite so beautiful.

'When I get you out of here, you and I need to talk about you coming to see my grandmother.' The fearful tone had left her voice. She was still anxious, but now she could actually see them both she obviously felt a bit more reassured.

'Your grandmother and I have reached an understanding,' he replied.

'What? What do you mean?'

He smiled as he craned his neck to turn his face towards her. 'I've been taking lessons.'

'Lessons in what?'

He held her gaze. He'd been practising and practising over in his head. He wanted to get it just right. 'This isn't exactly how I wanted to say this. But it's important. Probably the most important thing I'll ever say.' He concentrated hard. *'Kokoro no sokokara aishiteru.'*

There was a little gasp. 'What did you just say?'

'Kokoro no sokokara aishiteru.' This time he had more confidence. This time he followed it with something new. *'Aishiteru.'*

She didn't speak. She didn't say anything.

'Katsuko Williams, you have my heart. I love you. Last night I thought if I told you that, I'd be standing in your way. And I don't ever want to stand in your way. I want to stand by your side. You're unsettled. You think you don't fit anywhere. But I know where you fit. You fit with me. You are my perfect fit.' He stopped for a breath. The pain in his lung was constant but it wouldn't stop him from saying what he needed to say. 'I wanted to say this when I had my arms around you, not when we've been pushed apart. So get us out of here soon, so I can say it again. *Aishiteru.* I love you.'

Katsuko started sobbing. 'You tell me now? You tell me like this?'

'I've spent so much time wondering if I can be what you need. I've never been somewhere I don't want to leave. I've never been with someone I don't want to leave. But you're perfect for me. I want to make this work. I want to do anything at all to make this work. I love you, Katsuko, and get used to hearing it because I can say it in two languages now.'

'Avery Flynn, you are the most annoying man I've ever met.'

His heart skipped a beat, then she continued, 'And the most adorable. And the most infuriating. That kiss. That kiss in the middle of Hachiko Crossing. It blew my mind. I couldn't think straight. I haven't thought straight ever since. I want to be kissed like that every day for the rest of my life.'

'And I want to be the man to do that.'

Something shook around them. Avery frowned. 'What's that?'

It happened again. And again. Then again.

Her face pressed back up at the hole. 'It's me,' said Katsuko. 'I'm getting you out of there. I need to be kissed again and I don't want to wait.' He heard her shout in Japanese to the others and the thudding intensified. He turned towards Hiroko. Tears were streaming down her face.

'Hiroko? Are you okay? Are you in pain?'

She shook her head. 'No.'

He blinked. She'd just answered in English. Was he hallucinating? Maybe his oxygen level was lower than it should be.

'I love her,' he said. 'I promise you I'll take good care of her. I know you don't want her to marry an American. I know you didn't want your daughter to marry an American. But Katsuko is the woman for me.' He gave her a smile. 'She has my heart.'

Hiroko didn't speak. She just gave him a gracious nod.

A hand broke in and grabbed his shoulder. 'Come on,' shouted Katsuko. 'Hold on, honey. Not long now.'

He was almost relieved when the pounding stopped. The rescuers were too close to use the axe now. But they seemed to use every other tool they could find to try and break the thatch apart to get to them. More and more hands appeared, pulling at the edges of the thatch and doing their best to break it apart. It was tough. Avery could see that. Something that had lasted this long didn't want to give up now.

Finally there were arms around his shoulders. Katsuko let out a shriek. 'Avery? What's wrong? You're hurt. Why didn't you tell me?' He winced as her hand came into contact with his side and came up smeared in red. He sucked in a breath and she must have noticed his uneven breathing straight away. 'You have a pneumothorax?' She signalled to the driver as she pulled at his shirt. 'Get the rest of this thatch away. I need to check him over and get him out of here,' she shouted to the rescuers.

She stopped for a second and turned her attention to her grandmother, speaking to her in a low voice in Japanese and examining her as best she could.

He couldn't help but smile. This was her—the woman he loved. Taking charge. Her emergency skills shone through. She would excel in Afghanistan and he would be right by her side.

When she came back to him he whispered in her ear, 'You'd better have pressed send on that application because I pressed send last night.'

She pulled back, her eyes wide. 'You did?'

'Of course I did. Do you know how many guys will love you over there?'

She raised her eyebrows. 'But I'm only interested in one guy. The thing is, he can't get over his family history. He doesn't seem to know that he and I can make our own history.'

An oxygen canister appeared from somewhere and Katsuko slid the mask over his face. He pulled it aside. 'You have your work cut out for you. I might be a slow learner but someone in my family has got to set a good example. I figure it should be me.'

He slid his hand into hers. '*Kokoro no sokokara aishiteru.* I'd like to have our own saying. How about always and for ever? How does that sound?'

Her brown eyes met his and she put a hand on either side of his head as she leaned in to kiss him. 'That sounds perfect.'

EPILOGUE

THE BRIDE AND groom had decided to come back to Tokyo to get married. Hiroko was too frail to travel and Katsuko wouldn't get married without Don being there to give her away.

Avery had reluctantly invited his parents with their new partners, and his sister with her new baby. 'Don't worry,' promised Katsuko with a wink. 'Any one of them gets out of order, the new Mrs Flynn will deal with them.'

Avery couldn't be prouder. His bride, in a bright red gown, was stunning. They'd returned from Afghanistan a captain and a major. Katsuko had blossomed in the intense environment. Next stop was the San Antonio Military Medical Center, the biggest and most advanced military hospital in the US.

He lifted the glass of champagne to the room filled with their family and friends. 'I'd like everyone to raise their glasses with me. I want you all to raise a glass to the man sitting in the corner of the room—a man most of you won't know.' He gave a nod of his head. 'This, ladies and gentlemen, is Dwayne Cooper. Dr Dwayne Cooper, who was supposed to take up his posting eighteen months ago in Okatu, Japan. Dwayne, however, had other ideas and decided to come down with malaria instead, meaning— with one day's notice—I was the one who climbed on that plane at Hill Air Force base. I had no idea what would lie ahead. I had no idea I'd meet the love of my life and find a woman that I'd want to spend the rest of my life with.'

Katsuko was beaming. Don was sitting beside her in his dress uniform and couldn't look prouder. Her grandmother was next to Avery and had shed a tear during the ceremony.

Katsuko stood from her seat and wrapped her arms around his neck, kissing him on the lips. She lifted up her champagne glass from the table and showed it to the guests. 'To Dr Dwayne Cooper. My colleagues tell me that you're wonderful to work with, but you'll forgive me if I have a bias towards Major Flynn.'

The guests laughed and sipped their champagne.

Avery slipped his arm around his wife's waist. The wedding dinner had run later than expected and the hotel's full-length windows showed the dark sky outside. He lifted his glass again. 'One more thing, most of you will know my wife's nickname. So join me, everyone, in raising your glasses to my own *faiyakuraka*—Captain Katsuko Flynn.'

He gave a little signal to someone and a few seconds later the sky lit up with fireworks behind them.

Her eyes widened as she turned towards him and put both hands on his shoulders. 'You got me fireworks?'

'Of course I got you fireworks,' he bent to whisper in her ear. 'Now, how about we re-enact Hachiko Crossing?'

She grinned at him. 'I can't think of anything I want to do more.'

And so they did.

As the multi-coloured fireworks streaked across the sky and the guests cheered.

* * * * *

THE COURAGE TO
LOVE HER ARMY DOC

BY
KARIN BAINE

MILLS & BOON

Published in Great Britain 2016
By Mills & Boon, an imprint of HarperCollins*Publishers*
1 London Bridge Street, London, SE1 9GF

© 2016 Karin Baine

ISBN: 978-0-263-91516-7

Our policy is to use papers that are natural, renewable and recyclable products and made from wood grown in sustainable forests. The logging and manufacturing processes conform to the legal environmental regulations of the country of origin.

Printed and bound in Spain
by CPI, Barcelona

Dear Reader,

I'm a big fan of modern-day adventurers and those TV programmes in which they're dropped at remote locations with nothing but a camera and the will to survive. Mainly because I come from the 'What if?' school of thought, and prefer a cosy seat in my comfort zone to camping in the potentially spider-infested unknown. I admire that devil-may-care attitude to life—even though I watch those shows wondering why people would put themselves in unnecessary danger.

When ex-army doc Joe came to my mind he had that same adventurous spirit. He flits from one exciting escapade to another with no intention of settling down. Until he meets GP Emily, who is trying to break free from her own boring world, and begins to see the attraction in having someone to share his experiences with.

Although the remote island where they both arrive to volunteer their medical services is beautiful and welcoming, Emily's insecurities are in danger of stifling her enjoyment. Thank goodness Joe is there to give her a little nudge forward when she needs it.

Now I come to think about it, he kind of reminds me of my husband…

I do hope you enjoy going on Emily and Joe's exotic adventure with them. It was certainly fun to write!

Lots of love,

Karin xx

For the ladies who've shared this adventure with me—
Ann, Cherie, Donna, Doris, Heather, Joanne, Julia,
June, Kiru, Michelle, Rima, Sharon, Stacy, Stephanie,
Sukhi, Summerita, Suzy, Tammy, Teresa and Xandra.
UCW was where it all began.

With thanks also to the residents of Los Balcones
and the members of 'The Monday Club'
who bring a little sunshine into my life.

And to George—the other half of me.

Praise for
Karin Baine

'The moment I picked up Karin Baine's debut medical
romance I knew I would not be disappointed with
her work. Poetic and descriptive writing, engaging
dialogue, thoroughly created characters and a tightly
woven plot propels *French Fling to Forever* into the
must-read, highly recommended level.'
—*Contemporary Romance Reviews*

'This is a wonderfully written book and one I could
not put down and had to finish. You will not be
disappointed in Karin Baine's writing.'
—*Goodreads* on
French Fling to Forever

'*A Kiss to Change Her Life* by Karin Baine is a
well-researched, well-written, emotionally touching
story… One Mills & Boon Medical Romance you do
not want to miss!'
—*Goodreads*

CHAPTER ONE

PARADISE. IT WAS the only word to describe these sun-drenched islands that Emily Clifford hoped were going to change her life. Unfortunately, she hadn't accounted for the distance she would have to travel to find her solace.

Travel sickness wasn't something she'd ever suffered before or she would've had one of her colleagues at the GP practice prescribe her something before she'd left England. If she'd been thinking clearly she might have realised that accessing one of these remote Fijian islands would take more than a taxi ride. Her first day after landing at the airport on the main island, Viti Levu, walking through the markets, and her night at a luxurious five-star resort now seemed a lifetime ago.

Today's white-knuckle charter flight, followed by a bone-jangling cross-country drive and hours of sailing these waters, had taken their toll.

The only thing she was looking forward to more than a shower and bed was seeing Peter, her stepbrother, waiting for her. He was the reason she was even attempting this adventure. The chance to prove her ex-husband wrong about her being *boring* was simply a bonus.

She and Greg had been together since high school, married for ten years, but it hadn't been enough. She hadn't been enough.

When Peter had told her about the mission out here and how they were struggling to find medical professionals to volunteer, she'd jumped at the chance to help for a while. Not least because this fortnight away meant she'd be occupied while Greg and Little Miss Bit-on-the-Side held the wedding of the year.

Another swell of nausea rose as the boat bobbed again but this had to be better than sitting at home, crying over her wedding photographs and wondering where it had all gone wrong.

As they finally reached the far side of the island and prepared to go ashore, she could see a figure sitting cross-legged at the water's edge. She waved manically, desperate more than ever to get off this boat and find comfort in the arms of her big brother.

With her hand shielding her eyes from the glaring sun, she squinted at her welcome party of one slowly getting to his feet. He appeared to have grown in the two years since she'd last seen him, and he was leaner than she remembered, as though someone had stretched him like golden-coloured toffee.

Eventually she had to come to terms with the fact that no amount of sand, sea and sun could cause such a physical transformation. Disappointment settled in her belly as she realised it wasn't Peter at all. She was going to have to wait for her tea and sympathy for a bit longer.

She'd done her best to be strong over this past year and a half, holding it together as she'd moved out of her marital home and keeping a smile in place for all her patients when she'd been dying inside. For a short time she wanted to stop pretending she wasn't crushed by the rejection and it didn't take every ounce of strength just to get out of bed in the morning and face the world. Ten minutes of being the baby sister, crying out her pain to her big bro, would help reset the factory settings. Two weeks doing what she loved, what she was qualified to do, would remind her she was more than a redundant wife. She'd lasted this long for a shoulder to cry on so waiting a few extra minutes wouldn't kill her. Although she couldn't swear the pent-up anger and emotion she'd been gearing up to release wouldn't seep out somewhere along the way.

Her bejewelled sandals and floral maxi-dress flapped through the water as she stepped ashore. In hindsight, it hadn't been the ideal choice of travelling outfit. Her feet ached, her dress was creased and as she came face-to-face with the hunk on the beach she was pretty sure the flower in her hair was wilting. What had been an attempt to get into the holiday spirit had probably succeeded in making her appear even more ridiculous than usual, like a stereotypical tourist instead of a qualified professional hoping to fit effortlessly into society.

With his close-cropped brown hair and dressed in mid-length khaki shorts and navy T-shirt, her greeter looked more action man than island native. There was no sign of a grass skirt anywhere. Unfortunately.

'Hi. I'm Emily.' She held out her hand for him to shake but he bypassed the traditional greeting to head for the boat. The bit of research she'd done said they mostly spoke English here on Yasi island but perhaps she'd found the one local who didn't.

He began unloading her luggage, muscles flexing as he hurled her case and boxes of supplies onto the white sand.

'*Bula.*' She tried again, using the one Fijian word she'd picked up on her travels so far.

The Peter impostor waved off her last link to civilisation and came back to join her.

'*Bula* to you too.' The cut-glass British accent didn't fit with the swarthy skin but the familiar tongue and the glimpse of a smile put her mind at ease about being stranded here with an uncommunicative stranger.

'You're English?'

'Yeah. From Oxford, actually. I'm Joe. Joe Braden.' This time he did shake her hand, the firm grip showing the strength behind those muscles.

Emily shivered, regardless of the tropical heat. Clearly she'd been on her own too long when a single handshake was enough to get her excited. Not that she was ready for the dating game. In the day and age when physical attributes held more value than loyalty or commitment, she was in no rush to put herself through any more heartache.

'Joe Braden… Why does that name ring a bell?' They'd never met. She'd have remembered if they had.

'I served with Peter in Afghanistan.' The smile disappeared as quickly as it had formed.

That made sense of the military haircut and the no-nonsense attitude. She'd heard that name in conversation and she was sure there was an extra nugget of information tied to it that was just out of reach in her subconscious.

'Where is he? No offence, but I had hoped he'd be here to meet me.' She didn't want to get into a conversation about their time in combat and she doubted he'd be keen to rehash the whole experience either. It had been hell for all those involved, including the families waiting anxiously at home for their safe return. Peter's decision to leave the army and begin a life dedicated to his faith had been a relief to everyone who loved him.

'None taken. We couldn't be sure exactly what time to expect you and Peter had a service this evening. I volunteered for lookout duty.' He handed her a suitcase and a holdall while he hoisted the large box onto his shoulder.

She didn't dare ask how long he'd waited. His lips, drawn into a thin line and his apparent hurry to get moving, told her it had probably been too long. Not exactly the welcome she'd been hoping for.

Joe was already taking great strides across the beach,

so Emily traipsed after him as fast as she could with a holdall hooked over one shoulder and a suitcase in the other, waddling like a colourful penguin. There was no immediate sign of human habitation nearby and she didn't relish the thought of being left behind.

'What brings you out here anyway?' She caught up with him at the bottom of a steep, grassy slope. Their journey apparently wasn't going to be an easy or short one. Some small talk might help it pass quicker.

'Your stepbrother.'

'You're visiting Peter?' He hadn't mentioned having company in his emails. She hadn't counted on sharing his attention. As pitiful as that sounded, she hadn't seen him in two whole years and wanted to make up for lost time. Who knew where he'd be going next or how long he'd be gone? Quality time with him wasn't going to be quite the same with surly soldier dude tagging along.

'I'm here as a medical volunteer, the same as you. I'll be here for another month. Maybe. I prefer to keep on the move. What you would call a modern-day adventurer, I guess. This is the longest I've actually spent in one place since leaving the army, which is entirely down to your stepbrother's powers of persuasion.' He didn't even slow his pace to deliver the news, leaving her staring open-mouthed at him.

There were two things wrong with that statement. First of all, it meant he had personal intel on her already if he knew why she was there. She didn't have her stepbrother down as the gossipy type since he hadn't seen the need to share information concerning her new companion, so perhaps soldier boy had insisted on a debriefing before meeting his assigned target. Goodness knew what went on between ex-military buddies, they had a bro code mere mortals could never infiltrate, but she hoped any discussion about her arrival hadn't included details of her failed marriage. That shame was exactly what she was trying to escape.

Secondly, his introduction undoubtedly meant she'd be working alongside this man for the duration of her stay. Trying to get more than a few words out of him on this trek was proving hard enough.

In her version of this medical outreach programme she was simply transferring her cosy GP office to an exotic location without interference from third parties. Peter had sounded so delighted to hear she was coming she'd assumed she'd be the sole medical professional in residence. This Joe was stealing all her thunder.

'Do I call you Dr? Sergeant? Joe…?' She was going to have serious words with her stepbrother about dumping her on a complete stranger without a word of warning. It immediately put her on the back foot when Peter should have known how important it was for her to feel comfortable in her surroundings.

'Joe will do just fine.'

She couldn't work out if the reluctance to engage in conversation was personal or he was simply trying to conserve energy. The hike up this hill was a test of endurance in itself, never mind the heavy box he was balancing on his broad shoulders. She was starting to regret packing the weighty school books she'd brought with her as a gift.

'Isn't there someone who could give us a hand?' She was tired, achy and full of guilt, watching him shift the burden from one shoulder to the other.

'Did you bring the *yaqona*?' He ignored her question to stop and ask one of his own, as if hers wasn't important enough to deserve the few seconds it would take to answer it. With any luck this place was big enough to house two independent clinics. There was no way she was spending the duration of this trip with someone so rude.

'Yes. It's in this bag.' She, however, was polite enough

to answer him. Peter had at least given her the heads up about bringing gifts with her, including the root of this pepper plant. Apparently it was some sort of payment for her stay among the villagers, even though it did look kind of funky to her. She would have preferred to give him a pot plant or a nice bottle of wine with a thank-you card.

'Good. We'll go and make *sevusevu* now with the chief.'

'Can't we do that later? I really need to shower and freshen up.' By the time they reached their destination she wouldn't be fit to be seen in public.

'No can do. You have to show your respect to the tribal leader before you can integrate yourself into village life. If you respect the customs here it'll ensure you become part of the community.'

Right now, the heat and humidity were making her feel as though her face was melting. She was very wary of her potentially sliding make-up and the fact he was telling her she wouldn't get the chance to redo it. The heavy, thick concealer she wore to cover her birthmark was the one essential from home she couldn't do without.

She was self-conscious of the deep red port wine stain dominating the left side of her face, so noticeable against her otherwise pale skin. It was something that had caused her a great deal of distress over the years. And not only from uneducated, tactless strangers. Her own mother had been ashamed of her appearance. She'd told her that when she'd forced her through painful, ineffective laser treatment as a child. She'd shown it when she'd left the family home without her. In the end it had been the camouflage make-up and the love of her father's new family that had helped her live with it.

This was a big ask for her anyway, to come to foreign lands alone, never mind leaving herself exposed and open to scrutiny from strangers.

As they crested the hill she could see the settlement nestled below. It was now or never.

She stopped and dropped her bags. This trip was always going to be about improvising and making use of whatever resources she had at the time.

'What are you doing?' Joe raised an eyebrow at her as she rooted through her belongings for her mirror compact.

'I need to look my best if I'm going to meet someone of such great importance.' She made a few repairs before she scared small children and animals, ignoring Joe's shake of the head.

'You know, that's really not necessary. You should let your skin breathe and I'm sure you look just as amazing without it.'

There was no time to linger on the fact he'd paid her a compliment as he spun on his heel and started walking again. Besides, he'd be running if he knew what really lay beneath. She took one last glance in the mirror to check for any errant red patches shining through the layers of powder and paint and packed her precious cargo away again to follow him. Now she'd had a chance to boost her confidence again she could face any new challenge.

Joe couldn't hang about to watch her plaster that stuff over her face. He knew why she did it, of course, he'd seen the photographs of his kid sister Peter had kept with him out in Afghanistan. It simply irked him that someone had made her feel as though she had to use it to keep her real self from view. He knew how it was to have people devalue your worth so readily over a minor flaw.

Okay, his hearing had taken a hit along with the rest of him on the front line but that didn't mean he should have been written off altogether. The army might think all he was good for now was a desk job or teaching but he had no intention of sitting still. Fiji was just one stop on the list of adventures he'd embarked on since taking medical retirement.

According to Peter, Emily had had a rough time of it lately but Joe knew how empowering these trips abroad could be. His time trekking in Nepal, island hopping in the Philippines and swimming on the Great Barrier Reef had kept him from focusing on all the negatives in his past. With any luck she'd return at the end of this mission equally as upbeat, not caring a jot about other people's perceptions of her.

Although how she could think she was anything other than stunning he didn't know. The second she'd stepped ashore he'd known he was in trouble.

His decision to volunteer as official island greeter had been born of curiosity. He'd seen the worn photographs of her and Peter as kids, the shy Emily always hiding behind her stepbrother, and he'd wondered about the woman she'd become. The doctor he was going to be working along-side for the foreseeable future.

In the four weeks he'd already spent in this island para-dise she was the most beautiful sight he'd seen yet. With the golden waves of her hair shining in the sunlight, her turquoise eyes the colour of the water and her slender form draped in azure, she could've stepped out of a shampoo advert. It was too bad she was his mate's little sister and nursing a broken heart. Two things that immediately put her off limits. Even if hearing-impaired ex-army docs were her thing.

He'd let enough of his army buddies down without fail-ing Peter too. Neither was he in the market for any sort of emotional entanglements. Emily was literally carrying more baggage than he was prepared to take on. He was more of a backpacking guy, travelling light with no inten-tion of setting down roots. Although he helped out with these outreach programmes now and then when people were in dire need, he was better off on his own. It meant no long-term responsibility to anyone but himself.

The last time he'd been charged with the welfare of people close to him, it had cost two of his colleagues their lives. When the IED had knocked him to kingdom come he'd failed to be there for the men he'd had a duty of care for. Next to the young families left without fathers, his loss seemed insignificant. These days he preferred to keep his wits about him rather than become too complacent and safe in his surroundings.

'Are we there yet?' Emily was smiling as she jogged to keep up with him.

At least when she was close he could hear her or interpret her facial expressions. He only had a six per cent loss of hearing but sometimes it meant he missed full conversations going on in the background. More often than not he chose to let people think he was an arrogant sod over revealing his weakness. He and Emily had their pride in common.

'Very nearly. Now, there are a few protocols to be aware of before presenting the *yaqona* for the kava ceremony. You're dressed modestly enough so that shouldn't be a problem.' He took the opportunity for a more in-depth study of her form, though he wasn't likely to forget in a hurry how she looked today.

'What's the kava ceremony?' She eyed him suspiciously, as if he might be luring her to the village as some sort of human sacrifice.

'Basically, it's a welcoming ceremony with the most senior tribal members present. They grind the *yaqona*, or kava, and make it into a drink for you to take with them in a traditional ceremony. All visitors are invited to take part when they first arrive on the island.'

'It's not one of those hallucinogenic substances you hear about, is it? I don't want to be seeing fairies dancing about all night in front of my eyes. I'm not even a big drinker because I don't enjoy that feeling of being out of control.' She was starting to get herself into a flap for no reason.

Joe hadn't even asked questions when he'd taken part in his first kava ceremony, he'd just gone with the flow. He embraced every new experience with gusto, whereas Emily seemed to fear it.

'Don't worry. It's nothing sinister, although the taste leaves a lot to be desired. There shouldn't be any fairy visions keeping you awake. If anything, it's known to aid sleep, among other things.' He kept the claims of its aphrodisiac properties to himself rather than freak her out any further.

'I don't think that's something I'm going to have a problem with tonight.' She set her case down and rubbed her palms on her dress before lifting it again. The heavy labour in less-than-ideal circumstances was something she was going to have to get used to and only time would tell if she was up to it.

He, on the other hand, had a feeling his peace of mind here had suddenly been thrown into chaos.

It was just as well he thrived on a challenge.

CHAPTER TWO

ALL EMILY WANTED was a familiar face and familiar things around her. It wasn't a lot to ask for and the sooner she got her bags unpacked and her clinic in the sun set up the better. Then she might be able to finally relax. She'd had all the excitement she needed just getting here.

Her pulse skittered faster as the ramshackle buildings with their corrugated-iron roofs came into view. This was as far from her humdrum life as she could get and a definite two-fingered salute to her ex.

'Can I refuse to take part in this kava thing?' She'd used up her quota of bravery already. Drinking unknown substances with strangers was the sort of thing that could make her the subject of one of those 'disappearances unsolved' programmes.

Her idea of living dangerously was putting an extra spoonful of sugar in her cuppa at bedtime, not imbibing a local brew of origin unknown to her. It wasn't that she'd heard anything but good things about these people, she was just scared of all this *newness*. This would've been so much easier if Peter was here with her instead of the scowling Joe.

'You have free will, of course you can refuse. It would, however, show a distinct lack of respect for your hosts.'

That would be a no, then. It was going to be difficult

enough fitting in here, without incurring the wrath of the community from the get-go.

Trust and respect were vital components between a doctor and her patients. It had taken her a long time to gain both from her colleagues and the locals when she'd first joined the GP practice at home. Only years of hard work, building her reputation, had moved her from being last option to first choice for her patients.

With only two weeks to re-create that success here she'd have to take every opportunity available to ingratiate herself. Even if she was breaking out in a cold sweat at what that meant she could be walking into.

They passed a white building, larger than the rest, which her tour guide informed her was the village school. Although lessons were surely over for the day, the children were congregated on the patch of green surrounding it, playing ball games. There was a chorus of '*Bula!*' as the youngsters waved in their direction.

Unfortunately, one boy by the volleyball net was too distracted by their arrival to see the ball coming straight for him. The loud smack as it connected full in his face even made Emily flinch. As the child crumpled to the ground, for a split second she wondered if there was some sort of protocol she should follow as she hadn't been officially introduced. Common sense quickly overrode her worry and she dropped her bags to run to him. It was only when she was battling through the throng of children to reach him that she realised Joe had followed too. They knelt on either side of the boy, who was thankfully still conscious but clearly winded.

'If you could just stay still for us, sweetheart, we want to give you a check over. That was quite a hit you took there.' She couldn't see any blood or bruising as yet but she wanted him to stay flat until they'd given him a quick examination.

'Hi, Joni. This is Emily, the new doctor. You know, Pastor Peter's sister?' Joe made the introduction she'd omitted to do herself, and was already checking the boy's pupils with a small torch he'd retrieved from one of his pockets.

She'd bet her life he had a Swiss Army knife and a compass somewhere in those cargo shorts too. He was the type of guy who was always prepared, like a rugged, muscly Boy Scout. The only survival essentials she carried were make-up, teabags and chocolate biscuits, none of which were particularly useful at present. The few medical supplies she had with her were packed somewhere in her abandoned luggage.

Life as an island doctor certainly wasn't going to run to the office hours she was used to. She was going to be permanently on call and if she didn't come equipped, deferring to her army medic colleague was going to become the norm. That feeling of inadequacy could defeat the purpose of her personal journey here if she didn't get with the programme. This trip was primarily to bring medical relief to the people of the island and she could do without uncovering any new flaws to obsess over.

'Do you know where you are, Joni? Or what happened?' She wrestled back some control, determined not to let the issue of a pocket torch spiral into a major meltdown in her neurotic brain.

That earned her an *Are you serious?* glare. 'I'm lying on the ground because you two won't let me get up after I got hit in the face with a ball.'

Joe snickered as she was educated by her first patient.

'Dr Emily's making sure the bump on the head hasn't caused any serious damage, smart guy.' He ruffled the boy's hair, clearly already acquainted with the child.

She figured he was using her first name to break the

ice a little because she was a stranger. Either that or he
didn't know what surname she was currently going under.

It was a subject she hadn't fully resolved herself. Greg
Clifford was going to be someone else's husband soon.
She no longer had any claim over his name, or anything
else. Yet reverting back to her maiden name of Jackson
was confirmation that her marriage had failed. She'd been
returned unwanted for a second time, like a mangy stray
dog. The idea of going back on the singles market felt
very much like waiting for someone to take pity on her
and find her a forever home.

She tried to refocus her attention back from her ex
to the present. He didn't deserve any more of her time
since all the years she'd given him had apparently meant
so little.

'Do you have any pain in your neck?'

Her choice of words had her patient sniggering at her
again.

'Come on, Joni. We're trying to help you here. We
need to know if you're hurting anywhere before we get
you back on your feet.'

It was comforting to find Joe had her back this time,
even if his apparent seniority here was irksome.

'I'm okay.' As if to try to prove their fears unwar-
ranted, Joni jumped to his feet, only to have to reach out
and steady himself by grabbing Joe's arm.

If Emily was honest, she'd have made a grab for the
strong and sturdy desert island doc too in similar circumstances.

'Really?' Joe arched a dark eyebrow as he glanced
down at his new small-child accessory.

Joni shrugged but made no further wisecracks.

'We should really get him checked out properly.' Although he bore no immediate signs of concussion, it didn't
mean they should rule it out altogether.

As well as getting a cold compress to prevent swelling, she'd prefer to keep him under observation in case of headaches or vomiting. He'd taken quite a wallop and although the skull was there to protect the brain there was always a chance the knock could cause the brain to swell or bleed. She didn't like taking unnecessary chances.

'The best option for now is to get him to Miriama's.' Joe crouched down for the patient to jump on his back. A piggyback was apparently the equivalent of an ambulance around here.

'Isn't there a medical centre we can take him to?' A small bird of panic fluttered its wings in her chest. She'd been led to believe there'd be some sort of facility for her to practise from. He might be used to treating people in the field but she certainly wasn't.

'Of sorts, but Miriama is his grandmother and the closest thing they have to a medic. She can keep an eye on him until you make *sevusevu* and if his condition changes we'll only be a few minutes away.'

It didn't slip her attention that he intended coming with her. In the absence of her brother she supposed he was going to have to do as backup. At least this incident showed he could be a calming influence when the need arose and she trusted he would keep her grounded until she tracked down her sibling.

'What about my things?' As they followed the dirt trail further into the village she fretted over her worldly possessions abandoned on the hillside.

'No one's going to steal them. We'll come back for the *yaqona* and send someone to take the rest back to Miriama's later.' He strode on ahead, unconcerned with her petty worries or the weight strapped around his neck.

She could picture him in his army gear, bravely heading into battle with his kit on his back, and it gave her chills. The idea of her brother in a war zone had always freaked her out and there'd been no greater relief than when he'd left the army. She was glad he was no longer in danger. Joe too. Life here might be more unconventional than she was used to but she didn't have to worry about anyone getting shot or blown up.

With her imagination slowing her down, she was forced to run and catch up again. The sandals slapping against her bare feet really weren't suitable footwear for chasing fit men in a hurry.

'Why should my luggage end up at Miriama's?' That obscure snippet of information hadn't passed her by.

'That's where you're going to be staying for the next fortnight. Miriama's your host.'

Although she hadn't expected the luxury of last night's five-star resort, she'd imagined she'd be staying with her brother rather than another stranger.

'Peter's staying with the village chief. He's earned a great deal of respect from the community for his endeavours here.' Joe headed off her next question before she could ask it. She couldn't help but wonder what his own arrangements were.

'And you? Where do you lay your head at night?' Only when the words left her lips did she realise how nosy that sounded. She hadn't intended prying into his personal life but this was all new to her. She didn't know if he was presented with pretty young virgins and his own house to thank him for his services. It would certainly explain her brother's reluctance to leave the village.

He cocked his head to one side, his mouth twitching as he fought a smile. 'Well, there's a new arrival in my bed tonight—'

She held her hand up before he went into graphic detail. 'I shouldn't have asked. It's none of my business.'

'So I'm moving from Miriama's into the clinic.'

It took a second for the image of Joe cavorting with exotic beauties to clear and let his words sink in.

'I'm taking your bed? Honestly, that's not necessary. I'm more than willing to take your place at the clinic.' She didn't know what that entailed but she'd take it over the lack of privacy in someone else's house.

Joe shook his head. 'The clinic's a glorified hut with two camp beds and a supply cupboard. You'll find no comfort there. I, on the other hand, am used to kipping in ditches, or worse. It's no hardship for me. Besides, you'll be doing me a favour.' He gave a furtive glance back at his charge to make sure he wasn't listening. 'I don't want to offend Miriama but I prefer the peace and quiet of being alone. I'm not used to domesticity.'

Perhaps it was because he was the first man to get so close to her in well over a year or the picture he painted of himself as some wild creature who couldn't be tamed but the shivers were back, causing havoc along her spine and the back of her neck.

Okay, she wasn't happy with the arrangements made on her behalf but she couldn't deny him his bed choice when he'd gone so far out of his way for her already. She couldn't form a logical argument anyway when her brain was still stuck on a freeze frame of caveman Joe.

The smiling Miriama was as welcoming as anyone could hope for. Until she found out Emily had yet to meet with the tribal elders and shooed them both back out of the door. She'd unhitched her grandson with the promise of getting some ice for the bump on his forehead and accepted some paracetamol, which Joe had produced from his shorts of many pockets. This new informal approach to treatment would take some getting used to. Just like her new co-worker would.

They retrieved her gifts for the community on the way

back to the chief's house and dispatched the rest of her belongings back to her temporary lodgings with the children. Trust didn't come easily to her any more but she was willing to take a leap of faith safe in the knowledge there were few places on the island to hide. She'd found that out the minute she'd set foot on the beach.

Now she was standing on the doorstep of the most important man on Yasi as Joe entered into a dialogue she assumed involved her arrival. It was hard to tell because they were conversing in Fijian, another skill he'd apparently acquired in his short time here and one more advantage over her. Languages had never been her strong point. Along with keeping a husband.

She was hanging back as the menfolk discussed her business, still hoping for a way out, when a hand clamped down on her shoulder.

'Hey, sis. Long time no see.'

In her desire to be accepted she thought she'd imagined her stepbrother standing beside her in a garish pink hibiscus shirt but there was no mistaking the bear hug as anything but the real deal as the breath was almost squeezed out of her.

'Peter?' The tears were already welling in her eyes with relief to have finally found some comfort.

'I wouldn't miss this for the world. Now, Joe will be acting as our "chief" since he's the eldest of our group, or temporary tribe. It's his job to present the kava root to the elders. We'll talk you through everything else once we're inside.'

He instructed her to remove her sandals before they entered. Sandwiched between her brother and Joe was the safest she'd felt in an age. They sat down on woven mats strewn across the floor of the main room, surrounded by those she assumed were the elders of the village.

'I take it everything met with their approval?' She

leaned over to whisper to her unofficial leader sitting cross-legged beside her.

Joe kept his gaze straight ahead, completely ignoring her. She didn't know if pretending she didn't exist was part of the process until she was accepted into the community or if he was completely relinquishing all responsibility for her now Peter had appeared. Either way, it hurt.

She leaned back the other direction toward Peter. 'Am I persona non grata around here until the ceremony's over?'

He frowned at her. 'What makes you say that?'

She nodded at her silent partner. 'Your friend here can be a little cold when he wants. Thanks for landing me with a complete stranger, by the way. Just what I needed to make me feel at home. Not.'

The cheesy grin told her he'd done it on purpose. 'I thought you two could do with some team bonding since you'll be working together, and he volunteered in the first place. I should probably mention he's a bit hard of hearing, especially if you're whispering.'

'I had no idea!' Shame enveloped her. It had never entered her head that hearing impairment could've been an issue with Joe when he was so young and capable. She of all people should've known not to make assumptions based on people's appearances.

'Yeah. IED blast. The one where we lost Ste and Batesy.'

The pieces she'd been scrambling to put together slowly fitted into place. Of course, she'd heard of Sergeant Joe Braden. He'd been one of Peter's best friends and that blast had made her brother finally experience for himself the worry and fear of losing someone close. It hadn't been long after that he'd made the decision to change his career path completely. She hated it that his friends had suffered so much for him to reach that point and now she'd met the man behind the name, that blast held more significance than ever.

She sneaked a sideways peek at him. His strong profile gave no clue to his impairment. There was no physical evidence to provoke a discussion or sympathy. Unlike her, whose scars were there for the world to see and pass judgement on.

Over the years she'd heard all sorts of theories whispered behind her back. From being scalded as a baby to being the victim of a house fire or an acid attack, she'd heard them all. In the end it had been easier to simply cover the birthmark than to endure the constant rumours.

Joe came across as a stronger, more confident person than she could ever hope to be, but that kind of injury must've caused him the same level of anguish at one time or another. Someone like him would've seen it as a personal weakness when their whole career had been built on personal fitness and being the best. She barely knew him but she could tell that the word 'courage' was stamped all over his DNA. She was even more in awe of him now she knew something of his past.

As though he could sense her staring at the sharp lines of his jaw and the soft contours of his lips, Joe slowly turned to face her. 'There's a certain guide to drinking kava. You clap once with a cupped hand, making a hollow sound, and yell, '*Bula*!' Drink it in one gulp, clap three times and say, '*Mathe*.' You'll be offered the option of high tide or low tide. I strongly advise low tide for your first time.'

'Okay…' She might've put this down as some sort of elaborate practical joke if it wasn't for the twinkle in his eye and his excited-puppy enthusiasm while waiting for the ceremony to begin. In contrast to her reservations about the whole palaver, he clearly relished being a part of the culture.

He fell silent again as the villagers began to grind up the kava in the centre of the room. There were few women present but as the proceedings got under way she didn't feel intimidated at all. The relaxed atmosphere and the men playing guitar in the corner of the room gave it more of a party vibe. Despite her initial reservations, she was actually beginning to relax.

After they ground the kava, it was strained through a cloth bag into a large wooden bowl. It looked like muddy water to her but the chief drank it down without hesitation, as did Peter and Joe. She was thankful for the advice when it came to her turn. Requesting 'low tide' ensured the coconut shell she was offered was only half-full.

It didn't taste any better than it looked. Like mud. Bitter, peppery mud. Definitely an acquired taste but she drank it in one gulp and did the happy, clappy thing which seemed to please everyone. For unknown reasons the proud look from Joe was the one that gave her tingles.

In fact, it wasn't long before her mouth and tongue seemed to go completely numb.

'Whath happenin'?' she lisped to Peter as her tongue suddenly seemed to be too big for her mouth.

'That'll be the kava kicking in. It's a very mild narcotic but don't worry, it'll pass soon.' Something that wasn't bothering her God-fearing brother as he accepted another bowl.

She declined to partake in any further rounds, which her hosts accepted without any offence. Clearly she'd already proved herself as a worthy guest. Thank goodness. Any more and she'd either pass out or lose control of the rest of her faculties. All she wanted now was for Joe to take her to bed. Home. She meant home…

Joe had become accustomed to the bitter-tasting celebration drink to the point even a second bowl had had no effect. He was aware, however, that it might not be the same for Emily, especially as she was probably tired and hungry and currently running her fingertips across her lips. Numb no doubt from the small taste she'd had. He watched as she darted her tongue out to lick them, drawing his attention and thoughts to where they shouldn't go.

Emily was his best friend's sister and obviously running away from her demons to have come somewhere so clearly out of her comfort zone. She wasn't, and couldn't ever be, someone he could hook up with. Normally he didn't hesitate to act on his attraction to women on his travels. Life was too short and so was his stay in their company when he was always on the move. This was an entirely different situation. Peter would always be part of his life and he wouldn't jeopardise that friendship when he invariably moved on. There was no point thinking of her as anything other than a hindrance, a soft soul who'd probably never left her cosy office and would only get in his way. A liability he didn't want or need.

Now she had been fully accepted into the community the villagers soon let their curiosity shine through and asked the questions he already knew the answers to.

'Do you have a husband?'

'What about children?'

The first question had thrown her, he could see it in her wide aquamarine eyes and knew why. Peter had confided in him about her marital problems long before her arrival because he'd worried how she might've been affected by it all. He'd taken her acceptance to help out on the mission as the first step to her recovery and had sworn Joe to secrecy. Not that it was any of his business anyway and he'd no wish to embarrass her by answering for her now. This was her call.

She took her time in finding an answer she was happy to give them. 'No husband or children.'

It didn't surprise him to find her divorce wasn't a subject she intended to discuss. She wasn't the only one who

preferred to keep private matters out of the public do-
main. Only Peter knew about his past in the army and
the fallout from the IED, and that's the way it would stay.
Much like Emily, he'd decided he didn't need sympathy
or pitying looks.

The gathering and the kava seemed to relax her more
as the evening wore on, and she fielded their questions
about her work without giving away too much personal
information. A single, female doctor was something of a
novelty out here and he understood their fascination. He
was caught up in it too.

As usual, the evening ended with music and dancing, with both he and a yawning Emily watching from
the sidelines.

'You can go any time you're ready.'

'Really? They won't mind?' In contrast to her earlier
attempt to cry off from proceedings, she now seemed
apprehensive about potentially upsetting her hosts. That
was the beauty of the people here. They were so warm
and friendly it was impossible to feel like an outsider for
too long.

'Sure. You've done everything right and they'll understand you're tired. This could go on all night.' He got up
and helped her to her feet.

'Peter?' She waited for her brother to join her but he
wasn't as ready as his companions to leave.

Joe couldn't wait for some time out from the crowd.
Sometimes the white noise could be a bit overwhelming
when he couldn't pick out individual conversations.

'You could see Emily to Miriama's, couldn't you? It's
on the way back to the medical centre.'

He couldn't fault Peter's logic since he was staying
with the chief anyway but it meant prolonging his role as
escort a while longer. This was beyond the remit of his
volunteer medic/best friend duties and he didn't want it

to become a habit. He'd only known Emily a few hours and for someone who considered himself a lone wolf he'd already taken on too much responsibility.

'Fine.' He sighed with just enough sulkiness to let Peter know he wasn't happy playing babysitter any more.

The only thoughts in his head about Emily should be to do with the clinic and how they were going to make it work together. Now there was no chance of forgetting how beautiful she'd looked, sitting cross-legged, utterly transfixed with island life, if she was going to be the last thing he saw before going to sleep.

CHAPTER THREE

EMILY WAS STILL trying to shuffle back into her shoes as she trailed after Joe. If it wasn't for it being completely pitch-black outside without the streetlights she took for granted back home and the sense of direction that meant she shouldn't be allowed out of the house unsupervised, she'd totally have made her own way back without him. Joe's term as 'leader' had clearly ended given his reluctance to see her home. Not that she blamed him. She'd imposed long enough and as soon as she had five minutes alone with her brother she'd tear strips off him for palming her off on him all night.

Peter should have understood what a big deal it had been for her to come here and gone out of his way to look after her. She needed some TLC after everything she'd gone through, not being frog-marched home as if she'd broken curfew. This was supposed to build her confidence, not reaffirm that idea she spoiled everyone's fun.

'I'm sorry you've copped babysitting duties for the nuisance little sister again.' She made sure she spoke loudly and clearly for him to hear. She didn't know the full extent of his hearing loss. He wasn't wearing a hearing aid but he was the type of guy who wouldn't be seen with one even if he needed it.

'No problem. We can't have you stumbling about here

alone in the dark. It'll take a while for you to get your bearings but you'll be able to walk this island with your eyes shut in no time.'

She didn't correct him by admitting another of her weaknesses since he was probably pinning his hopes on it so he wouldn't have to do this again. However, without her chatter, the sound of his heavy footsteps dominated the night, reminding her he was trying to ditch her as soon as possible.

'So what was with all the questions back there? They're not planning on marrying me off to the chief's son, are they?' It was a pseudo-concern in an attempt at small talk. Mostly.

The footsteps stopped and she could hear him grinding the dirt underfoot as he spun round.

'You've watched way too many movies. These people are no different from you or me. They simply have a sense of tradition. They've accepted you as one of their own, there's no ulterior motive.'

She was caught so off balance by his passion as he spoke of his new friends that she stumbled. She made a grab for him in the dark to steady herself and found a nice sturdy bicep beneath her fingers.

'Sorry,' she mumbled, eventually letting go once the shock of coming into contact with bare male body parts wore off. Or at least when she thought the prolonged touching was entering the awkward and desperate phase. He may be lean but he was one hundred per cent solid hunk.

She was nodding her head and apologising as he defended his friends, in an attempt at a mature response, which probably shouldn't include going back for another squeeze.

'You're right. I…er…was thrown by the level of attention. I'm not used to it.' If anything she tried to avoid those kinds of situations where she was the focal point of interest in case people studied her too closely and spotted her secret shame.

She caught the glint of his smile in the moonlight as he looked down at her. Compared to her last port of call, she should've been more at ease under the cover of darkness but her birthmark may as well have been blazing under his night vision she felt so exposed here with him.

'You're beautiful and smart. Of course they want to know your story.' The tone of his voice was soft enough to snuggle into, never mind the unexpected compliment almost bringing her to a swoon.

Except he was back on the move again, not lingering for a romantic smooch under the stars. She definitely watched too many movies. Probably because reality was too damn anticlimactic. She sighed, forced to gather herself together and remember this was no holiday romance, as much as she wanted to get carried away as far from real life as possible.

He didn't elaborate on what had prompted the ego boost and she had to hold her tongue to stop herself from pushing for more praise. How had he reached the conclusion she was either of those things? And did he have any interest in her beyond work and doing favours for her brother? Would it matter if he did?

The resulting silence between them stretched out to Miriama's house, giving her time to get her head back out of the clouds. He hadn't seen her true, vivid, scarlet colours. His assessment of her looks and personality was based on a lie. He knew nothing of the scarred woman beneath who'd been rejected time and time again.

By the time they reached her doorstep she'd firmly landed her backside back on earth with a thud. All he'd been trying to do was illustrate how ridiculous her assumptions had been. He probably hadn't even meant what he'd said but it had been so long since a man had paid her a compliment she'd taken it and twisted it into something it wasn't. She blamed the kava. Apart from the numbness and the tingles, she'd add delusions to the list of side effects. She'd have to remember to ship a crate of the stuff back to England with her.

To Joe, the short walk to Miriama's seemed twice as long as usual. That was the trouble with island life. It was too easy to get caught up in the beauty of the surroundings. They should really think about investing in some street-lights here. The electric hum and fluorescent orange glare might have made this feel less like a walk home after a first date than the moonlight and the sound of the sea.

All he'd intended to do was put her mind at ease that the people here weren't perhaps as…duplicitous as those she may have encountered recently. Instead, those careless few words had given away his less-than-platonic thoughts about having her here. Now he was watching her in the dim light of the doorway, pouting and tracing the outline of her lips with her fingertips.

'What are you doing?' He cocked his head to one side, fixated by her fascinating courtship display. If this was designed to pique his interest even further, it was working. His whole body was standing to attention as he followed the soft lines of her mouth, envying the manicured nail that got to touch them.

'Just checking my lips are still there since I can't feel them any more.' She poked her pink tongue out, parting her lips to dampen them, leaving them moist and a temptation too great to ignore any longer.

He stepped forward to give her a soft peck on the lips. Enough to satisfy his curiosity but insufficient to quell the rising swell of desire inside.

If he didn't break away soon this would change from

a simple goodnight kiss into something steamier and liable to offend Miriama. Especially as Emily wasn't protesting against this.

'Yup. They're still there. Goodnight, Emily.' He turned his back on her and walked away so he couldn't see the dazed look in her eyes and her still-parted lips, although the sight and taste of her would probably be seared in his brain forever.

He ditched all thoughts of going to bed and chose the path back down to the beach instead. There was no point trying to go to sleep when adrenaline was pulsing through his whole body. That had been a dumb move, an impulsive one, one born of pure instinct and lack of judgement. He'd wanted to kiss her so he had, without any thought to the consequences of his actions. That spur-of-the-moment thinking was fine when it came to picking a new place to visit where no one but him would come a cropper if he made the wrong decision. When it came to kissing emotionally fragile divorcees related to his best friend it had the potential to get messy.

He lifted a pebble from the beach and threw it, watching it skim the surface of the water before disappearing into the darkness along with his common sense. He pitched another and another, venting his anger at himself in the only way possible without punching something. In the end he stripped off his clothes and chucked himself into the sea to cool off. Late-night skinny-dipping had often been a way for him to unwind but tonight it was his attempt to cleanse himself of his transgression. He didn't kiss women because he'd made an emotional connection with them, he kissed them because he wanted to. This was a woman he was going to be working with closely for the next two weeks and he was in serious trouble if he couldn't go one evening without controlling himself around her.

He dipped his head below the surface but even as he scrubbed his face with his hands he knew the cold salty water couldn't wipe away the taste and feel of her lips on his. The damage was already done. All he could do now was add it to the list of mistakes he carried with him and hope Emily didn't expect anything more from him than medical input and local knowledge. He'd hate to disappoint her as well as himself.

Emily suspected the local brew had a lot to do with her falling asleep the minute her head touched the pillow and the weird dreams that followed. She spent the night imagining she was stranded on a desert island with a hunky sea captain who looked suspiciously like Sgt Joe Braden coming to her rescue. There was no need to overanalyse it. It was simply her mind trying to make sense of the day's events, and better than spending all night worrying about what sort of creatures lurked in her small room, or thinking about that kiss.

Joe more than likely left dazed women in his wake with his throwaway kisses every day and would have no clue of the impact it had made on her. It was silly really to obsess over something so fleeting, but up until last night her husband had been the only man she'd ever kissed.

She remembered every tiny detail of the brief connection between her and Joe. The firm but tender pressure of his mouth on hers, the bitter taste of kava lingering on his lips and her body frozen while her veins burned with fire.

The past eighteen months had made her a jaded divorcee so she shouldn't have had her head turned so easily. She really needed to work on building up those walls if she was being a fangirl over a peck on the lips from a glorified babysitter.

Today was the start of her placement alongside last night's fantasy figure. There was no room for schoolgirl crushes when she was already on edge about working here. She'd risen with the sun, showered with the aid of a bucket of cold water, breakfasted on bread and jam with Miriama, and checked on Joni, but she couldn't put it off any longer. As she walked towards the medical centre she tried to focus on the positives instead of the nerves bundling in her stomach.

The sky was the brightest blue she'd ever seen, her skin was warmed by the sun and she'd swapped her usual restrictive formal attire for a strappy pink sundress and flats. She was confident in her work and her capabilities, it was more the personal aspects causing her anxieties. Last night she'd mixed well with the community but that had been in an informal setting. It hadn't escaped her attention that very few women had been present at the kava ceremony and they'd had to wait until the men had taken their fill before they'd been served. She hoped it was another nod to tradition rather than any prejudiced attitude towards women's role in society.

Joni had shown her the route back to the medical centre on his way to school and it really was nothing more than a glorified hut on the edge of the village. Thankfully the boy had shown no signs of concussion this morning but in her line of work it was always better to be safe than sorry when it could mean the difference between life and death. It was a shame that same adage had caused the end of her marriage. Playing it safe in her personal life had driven Greg away and made her sorrier than ever for the risks she hadn't taken.

Still, her love life, or lack of it, wasn't the sole reason she'd come all this way. Joe Braden certainly wasn't the risk she wanted to start with. She was here to help a community that didn't have immediate access to medical facilities, nothing more.

Once she set foot inside the designated workspace she

realised how difficult it was going to be to avoid further close contact with him.

'Welcome to your new clinic, Dr Emily.' A grinning Joe greeted her, his outstretched arms almost touching both sides of the hut.

The sun shone in behind him through the one window in the room, the rays outlining the tantalising V-shape of his torso through his loose white cotton shirt.

'You've got to be kidding.' She hadn't meant to vocalise her thoughts and for a shameful second she wished this was one time he hadn't heard her. No such luck.

'Hey, we gotta work with what we've got. I know you're used to all the mod cons at your practice but you have to remember the context here. Me, you and this equipment donated by the church is more than these people usually have.'

The good news was he thought her only concern was her new working conditions. The bad news was…her new working conditions.

There were two basic camp beds, not unlike the one she'd been put up in at Miriama's, a couple of medical storage lockers and chairs, some old IV stands and monitors and some sort of curtain on wheels she guessed was supposed to be a privacy screen. There were adequate facilities for routine health checks and not much else but enough to divide the workload and shared space.

'I think this will work best if we treat this as two different clinics and double the output. You do your thing and I'll do mine.' Never the twain to meet and make body contact ever again.

She moved one medical trolley to one side of the room and claimed her half by wheeling the screen between the two beds.

'If you say so…' Joe didn't sound convinced but at least he wasn't getting precious about this being his territory. Chances were he was happy to block her out anyway after being forced to lead her around by the hand all day yesterday.

'I do. This is going to work.' This new set-up enabled her to take back some control of her life here and already made her feel less nauseous about the days ahead.

This was never going to work. Joe had been here long enough to understand the logistical nightmare of putting her idea into practice. There simply wasn't enough room to create two viable working spaces, although he didn't try to dissuade her from attempting it. She'd work it out for herself eventually without him coming across as a tyrant by refusing to cooperate with her plans. It was his fault she felt the need to put a barrier between them in the first place.

After his antics last night he was lucky Peter hadn't rounded up a posse to turf him off the island for laying lips on his sister. He'd been beating himself up over it all night and this display of skittish behaviour wasn't easing his conscience at all. By all accounts Emily was recovering from an acrimonious split and definitely wasn't the sort of woman he should be kissing on a whim.

His one saving grace was their apparent mutual decision not to mention it. Perhaps his casual walk away had lessened the significance of the event. He might start kissing everyone goodbye and make it out to be more of a personal custom rather than the result of his attraction to her. Although there was something intimate about seeing her fuss around the bed where he'd been lying, thinking about her, last night.

He'd been honest when he'd said he preferred the quiet out here to Miriama's busy household. There was also the added benefit of being able to see the door from his bed. Combat had made him hypervigilant about his surroundings. He wasn't comfortable in a room where he couldn't see all entry points. Army life taught a man that concealed entrances were all potential ambushes where the enemy could attack. That level of paranoia had been essential in his survival but it hadn't left him even after his medical retirement to civilian life. It was simply part of his make-up now and another reason he took to the open road rather than remain cooped up in a two-up, two-down suburban prison.

'So, do we have any particular schedule, or is this more of an A and E department we're running?' Emily encroached on his half of the room, arms folded across her chest.

'I thought we'd break you in gently today and run more of a walk-in clinic. We can organise something more formal once you're settled, if you prefer.' He operated a casual open-door policy every day but he got the impression this GP would expect something more…structured.

Emily struck him as the type who preferred knowing exactly what she'd be doing from one day to the next without any disruption to her routine. The complete opposite of how he lived his life.

'I'd like to set up a few basic health checks. We could start with taking blood pressure, maybe even a family planning clinic.' She was drifting off into the realms of her own practice but it was a good idea.

Specific clinics might draw in more of the community for preventative check-ups as opposed to waiting until something serious occurred when it was too late to get help from the mainland.

'I think the female population might be more open to you too. Perhaps you could think about running a women's wellness clinic? It's not every day they have someone to talk to them about sensitive subjects such as sexual health or female-specific cancers.' It was as much about educating patients as treating them and he would happily defer to Emily in areas where she had more experience.

'That's a great idea. I'm sure I can put something together for later this week.' Her eyes were shining with excitement rather than fear for the first time since they'd met. Well, if he didn't include last night on her doorstep.

His gaze dropped to her mouth as he relived the memory and the adrenaline rush it had given him. Was giving him. Only her nervous cough snapped him out of his slide back into dangerous territory. He certainly didn't want to freak her out after they'd just established their boundaries.

'Good.'

'Glad we got that sorted.'

It was better all around if they kept their lips to themselves, on different sides of that screen.

There'd been a steady influx of patients throughout the day, more minor ailments than emergency medicine to deal with. Not that she was complaining. Coughs and colds were manageable and it meant she didn't have to call on her colleague for an extra pair of hands. She had, however, handed out a vast amount of paracetamol and antibiotics, not to mention sticking plasters. It was probably a combination of not having these drugs readily available and the novelty of a new, female doctor in residence. At least it showed she'd been accepted in her role and she'd kept busy. That was better than sitting fretting in the corner with nothing but tumbleweeds straying into her section of the clinic. Worse, she'd have had time to over-analyse that kiss some more. Every time he so much as looked in her direction her body went up in flames at the memory. While she was investigating the swollen glands of a pensioner she wasn't thinking about Joe. Much.

'Say "Ah" for me.' She bent over the side of the bed

to peer into her patient's mouth and felt a nudge against her backside.

She turned around to read the Riot Act to whoever it was getting handsy with her when she saw the shadow on the other side of the curtain. Joe was innocently tending his patient too and proving that having little room to manoeuvre was going to be an issue if the butt-bumping became a regular occurrence. It mightn't faze him but she was finding it pretty distracting.

'Your tonsils are quite inflamed but it's nothing a course of antibiotics won't clear up.'

She heard Joe prescribe the same treatment she'd been dishing out all day. It wasn't unusual for viruses to spread like wildfire in such a small community and she was glad of the extra supplies she'd brought with her. They were going to need them, along with the hand sanitiser and vitamin tablets she'd be using to prevent succumbing to it herself. The last thing she needed was Joe having to tend her too.

If the claustrophobic room wasn't hot enough, the thought of her next-door neighbour mopping her fevered brow was enough to bring on the vapours.

Emily moved closer to the oscillating fan before the heat in her cheeks eroded her camouflage make-up and caught sight of a young woman running up the path with a baby in her arms.

'Help! She's not breathing!'

The baby, no more than nine or ten months, was conscious but not making a sound, even though her limbs were flailing in a panic. Not hearing a baby cry in this situation was heart-stopping for her too, indicating the child's airway was completely blocked.

'Give her to me. Quick.'

The child's lips and fingernails were already turning blue but there was no visible sign of obstruction in her mouth.

Joe was at her side in the blink of an eye. 'What happened?'

'She… We were eating breakfast. She grabbed some bread off my plate. Is she going to be okay?'

Emily slid one arm under the baby's back so her hand cradled the head. With her other arm placed on the baby's front, she gently flipped the tiny patient so she was lying face down along her other forearm. She kept the head supported and lower than the bottom and rested her arm against her thigh for added support. With the heel of her hand she hit the baby firmly on the back between the shoulder blades, trying to dislodge whatever was stuck in there.

Delivering a blow to such a small body wasn't easy to do without guilt but the pressure and vibration in the airway was often enough to clear it.

Unfortunately, after the recommended five back blows there was no progress. Time was of the essence as the lack of oxygen to the brain would soon become critical. She rushed over to lay the baby on the bed, paying no mind as Joe kicked the screen away so he had room to assist. He cradled the infant's head, murmuring soothing words for child and mother as Emily started chest thrusts.

With two fingertips she pushed inwards and upwards against the breastbone, trying to shift the blockage. She waited for the chest to return to its normal position before she repeated the action. Her skin was clammy with perspiration as she fought to help the child to breathe. If this didn't work they'd run out of options.

Joe reached out to touch her arm. 'I've done a few tracheostomies in my time if it comes to it.'

He was willing to step up to the plate with her and she found that reassuring. She'd never performed one and hoped it wouldn't come to that. The idea of making an incision for a tube into the windpipe of one so small was terrifying.

'Thank you.'

With her surgical inexperience and the primitive facilities she was glad to have the backup but it was absolutely the last resort. His calm demeanour in the face of a crisis helped her to centre herself again and deliver another chest thrust.

She checked inside the mouth again. If this didn't work she would repeat the cycle before letting Joe take over. After another chest thrust she felt movement beneath her fingers and heard a small cry.

'You've got it!' Joe's shout confirmed her success and she stopped so he could retrieve the chunk of bread causing the trouble.

The colour slowly returned to the baby's face and Emily had never been so relieved to hear a child cry.

'Thank you. Thank you.' The weeping mother alternated between hugging them and stroking her daughter's face.

'I just want to sound her chest.' Emily unhooked her stethoscope from around her neck so she could listen to the baby's heartbeat and make sure there was no resulting damage from the trauma. Her lungs were certainly in good order as she raged her disapproval.

Once she'd carried out her checks and made sure all was well, she gave the relieved mother the go-ahead to comfort her child.

'I think I need to keep you all under observation for a while. Emily, if you don't mind, I'm going to break into that stash of tea and biscuits I saw you put in your locker earlier. We all need it for shock.' Joe's worried frown had evened out into a relieved smile to match her own. She sat down on the bed and waited for the much-needed cup of tea, still feeling a tad shaky herself after the ordeal.

Having a partner here mightn't be all bad. He'd let her take the lead today while still providing support, and tea, when she'd needed it. It made practical sense for them to work together. If only she'd stop overreacting to the slightest body contact. And staring at his backside as he bent down to retrieve her precious cure-all.

CHAPTER FOUR

'I THINK WE deserve a break,' Joe waved off their first emergency patient and her mother at the door once they were sure she had fully recovered.

'I was under the impression we'd just had one.' While it had all been very dramatic and draining, saving lives was part of their job. It shouldn't be an excuse to shut up shop and act unprofessionally. If anything it highlighted the need for them to keep to a schedule so people knew where to reach them at any given time.

'Even busy doctors are entitled to a lunch break. Are you telling me you don't take one back home?' His raised eyebrow and smirk dared her to deny it.

'Of course I take my regulation breaks. Just not usually all at once.' She omitted to mention she took a packed lunch and did her paperwork through those breaks since it made her sound as if she had no life outside work.

He made a derisory '*pfft*' sound through his teeth. 'Ten minutes off our feet, keeping a baby under observation, isn't a real break. We need a proper time out to de-stress before our next patients, otherwise how can we do our jobs effectively? You need to learn how to go with the flow, Emily.'

His cheeky wink only served to irritate her further.

'I thought that's what I *was* doing.' The sigh of self-pity was entirely justified, she thought, after coming all the way out here and taking part in everything thrown at her thus far. If she let herself get carried away too much there was a danger she'd end up completely lost at sea.

'It's lunch, Emily. It's not a big deal.'

It *would* seem silly to him but in her head it translated to something much bigger—ditching their responsibilities for their own gratification. That was exactly what Greg had done and she'd been the one left to deal with the consequences. It wasn't a situation she intended to recreate any time soon.

'What about cover? We can't abandon our post here and leave people without adequate care.'

'We can put a note on the door but, honestly, we won't be that hard to track down if something happens. Yasi Island has survived all this time without us and I'm sure they'll cope over one lunchtime.' He was already scribbling on a piece of paper now he'd made her concerns seem ridiculous.

She was here for two weeks, had treated one emergency patient so far, and was trying to avoid a shared break under the cover of her 'they can't live without me' excuse. It was no wonder he wasn't buying it. This was about him, and her fear of spending time with him, and nothing else. She had to get over it or the next fortnight was going to be hell.

'Is there some place we can buy lunch? I don't recall seeing any fast-food restaurants nearby.' Her tongue-in-cheek comment was intended to make her seem less of a jobsworth but the practicalities of his proposal were no less important to her. While it was refreshing not to have a coffee shop or burger joint on every inch of land, there was also a distinct lack of grocery outlets. She had literally nothing to bring to the table and it wouldn't be polite to help herself to Miriama's meagre provisions.

'Lack of refrigeration is a problem on the island when the only electricity available is via the odd generator here and there so most of the food is fresh. There's none of your fast-frozen, pre-packed, no-taste, processed muck here. The gathering of food is a communal effort, as is eating it. There'll be no shortage of hosts to take lunch with.' He pinned the note to the door and hovered, clearly waiting for her to leave with him.

She was certain the idea of turning up at people's homes uninvited and unannounced was something he did all the time, given his nonchalance now, but she was used to a certain etiquette. Dinner parties and organised soirées were more her thing than breaking bread with strangers. Honestly, this man had no shame.

'Should we take a gift?' Something to break the ice and make it seem less like begging for food. She'd rather starve than face any humiliation.

'You've already donated supplies to the school and I thought we could head there first. The children will be thrilled to meet you. They enjoy showing off and I know for a fact this is their lunchtime too. So…' He gestured for her to make her way out in front of him but she wasn't entirely convinced by his argument. That 'first' comment alluded to the idea there'd be more than one stop.

'You could take your medical bag with you if that makes you any more comfortable about leaving.' He pre-empted her next attempt to back out.

'A mobile clinic?' It wasn't a bad idea to combine work and lunch, and accepting their hospitality in exchange for her medical skills was much more palatable than simply pulling up a chair and waiting to be served.

'If that's what you'd prefer.' His voice was a mixture of amusement and exasperation.

'It is.' She knew she could be hard work when people seemed to tire of her so easily but at least Joe nudged her with encouragement rather than criticism. It left her free to make decisions on her own terms.

Negotiations over, she grabbed her bag and followed him out the door. Despite her initial reservations, reaching this compromise felt like a win. With a little forward planning she could *do* spontaneity. Somewhere between Joe's laid-back attitude and her regimented approach to work they might find a way to actually make this work. Perhaps if she found that happy medium in her personal life, she might make that work again too.

Joe had been right again. It was becoming a habit. And very annoying. Every time his cool, calm and rational thinking was proved correct it made her fears seem all the more neurotic.

Their impromptu visit to the school had caused such a commotion the children had immediately abandoned their lessons. She would've felt terribly guilty about the disruption if their teacher hadn't been equally animated by their arrival.

'*Vanaku*. Thank you for coming to see the children.'

The pupils all stood to attention behind their desks as though someone of great importance had entered the room. It was difficult to come to terms with the fact that person could be her.

'I, er…we thought I should come and introduce myself. I'm Emily, the new doctor.' She shook hands with the pretty young teacher.

'I'm Keresi. We're so grateful for your wonderful gifts to the school. Aren't we, children?'

They were prompted into an enthusiastic chorus of agreement that managed to suffuse Emily's cheeks with heat.

'It's nothing, really.' She'd only brought a few stationery supplies at the last minute. Nothing that would've warranted such an outpouring of gratitude at home. It was humbling to be reminded how lucky she was in the grand scheme of things and how much she took for granted. Okay, her heart had taken a mauling recently but she'd had a university education that enabled her to live a life of luxury compared to many here.

'We would really like to do something for you.' The effusive teacher clapped her hands to assemble the kids along the back wall of the classroom.

Emily stepped further into the room to allow Joe in on whatever was about to happen. No matter how hard she tried to make this a solo adventure they were destined to share these experiences and if she was honest, everything seemed slightly less intimidating when he was close by. This morning had been a prime example. She'd coped with the emergency largely on her own but having him there had been a comfort when she was so far from the medical support she was used to. Joe had been the first person in a long time to make sure she hadn't felt alone.

The children launched into a repertoire of songs and dance, so well choreographed she understood this must be something they performed on a regular basis for tourists—and hungry doctors. It enabled her to stop over-analysing what people would think of her for turning up uninvited and enjoy the proud display of talent. Old and young alike had made it impossible not to be a part of the community here.

Once the show was over, she and Joe broke into applause.

'That was just…lovely.' The tears in her eyes and lump in her throat arrived unexpectedly.

'Yes, thanks, everybody.' Joe lifted his hands above his head and gave them another round of applause.

'We're going to take our lunch outside now, if you'd

care to join us.' Keresi motioned her class outside as she delivered the invitation Joe had prophesied.

'That's so kind of you. We'd be honoured. Wouldn't we, Emily?' He didn't even attempt to hide his glee at being proved right.

'Sure, and in return we'd be happy to do a free health check for everyone while we're here.'

She'd call that an even trade and a conscience salve all in one.

With everyone in accordance and no one beholden to anyone else, the trio of adults joined the rest of the class outside on the grass.

Joe had made it sound as though lunch would be some grand affair with buffet-style tables of food, or at least that's how she'd interpreted it. Instead, the children were cross-legged under the shade of the trees, tucking into their food boxes.

'What are we going to do? A lunch-box raid?' she murmured, before catching herself.

She cleared her throat to draw his attention and spoke again. 'I'm not taking food from the mouths of babes.'

'Will you chill out? I can guarantee you'll neither have to ask for food while you're here nor starve. Honestly, you put yourself through so much unnecessary stress you'll make yourself ill. You should take a leaf out of your brother's book and take this all in your stride.' He rested his large hand on her shoulder in an act that should've been easy for her to shrug off along with his advice, but his warmth on her bare skin stole away any snarky retort. His touch had distracted her even from the arrival of her stepbrother, who was strolling towards them.

'Hey, you two. I saw your note and figured you might want to share a bite to eat.' He held up a basket of fresh fruit and other foods not readily identifiable to Emily. At this moment she didn't care. Her stomach was rumbling and Peter was family. She was entitled to take food from him guilt-free.

'Oh, ye of little faith.'

Joe was really going to keep this gloating going all day.

Thankfully he did release her from his thrall, abandoning her shoulder in favour of a banana. There was definitely a happy vibe about him, her brother too, which was surprising given their previous life before Yasi. It showed a definite strength of character in both of them to have come through the darkness that time in Afghanistan had surely brought to their door.

She kind of envied this enlightened attitude they'd found where they no longer sweated the small stuff and trusted that everything would somehow work out in the end. Although not the path, or the losses they'd endured to reach this Zen place. A place that seemed so far beyond her reach when even the timely food delivery was causing concern.

'Er…what is this?' She prodded the leafy parcels that were apparently the main component of their meal.

'*Rourou* and cassava,' Peter declared, as though that helped her identify what he expected her to eat. Time apart had made him forget who he was dealing with here. This was the girl who'd taken a great deal of persuading to partake of the mildest curries when they'd gone to an Indian restaurant for the first time. She needed any new dish explained in simple layman's terms and a tasting demonstration before she ventured into new territory.

Joe had no such qualms as he dug in with his fingers to take a sample. 'They're *dalo* leaves with boiled tapioca.'

'Just like real school dinners, then?' With her food taster apparently unharmed, and Peter helping himself too, Emily braved the unknown. It wasn't as bad tasting as she'd imagined and the starchy snack would fuel her for the rest of the afternoon, along with the more familiar fruit she took for later.

'I know you'd rather have a pasta salad and a fruit smoothie but this is the next best thing. You'll get used to it. I have.' Peter took a second helping to prove his point.

'I see that.' She also saw the way his gaze kept drifting past her to watch the pretty Keresi in the background.

'Did you make these, bro?' Joe scooped up the last food bundle after she declined it.

Her taste buds had been enjoying the sweet and stodgy delights of comfort food these past months so it was going to take some time to adjust.

'No. The young mother whose baby you saved this morning sent them over to say thank-you. You two are her new heroes.'

'Hey, it was all your sister. This girl knows her stuff and I wouldn't want to get on the wrong side of her by claiming credit for what she did. She can hit pretty hard when she wants to.' Joe held his hands up and deflected the praise back to her.

'Oh, I know all about it. She can be vicious if you take her toys without permission and as for her chocolate stash, if you touch that your life won't be worth living.' Peter made it sound as though they'd had a tempestuous relationship growing up when nothing could be further from the truth. She'd been so happy to be accepted by him and his mum, Shirl, she'd followed him like a puppy. He'd have been justified in pushing his pesky shadow away but he'd never once made her feel like a nuisance or his ugly stepsister. She'd often thought how different her life could've been if Shirl had been her *actual* mother, avoiding all the unpleasantness of her early years.

Peter rubbed the invisible evidence of their imaginary argument on his leg but his eyes were still focused on something, someone else. That someone who was making her way over to their little group.

'Can I get you a drink?'

'That would be—'

'I'll help you.' Peter cut her off as he stumbled to his feet in a hurry.

'Could he be any more obvious?' Emily's eye-roll was born out of her irrational jealousy that there was now a third party competing for his attention. She may as well have been back in high school when he had been the popular kid and she'd been the newbie with no friends of her own.

'Give him a break.'

'I thought he was here to spread the word of God, not get romantically involved with his congregation.' She'd never seen him so smitten as he trailed after his love interest into the school, his tongue practically hanging out, but she shouldn't be a brat and put her own happiness above Peter's. This lovestruck bohemian was a far cry from the traumatised veteran she'd last encountered and his healing was all that mattered.

'He's a red-blooded, single man, not a monk, and this place is doing him the world of good. He'll be settled down with two point four kids before you know it.' Joe plucked a blade of grass from the ground and wound it around his finger until the circulation stopped and it turned white.

Despite his wise words on the subject he didn't look any more thrilled about that prospect than she did. He was supposed to be the fly-by-the-seat-of-his-pants adventurer, not a stick-in-the-mud who hated change like her.

'And you? Are you planning on settling down at some point?' Her heart fluttered as she asked the question, which had been on her mind since he'd kissed her.

His snort-laugh cut any hope dead that she could be

the one to make him think again about his nomadic life choice but it was better to face that truth now before she got carried away over the next few days and considered that a possibility.

'No chance. These itchy feet of mine don't let me hang around long enough to develop that kind of attachment.'

'Why's that?' It would've made more sense to her that someone who'd been in a war zone would've been glad of the normality and stability that a family could bring.

He was pulling the grass out in clumps now. 'Life's too short not to get out there and experience everything the world has to offer. I'm never going to be the pipe-and-slippers type to sit and vegetate in front of the telly with his missus.'

There was the crux of Emily's ill-judged attraction to-wards him. If you swapped the pipe for a bar of chocolate he'd just described her idea of a perfect night in.

He hadn't mentioned the events leading to his retire-ment from the army but she guessed that was part of the reason for his compulsion to live life to the full. In that sense he and her brother were very alike. The blast had had a profound impact on how they lived from day to day and she was in awe of their courage when any new ex-perience brought her out in a cold sweat. If, on the other hand, this drifting from one place to the next had been the guys running away from dealing with what had happened, setting down roots was a huge step forward. Still, long-term relationships didn't always equal a happy-ever-after.

'Yeah, marriage sucks,' she said, trying to convince herself she didn't want or need it any more either.

Joe raised his eyebrows at her as he stood and brushed the grass from his hands. Now she was going to have to explain herself and confess she was one of those losers who'd tried and failed at it.

'I'm divorced. Greg left me for another woman.' Even

in the shade she was burning with the shame of her husband's rejection. Although it was almost a relief to say it out loud.

Colleagues and friends knew about the split but she hadn't divulged the gory details. Blurting it out to a man she'd only met and most likely would never see again was liberating. She could vent without fear of repercussions.

He held out his hand to help her up and without missing a beat said, 'He's an idiot.'

Those three simple words brought a smile to her lips and a lightness in her heart. There was no changing of the subject or querying the circumstances, he'd simply decided in her favour. Greg *was* an idiot and she should stop wasting any more of her life on him.

Joe's lifestyle sounded too lonely for her but she could appreciate its merits. There was an attraction in walking away from a relationship before things got too serious and certain expectations grew around it. Such as being together for ever. Avoiding love was the best way to protect your heart. Thank goodness she no longer trusted anyone with hers.

CHAPTER FIVE

JOE'S PLAN TO get outside of their confined workspace into the great outdoors to create some distance between him and Emily had backfired spectacularly. Somehow mingling with a large group of excited school children had led to lunch together discussing their private lives, or in his case a lack of one. Where Emily's was concerned he'd call it a lucky escape.

Peter didn't usually take against people without due cause but when he talked about his ex-brother-in-law it had never been with any degree of affection. It would take a certain kind of someone to get him offside when he was such a people person. The sort who imagined he could do better than Emily. *Idiot* wasn't a strong enough word to describe what Joe thought of the guy but it was the only tag he could give him in the presence of children.

Although it was early days to be thinking of Peter and the schoolteacher as being in a serious relationship, leading to something more permanent, it certainly seemed to be heading that way. It caused him mixed emotions. He was happy to see his friend in such a great place after struggling with his faith in the aftermath of Afghanistan and it meant he himself was no longer obligated to stick around as his sole support system. Peter settled down would give him the freedom to move on to his next ad-

venture free from residual responsibility that kept him tied
to his old army pal. It certainly shouldn't create the extra
hole in his heart and a pang for the life he'd never have.

He couldn't afford to have a wife and children relying
on him when he couldn't even depend on himself, on his
own emotions. He'd heard somewhere that grief was the
price you paid for loving someone but he really didn't
want to go through it again. He'd loved Batesy and Ste
like brothers, grieved for them as part of his army family,
and shouldered responsibility for their loss as any other
medic who'd lost patients would have. It was impossible
not to become that close to anyone and not feel compassion again. He was risking his heart and his sanity by re-
maining in the medical field but it was still his calling.
These pop-up clinics were a compromise, his answer to
preventing further long-term damage to his soul while still
being able to treat those in desperate need. Listening to
Emily's tale of marriage woe was enough to strengthen
his resolve on the matter. Commitment to anything beyond a casual arrangement did more harm than good.

Hence this afternoon's impromptu alfresco lunch.
Working side by side in that hut had not only led to inadvertent body contact but a growing admiration for his
co-worker. This morning had shone a light on her profes-
sionalism in what had been a highly emotive and dramatic
case, the like of which she probably wasn't used to in her
day job. He shouldn't be surprised, she was a qualified
doctor after all, but he'd clearly been thinking about her
in a less than professional manner.

Romantic picnics in the park weren't going to help
get his mind back in the game but the clinic idea at the
school had helped re-establish the boundaries of their relationship. For the past couple of hours they'd been busy
chatting to the children and making sure they were all in
tip-top health, with Emily on one side of the room and him

on the other. Except now her queue of children had come to an end and she was making her way over to his table.

'Well, Dr Braden, anything to report?' She was totally at ease here. He could see it in her relaxed body language and the big smile on her lips.

He should really quit paying attention to what her lips were doing at any given moment. It wouldn't help him forget how they felt against his: soft, pliant, agreeable...

There was no way he trusted himself not to try and experience it again if they were holed up in that close space for another two weeks.

'Just another A-star pupil.' He gave his last patient a high five and watched him run off with his last excuse to hang around.

'They're a pretty happy, healthy bunch all round.'

'And more than willing to have a bit of fuss from the glamorous new doctor.' He hadn't missed the girls' fascination with her blonde hair, or the fact she'd let them braid it while she'd worked. The boys too had been more interested in what was going on at that side of the room, which had made their eye checks challenging.

Emily's laughter reached right in and twisted his insides. It was the first time he'd heard it since her arrival and he knew he wanted to hear more of it.

'*Glamorous* isn't the word I'd use right now.' She was finger-brushing the various plaits and knots her army of hairdressers had created, leaving her tresses wavy and unkempt and looking a lot like bed hair.

It conjured up images of her in the morning, in bed, and brought a lot more adjectives to describe her that weren't appropriate in a classroom. Joe had to turn away and pack away the ophthalmoscope and otoscope he'd been using to check the children's eyes and ears before he said or did something stupid. Again.

'Thank you for doing this.' Keresi interrupted Joe's wayward thoughts to shake hands with him and Emily.

'Thanks for letting us disrupt your lessons today. We're going to take our travelling sideshow further afield but I'm sure you could get Peter to track us down in an emergency.' He'd disappeared during their clinic but Joe had a hunch he'd return before the end of the school day.

'Since when?' Emily's mouth flattened out into an unimpressed line once they were alone again. Her mouth was puckered now, her turquoise eyes blazing with flecks of amber fire and her arms folded across her chest as she made her disapproval known. He supposed it would be totally out of order to comment on how hot she looked.

'We've had such a great response here I thought we could venture further around the village with our mobile clinic. A meet and greet with those who might be too busy to attend isn't a bad idea.' In the army he'd learned to think on his feet, and forced with their imminent return to the claustrophobic hub of medical operations he'd made an executive decision. Not to.

'You really need to stop making decisions for other people. You're not in the army now and you're certainly not my superior,' Emily huffed, as she made the scarily accurate call about his thought process. He was railroading her into taking a trail away from his temporary lodgings when they were supposed to be equal partners but separating her from his bed space would be beneficial to them both in the long run.

'Sorry, I'm not used to working with a partner. I should have asked if you would prefer to spend the afternoon bumping into each other and waiting for people to show up or go out and drum up some interest in your clinic.' He didn't think of it as emotional blackmail, more as forward planning. Once Emily had her own patients set up they could alternate between running both static and mobile practices. With some organisation he could engineer the rest of her stay so they spent minimal time in each other's company.

'When you put it like that I guess it's a no-brainer.' She stuck her tongue out at him in a manner more like that of a friend than a professional colleague. Definitely time to make that distinction between them. There wasn't room in his life even for a friend. He already had one more than he needed. It was the only reason he'd stayed on Yasi as long as he had. He would never have stood back and ignored Peter's pleas for help out here when he still felt as though he had a huge debt to repay. As soon as his stint here was over and all necessary referrals to the hospital on the mainland had been made, he was gone. Ready to disappear into anonymity again and start over somewhere where they didn't know his history.

Their stroll through the village in the daylight was taken at a more leisurely pace than last night's constitutional. Out here in public view with the sights and sounds of island life around them somehow felt less intense, safer. Even if it hadn't taken away the urge to kiss her.

'What's that growing on the roof up there?' Emily pointed at the rows of brown string covering which, to the untrained eye, could've been mistaken for decaying foliage.

'That's coconut husk. They dry the strands in the sun before they braid it. *Magimagi* is the main source of income here. Children are taught the skill from a very early age. Unfortunately, even with all the hard work that goes into it, it sells for a pittance. You're talking only a few dollars for about twenty-five yards of hand-made rope.'

'Wow. I don't know whether to admire the work ethos or pity the folks who do it. I'll never complain about my long hours again. At least I get paid a living wage.'

'Both. It's part and parcel of living here. Unless you're a blow-in, of course, who's benefiting from the local hospitality.'

'Don't make me feel any guiltier about accepting food and lodging than I already do.'

Her genuine outrage made him chuckle. Emily would no more take advantage of people than her generous-spirited stepbrother. From what he'd gathered about her personal life, he suspected it was probably the other way around. It would be so easily for a manipulative sort to tie her soft heart into knots to suit their own agenda. She'd had enough of that in her life for him to do the same. His actions were merely to protect her as well as himself.

'I'm only joking. Everything given to you here is simply payment for all the work you're doing to help the community. Think of that as your wages, then there's no need to feel guilty.' At least, that's how he viewed it when the doubts crept in about accepting so much from those who had so little. It wasn't as though rejecting their gifts of friendship was an option when it would cause even greater offence.

'I'll try to remember that,' she said, a tad more brightly, clearly never having considered the work she was doing here as anything more than the job she was born to do. That humility made her all the more special.

She had that same warrior spirit of every man he'd ever fought alongside—selflessly giving of herself without expecting anything in return. Unfortunately she didn't recognise her own strengths, only her weaknesses. The sooner she found them herself, the sooner he'd be off the hook.

'You should. You'll definitely earn your keep over the next two weeks. The community as a whole will make the most of having qualified medical personnel, even if there are a few too busy trying to make a living to visit.'

'The *magimagi* weavers?'

'And the rest of the arts and crafts community. The economy here is based on the sale of handmade goods such as wooden sculptures and woven mats. If you're lucky you might get to try making some for yourself.' He was counting on it. Okay, so his service to the community wasn't as selfless as Emily's. He'd been part of the scenery here long enough to know that taking her out to that part of the island would be another excuse for a social gathering.

Not only was he spreading the word about the clinic by introducing her but it would certainly help them pass the afternoon. In company.

Emily knew exactly what Joe was up to. He was trying to get her out of his way, palm her off onto someone else. It was the only plausible explanation as to why he was so reluctant they return to what was supposed to be their base of operations. She didn't totally buy this notion of extending personal invitations to her practice when news seemed to travel so quickly across the island anyway.

The kava ceremony was supposed to have been her introduction to society and unless he was using this to ensure he had a dinner invitation too, it felt like a futile exercise. She was only going along with it so she could get a bearing on her surroundings and those she'd be potentially treating. Once she'd established her own list of patients and could manage a conversation without an introduction from her self-appointed leader, she could stop relying on him to get her through this. She wasn't swapping one man-sized crutch for another. This was no journey of self-discovery if Joe was always there showing her the way.

He was a man who craved excitement, thrived on it. The more he did for her, smoothed the way for her, the less interesting she would become to him. As they spent more time together the last thing she wanted was for him to find her just as boring as her husband had.

She'd come here with the idea of reinventing herself as a fearless trailblazer, an inspiration to life's other rejects too afraid to step back out into the sun, only to find herself falling into step behind Joe and following that safe path.

With the warmth of the islanders she was beginning to shed her nerves. There'd been nothing but support for her so far and this morning's drama, although traumatic, had proved her professional worth. The children had been wonderful too, and although another random house call could be seen as skiving she was kind of looking forward to it.

Ten-minute appointments with patients passing through her office on a conveyor belt was frustrating to say the least. At least here she wasn't restrained by time limits or budget; she was free to diagnose and treat anyone who needed her help.

The way of life here was so fascinating and such a far cry from the frantic digital age where she spent more time on the phone or answering emails than getting to know the people she was treating. Time out here had a different meaning, more significance, and gave her extra opportunities to be the best doctor she could be.

'They do say hobbies are a great way to relieve stress. Perhaps I'll find a new creative outlet for my frustrations and irritations.' She batted her eyelashes and smiled a saccharine-sweet smile, enjoying Joe's obvious bewilderment at her sudden compliance.

When it came to interpreting her thoughts and feelings regarding her chaperon she was just as confused. Apart from her own neuroses, he was the main stumbling block between her and her new super-identity. But she'd be lying if she said she didn't appreciate having him as a safety net at times, knowing she could rely on him if she needed support. Plus he was great eye candy. She might have put her heart under lock and key but that didn't mean she was made of stone. She could still appreciate the sight of a perfect male specimen. Especially one flashing his rippling torso as he lifted the hem of his shirt to wipe his brow.

Shallow. So very shallow. She of all people should've resisted objectifying another human being but that flat, toned body deserved recognition. Hell, it deserved its own social media account. She fanned herself with her hand. The heat was starting to get to her and it wasn't entirely down to the fires lining their path through the encampment.

When she managed to drag her gaze away from his midsection and back up to meet his eyes she could see he was more amused than appalled by her visual appreciation.

Busted.

'So, what do they do here?' She coughed away the stirrings his naked chest had caused with a question about the other sights of interest. Okay, steaming pans and bubbling pots weren't nearly as interesting as cheese-grater abs but were infinitely less likely to get her burned.

'This is where they boil the *pandanus* leaves to make them soft enough to weave. They fade from green to white once they're left to dry in the sun before the cloth they make is painted to make colourful mats. It's quite an art.' Joe gave her a quick run-down of the process, displaying more local knowledge than a mere tourist should be privy to.

He might claim to have no attachment to Yasi other than another pin tack on his wall map but it had already become a part of him. Emily wondered if its mystical healing powers would work on her too. Her brother had certainly found his peace on the island and Joe was way too involved in the way of life for someone who'd probably been strong-armed into volunteering here in the first place. If all her wishes came true too this magical isle would conjure up her own successful, independent practice and someone other than her stepbrother who loved her and accepted her for who she was.

The second of those was never going to happen since there was no way in hell she'd forgo her camouflage and let anyone see the *real* her. The best she could hope for was a holiday tan and a good time. After the last year she was willing to settle for that.

He introduced her to Sou and a few of her friends, sitting cross-legged on the floor painting the mats. They welcomed her and immediately invited her to stop clutching her medical bag as though she'd come to sell them encyclopaedias and join them.

Furniture was overrated anyway. Along with the internet and hot running water. And abs. A girl could live without all of them. If she had to.

She didn't want to interrupt their working day but they were keen to start a new mat in her honour and have her be a part of it.

'What kind of paint is this?' she asked as the ladies coloured black geometric shapes with earthy red tones.

'The black is made from ash and coal from the fire mixed with water. It can be messy.' Sou gave her a toothy smile as she prepared the primitive materials in a bowl with her hands.

'The red is actually from clay found on the island. It's scraped and rinsed with water to create various shades.' Although this activity appeared to be primarily women's work, Joe happily took up a place beside her on the floor.

'You've done this before?' Was there anything left for her to explore on the island that he hadn't already laid claim to? She wanted to be annoyed at the unintentional

one-upmanship but it was impossible when he didn't have
a bad bone in his body. And she'd thoroughly inspected it.

He didn't seem to care about losing face at sitting in
the midst of all the women, when his joy at sharing his
newly acquired skill with her was plain to see.

This mat-painting session was Yasi's equivalent to a
coffee morning, as Emily soon found out. The ladies spent
their time swapping anecdotes and chatting among themselves but she was finding it tough to pay attention to everything going on around her when her gaze was locked
onto that of the smiling hunk next to her.

'You dip your finger in the clay mixture.' He took her
hand in his and pressed her fingertip firmly into the red
sludge. 'Then it's simply a matter of colouring between
the lines.' He leaned across to guide her between the thick
black outlines.

His breath was hot against her neck and her own was
caught somewhere between a squeak and a squeal as it
brought goose-bumps along her skin. Somehow she managed to daub enough paint on to fill the small triangle
she'd been assigned. Amazing when his touch had turned
her into a ragdoll with no control over her floppy limbs
except by his hand.

Only when he excused himself from the group to go
and visit the wood-carving menfolk outside was she able
to breathe and move freely again. She could inhale a lung-
ful of fresh air no longer contaminated by his spicy, exotic scent, which had made every breath feel as though
she was taking part of him inside her.

'That man is handsome!' Sou's unlikely outburst was
accompanied by the giggles of grown women with a girl-
ish crush.

Emily gave a nervous laugh along with them, grateful
she wasn't the only one finding his charms irresistible.

'And single!' There was another titter of female appreciation. Clearly, getting het up around this man was a normal reaction and nothing for Emily to worry about.

'Are you two together?'

It took a moment before Emily recognised they'd stopped gossiping among themselves and were addressing her directly. Four pairs of eyes were watching her unblinkingly and waiting for her answer.

'No. No.' She couldn't keep the hint of regret from her voice when she was still recovering from her up close and personal painting tutorial.

'Why not?' Sou tilted her head to one side and stared at her as though she was trying to work out what was wrong with her.

'We're colleagues and I only arrived twenty-four hours ago.' Emily dodged eye contact and concentrated on staying between the lines so no one would see the naked desire for him she was fighting with every breath.

As she stared at her discoloured fingertips and shuffled position so her legs didn't fall asleep, it struck her how off track her itinerary for this trip had gone. Other than the ladies promising to drop in at the clinic, this had nothing to do with her duties as a doctor.

Sou made a strange grunting noise, which sounded like something between disbelief and bewilderment. 'I can tell he likes you.'

The others nodded and clucked their agreement like hens around her.

'Really?' As much as Emily was uncomfortable about her and Joe being the topic of conversation, their reassurance created a warm glow inside her. She wanted him to like her, to see her as more than his mate's kid sister he was obliged to take under his wing, and to think of her as more than a colleague. The way she was doing about him.

There was more clucking.

'I can see it in the way he looks at you. The way he touches you.'

'Oh, yes!'

'Mmm-hmm.'

Another chorus of oohs and laughter sent Emily's temperature rising with the heat of being in the spotlight. Perhaps it hadn't simply been a case of wishful thinking after all.

She cast her mind back over their interaction with a different eye. Had there really been a need to hold her hand? Or sit that close? There was also the matter of that kiss. Dared she hope there'd been more to it than she'd convinced herself? And what if there was? Did she want to go there and start kissing a man she barely knew and wouldn't see again?

Every time she envisaged going through the same heartache Greg had caused her, she pictured Joe instead with his smile and gentle consideration. The answer was overwhelmingly yes, she wanted to kiss him again.

It was the possibility of rejection that frightened her, that abandonment she'd suffered too often, but at the end of this trip *she* would be the one walking away. The whole idea was that she went back to England a stronger person, a braver one for the risks she *should* take. It was time to woman up and live dangerously, and there was nothing more terrifying than the prospect of dipping a toe back into the dating pool. What better way to reintroduce herself than with a holiday romance?

She smiled to herself.

The room erupted into laughter around her.

'Just co-workers, huh?'

'Emily, you've got it bad.'

Yes, yes, she had and it was within her power to turn it into something good.

CHAPTER SIX

JOE SWUNG THE axe and brought it crashing down to split the timber in two. It was a powerful blow designed to be effective both physically and mentally. He'd needed to be in the company of men, doing manly things. Not more hand-holding and making memories with his pretty co-worker. It was all very well making sure they were in a public place but it kind of defeated the object of avoiding close contact if he couldn't leave her side.

He'd been carried away with the whole tour-guide demonstration with the *masi* process because she'd been so open to it. A complete attitude turnaround since the kava ceremony and he hadn't been able to resist capitalising on her new willingness to participate in the local culture. It wasn't often he got to share new experiences with anyone and showing her how to paint the mats had given him the same buzz as when he'd tried it for the first time.

So engrossed in that moment of her new discovery, he'd forgotten the reasons they were there in the first place. Patients. Work. Education. Definitely not taking part in couples' activities as if they were at a holiday camp together. He'd remembered that too late—after the touching and the quickening pulse as he'd leaned too close to the flame.

He'd made a bolt for it in an attempt to direct the adrenaline coursing through his body toward something more practical than neck-kissing his colleague in public. The sculptors had given him the job of sanding the wooden bowls they sold for mixing kava but the smooth, silky texture hadn't really detracted his thoughts away from Emily's skin beneath his touch. So he'd moved on to the more demanding task of preparing the raw material for them in the hope he'd be too exhausted to keep thinking about her. It clearly hadn't worked.

His time hadn't totally been wasted as he'd persuaded a few of the men to stop by the clinic before the end of the week for blood-pressure checks and a general 'MOT'. If Emily had stuck to the plan she'd have a few more recruits on her side too.

'I think we have enough now, Joe, and the light's starting to fade.' Tomasi, Sou's other half, was the one to finally call time.

Joe had been concentrating so hard on making sure he chopped the wood in half and not his foot, he hadn't noticed the sun beginning to set. In the name of health and safety he would have to call it a day. Besides, they had enough wood stacked now to last for weeks.

'I guess I was enjoying my workout too much.' He snatched up his shirt from the top of the wood pile where he'd thrown it after working up a sweat.

'Sou says we're welcome to stay for dinner…'

Joe glanced up as Emily's voice trailed off at the doorway to find her staring again, her mouth open but no further words forthcoming. Her eyes travelled up and down his body without ever reaching his. There was no other word for it. She was *ogling* him.

He made a bigger deal of unfolding his shirt and pulling it over his head than he really needed to, giving her more time to look. No woman had stared at him with such naked desire since the explosion, or if they had he hadn't noticed or found it quite so enjoyable.

He'd flirted and slept with women since leaving the army but a part of his male pride had died along with all his other losses. Although it was only his hearing that had been damaged in the blast he'd stopped thinking of himself as a 'whole' man. With Emily watching him dress as though he could've been the world's sexiest male model instead of a disabled ex-soldier, he made the most of every second of it. She was a doctor who'd probably seen better bodies than his over the space of her career but her apparent fascination was proof this attraction wasn't one-sided. Not that he knew what he should do about that, if anything, when it would only complicate everything.

'Sou has…er…invited us inside for a bite to eat.' Emily slowly came out of her trance now that those hypnotic abs of steel had been hidden from view. Thanks to the T-shirt's shield of invisibility, his hold on her was temporarily suspended. She pretended she was squinting into the semi-darkness, trying to see him, rather than getting her rocks off staring at him half-naked.

'Is that what you want to do?'

Damn him, he'd deployed that adorable smile to disguise his dirty tactics. He was forcing her to make the decision.

'It would be rude not to.' She'd spent the past couple of hours in their company, being part of their group, as Joe had done with the men. It wouldn't be right to shun their invitation now, especially when she had nothing to rush back to. Unlike her *real* life, she wasn't planning her evening to catch up on paperwork or binge-watch episodes of her favourite TV shows.

Dinner with friendly islanders and a hunky ex-serviceman could be the most exotic meal she'd ever have in her life.

Take that, boring old Emily Clifford!

It turned out to be every bit as extraordinary as she'd imagined. The men and women all gathered inside Sou and Tomasi's house and took up their places on the floor mats. The women had put together a feast while Emily had finished up her painting and Joe had been flexing his muscles outside. Although she remained wary about the contents of the dishes laid before her, she had Joe on hand to sample the menu for her first.

With no cutlery available she had no choice but to follow suit and eat with her hands. She chose a pork dish and something delicious called *palusami*, which Joe explained was spinach prepared in coconut cream, and washed it down with a cup of black tea. With her belly full she realised she was getting the hang of this immersion into Yasi society. The only times her nerves had bunched together to remind her this wasn't the norm for her had been when Joe had brushed against her and made her tingle with sexual awareness.

It was a blessing the others hadn't continued with their teasing because she was pretty sure she was doing a bang-up job of making a fool of herself without their help. She'd been positively drooling as she'd watched his topless axe work and tensed every time he leaned in to explain the menu to her, like some virgin schoolgirl with a crush on her teacher. Her emotions had been stretched to every conceivable extreme today and although she was glad to end it in such good company, the walk home was playing on her mind. Their last one had ended in *that* kiss and she was so tightly wound after this evening she might explode if she didn't get the release she'd been craving since his lips had first touched hers.

'Don't forget to take your *masi* with you.' Sou presented her with the finished mat, which already held so many memories for her, when she stood to leave.

'Thank you. That's so kind of you.' They'd spent hours working on it. Time that should have been channelled into their livelihood. It was a wonderful gesture that choked her up even though she should expect this level of kindness by now.

'A souvenir of your time here.'

Emily didn't miss Sou's gaze flicker between her and Joe, a silent insistence she attributed significance to *all* of tonight's events.

'I'll cherish the memories of everyone here,' she assured her with a wry smile. Tonight wouldn't easily be forgotten, with or without the satisfactory conclusion of a second, perhaps more passionate lip-lock.

Emily retrieved her long-forgotten medical bag from the corner of the room. If today had taught her anything apart from her apparent weakness for muscular medics, it was that an office and an appointment book was no substitute for getting out and experiencing life. It was no wonder Greg had grown tired of her if this was what he'd been doing while she'd remained stagnant.

After all the sweetness she'd tasted today, the thought that her inability to spread her wings beyond her own living room had killed her marriage left a sour taste in her mouth. The only consolation she had was that wherever Greg was, whatever he was doing, it couldn't compare with her current adventure.

'Is everything all right, Emily? I know you didn't particularly want to leave the clinic but, honestly, we'd have heard about any emergency.' Joe's concern as they waved their goodbyes reinforced the idea she spoiled everyone's fun by always playing by the rules.

She'd gambled a few times over this last couple of

days and the world hadn't stopped turning because she'd swapped her sensible shoes for some frivolous flip-flops. Far from creating a catastrophic shift in the universe, these spontaneous acts had added a new, fun dimension to her existence.

Each new accepted challenge had enriched her time here with new friends, new skills and tastes, and the new memories were starting to dim the unpleasant ones she'd accumulated recently. One of which topped them all. Every time Greg's cruel words came back to haunt her she'd replace the image of his mouth curled in a sneer as he turned her heart inside out with one of Joe. His lips soft and tender on hers and leaving her fuzzy inside instead of cold.

She sighed. 'It's not that. I just couldn't help thinking that perhaps if I'd been a different woman then, this woman, perhaps Greg wouldn't have left me for someone else.'

Joe frowned at her with a scorn she hadn't expected after their evening playing nice. 'Is that what you want? To waste your life on someone who doesn't appreciate you for who you are? Did you ever think that *he* should've been a different man, a better husband, someone you weren't afraid to try new things with?'

Someone like Joe.

She'd never considered that take on the situation and had simply accepted the blame for the breakdown in their relationship as she had when her mother had left. Neither had wanted to be with her any more and since she had been the common denominator it was logical to assume she had been the root cause. They had wanted her to be someone else to suit their needs but she hadn't found that out until it was too late.

The truth was she couldn't pinpoint one specific reason why Greg had cheated on her and effectively ended their marriage. Yes, he'd said she was boring but she'd been the same woman he'd married. She hadn't changed, he had. One morning he'd simply woken up and decided he could do better. He'd simply grown tired of her and decided he no longer wanted her in his life. That thought had kept her awake and tearful for a long time. It didn't do a lot for a girl who was faced with her own faults in the mirror every single morning. She didn't want to hold on to that negativity any more.

'No.' To all of it. Including Greg.

'Good.' Joe took the mat and helped share her load.

She'd been clinging to the idea of marriage, not the realities of it. Working long days and being expected to have dinner waiting for her husband the minute he walked through the door had been a juggling act. In order to be the perfect wife she hadn't even confronted him on those times he'd arrived home late without an explanation, food ruined and a complete waste of her time cooking it. After the shock of his infidelity those overrunning meetings and last-minute business trips had taken on a sinister new meaning. She'd taken his word his absences were work-related, too trusting to even contemplate it was all lies to cover his dalliances with another woman. Or women. Her trust had been shattered to the point she'd no longer known who it was she'd married.

She'd never forgive him for what he'd put her through, regardless of how much he'd insisted it was her fault he'd chased excitement elsewhere. A marriage was supposed to be a partnership based on love, trust and communication. None of which it turned out they'd had. He hadn't even given her the chance to fix anything when he'd ditched her rather than discuss their problems like a normal couple. Although it hadn't seemed like it up until now, being on her own was probably better than going through the motions of a sham marriage. It had only taken some good company and straight talking for her to finally see that.

She didn't want to waste another second on regrets. That included not acting on the sexual chemistry between her and Joe. Not that she was intending to seduce him or anything, that would be a step too far, but even initiating another kiss seemed such a thrilling prospect it was all she could think about. The spectre of rejection always haunted her actions but he'd kissed her first, looked at her the way she'd lusted after him and lessened the chances he'd spurn her. It was the next big step in becoming Emily Jackson again.

Except she'd spent so long overthinking how she should approach this they were almost back at her door. So much for being spontaneous. She'd never learned how to flirt, had never had reason to. The ugly duckling would've been laughed out of high school if she'd even attempted it and it had been Greg who'd done all the running after they'd first met. She tried to convince herself this was only carrying on from where they'd left things last night when Joe had started this chain reaction inside her. He'd lit the fuse so he'd have to take responsibility for the fallout.

'I had a good time today.' She stopped short of Miriama's house so they weren't under the porch light and reduced the pressure to make something happen there and then.

'Me too.' Joe's bright smile lit up the semi-darkness and took the chill off the evening air.

She reached out to take the mat from him and Joe brushed his thumb along her fingers in the handover. The only sound she could hear was her own breathing as he watched her intently with no sign of backing away. It was now or never. She swallowed hard as she took a step closer to him.

They were both holding onto the mat as she closed her eyes and offered her lips up to his.

For a heart-stopping moment there was only cold air to meet her. Then the weight of his mouth was on hers, accepting her, loving her and bringing her almost to tears with relief. Each caress of her lips, every flick of his tongue to match hers made her confidence stronger and her body weaker. She'd taken a gamble and this was her reward. In future she'd remember how utterly satisfying, and hot, victory tasted.

It was a triumph over her anxieties, her fears and, above all, her old self. This was anything but boring, as her fevered skin would testify.

'I don't want this.'

Her new fairy wings disappeared and left her plummeting back down to earth as Joe did the one thing she'd feared from the start.

'I, I…' She didn't know whether to apologise or say goodnight but either would be better than dissolving into a puddle of tears, which was exactly what she wanted to do. Her determination to prove she was still attractive to someone, that she could change, had obviously built this up into something Joe hadn't been expecting. The celebrations heralding the brave new Emily had been premature. Nobody wanted *her* either. The difference was she would no longer let other people's opinions define her.

Joe wanted Emily more than anything else in the world right now. That was the problem. It was one thing for him to snatch a kiss from her and walk away but quite another for her to initiate one. Double standards for sure but what was a moment of madness for him could mean something entirely different for her. They were already too close when every attempt to create some distance between them only succeeded in them spending more time together. To what end? She wasn't going to find peace with him when he couldn't find his own.

'Okay, I do want this, there's no point in denying it.' Not when he could see how much hurt he was causing her by doing so. That tilt of the chin didn't fool him when she was clutching her medical bag like a security blanket and her eyes were glassy with tears.

'So why do it? Why keep pretending there isn't something more than my brother or work binding us together?'

He admired her strong stance, facing him out over his cowardice despite her wobbly voice. She deserved the truth. He dug his nails into his palms to stop from reaching out to her. This was exactly why he should have avoided kissing her in the first place.

'I've told you, I'm not boyfriend material. You'll end up just another holiday memory when I move on and after everything you've been through you need more than that. I don't want the level of responsibility that comes with being the rebound guy. I'm not going to be the one to restore your faith in men or be your emotional crutch until you're over Greg, and I won't pretend to be.' Cards on the table, he braced himself for her reaction. He doubted any woman wanted to be told the man they were kissing was emotionally unavailable, and since he hadn't found it in himself to walk away he was counting on her to make that call.

Emily closed the gap he'd created between them. 'I don't remember saying I wanted any of those things from you but thank you for your honesty. I guess we both know where we stand.'

Too close for him to think straight. Alarm bells were ringing in his head with her breathy acceptance of his terms but it was no longer his head he was listening to.

'I don't want this,' he repeated, even as his lips inched towards hers.

'Neither do I.'

Their mouths collided in a crushing kiss as if they were trying to exorcise this need for one another. The very opposite happened to him as his brain short-circuited and erased the reason he shouldn't do this. Something about him being an idiot and Emily accepting it.

The medical bag and mat fell in the dirt as they clung to each other tighter, her hands around his neck, his around her waist, their legs entwined as they tied themselves into a love pretzel, obliterating all pretence for good.

There was so much fire as she came back time and time again for more, exploring him with her tongue, her passion took him completely by surprise. This naked display of desire for him from a woman who worried about every move she made was such an aphrodisiac his body was already racing on to the next stage. Neither of them were ready for that. At least, not here, not now.

He loosened his hold and gradually let the intensity of the embrace subside. Eventually he had to break free before the most demanding part of his anatomy wrestled sole charge of the situation.

'Glad we got that sorted. It stops any future misunderstanding.' The only way he could survive this was to make a joke of it and diffuse the crackling sexual tension for the moment. Neither of them wanted this but it was happening and there was clearly no escape from it on this tiny island.

'Yeah. We wouldn't want things getting awkward at work.' Emily teased him back but she was already collecting her things from the ground, the moment over.

'Goodnight, Emily.' He kissed her on the cheek, avoiding her lips in case his chivalry died altogether.

'Goodnight, Joe,' she whispered directly into his ear. Even if he hadn't heard it, the deliberately provocative breathy goodbye would still have had the same effect on his libido. Deadly.

This surge in Emily's confidence had the potential to be one of the greatest challenges of his life if he kept resisting his natural response to her. If she was really the sort of girl who could hook up with a stranger on a whim they'd have got it on as soon as she'd set foot on the beach. The attraction had been there from the start. She'd had no more casual flings than he'd had ex-wives. They were completely incompatible. Except where it counted.

He was a thrill-seeker because he needed that reminder he was still alive, and his life hadn't ended in that blast. There'd been no greater example of that than when he'd had Emily in his arms, his heartbeat thundering in his ears as she'd kissed him.

It would be madness to carry on with this reckless attraction, let it develop beyond stolen kisses in the moonlight and risk anyone getting hurt. Then again, he was an adrenaline junkie. Playing it safe simply wasn't his style and, it would seem, no longer Emily's.

CHAPTER SEVEN

'SOMEONE'S HAPPY THIS MORNING. I heard you up, singing with the birds.' Miriama peered at Emily over the breakfast of sweet rolls she'd provided.

Emily wolfed them down, ravenous after a good night's sleep and some very pleasant dreams.

'I'm loving my time here, that's all,' she said, washing her white lie down with some lemon tea. Whilst she was happy to be here, this morning's mood was solely down to one man on the island.

'And we love having you here. Perhaps you could stay a little while longer?' She had such hope in her eyes it was a shame to let her down. It wasn't everyone who would open their homes up to a complete stranger in the first place and it was lovely for Emily to hear someone wasn't sick of the sight of her. Not yet anyway.

'I wish I could but I've got my own clinic, my own patients, waiting for me at home.' There was no place she'd rather be than Yasi Island right now. It had made quite an impression on her.

She traced the outline of her mouth with her fingertips absent-mindedly, replaying the moment it had all been worth it to come here. It was no wonder Miriama was staring at her as if she was mad. She couldn't stop smiling.

There was no way of telling if it was down to this place

or merely being away from the toxic environment of a life she'd shared with her ex, but she was beginning to feel like a new person. A woman who could override her fears with a burst of courage when it was required. The benefits she'd received in doing so would only inspire her to keep challenging herself.

Until last night she would never have entertained the idea of making a move on a man but she was glad she had. A lovely shiver tickled the back of her neck at the thought of her reward. She didn't know if anything more would come of it and constantly worrying about it would only spoil things. As with any other holiday memory the kiss was simply something to look back on fondly. A fantasy designed to give her a boost when real life became a drudge, not take seriously.

'Oh, well. You're ours for a while at least, so you should go make the most of your time here. I'm sure Joe is waiting for you.'

She tried to block out her inner worrywart, who always did her best to sabotage the good things that came her way, and focus on the positives as she made her way to work. Such as the reserves of courage she hadn't known she'd had to make a move on him in the first place.

'Hey.' Her breakfast did a backflip in her belly at the first Joe sighting of the day.

'Hey,' he said back, every bit as bashful as they faced each other from either end of the hut.

It seemed they were back to yesterday's avoidance tactics again and although it was probably best when they had to work together, there was still that sinking feeling in her stomach that their moment had passed.

They kept themselves busy by setting up what minimal equipment they had and she was glad when Sou made an appearance to interrupt the awkward atmosphere.

'Hey, Sou. What can we do for you?' Joe asked.

'If it's a general health check you want we can start with your blood pressure.' Emily turned back to fetch the blood-pressure cuff, only to collide with that solid wall of muscle again.

'Excuse me,' she said, attempting to duck past Joe.

'Of course.' He moved aside but she promptly ran into him again.

'Sorry.'

'Sorry.'

'If you two have quite finished, is there somewhere I can set these before my arm drops off?' Sou shoved a plate of sweet desserts between Emily and Joe's clumsy tango.

'You can set them over here.' She cleared a space on the table for Sou's offering and prayed it wasn't completely obvious that she and Joe were dealing with personal issues. It was taking all her mental strength to relegate their ten minutes of sexy times to the past when she was still trying to regulate her breathing and her heart rate, but she would never bring her personal business into the workplace.

'I'll go...do something else.' Joe backed out of her personal space and her skittishness immediately began to dissipate.

Good. It would help her get back to the day job if she couldn't see him. They couldn't let things between them affect their work.

'Take a seat, Sou. I wasn't expecting to see you so soon. What can I do for you?'

Yasi Island, and Joe, were making her forget who she was *supposed* to be.

She wrapped the cuff around Sou's upper arm and watched the dial as she inflated it.

'I haven't been myself at all lately and I thought it was about time I saw about it. If I'm honest, it's only because you're here that I'm bothering at all.' Sou rested her hands on her lap and that sparkle she'd had in her eye when she'd first walked in began to dim. There was clearly something bothering her more than she wanted anyone to know.

'Well, your blood pressure's fine. We'll start with taking a few measurements and then we'll discuss whatever problems you're having.' Emily unfastened the cuff and started a file for her new patient. She plotted her height on the wall chart and pushed the scales out to get a quick weight reading.

Sou was fifty-eight, and very overweight, which could lead to all manner of health issues.

'I'm tired and thirsty all the time. I know I'm not getting any younger but I'm exhausted.'

'Are you passing urine more frequently too?' Alarm bells were already ringing in her doctor brain.

'I thought that was because of the extra drinks?'

'It could be but we have to look into all possibilities. Tell me, Sou, do you know if there's a history of diabetes in your family?' It would certainly explain the symptoms but Emily didn't have the means to treat it effectively here. She would have to refer Sou to hospital on the mainland for the kind of long-term care that would require and she'd have to be certain of her diagnosis before she started the ball rolling on that score.

'My mother had it but she hated the hospital. She didn't always do everything they advised. She was a stubborn lady and I miss her.' The fear in her voice came from someone who didn't want to follow that same path but neither did she want to face the scary truth. It was important for Emily to treat her with kid gloves so she didn't scare her off back into denial.

'If it is diabetes we're dealing with, we *can* manage it effectively. First things first. We'll do a wee sample to test your blood sugar levels. You'll feel a little prick in your finger as the needle draws the blood but it'll all be over in seconds. Okay?' She only had the small reading device at her disposal and any in-depth analysis would have to be done in the hospital labs but it should give her a good indication if there was a problem.

Sou nodded her head and slowly extended her hand. While Emily was used to this sort of test she understood this wasn't something her patient would be too familiar with and counted to three before she clicked the needle into the skin.

Unfortunately her hunch proved correct. The glucose levels exceeded those she'd hoped for.

'Going by the reading here, diabetes is a definite possibility. I'd like to repeat the test tomorrow if you could fast in the morning for me. We'll take a urine sample first thing too to make sure this isn't some sort of anomaly. If there's no change we're going to have to refer you to the hospital to arrange long-term care for the condition.'

She rested her hand on Sou's, wishing this lovely woman had better news coming to her. 'You can do a little something to help yourself in the meantime. If you could cut out the sweet stuff and take up even the smallest exercise, it can make all the difference.'

Sou's long stare was that of a woman who may as well have been handed a death sentence. Emily understood how much food was a part of the culture here but Sou needed to help herself when there wasn't immediate access to medical facilities and drugs on the island. Diabetes unchecked could lead to all sorts of other health complications, which were often more difficult to treat. Prevention was always better than cure.

'We can work together to come up with a healthy eating plan if it would help.'

'Yes, please.'

That would be her homework tonight, to try and devise a meal plan that could work in a place where food supplies were already limited. With any luck Joe would help her. Putting their heads together for the sake of their patients was the perfect excuse to cosy up this evening.

'I know it's easier said than done but try not to worry about it. Carry on as normal tonight. We'll do more tests tomorrow, then take it from there.' She'd get his advice on hospital referrals too when he'd finished with his own patient. Joni was currently monopolising his time with another sports injury of some sort.

'Can I still drink kava?'

If this had been a patient at home she wouldn't be encouraging alcohol but not overwhelming Sou with too much change was just as important. They'd take this one step at a time together.

'I'm not going to stop you partaking tonight but we will look into your alcohol intake as part of this lifestyle change at some point. Everything's possible in moderation. Now, go home, talk this over with Tomasi and I'll see you back here in the morning.'

Sou rose slowly from the bed. It was no wonder she was still in a daze after the bombshell she'd just had dropped on her.

'I'm here any time you need to talk or if you have any questions.'

'Thanks, Emily.'

'No problem. We'll get you back to your old self as soon as we can.' She wrapped Sou in a bear hug, another thing she'd never have dreamed of doing in her own practice. That line between patient and friend had been blurred around the same time as the one with Joe.

She made a note to call in and check on Sou later as she waved her off. It was a lot for her to take in and meant huge changes in her life, something that was always difficult to come to terms with even when it was for the best. She was a prime example herself of someone who'd resisted adapting to the new hand fate had dealt her and was only now reaping the benefits of that evolution. It would've been nice if she'd had someone to hold her hand and assure her things would be okay and her world wouldn't come to an end because of one event.

Perhaps she wouldn't have been in the right head space to hear those platitudes about life going on after Greg but it had, and in quite dramatic fashion. In those dark early days she'd never have imagined flying to a remote island, treating patients with rudimentary equipment and snogging the local totty. She was proud of herself for all of it. Sou would be too if she made a few simple changes to improve her lot. Although Joe was definitely out of bounds, she would find her courage rewarded in other ways.

Her attention inevitably returned to her army medic, who was patching up Joni's knee. She could hear the pair of them laughing and was automatically drawn towards the easy camaraderie after the difficult start to the day.

'Have you been in the wars again?' she asked the patient, who was lying on the bed with his hands behind his head as relaxed as could be.

'The perils of running and not paying attention.' Joe grinned at her over his shoulder, sending her pulse skipping off into the sunset with her common sense.

'It's as well you're made of tough stuff around here, huh?' Her attempt at playful banter fell flat as Joni was staring at her unblinkingly, clearly disturbed by her presence.

He sat up, his face screwed up as he peered closer into her face, his nose wrinkled in disgust. Emily moved away from the bedside taken aback by the boy's sudden change in demeanour. She could sense Joe tensing next to her too and she panicked she'd made a mistake in coming over and interrupting their male bonding.

'What happened to your face, Doc?'

It was the kind of blunt questioning she should've been used to by now but it still managed to knock the air out of her lungs. This was why she took great steps to make sure she kept her birthmark covered and avoid this sort of confrontation. Joni had reacted so strongly there had to be something wrong with her usually foolproof camouflage.

She'd been so high on life this morning she barely remembered anything before coming to work. Her routine never differed—shower, dress, make-up, breakfast. Except this wasn't any ordinary day and this certainly wasn't the usual running order. She'd swapped her hot showers for buckets of cold water, dressed according to the weather instead of her job title, and…she didn't recall performing her twenty-minute beauty regime while she'd been singing and daydreaming about the night before. That would teach her to get carried away with romance. Now stark reality was staring her right in the face. This fairy-tale was well and truly over.

'I…uh…' She scrabbled around for her bag. There should be an emergency compact in there and she'd handle this better if she wasn't so exposed.

She couldn't even look at Joe now her big secret had been revealed in its full gory glory. Goodness knew what he was thinking. Probably how much of a lucky escape he'd had.

'It's a birthmark. Just a different coloured patch of skin Emily was born with. We're lucky she feels comfortable enough with us to stop hiding it under her make-up.' Joe shot her a smile warm enough to thaw out her bones, which were chilled after being called out on her deception. Bless him, he was trying to make this easy on her when he'd been the one kept in the dark.

She was torn now between doing a last-minute cover-up, pretending this had never happened, or playing along that this had been a deliberate move on her part. Joe wasn't stupid, he'd have known she'd never have intentionally 'come out' and left herself open to such scrutiny. It was testament to his strength of character for trying to save her blushes when it must have been a shock to his system to see her like this. Greg wouldn't have been so accommodating. He would've escorted her to the nearest mirror to rectify her glaring blunder. Although he wouldn't have let her leave the house make-up-free in the first place, never mind make excuses for her. He'd always made her feel as though she earned more respect from people when she perpetuated the lie about her true appearance.

She was lucky to have met a man who didn't need to put her down and always did his best to make her comfortable in her surroundings. No matter what the circumstances. That total acceptance of her as a person was something rare in her world.

'Does it hurt?' Joni was still staring at her face, which was aflame with the continued line of questioning.

'No. I forget it's even there.' That wasn't strictly true. Apart from today when it had apparently gone completely out of her head, that wretched port wine stain was the bane of her existence.

It was a boring enough answer for the child to lose interest.

'Will I have a scar?' he asked as Joe finished dressing his knee.

'No. You should be all healed up in a day or two. Now, get yourself off to school before your teacher sends out a search party for you.'

Joni looked remarkably disappointed not to have a long-lasting reminder of his injury as he hopped down off the bed. 'I suppose I'll see you later, then.'

At least when he was engrossed in his own woes it stopped him gawping at her as though she was a sideshow attraction. The novelty usually wore off but that initial shock and revulsion was always difficult to stomach. Sometimes children could be the worst, laughing and pointing at her affliction, too young to understand the pain it would cause, but Joni had been quite straightforward about the matter. He'd asked questions and once they'd been answered it was no longer an issue. He'd made no judgement on her as a person because of her physical disfigurement.

It suddenly struck her that Sou and Miriama had also seen her without her camouflage. That explained the curious stares that she'd put down to her Joe-enhanced mood but they'd just been too polite to comment.

A woman with a dark red birthmark apparently wasn't anything the people of Yasi were going to waste energy thinking about when they were working so hard to just get by themselves. Physical attractiveness didn't hold much meaning out here because it had no effect on their quality of life. That's the way it should be; the way Emily preferred it. Except when she was unashamedly ogling Joe, of course. She was aware of the irony.

Joe. He'd seen her long before Sou or Joni had come onto the scene and he hadn't blinked, hadn't felt the need to point it out to her.

She opened her mouth, trying to find the words she needed to express what that meant to her, and failing. His easy acceptance was already making her tear up.

'Is everything all right with Sou? I think Joni was only trying to avoid class. He spends so much time here we should probably find him a job.'

She couldn't believe he wasn't even going to mention her birthmark. Honestly, she was finding his nonchalance even more disturbing than the boy's reaction. It wasn't the norm and, as such, she didn't know how to handle it.

In the end she decided to go with honesty and straight

talking. Another new first when it came to relationships for her.

'Are you really going to stand there and pretend nothing's wrong?'

'What are you talking about?' His naivety on the subject was annoying her now. No one could possibly be that oblivious to her predicament.

'This.' She couldn't believe she was voluntarily pointing out her flaw.

'Oh, your birthmark? I see it. So what?' He shrugged, increasing the chances of her giving him a good shake.

'So what, he says. You could have given me a heads up I'd gone out in public like this.' She didn't know why she was taking her mistake out on him when he'd been nothing but supportive. Her lashing out might have had something to do with this being the most vulnerable she'd felt since arriving on the island.

'As I said to Joni, I'd assumed you were actually comfortable enough around us to stop hiding away.'

'You weren't shocked? I mean, this ugly big mess can take some getting used to.' Nearly thirty years of living with it hadn't made it any easier for her so she didn't expect anyone else to take it in their stride the way Joe had.

'If I'm honest, I knew about it. I've seen the family photos Peter carries around with him but even if I hadn't it doesn't make any difference to me.'

Emily had to admit that took the shine off his brilliance somewhat. He'd had time to prepare himself for the great revelation. Unlike her discovery about his hearing problem. Perhaps the knowledge of her struggles with defective body parts had been what had drawn him to her in the first place and had made her seem attractive as another damaged soul. If something appeared too good to be true, it usually was.

'Hey. Your birthmark is part of you. How could it be

anything other than beautiful?' He tilted her chin up so she had to look in his eyes and believe what she saw there—pure, undiluted desire.

Whether he'd had advance warning or not, whether she covered up or not, he always looked at her as though she was the sexiest woman alive. There was no greater compliment for a woman like her. When he'd said her birthmark didn't matter to him, holding her gaze this way, she was more inclined to believe it.

Joe leaned forward and placed a light kiss on the exact spot between her cheek and her nose where her greatest weakness blazed brightly. She held her breath. It was one of those moments she'd dreamed of, when someone would embrace her, warts and all, not shy away from any part of her. She'd never had that complete acceptance from Greg and, despite being together so long, she'd always been slightly on edge. With good reason, it had turned out.

Joe was different. He believed in qualities and causes that mattered, not superficial nonsense that held no significant meaning. He was a special person. One with whom her time was limited.

Typical.

If she was only to encounter this kind of acceptance once in her lifetime she should really immerse herself in the experience. No holding back. No regrets. Be herself without conditions.

For the first time in her life she was seriously considering ditching her camouflage on a permanent basis and really letting loose. It was a bold move she would never have undertaken without Joe's unconditional support, and she was keen to share the rest of the adventure with him.

CHAPTER EIGHT

THERE WERE TIMES when Joe needed his medical work to give his life meaning and other times it was something he felt compelled to do. Today it felt like the latter. He'd volunteered to come to Yasi because he'd genuinely wanted to help, and he still did, but the success of the clinic had curtailed his personal life. That hadn't been a problem up until now. He'd spent all day treating one patient after another with Emily almost within arm's reach. It was torture if he was expected to forget everything that had happened between them.

He shouldn't complain, though, when their outreach yesterday had garnered so many follow-up appointments. It would go a long way towards improving the long-term health of the inhabitants. At one point they'd had a queue outside of people waiting to be seen for check-ups, which hadn't happened since he'd set up the clinic. Such an influx could've been overwhelming for Emily, especially since she'd chosen not to cover up her birthmark again. Of course there'd been comments and stares but she'd dealt with them all without any upset or drama, as if she'd reconciled herself about living without the make-up.

When she'd turned up this morning, her natural beauty shining through, all he'd wanted to do was take her in his arms and kiss her. It didn't matter it had turned out to have been an oversight on her part, her actions since had established her bravery and made him want her more. Every inadvertent brush against each other since had simply increased his desire to act on that impulse—impossible given their circumstances, not to mention the room full of people between them for most of the day. He couldn't afford to let anyone else down when he was still coming to terms with the last time he'd failed people who had needed his help.

They were making a difference here and that's what was important. Along with minor ailments and a test of his suturing skills on one of the local craftsmen, who'd whittled his hand instead of the wood he was supposed to be carving, they'd uncovered a few more serious health issues in the older population. Emily had confided in him about Sou, but diabetes, along with hypertension, wasn't an uncommon problem in remote regions like Yasi. Without adequate primary health care access and education, the rates of non-communicable diseases were often high and many cardiovascular risk factors also went unchecked. He already had a list of patients who'd require further investigation and treatment in proper hospital facilities.

In turn, the island was also doing Emily the power of good. That creep of an ex-husband had taken a sledgehammer to her confidence with his callous behaviour but she was flourishing out here. The same woman who forty-eight hours ago had been unable to walk more than twenty paces without touching up her make-up and had wanted to hide from company was fresh-faced and joking about with the locals.

She'd told all manner of tall tales to explain the birthmark, making light of it to avoid any awkwardness. He'd even heard her tell one curious patient it was the result of dodgy suncream application. By the time she revealed the truth it didn't seem to matter any more. Talking about it somehow made it less of a big deal and it was great to see Emily comfortable in her own skin. She didn't need him to wrap her in cotton wool when she was making such great progress on her own. It made his life easier too if she wasn't relying on him to act as intermediary any more.

'I've got another patient to add to the list of referrals. His heartbeat is irregular and he's out of breath. I'd be happier if he had an ECG to see what's going on in there.' Emily was all business as she approached him during a lull. She'd wound her hair up into a topknot and Joe's hand twitched to reach out and pluck out the pen holding it in place.

He gave himself a shake to rid himself of the image of her shaking her hair loose and showed her he could be just as professional. 'If you jot down all his details I'm going to make a few calls on the satellite phone later to the medical outreach co-ordinator and the hospital to get people here as soon as possible. Perhaps they can arrange communal transport to save money and effort in the transfer.'

'Like a community day trip? I suppose they could take a picnic and do some sightseeing on the way.' The corner of her mouth curved up as she teased him.

'Careful or I'll appoint you as tour rep.'

'I'd say you're the man for the job, not me. I imagine you'd be really good.'

He knew she was referring to the introductions he'd made for her around the island, yet the unintended innuendo immediately brought a groan from his inner Neanderthal. Given the chance with Emily he'd show her just how good he could be.

Her cheeks flushed scarlet as though she was reading his X-rated thoughts. The only thing more frustrating than not being able to act on his attraction to Emily was being aware that she wanted him too.

She made a move towards the new batch of patients hovering nearby, but Joe was finding it hard to let the moment pass without recognising the frisson of sexual energy they'd created in the space of a few seconds. Despite the buzz and whirr of the neon danger signs around her, he enjoyed Emily's company and the adrenaline rush he got simply from being around her.

He leaned down to whisper in her ear as she passed by. 'Why don't we get together tonight?'

Her eyes nearly popped out of her head at the suggestion. Clearly her thoughts were as muddled as his own about his motives. 'I, er…'

'You know, to catch up on that patient transfer list.' They could play it safe, didn't have to do anything other than chat about their working day. It would be novelty enough for him to entertain a guest, without getting into trouble with Peter's sibling and causing all manner of problems.

'Oh, yes. Of course. I'd also appreciate your help in devising some sort of healthy eating plan for Sou. We could even draw up an easy-to-read guide on healthier living for everyone to explain the basics.'

'Why don't we do it over dinner?'

'Here?'

'Sure. Leave it with me. As soon as we wrap up here you go and get freshened up and I'll rustle up some food for us. Just a quiet dinner for two.' So far, all their meals had been very public affairs where she'd found it difficult to relax. He wanted to change that for her without the pressure of structured proceedings. Just work talk and chill.

'That would be nice.'

'So it's a date, then?' He couldn't stop himself from teasing her one last time.

'It's a date,' she confirmed, before resuming her work

duties. The smile on her face eased the sense of loss as she turned away, knowing he'd been the one to put it there.

He had no expectations for anything beyond a nice evening together. A working dinner sounded more manageable for both of them long-term than an appointment for hot, unforgettable sex. Although he imagined that's exactly what would happen if they ever gave in to temptation.

That thought wasn't going to help this day go any faster.

The butterflies in her stomach might be older and more cynical than they had been fifteen years ago when she'd gone on her first date to the cinema, but they weren't any less mobile on this *non-date*. She was playing with fire tonight and she knew it. Joe had made it clear he didn't intend anything other than work-related conversation, but their apparent chemistry had a way of throwing them off track. She took full responsibility for last night's descent into madness and she wasn't ashamed of it. Taking the initiative had given her a confidence boost, especially when he'd been so responsive to her advances, but she wasn't sure she wanted to take things any further than that. Joe was an experienced man of the world who'd invariably expect more than a kiss in the moonlight.

Although she'd initially been disappointed they hadn't carried on where they'd left off, it was probably better they let things cool off. As much as she wanted to exorcise her demons once and for all, she wasn't ready to sleep with anyone yet, not even someone who was so accepting of her, flaws and all. While the idea of sharing Joe's bed was appealing on the surface, it would probably only give her more issues to worry about. Including all the ways in which he could find her lacking as a lover, given her limited experience.

Until she fully overcame her personal issues she'd have

to make do with the exhilaration of anticipation instead. This was the most alive she'd felt since the divorce, when all hope inside her for the future had seemed to have died along with her marriage. Even the idea he might want to sleep with her had definitely got the blood pumping back in her veins and that was enough for now.

She'd come armed as she entered the battlefield tonight where hormones would fight against her battered heart for supremacy. Flowers and chocolates were usually the gifts to bring on such an auspicious occasion but stationery was her particular weapon of choice this evening. An armful of paper, glue and coloured markers seemed like a good distraction from the beds that would dominate tonight's dinner venue.

She'd informed Miriama she'd be working late and wouldn't be around for supper when she'd gone back to change. There wasn't much to choose from in her limited wardrobe but she'd gone with Capri pants and a navy and white polka-dot halterneck for what she hoped was a touch of vintage glamour. It had taken longer for her decide on her make-up for the evening. While using her thick foundation could be seen as taking a step backwards, there weren't many women who'd get ready for an evening in male company without a little extra help. After much debate she'd decided a sweep of mascara over her eyelashes and a dab of lip-gloss would do just fine.

She'd taken so much time and care over her appearance she hadn't given a thought to how Joe would look tonight. When he opened the door to her she hadn't expected to see him in anything other than his casual T-shirt and shorts combo. So the more formal cream-coloured linen trousers and unbuttoned white shirt he was rocking had her eyes out on stalks.

'What? You don't think I can scrub up well too?'

'You look great.' She appreciated the effort he'd gone

to for her and that appreciation had reached deep inside and touched somewhere that definitely went beyond the friendship realm.

'So do you.' He leaned in to give her a welcome peck on the cheek, his skin smooth against hers and smelling of aftershave and soap.

She closed her eyes and breathed him in, the combination of familiar citrus tones and spicy musk seeming to complement his personality perfectly. Like him, his cologne was comforting with a dangerous hint of the exotic. Not to mention so very moreish. But standing on the doorstep, sniffing him, wasn't supposed to be the highlight of her evening.

'I'm intrigued to find out what you have planned for dinner.' She didn't have much of an appetite, at least not for food, but she was curious about how he'd sourced it, or if he'd cooked it himself.

'Come in and be prepared to be blown away. I can guarantee you the best meal you've had on the island, all cooked by my own fair hand.' He ushered her inside with the urgency of a man keen to show off said cooking skills.

'Bold claims. You're going to have to go a long way to top Sou's spread last night. I hope you've had some training.' She was still battling her fear of new foods, especially when not all of them here were to her taste. Except the coconut spinach thing.

Please, let it be the coconut spinach thing.

'I'll have you know I've cooked this very same meal while trekking through the Amazon rainforest. I'm a very capable chef who has whipped up a veritable feast even in the most trying circumstances.'

'In that case, I'm most honoured to be your guest.' And impressed with the casual mention of what must have been the most epic of adventures. Time spent in the jungle put her island escape well and truly in the shade.

Conditions here were probably luxurious compared to what he'd endured and she was panicking about what was on the menu. She should think herself lucky people were happy to keep feeding her. If left to her own devices she'd probably starve once her biscuit stash ran out.

'Take a seat and make yourself comfortable. You can set your things over there in the corner.'

She thought it was his idea of a joke when her bones were still protesting against this tradition of sitting on hard wood floors until she saw what he'd done with the place. The room was lit with the lanterns she'd seen in all the other houses, which somehow here they took on that air of intimacy a candlelit dinner for two demanded. He'd pushed all the medical equipment to the side and pulled the table, now covered with one of the painted *masa* mats, into the middle of the room. There were even two crude wooden chairs, one either side of the makeshift dining table. Bliss!

'I thought we were doing paperwork.' She clutched her armful of stationery closer. It was her security blanket, supposed to keep her grounded and stop her from getting carried away with the idea of romance.

'We are but we'll think better on a full stomach.' He eased the supplies from her grasp and set them on top of the medicine cabinet.

'It might be an idea to make a food pyramid to explain the basic principles of healthy living at a glance. You know, one of those colour-coded posters that starts with a small amounts of fatty foods bad for the body and ends with encouraging more fruit and veg in the diet.'

'Sure. I'm no artist but I'm sure we can manage a simple pictograph between us. Now, if you'll excuse me I must go and check on dinner cooking on my camping stove out the back.' It was only when he padded away from her that Emily noticed he was barefoot. He had his

very own brand of sophistication that, while traditionally handsome, still paid homage to his bohemian nature.
The best of both worlds from a spectator's point of view.

He gave a half-bow before ducking back outside. Emily
took the seat facing the door in order to see this specta-
cle as it unfolded. He'd certainly gone to a lot of trouble
but nothing so far indicated what she should expect on
her plate. Her suspense was prolonged even further when
dinner did arrive as he kept it covered, using an upturned
wooden bowl as an improvised cloche.

'Ta-da!' He lifted the cover with a flourish.

Emily released the breath she'd been holding in a splutter of disbelief. 'Beans on toast? Where on earth did you
get that?'

The welcome sight of an old British favourite, baked
beans in tomato sauce, was a little piece of home that immediately brought her comfort. He'd even taken the care
to toast the rustic bread to keep it authentic.

'We explorers always carry a few emergency supplies.'
He produced an empty tin, which he'd obviously brought
with him from England.

'This beats a fancy restaurant any day of the week.'

'Wait. You haven't seen anything yet.' He disappeared
again, returning with two tin cups full of what looked
suspiciously like English tea.

She took a sip of sweet heaven. 'But how…?'

Joe sat down too. 'I told you, I have a few essentials
and I called in a few favours for the rest.'

She wanted to tell him he shouldn't have gone to so
much trouble for her but she was too grateful to him for
sacrificing his supplies for her. And her mouth was wa-
tering to taste something familiar.

'I've never eaten beans and toast with my fingers.'

'You don't have to. Unless you want to.' He reached
into his pocket and pulled out a set of small stainless-steel

cutlery. The kind no good Boy Scout would ever leave home without. It also proved his commitment to being part of the community here when he'd chosen to forgo using them until now.

Emily reached out and snatched a knife and fork from him. 'It's the little things that mean the most.'

That first bite of hearty nostalgia seemed to go in slow motion as she savoured the taste of home, enjoying the textures and flavours she knew so well. After that, she practically devoured her plate in hunger. When she was done she wiped her chin to make sure she hadn't embarrassed herself by dripping tomato sauce down herself.

'I aim to please.' He set down his cutlery on his clean plate with every reason to look smug after pulling out all the stops tonight. She wouldn't have been more pleased if he'd wined and dined her at The Ritz.

'I can't believe you did this. More to the point, I can't believe you wore white, knowing this was what we were eating. That's a laundry nightmare waiting to happen.'

He leaned forward, his intense gaze holding her captive in her seat, that desire they'd been trying to swerve all day flaring back into life. 'What can I say? I live right on the edge of danger.'

They both did if the sparks between them were anything to go by.

'Maybe we should get started on our craft project?' Before they cleared the table and lunged at each other in a fit of passion.

'There's no rush. Now, I hope you have room for dessert?'

'Always.' It was usually her favourite part of a meal but there wasn't much that could possibly top that main course.

Except the two chocolate bars he was waving in her face. All her Christmases had come at once.

'I was saving them for a special occasion.'

'Well, now's not the time to be selfish,' she said, holding out a hand for her share, secretly pleased he deemed an evening in her company 'special' when she was thinking exactly the same thing about him.

He was good-looking, generous, thoughtful and funny. Everything a woman could want in a man.

Joe Braden spelled trouble with a capital 'T'.

'Hmm, I don't think I'll ever make it as an artist.' Emily chewed the end of her pen and squinted at her depiction of Fijian desserts in the 'Eat Less' section at the top of the food pyramid. The only reason she didn't feel a hypocrite after scoffing down that chocolate was because it was the only indulgence she'd had in three days.

After their feast on comfort foods they'd got their heads together to create a diet plan for Sou and had now taken up residence on the floor to work on their healthy eating poster. The idea that there'd be more room to spread out had actually led to the two of them sitting almost on top of each other as they drew on the same piece of paper.

Joe glanced up from his scribbling to see her efforts for himself. 'Don't put yourself down. That's an excellent cheese wedge.'

'It's supposed to be coconut cake.'

'Maybe we should label everything.'

She gave him a dig with her elbow, making him give his perfectly drawn apple an extra-long stalk on the 'Eat More' shelf as he laughed at his own joke.

'I think they'll get the gist of the message and we'll explain it as part of the general physical exam anyway.'

'I'm only messing with you. I reckon we've done a great job. This artwork will still be hanging here displaying the info long after we've gone, essentially doing our job in our absence.' Joe hammered his fist on the sheet of A4 paper in passionate defence of their initiative.

'That's a scary thought,' she said with a giggle. He did make her laugh. And swoon.

'Which bit? The quality of our legacy or the idea of us leaving this place?'

Just like that the jovial mood gave way to something more serious, something more intense. Leaving Yasi meant leaving Joe behind too and she wasn't ready for that. He held her gaze and right there and then she knew she didn't want this to be over. She wanted this to be the beginning.

'Both.'

It was impossible to tell who'd made the first move when they'd both leaned in for the kiss.

Joe fastened his lips to hers with such stunning conviction she knew he'd been waiting for this too. She was starting to forget why she shouldn't let this happen when he knew her secret already and embraced it with more passion than she'd ever expected. He hadn't looked at her with any kind of pity today, only desire. Unless he was a very good actor or did charity work as a self-esteem booster for unfortunates, he didn't seem bothered by her *au naturel* appearance.

She scooted closer to deepen their connection and sample the best course of the evening in her opinion. Kissing him was even better than chocolate but every bit as delicious. Every romantic bone in her body melted as he pulled her close and reached out to cup her face in his hands, possessing her completely. It could've been a scene taken directly from one of those over-sentimental chick flicks she'd overindulged in recently. It was perfect.

Too perfect, that small voice of doom piped up.

It wasn't real; they weren't going to run off into the sunset together at the end of this.

Shut up, Miss Stick-in-the-Mud, and let me enjoy my wild side for once.

While the inner debate went on in her head, her body was making the next move for her. With her arms snaked around his neck and the rest of her draped over him like a silk scarf she was getting the full Joe Braden experience. He was all hard lines and smooth planes, the ideal structure to support her melty bones. They fitted together so well, felt so natural together, she didn't know why she'd worried so much. This dance around each other since her arrival had only been delaying the inevitable and they didn't have much time left together to waste. From now on she was going to take his advice and go with the flow, whatever direction it carried her.

Emily's knees were sliding from under her as he lowered her back onto the floor; their project quickly becoming a victim of their desire beneath their entangled limbs. Joe's body was heavy against hers but she'd never felt more secure, either with herself or another. Despite all her earlier anxieties, anticipating this moment, there was nowhere she'd rather be than here lying with him.

That didn't mean she wasn't a little skittish. She gasped at that first intimate touch as Joe slid his hand under her top to caress her breast, the skin-on-skin contact a shock to her system after all this time.

'You okay?' He immediately withdrew, leaving her feeling cold without the warmth of his touch.

'Mmm-hmm.' She nodded, keen to reconnect before she lost her bottle. It was better if she didn't have time to overthink and when his hands were on her she couldn't think about anything other than how good he made her feel.

'Tell me if this is going too fast,' he whispered against her neck, nuzzling that sensitive skin and stealing any potential argument from her.

'No.' Her breathy impatience saw him seek her out once more, kneading that soft mound into a hardened peak. Far from her usual cautious nature, she wanted to throw herself completely into the moment. She was too busy *feeling* to think or worry and it made her positively wanton, grinding her body against Joe's, aching for more.

His shirt came away easily beneath her busy fingers to reveal the well-defined torso she'd only ogled from afar until now. Up close it was even more impressive as she slid her hands over the bumps and contours of his body. It was amazing that one man was in possession of so much inner and outer beauty and she counted herself lucky she got to experience all of it.

The cool air puckered her nipple ever harder as Joe exposed her fully to his gaze. And his tongue. She moaned and arched up off the floor as he drove her to the brink of insanity with every flick. That little bud seemed to contain every nerve ending in her body, tightened with complete arousal and straining for his touch.

Eyes closed as she surrendered to her needs, she let her hands survey the rest of Joe's body. They slipped easily along his smooth skin until they met that trail of hair leading into the waistband of his trousers. Suddenly her nakedness didn't matter as much as his. She wanted to see all of him, feel all of him pressed against her. Into her.

He sucked in a breath as she unfastened the button and dared to go ever lower to trace the hard ridge of his erection. It was her turn to gasp. There was no denying the strength of his desire for her when the steely evidence was right there beneath her fingertips. The knowledge that the flawed Emily still had the ability to turn him on to this extent was a powerful motivator.

She explored his length and self-control through the fabric of his briefs, enjoying the groans of pleasure and frustration she drew from him with every feathery stroke along his shaft. However, teasing him also meant she was testing the limits of her own restraint and she was never one to inflict unnecessary pain on herself.

She squeezed his taut backside and Joe closed his eyes and tilted his head back in ecstasy. This shameless need to follow her desire and to hell with the consequences was new, exciting, and though she wanted to reach that final peak she didn't want this feeling to end. Although she might spontaneously combust if they didn't bring this to its natural conclusion soon.

She was scrabbling to undo the zip on her own trousers when the door burst open.

'We need your help!'

Emily screamed.

Joe swore.

'Get out!' he shouted, throwing himself on top of her to save what was left of her modesty.

'I'm sorry. Holy—'

She didn't hear the rest as the door closed again but she imagined there was probably an expletive missing at the end of the sentence.

'Was that—?'

'Yeah,' Joe confirmed her worst fears as he leaned his forehead on her chest and swore again.

The best moment of her life had transformed into one of the worst. Her own stepbrother had just walked in on her about to have sex with his best friend.

Lying here half-undressed with an almost naked Joe spread-eagled across the top of her suddenly became tawdry when she viewed it from Peter's perspective. The cold dose of reality brought back all the reasons this should have remained nothing more than a bad idea.

'I need to get up.' She pushed Joe off and covered herself up again, the thrill of the evening well and truly having worn off. It was unfortunate that after everything she'd gone through to reach this point she was back to being a disappointment.

Emily was hunched over, hugging her knees and almost rocking with the trauma of having Peter catch them at it on the floor. Joe knew he was going to have to man up and face the consequences with her stepbrother. The thought of that had killed his arousal stone-dead.

Once he'd relocated his shirt and pulled his trousers back up, he crouched down beside her.

'We didn't do anything wrong,' he whispered, desperate for her to come back to him. They'd acted on their mutual attraction, not committed a crime.

'I know.' She said it so softly and with so little conviction he'd had to read her lips. He could see the shame clouding her face and curling her body into a ball.

If it had been anybody else who'd burst in uninvited he would've read them the Riot Act, but on this occasion Peter had claim on the victim role. He needed to go and do some damage control but he was reluctant to leave Emily there, reflecting on the embarrassment she'd been subjected to because of him. He should've taken better care of her.

He dipped his head to drop a kiss on her lips, hoping to keep that connection alive. They'd come this far and risked so much to get to this point that it would be a shame to take two steps back now, but she remained motionless, unresponsive to the gesture. This sudden impassiveness wasn't something he was simply going to accept after the fire he'd just witnessed from her. He wanted her to stay with him and not give in to unnecessary guilt. She'd had enough of that recently.

With her face cradled in his hands, he teased her lips apart with the tip of his tongue, searching for that woman who'd had her hands down his pants not five minutes ago. Slowly but surely she began to respond, tentatively meeting his tongue with hers and opening her mouth to invite him further. He wanted to scoop her up and carry her off somewhere peaceful and private, preferably with carpet on the floor and a king-size bed. They needed somewhere with no distractions, no outside influences interfering in how they expressed their feelings for one another. Emotionally they mightn't have it all figured out, but until Peter had arrived they'd been happy for their bodies to make their decisions for them.

The sound of banging on the door reverberated around the room.

'Guys, I know this is…er…bad timing but we really have an emergency out here. So if you could postpone this for now and get your clothes on, I'd really appreciate it.' Peter was shouting so loudly it wasn't hard to figure out what he thought of this match. Seeing Joe rolling around half-naked with his stepsister might have played a part in colouring that judgement.

'We have to go. Peter definitely wouldn't be hanging around unless he really had to. It must be serious.' It was Emily who finally became the voice of reason. Someone needed their help, and everything else would have to wait.

Joe was dreading coming face-to-face with Peter more than whatever crisis was going on beyond this one.

'Are we good?' He wanted confirmation before they took this outside.

Emily nodded and attempted a smile. It would have to do until they were alone again and able to speak freely.

There was no putting this off any longer. They couldn't afford to let any awkwardness take precedence over someone's health. Joe opened the door to a scowling Peter.

'It's the chief's son. You'd better come and see him.' He turned on his heel, barely able to look at either of them.

Joe could hardly blame him. He was lucky he hadn't been on the receiving end of a fist. Although there was still time. He quickened his pace to keep up with his probably now ex-mate, aware that Emily was content to hang back.

'What's wrong with him?'

'He's running a fever, vomiting, and generally in a really bad way.'

In this region there was always a chance those symptoms could be more serious than a run-of-the-mill stomach bug. Malaria, typhoid and dengue fever were also commonplace alongside the usual culprits. They were also potentially deadly. He'd seen them all on his travels, along with the variable outcomes.

Joe stopped abruptly.

'We'll need medical supplies if he's too weak to come here for treatment.' It was the first thing he should have checked before heading off, and showed how far his focus had strayed over the course of the evening. This wasn't a typical nine-to-five job where he could clock off and have romantic nights in when he felt like it.

'Of course. There's no way he'd make it back here.' Peter slowed too as if he should also take the blame for the oversight. They were obviously all a little shaken up and not thinking as rationally as they should in their rush to get away from the scene of the alleged crime.

'I'll go back and get them,' Emily piped up from the back.

'Pardon me?' He wasn't sure he'd heard her correctly. Volunteering to go back meant she would have to find her way out to the chief's house alone, in the dark. It was a clear sign how much she was dreading being left with her stepbrother, trying to make conversation. He wasn't looking forward to it much himself.

'I said I'll get what we need and meet you both out there.' She spoke louder, with a determination he couldn't very well object to.

'Will you be able to find your way in the dark?' It was one thing for two ex-soldiers who'd been living here for weeks to track their way back with very little illumination and quite another for Emily, who was still getting to know her way around.

'I'll be fine. I'll grab a lantern from the clinic.'

Oh, yeah, that made sense. He might have done that himself if he hadn't thought he'd need both hands to fend off an irate stepbrother. Peter was keeping it together for now but he knew him well enough to know that rage was bubbling somewhere under that apparently calm surface.

'We're probably going to need antibiotics, paracetamol, a blood-pressure cuff, maybe an IV line—'

'I'm sure I can handle it.' Emily wasted no more time as she spun round and walked towards the light coming from the clinic.

He'd been so busy trying to cover all possibilities he'd neglected to give her any credit as his medically qualified equal in the process. That was another member of the Jackson family he was going to have to try and make amends with later. It wasn't that he was *trying* to tick everyone off tonight, it had simply happened organically.

'You heard her. We'll go on without her.' There was the tone of a big brother/kid sister talk waiting to happen and it wasn't as if Joe could walk away and let them get on with it. He was very much a part of it.

'Mate, I know what that must've looked like.' He was literally cringing at having to remind Peter of what he'd just witnessed but he didn't want to ignore the obvious tension and have their friendship fester because of it.

'Unless I'm wrong, it looked like you were seducing my sister on the floor.' Peter's teeth were a glistening vision of naked aggression in the moonlight and Joe braced himself for imminent attack.

'You're partially right. Although I wouldn't have said

it was all one-sided. Emily's a woman who knows her own mind—'

'I don't want to know the details, thanks.'

'Right. I just mean we both like each other. We're having some fun together.'

They'd been having a lot of fun right up until real life had barged in on them and burst their bubble. Up until the moment his love interest's protective big brother had come looking for her, they had been discovering their own little piece of paradise. Alone in that room, in each other's company, in each other's arms it had been easy to forget their lives outside that door and not consider the consequences of their actions. Such as protection. They hadn't discussed it and Joe had definitely been too carried away in the moment to think about it. Although his body had protested at Peter's interruption perhaps it hadn't been as ill-timed as he'd first thought.

A pregnancy would not have been a souvenir either of them would want to take away from this holiday romance. Emily was just getting her life back on track after her ex-husband's betrayal and her bravery today was proof of that. She didn't need to be tied to him for the rest of her days and vice versa. His personal issues would forever cloud any sort of long-term relationship and while this was still only a fling there was no reason to start trying to explain them. Unlike Emily, he wasn't ready to share them publicly.

'I thought I could trust you, man. You know what she's been through.'

'Yeah, and she needs this time away to try and forget it. I promise I won't do anything to hurt her.' He wouldn't be able to live with himself if he did. There'd be no trek long enough, or climb high enough to help him forget intentionally hurting either of them.

'You'd better not. I'd hate to have to hand back my halo

and take up arms again.' At least there was a hint of humour in the thinly veiled threat.

Joe held his hand up. 'Hey, I don't want to be the one responsible for sending you back to the dark side.'

'Then stay away from my sister.'

Okay, there wasn't a trace of a veil hiding that one. If only it was as easy as keeping his distance. Been there, done that, ended up rolling around on the floor with her.

'Sorry, bro, but I'm not going to do that. I don't want any bad blood between us but I like Emily a lot.' Joe waited for the explosions to start as he defiantly went against his friend's wishes. He only hoped Emily was as steadfast in continuing the relationship after this or else putting his friendship with Peter in jeopardy was all for nothing.

Instead of further threats of fisticuffs, Peter let out a sigh. The resigned sound of his disappointment was almost as devastating to Joe's equilibrium as the right hook he'd been expecting. Although he didn't want to examine his feelings for Emily too deeply for fear of what he'd discover, it spoke volumes that he was willing to risk upsetting the very guy he'd come here to help.

'I guess it's my fault for pushing you two together but I thought I could trust you not to take advantage of her.'

Another blow where it hurt the most.

'I would never do that. I respect her too much.'

'It didn't look that way to me.'

Joe's insides shrivelled up with shame. It would be easy to misinterpret what had been happening between him and Emily as something tawdry when it had evolved so naturally and beautifully. He regretted Peter walking in on them but not a second of the evening up until then.

'I'm sorry if you saw anything untoward but at the end of the day Emily's a grown woman who makes her own decisions.' There it was, the comment that could finally break their bromance. He was effectively telling the guy to butt out.

'That lack of judgement is the reason she ran out here in the first place.' Another sigh. 'I could use a cup of kava right about now, and a bucket of eye bleach. Your bare backside is not an image I want to go to sleep with tonight.'

Joe exhaled a nervous laugh. 'In that case, what do you say we forget it ever happened? I promise not to hurt your sister and keep my backside covered at all times.' It was the best compromise he could come to and mean it. Anything more than that and he knew he'd have difficulty keeping his word. He and Emily still had unfinished business.

'Hmm. I guess that'll have to do but the first sign of Joe-related tears from my little sister—'

'I know, I know, I should start swimming.'

'As long as we're clear.'

'Crystal.'

It wasn't anything Joe hadn't expected. All things considered, he'd got off lightly. Yasi Island really had mellowed Peter out. In another time and place he wouldn't have thought twice about knocking him out and Joe wouldn't have blamed him. He'd spent many a long night on training exercises talking about his family, shared all the big achievements in Emily's life with Joe as he'd read about them in cherished letters he'd received in Afghanistan. It was only natural tonight would seem like a betrayal and only time would let him prove otherwise.

As they reached the chief's house he was glad they'd kind of cleared the air. Whatever was ailing the patient inside was undoubtedly going to be difficult enough to manage, without the added stress of a duel over Emily's honour. He glanced back, checking for signs of her following, and could just about make out a bobbing flicker of light snaking through the village in the distance. Whatever the rest of the night had in store for him, he knew he would get through it better with her at his side.

CHAPTER NINE

EMILY KNEW JOE would have everything under control until she got there. At least as far as the medical emergency went. There were no obvious signs of a scuffle as she followed in their wake to the chief's house. She hadn't stumbled over any bodies so she'd take that as a sign he and Peter had either worked things out or chosen to ignore the humiliation they'd all just endured. It was going to take her longer to get over it.

She prayed Joe's quick actions had covered most of her blushes but it hadn't been enough to disguise what they'd been up to. Peter definitely would not approve, not because he was a prude, he was an ex-soldier after all, but because she'd chosen his best friend to get over her break-up. At the same time she realised Joe wasn't something she was willing to give up. Not yet. That time would come soon enough and she didn't want to miss out on anything he had to offer.

Tonight had only been a taster of what they could have together and not something she would easily forget when her body was still thrumming with sexual awareness. As long as she remembered this wasn't real, that they were never going to be part of each other's lives away from here, she shouldn't have to worry about anything other than enjoying the moment with Joe. Well, apart from her stepbrother walking in on them after passion had taken hold.

A shudder ripped through her. She was an adult, one who'd gone through an acrimonious split from her husband and deserved some fun and excitement in her life. That didn't mean one frowning look from her stepbrother wouldn't regress her back to that role of naughty kid sister, even when she hadn't done anything other than let loose for once. They were going to have to discuss what had happened, what was happening, between her and Joe so she could reassure him she knew what she was doing. Even when it seemed so far removed from her normal behaviour.

Joe and Peter already had proceedings under way when she caught up with them at either side of the patient's bedside.

'We thought he'd be more comfortable in my bed and we've stripped him down to try and bring down the fever.' Her stepbrother didn't waste any time on small talk, which suited her fine. They could discuss personal matters later in private, or not at all—either worked for her.

The small room was cramped with the chief and the three of them crowded inside, so she stood back, trying to remain invisible until she was needed. No such luck when Joe had anything to do with it.

'I need a thermometer if you have one in there.'

She rummaged around her bag and produced one while he stood with his hand out, waiting, as if he was the lead surgeon and she was the theatre nurse. It wasn't much of a stretch, she supposed, in this scenario where she was a spectator rather than the one taking readings.

'You've got a temperature of forty degrees, so we really need to get that down. I'll need plenty of water to keep him hydrated and we could use something to keep him sponged down. It would really help if we could clear as many people out of here as possible. Emily, I'm going to need your help to get this under control.' The crowd parted like the Red Sea to make a clear path between her and Joe, everyone watching for her reaction. Probably for different reasons.

'I'll get the water.' Peter's gaze flitted suspiciously between them as though they were trying to engineer another reason to be alone.

He shouldn't have worried. Emily needed time to process what had taken place tonight before they ended up back in the same scenario. It seemed neither of them were able to control themselves when left to their own devices and as yet she hadn't decided if that was detrimental to her well-being or not. Physically, there was no doubt they were compatible. It was the more *personal* aspects of getting involved that caused her concern. Her emotions were still in recovery and she didn't think they could cope with another mauling, no matter how unintentional.

Eventually Peter made a move towards the door, with the chief soon following behind.

Although it didn't make the room any less suffocating as she had to face Joe and try not to mention the incredible time they'd had together before fate had intervened.

'Nete is presenting with fever, along with muscle and joint pain. Did you bring some paracetamol?' He put her to shame with his thoughts being solely for his patient and not lingering back at their love shack. From here on they were merely medical colleagues working together to treat their patient. Everything beyond that could wait until their patient was back on track.

'Yes. That should help bring that temperature down too.' Important in preventing fits and further complications.

'Can you sit up for me?' He put a hand on the young

man's back and eased him up from the bed amid a lot of wincing.

Joe gestured for her to stand beside him. It was only then that she noticed the rash dotted across Nete's flushed skin, little islands of white in a sea of red.

'Have you been near any stagnant water recently?'

Emily's mind had instantly gone to all of those childhood illnesses mostly eradicated via the vaccination programme back home, but Joe obviously had different ideas about the source of the rash.

'I was down by the river a few days ago.'

Joe frowned, clearly disturbed by the information.

She knew herself that areas of stagnant water were a breeding ground for mosquitoes, airborne viruses and bad news.

'Could you get me the blood-pressure cuff, Emily?'

'I'm just going to wrap this around your arm,' she said to Nete. 'There will be a tightening sensation as we inflate the cuff but there's no need to panic. It's just how we test your blood pressure.' She knew the patient was too lethargic to really pay attention to what they were doing but it was important for her to have a role here and not fall back into the old pattern of feeling surplus to requirements. Joe had specifically asked her to assist him and this kind of emergency was exactly why she was here.

The lines on Joe's forehead grew deeper with the low reading she recorded. Although low blood pressure could be a sign of good health and fitness in someone of this age, coupled with the other symptoms it could be an indicator of heart or neurological disorders.

Joe loosened the cuff, squinting at the arm beneath as he did so and refastening it. 'I'm just going to do something called a tourniquet test. This means the cuff will tighten again for a few minutes.'

Emily watched in silence as he inflated it to the midpoint between the systolic and diastolic blood pressures, unease snaking through her body. She'd read up on tropical illnesses before venturing out here to practise and the tourniquet test was used to diagnose something far more serious than gastroenteritis. Dengue fever, also known as break-bone fever because of the associated joint pain. It was no wonder he was whimpering with pain even in his dazed state or that Joe was becoming increasingly concerned.

There was the threat of potentially fatal dengue haemorrhagic fever or dengue shock syndrome, neither of which they were equipped to treat. There was no intensive care unit in which to treat him if he needed it. Neither was there access to laboratory tests to confirm the initial diagnosis, which was why they would have to rely on this tourniquet test. With more than twenty petechial red spots from broken capillary blood vessels visible per square inch of skin, Joe's hunch was proved right.

There was no part of that diagnosis she found positive. Not only had she missed it, they were going to have a fight on their hands if his condition worsened.

'Okay, we'll let you rest again but you're going to have to sit up and make sure you drink plenty. Emily and I will go and see where Peter got to with that water.' Joe undid the cuff and tried to make him comfortable again before gesturing for Emily to join him outside.

'How did you know it was dengue?' It would probably have been well down her list of possibilities causing the patient so much discomfort and she could've wasted precious time in reaching the same diagnosis.

'I've seen it a few times on my travels. It's a nasty one. The rash and the joint pain are usually the main indicators, along with the more common symptoms.'

'What's the best way to approach this?' She wasn't

afraid to defer to him on this subject since it wasn't something she'd ever come across before.

'We need to keep an eye on him through the night in case his condition worsens. For now the paracetamol and tepid sponging should help control the fever at least, and if need be we can hook up an IV to make sure his fluid levels are balanced. We don't want to give any NSAIDs, such as ibuprofen or aspirin, in case they aggravate the risk of bleeding.'

Peter arrived back to meet them outside the room with the water and cloths. 'Bad news?'

Their faces must've expressed their concerns that a secondary infection could complicate matters beyond their capabilities with the limited medical supplies they had available.

'Dengue.' Joe shared their suspicions with Peter, then went back into the house to break it to the rest of the family, leaving her alone with her stepbrother and an awkward silence.

In the end Emily decided in the spirit of her new bolder persona she should be the one to broach the subject causing the tension. Except she didn't know how to appropriately rephrase, 'I know you're mad at me for getting jiggy with your mate but I literally fancy the pants off him.'

'I really like him. Joe, that is.' She went with inarticulate phrasing in the end.

Peter screwed his eyes tightly shut as though he was still trying to rid himself of the memory. 'I think I got that.'

'I mean, we didn't plan anything but we're, er, enjoying each other's company while we're here.' Her cheeks were burning as she tried to explain her outrageous behaviour to her religious sibling.

'As it was pointed out to me earlier, it's your life, Emily. But I would hate to see you get hurt. I've known Joe a long time. He's a good guy but he's not the commitment type. You've only just come out of a long-term relationship, your only relationship, and I don't want you to think he's the answer to being on your own. He'll be back on his travels in another couple of weeks.'

'So will I. You don't have to worry, I'm going into this with my eyes fully open. I know you're all loved up with Keresi at the minute, but the last thing I want is to be tied to another man.' However this progressed she was under no illusion that she was going home as part of a couple. The most this could ever be was a fling, a temporary arrangement, if that's what they both wanted.

'It's that obvious, huh?' It was refreshing to see her stepbrother take his turn at blushing. This woman clearly meant a lot to him. On the plus side, it took the onus off her and Joe.

'Well, not in the "found half-naked together" sense of obvious, but, yeah, I can tell. Is it serious?'

'We've been hanging out a lot and, yeah, I think I'm in deep.' His bashful smile said as much.

Emily gave him a playful punch on the arm, careful not to spill any of the water he was carrying. 'I'm so happy for you. For us.' She wanted him to understand they were both where they wanted to be in terms of relationships, or non-relationship in her case. The jury was still out on the official classification of her status.

'I haven't decided if I'll be leaving with you at the end of the month. I might stick around a while longer.'

'You do whatever feels right. I can always come back and visit when I need a bro-fix.' She smiled for his benefit, even though her heart broke a little more at the thought of losing him to Yasi permanently. Not that she would begrudge him this island paradise or a chance at happiness. She envied it.

'I haven't made any decision yet.'

'Something tells me you'll find it hard to leave.' She knew she would. If she had the choice between her lonely existence, bound by the rules of her position and the confinement of her office, or the freedom to help people out here with Joe by her side, she knew which one she'd take now.

'All I can do is take each day as it comes.'

'Is that the island motto or something? They should print that on T-shirts and sell them as souvenirs,' she said with a touch of bitterness. It was easier to do that when your days weren't limited to double digits.

He gave a hearty laugh, which did nothing to alleviate this particular case of the green-eyed monster. The clock was ticking on whatever this was with Joe, and she didn't have the luxury of deciding its fate. Peter didn't know how lucky he was. For her the dream would all be over too soon.

With the pressure of time weighing heavily on her mind, she thought of her patient, to whom it mattered most tonight. The next hours would be crucial in determining the severity of his illness and how effectively they'd be able to manage it.

'I should get back to work and take this water in before it reaches room temperature.'

'I'll give you a hand.'

True to his word, Peter helped her to get Nete upright and helped him drink the water, while she sponged him down. It wasn't long before Joe came back to join them and sent at least one temperature in the room soaring back up again.

'Isn't there a drug or something we can give him to counteract this?' Peter quizzed them, as he struggled to keep the lethargic patient upright.

'If only.' There was nothing she wanted more than to be able to give this boy a tablet and fix everything that ailed him. That was the kind of medicine she was used to—diagnosis, treatment, cure. Rare illnesses such as dengue weren't something she came across very often and when they did crop up the patients were invariably referred elsewhere. That wasn't an option out here. Even if they could get him transported to hospital, the journey alone could kill him. Seeing Nete in pain, following his progress right through, somehow made it real and personal. It was down to her and Joe to get him through this and out the other side.

Joe took another temperature reading and shook his head. 'There might be one thing we can try…'

As Emily took a peek at the thermometer she knew they needed to try something more than they were already doing. 'What is it?'

Joe exhaled a hard breath and it was a few heartbeats before he spoke as if he was debating whether or not his idea was even worth sharing. 'I mean, it's not scientifically proven or anything but when I was in India I saw them use the juice from papaya leaves to treat dengue.'

'Papaya leaves?' Although it wouldn't do any harm to try, Emily wasn't convinced that would really make much difference to his condition.

'I know it sounds ridiculous but I did do some follow up research into the properties of papaya leaves after seeing them used. Apparently they are packed with enzymes that are supposed to help clot the blood and normalise platelet count. It's worth a shot, right?' He was the only one offering a blink of hope, no matter how far away it appeared from the current reality of the situation.

'Definitely, but where do we get them and what do we do with them?' It was at times like this she missed the luxury of twenty-four-hour supermarkets and smoothie bars. She was too used to the convenience of modern life, and making simple requests like this without them seem impossible.

'I'm sure someone will know where to find them, then all we have to do is crush them.' Joe made it sound so simple when it scared Emily to put her faith in anything other than conventional medicine. That was probably the beauty of them working together and combining their so very different experiences.

'I know where we can find some. I'll go. I'm sure you can manage without me.' Peter gave a wry smile as he left on his mission. He clearly wasn't about to let go of her embarrassment any time soon but a nod and a wink was better than a frowny face and a half-battered Joe.

The patient gave a soft snore, oblivious to events unfolding all around him. They'd let him sleep through the pain until Joe concocted his marvellous medicine. In the meantime, Emily took the small battery-operated fan she kept in her bag and set it by the bed. Every little bit helped.

'Are things okay with you two, then?' She figured it was safe to ask now the initial awkwardness appeared to have passed.

'Yeah. We're good. You?'

She nodded. They'd known their actions would complicate all manner of things and yet that hadn't mattered at the time. It shouldn't matter now either since they'd addressed Peter's concerns. 'I can't say he's ecstatic about it but he knows where we're coming from. I think he's dodging Cupid's arrows himself at the minute.'

'I would say that little sucker struck his target long ago.' Joe's laugh reached across the bed to her and all the way down to curl her toes. She was already missing that carefree couple of hours they'd had. Who knew when they'd get to spend time together again? Or if it would ever be quite the same now they'd always be on their guard?

'Well, I hope he didn't give you too much of a hard time.'

'Nothing I couldn't handle,' he said, with the sexy smile of a man secure in his own skin. He could look after himself but Emily knew he would never have lifted a hand to do anything against his best friend except in defence. Even then, she suspected, he might've let Peter vent his anger unchecked if it made him feel better.

'There wasn't any blood spilled so I'd call that a win. I wouldn't want to be the cause of any unpleasantness between you.' She was fully aware of the special bond they had and, as far as she could see, the only real friend each of them had. It would be selfish of her to think a holiday fling should mean more to Joe than everything he'd gone through with Peter.

Joe carefully laid the cold cloth he was holding across Nete's forehead and walked around to the side of the bed where she was standing. There was definitely a shift in the atmosphere as he took her hand and turned her to face him, as if by entering her personal space he'd pushed out all the negative space around her and replaced it with crackling sexual energy.

'For the record, it would've been totally worth it.' His voice was a gravelly aphrodisiac, taking her right back to that moment before Peter had interrupted them. She'd been hovering on the brink of something amazing and she knew she wanted to go back there some time soon once they knew their patient was out of danger.

'I'm glad you think so.' Her mouth was suddenly dry and she had to moisten her lips with her tongue before she was able to speak. It hadn't been intended as a provocative action but she didn't miss the flare of desire in Joe's eyes as he watched her. They'd better get a move on with that miracle cure.

'I know so.' He dipped his head and left the ghost of a kiss on her lips; too quick to make a solid physical impact but with enough intention to stop her fretting that their time had already passed. There was still hope they could explore this chemistry if and when the opportunity arose again. Despite all the obstacles, Joe still wanted her and that was the best medicine in the world for her.

Joe hated it that they were pinning everything on this bowl of green mush on his say-so. Perhaps he should have kept it to himself and simply passed this off as an energy drink. That way the consequences of its failure wouldn't rest entirely on his shoulders. If this didn't work, the boy's condition was entirely down to the fates. Best-case scenario, he would recover on his own anyway. Worst-case scenario could lead to organ dysfunction, toxic shock and other life-threatening complications that required hospital intervention. Not two travelling doctors with little more than a first-aid kit.

He crushed the leaves with the wooden pestle and mortar he'd borrowed and ground away his fears before anyone could see them. As he'd watched the medicine men in India do, he squeezed the juice out into a bowl with his bare, clean hands. They didn't dilute the juice with water or add salt or sugar so neither did he, unwilling to take the chance of reducing its benefits.

'We need you to sit up and drink this.'

Peter and Emily took one arm each to help Nete sit up while Joe tilted the bowl to his lips for him to sip at. He hadn't tasted the juice himself but the sight of it and the patient's puckered mouth told him it didn't have the sweet, palatable taste of commercial medicines.

It had taken Peter a good couple of hours to source the papaya leaves for him, during which time he and Emily had managed to set aside their unresolved personal feelings for one another and focus on their patient's recovery. They'd seen a small decrease in his temperature as a result of the course of treatment provided already but not enough to sit back. The fever itself, he knew, could be biphasic, breaking and returning, and any sudden disappearance could be one of the warning signs of dengue haemorrhagic fever, the next critical level of the condition.

'When will we know if this is working?' Nete was understandably anxious for an instant cure for his pain but Joe didn't want to make any definite promises.

'You'll have to keep taking the juice at regular intervals through the night, I'm afraid.' He shot Emily a look of apology too since this was the first time she was hearing the news.

'We're all in for a long night by the sound of it.' Emily threw her hat in the ring to become part of the night watch alongside him.

Peter, on the other hand, already looked dead on his feet after his mad dash across the island, to retrieve the precious foliage. He'd done his part and keeping him here wouldn't serve any real practical purpose.

'I think you could use a few hours' sleep, mate. If you want to grab forty winks while you can, we'll give you a shout if we need your help.'

'I'll be fine,' Peter protested, blinking his eyes open wide.

'The last thing we need is to be another man down because you've overdone it. Now, take the advice of *two* doctors and get some sleep. You can take the next shift. Scoot.' Emily was the one to finally shoo him away so they could concentrate on the one patient they already had.

They'd do that better without the spectre of their indiscretion lingering in the room between them. Peter's reluctance to leave them alone again was proof enough that he hadn't got over it yet, even if they'd decided to leave it behind them until they had time and space to deal with it. Or carry on where they'd left off.

When it came to Emily all his common sense seemed to go out of the window and he could no longer predict his own actions from one minute to the next. Ordinarily he thrived on that level of excitement but tonight's events had shown him just how destructive that lapse in judgement could be. By continuing relations with Emily he was playing a dangerous game but he didn't think it was one he could quit any time soon.

'I don't know how you managed to keep control of an entire regiment. One pig-headed male is more than enough to deal with,' Emily huffed, as she won the battle of wills and common sense with her stepbrother.

To her it was a throwaway comment more about man's inability to admit personal weakness, something he knew a lot about. To him, any reference to his role in the military was a stark reminder of all the people he'd let down when they'd needed him most.

'I'm not sure I did.'

'There's no need for modesty. I'm sure you saved the lives of countless men on the front line and I know you pulled Peter out of a few tight spots.'

The patient was sleeping soundly now between them, dosed with papaya leaf juice and paracetamol and as cool as they could get him for now, so Joe stepped back from the bed for a little more space. He took a seat on the floor in the corner of the room and sipped at the cool water the chief had provided for them. Unfortunately, Emily followed him, apparently determined to carry on this conversation.

He'd probably played a part in saving lives in close-quarter combat. There were fleeting memories of bullet-ridden and shattered men he'd patched up and sent back in Chinooks to the base hospital, who he knew had later recovered from their injuries, but those faded against the vivid images of the last ambush he'd been caught up in.

He'd had to rely on the expertise of other medical personnel through that one when he'd *become* one of the casualties instead of being the one helping them.

'I did what I had to.' Mostly.

He took another sip of water, even the thought of the desert heat and that feeling of powerlessness making his mouth dry. Emily was oblivious to his discomfort, leaning forward, her head resting on her chin, listening intently as though he was telling her a bedtime story and not recounting the horrors of war.

'Do you miss it? I mean, I know Peter found it hard to adjust to civilian life again. I imagine it must be harder still if you were battling to save lives every day and suddenly no longer practising medicine. That must have been a huge departure for you.'

'It wasn't my choice.' The injustice of the situation forced its way to his lips before he could stop the words forming.

Emily cocked her head to one side, no doubt waiting for an explanation. He sighed, resigned to the fact he was going to have to reveal his biggest shame. Worse than that, he'd have to watch her reaction to it. Details of his hearing loss weren't something he often discussed. Generally he didn't stay in company long enough for it to become apparent. Asking people to repeat themselves, or missing snippets of conversation altogether, only became an issue if it was an ongoing problem. He didn't see the need to highlight his weakness and face more discrimination, decisions made on his behalf because of a perceived disability. The only reason he was considering telling her about it now was because she'd been brave enough to face her demons in his presence. Now it was his turn.

He took a deep breath.

'I had to take medical retirement after the IED that killed Batesy and Ste.' He debated whether or not to go as far as spilling his guts over the guilt he felt over the incident but decided against it. No one would ever understand how much his failing had affected him, still affected him, and he didn't expect them to. That was his own personal wallowing pool.

When Emily didn't launch into her usual line of questioning, which he'd expected to draw the information out gradually, he was forced to elaborate.

'The explosion damaged my hearing and the army decided they didn't want to take the chance of having a partially deaf soldier on the front line who couldn't hear the enemy coming.' The irony was that it was the stealth of the insurgents that had done the damage in the first place.

'Couldn't you have continued your medical expertise in one of the hospitals or in some sort of training capacity?'

There had been no gasp of shock as he broke the news. Although he wasn't looking for sympathy, he had expected some sort of emotional reaction. Here he was, spilling a secret so easily to her that usually only came out when circumstances forced it from him, and she was treating it as a minor ailment that could've been remedied with some paperwork shuffling. She should've understood how great the loss of his career had been when she was so tied to her own. If it wasn't for her own medical expertise keeping her afloat in the aftermath of her marriage she might have felt just as lost as he had when he'd first left the army.

'I was a soldier as well as a medic. I belonged in the field, not cooped up in some *safe* place while the rest of my colleagues were risking their lives. That blast stole my career from me and left me half the man I used to be.' There, he'd spelled it out to her in case she was missing the bit about him essentially being worthless to the army.

'It may have felt like that at the time but you're so much

more than the army. You've proved that with the work you've done here, and everywhere else on your travels.'

Joe wasn't sure if he imagined her flinching at the picture he'd painted since she spoke so coolly. Too coolly. Too precisely. Now he thought about it, he hadn't once had to ask her to repeat herself or speak up since they'd first met. She always spoke clearly, facing him, so he could read her lips, even if he couldn't hear her every word.

'You already knew.' The realisation hit him hard. All this time he'd been trying to impress her and she'd probably been aware of his inadequacy all along.

'Sorry?'

'Peter told you why I had to leave the army?'

The blush gave her away even before she confirmed his hunch. 'Only because I thought you were being rude by ignoring me.'

'I get that a lot.' He managed a half-smile at the thought of how riled she must've been at him for Peter to have told her. It was some consolation he hadn't simply been the subject of gossip between them but telling Emily was a big deal for him. It should have been his decision, his privilege to tell her.

'I think that makes us even. My secret for yours.' Emily nudged him, trying to make light of the moment.

It would be easy for him to lose his rag and tell her it was none of her business but she wasn't to blame for his inability to deal with this. No one was, not even Peter. He couldn't hide away from his hearing issue for ever and if he took a leaf out of her book he'd front it out and people would simply have to accept it. The strength of her courage became even more apparent when he thought of shining a spotlight on his insecurity for the whole world to see. Still, he'd share details of his deafness before he'd let anyone in on the events of that fateful day and his responsibility for it.

'How about a pact never to mention either?'

'Done.'

'And in answer to your original question, yes, I do miss it. Not the heat or the injuries my friends suffered, but the excitement and that sense of belonging. I had a role, a reason to be.' He shut his mouth before he said anything more. It wasn't in his nature to take a dip in self-pity, and especially not with spectators. Coming across as a sad sack certainly wasn't going to improve his chances of finishing what he'd started with Emily tonight. He was supposed to be the fun, uncomplicated side of this partnership. A traumatised ex-vet who needed sex to justify his existence probably wouldn't seem as attractive.

'You have a role out here. You're needed here. But I guess that's why you don't stick around. It never gets dull for you if you're always moving from one place to another.' Emily hugged her knees against her chest as she psychoanalysed him. Joe guessed she found that harder to understand than him hiding his disability when stability and security seemed to be what she craved most in her life. Things she would never find with him.

'Exactly. New places, new people get the adrenaline pumping for me.' The closest he came to that without leaving the island was when he and Emily were alone together. That was when he felt most alive, most validated as a person.

Once she left Yasi there would be absolutely no reason for him to stick around.

CHAPTER TEN

'MORNING.' EMILY YAWNED a greeting to Peter and Miriama as she passed them in the hallway. She and Joe had managed to grab a few hours' sleep on a couple of makeshift mattresses close by when they'd volunteered to take over the early morning shift. She thought all was well since she'd been left to wake up in her own time, until she saw that Joe had already vacated his bed.

'Morning.' Peter handed her some lemon tea, its bitter zing guaranteed to wake her up.

She cradled the cup in her hands, letting the comforting warmth spread through her weary body before she took a sip. 'How is Nete?'

'He's a bit brighter today. Joe's with him if you want a professional assessment.'

She trusted Peter's word but she did want to see for herself. An early morning Joe fix might just set her up for the day too.

'Hey,' she said when she saw Joe, thinking how unfair it was that he still looked devastatingly handsome on so little sleep. No doubt she had the world's worst bed hair and panda eyes, while his crumpled clothes and morning stubble simply elevated his hunk status.

'Hi, sleepyhead.' He had the bright eyes and cheerful

demeanour of someone who'd been awake for a while, or had somehow got his hands on a shot of *actual* caffeine.

Either way, she would have preferred to have been included than not. 'You should have woken me.'

'You were sleeping so soundly I hated to disturb you. Besides, you probably wouldn't have heard me above your snoring.' He shared the joke with their patient, who was now sitting up unassisted and laughing at her expense.

'I do not snore!' At least, she didn't think she did, unless a year of sleeping alone had somehow caused it to manifest. She was sure Greg would've told her if it had ever been a problem. He'd never been shy about pointing out her faults and not in such a jokey fashion either. In fact, she could see now that he'd been downright cruel at times, playing on her insecurities until she'd hated herself for not being the woman he'd obviously wanted.

At least now she was beginning to see she wasn't the only one who'd failed at that relationship. If Greg had accepted her as unconditionally as Joe seemed to, there would never have been a need to constantly belittle her. In hindsight that was probably what had made her cling to stability as much as she had. She'd needed something to make her feel safe and secure, with her husband constantly undermining her. Now that she'd moved on, found herself at peace with who she was, she didn't intend to return to that dark, uncertain place.

'I'm only messing with you. You needed the rest. I'm used to getting by on very little sleep.'

She faked a smile as he reminded her of their contrasting lifestyles. He was always going to be the drifter, content to take life one day at a time, when all she wanted was her own bed and job security. If she was realistic they'd probably only made a connection because they'd been thrown together on this tiny island and she didn't want to be with another man for all the wrong reasons.

'So, how are we getting on?' She glanced over the readings Peter had jotted down during the night, keeping track of his progress.

'Fever's broken, fluid intake is steady, as is urine output, and he's hungry, which is always a good sign.' Relief was etched all over Joe's smiling face, even though he hadn't once given in to panic during their stint last night.

'I'm so glad to hear that.' At times it had been touch-and-go whether or not they'd get to this apparent recovery phase. They'd sweated right along with the patient through every painful stage of the illness. Not that it was over yet, but Joe was right, the outcome was looking more favourable now than it had done at certain low points of the night. It had been a long shift and she had a new-found respect for hospital workers for whom the long hours and clean-up were simply part of the job. All worth it, though, if it meant the worst had passed.

'I think it's safe for us to nip home and get freshened up, if Peter and Miriama don't mind taking over here a bit longer?' Joe was able to put his question directly to the other volunteers as they entered the room on cue.

'No problem at all,' Miriama assured them both.

Emily would never dream of taking advantage but even a bucket of cold water seemed like a luxury right now to someone in last night's clothes who'd spent most of the last twelve hours mopping fevered brows and vomit.

'Er…the chief might have other ideas for you.'

Peter interrupted her immediate plans with a worrying comment. If there was some sort of ceremony to celebrate renewed health, Emily hoped she could still grab five minutes' privacy for a wash and change of clothes.

'We won't be long. Tell him we'll be back in our rightful places in no time at all.' Joe added his support to her cause, clearly with the same need to feel human again. They couldn't possibly be taken seriously as medical professionals dressed in wrinkled date-night clothes as if they'd just stumbled in from a club.

'Yeah, yeah, you can still go and get changed. I mean he has plans for the rest of your day. He wants to throw a beach picnic in your honour for saving his son.'

'That sounds lovely.'

'There's really no need. Besides, we're not completely out of the woods yet.' Joe talked over her acceptance with some uncharacteristic reluctance to take part on one of the spontaneous gatherings.

Emily pouted as the menfolk battled to plan her day for her. 'I haven't seen the beach since the day I arrived. You're the one who's always telling me to chill, take time out for me and stop stressing about deserting my post. Or is that only when it suits you?'

This was coming close to their first real argument, but while she was bracing herself for a showdown, Joe clenched his jaw and bit back whatever retort was on his tongue.

'He really wants to show you his gratitude and we can hold the fort for you here until you get back. You both need the break.' Peter was so insistent it would be a shame to send him back to the chief with bad news.

'We'd love to, wouldn't we, Joe?' She pushed her luck that tiny bit further. Once he had time to think about it he'd see some fresh air, a paddle in the sea and a picnic lunch might be the best medicine to revitalise two weary medics.

Neither his scowl nor his grunt were in keeping with that theory but he didn't object verbally and she took that as an uneasy acceptance. A complete role reversal from their usual power play. This time she was the one pushing him to try something different. Emily understood his concerns but the others were well versed in the treatment to give in their absence. Bar chartering a private plane to get their patient to a hospital, there was little more any of them could do if his condition worsened. The next time this illness struck the island it was entirely possible Miriama would be the only person here to treat it anyway. At least, that's how Emily justified this time out to herself.

It wasn't long before she and Joe were heading back to get ready for their lunch date, regardless of his reluctance to join the 'keep calm and carry on' party.

'You shouldn't have done that.'

'Why not? I think we earned a break. Anyway, aren't you the one always reminding me how much I'll offend people by not participating in these things? It's lunch, not a mutiny. I'm still coming back to resume my doctor duties once I've been fed. It might not be up to the culinary standards of your beans on toast feast but I'm hungry, sleep-deprived and generally in need of some me time. That might sound selfish but I think a less grouchy me will benefit everyone in the long run. We'll be back before you know it.'

She could see why he was so concerned about leaving their patient but she genuinely believed Nete was over the worst of it and they wouldn't be gone for too long. It was never going to be a continuation of their ruined date with so many others in attendance but it would do them good to get out of there for a while.

'That won't be as soon as you think.'

'What makes you say that?'

'Their idea of a beach picnic is on another island. It's a beautiful place but not very practical for getting back to a patient in the event of an emergency.'

'Why on earth didn't you tell me?' She wanted to scream at him for standing back while she'd blathered on about what *she* needed. If she'd known it would come at the possible cost of their patient's welfare she never would've pursued this.

He shrugged, increasing the chances of her giving those shoulders a shake herself. 'You didn't give me much of a chance. You seemed so determined to accept and I didn't want to worry the others unnecessarily.'

But it was apparently okay to make her more anxious by keeping the details to himself until it was too late to do anything. She ground her teeth, stifling her exasperation.

'Now what do we do?' She'd landed them in a tricky situation, caught between offending the chief and potentially jeopardising his son's health.

'Now we go and put on our beach clothes and graciously accept our host's invitation. We'll leave instructions for the treatment we would've carried out ourselves and keep our fingers crossed this works out.' His smile didn't travel any further than his lips and Emily knew it was only to placate her.

She'd messed up but something told her Joe would be the one to accept responsibility should the worst happen.

So much for acting spontaneously. It never ended well for her.

CHAPTER ELEVEN

After her longed-for freshen-up, Emily decided to go with the outfit she'd worn when she'd first arrived on the island. The maxi-dress wasn't any more practical than the last time but it was comfortable and put her back in holiday mode. The deed was done, they were leaving the island, so she may as well enjoy it.

She met up with Joe where they'd had that initial encounter at the water's edge, although there were a few more island greeters this time. He was wearing the same outfit as he had that day too, which she put down to their strong connection—or karma. Or the distinct lack of wardrobe choices available to them on the island.

At least he was smiling properly this time as he walked towards her. 'I've left the locum doctors with enough papaya leaves to paper the room with and a promise we'll be back before nightfall.'

'I'm sure everything will be fine.' She was trying to convince herself since it was too late to undo her mistake without causing panic.

They joined the small band of locals weighed down with armfuls of food for their day out. It seemed an age since she'd landed here with no knowledge of what she'd been getting herself into. Only a few days later she had friends who wanted to throw her a celebratory lunch, and a man who seemed to like her. If they ever found themselves alone again they might actually get to explore what that meant.

'You look beautiful, by the way,' he said, and pressed a kiss to her cheek, drawing a few giggles from the kids in the assembled crowd.

'I'm actually quite excited about this.' She meant about their island hopping but it worked for Joe kisses too. No matter how chaste, or not, the second his lips touched her she was on fire with desire for him. Sooner or later she was going to have to let it burn itself out or extinguish the flames altogether. In the end there would be nothing but ashes left anyway and a memory of what could have been.

'So are they.' He nodded in the direction of their happy travelling companions who'd come together in their honour. Those who could afford to take some time out of their busy day, at least. She and Joe really were very privileged to have such generosity bestowed on them when resources were so limited out here. That kind of respect and appreciation meant more to her than monetary bonuses or finishing work on time every night. There was a definite attraction to the laid-back lifestyle out here that wasn't just about her co-worker.

'Where is this place we're going to?' Her adventurous spirit hadn't completely run away with her. On seeing their mode of transport, a couple of dinghies that looked as though they'd been washed ashore during the last hurricane, she was suddenly keen to remain within swimming distance of Yasi. They definitely weren't in any condition to go out on the open sea but the chief was beaming with so much pride as he ushered them on board he could've been giving them a tour of the islands on his private yacht.

'Not too far. There's a small uninhabited island just across the bay.'

'A *real* desert island?' That was something she'd only

seen in the movies, usually involving starving castaways driven mad by heatstroke and loneliness. It wasn't a thought she relished on her own but with food and company, and the means to leave again, she knew it could turn out to be one of the highlights of her trip. Once she stopped imagining falling overboard and being stranded with nothing to eat but coconuts, she was able to focus on the merits of such a setting. Sand, sea and a sexy sidekick were the makings of a very different kind of film.

They all piled into the two boats, with the majority of the islanders in one dinghy, and Emily, Joe, the chief and the food in the other. This was obviously a treat for everyone and not something they did on a whim, given the level of excitement as the engine spluttered into life. It seemed this was the Yasi equivalent of first class and she should feel honoured, not clutching the side of the boat and praying.

'Stop worrying.' Joe prised her fingers loose and set her hand back in her lap, with his resting on top.

She closed her eyes and did her best not to imagine a watery grave as he gave her hand a reassuring squeeze, and she knew he'd keep her safe no matter what. The wind whipped through her hair, blowing away her residual fears as they skimmed the waves towards sanctuary. It was easy to imagine this was all an illusion created by her lack of sleep but the sea spray splashed her face, reminding her this *was* real even when it seemed too fantastic to be true. Nonetheless, when they cut the engine and came ashore, she had to restrain herself from jumping overboard and kissing the sandy ground. She took off her sandals as Joe helped her off the boat so her footprints were the first to mark the untouched beach.

Not for the first time she wished she'd brought a camera to document her travels. At the time of leaving England she'd been so eager to distance herself from reality she'd left all traces of the modern world behind her, including her phone. There was something so symbolic about that single track of footprints in the sand, marking her bold journey into the unknown, she'd never forget it.

When she reached a line of trees and looked back to see Joe making his way across the beach, leaving a second set of prints alongside hers, it didn't lessen the powerful image. He'd been very much a part of this adventure with her, coaxing this slightly braver Emily to explore beautiful new vistas. She didn't want to leave any of it behind in case she forgot it, or vice versa. Everything here had made such an impact on her for the better and she hoped she'd made some sort of lasting impression on Yasi, on Joe. It didn't seem fair to be falling so heavily for someone if she turned out to be nothing more than a side note in his travel journal.

She knew that's what was happening when she was so conflicted about what she wanted from this trip and from him. If he hadn't already claimed a piece of her heart she wouldn't be overanalysing every move about how it would affect her and simply go with her natural urges. It almost didn't matter if they took that next step together when the damage had already been done. He'd breached her defences and left her vulnerable.

'It's beautiful here.' She tried to keep upbeat even though the shock of her discovery was enough to bring her to tears. The sky might be bluer than she thought naturally possible, the white sand warm under her feet, but she was still a fool when it came to men.

Joe had warned her off against getting into anything she couldn't handle but she'd convinced herself she was tough enough to deal with whatever happened. Now, after little more than a few snatched kisses, she knew her heart had lied to her. It hadn't been broken beyond all repair after Greg, or why else would it ache so much for another man?

'I've been here a few times. It's a good spot to unwind. Mind you, there's work to be done if we're going to eat any time soon.' He pointed down at the rest of the islanders coming ashore in single file, carrying the food supplies, like an army of ants.

'I'm so sorry. I was so pleased to get here I didn't even think about helping to unload the boats.' She must seem so shallow and privileged to everyone else, used to mucking in and doing their bit as part of the community. She'd been living alone too long, concerned with nothing but her own survival until now.

'It's okay. Everyone is assigned jobs to do. Ours is to collect palm leaves.'

'Palm leaves? That's not lunch, is it?'

His laughter calmed her new food fears before they fully formed. 'No. They're used for weaving into plates for the food and as a makeshift picnic table. It means there's no litter left behind when we're finished here.'

They carried out their new duties in silence, with Joe cutting the leaves while she gathered them. She should have known this would be more than the tartan rug and plastic accessories she was used to in a basket. Then again, lunch here was bound to be more than a soggy sandwich and a packet of crisps. Even a simple picnic turned into something exotic and exciting when it was on one of these islands.

Never more so than when she saw how they were preparing the food. The *lovo*, as Joe explained to her, was an oven built in the sand. Emily watched with fascination as the men set a fire in the small pit and stacked rocks on top until they were hot enough to cook the food on. Banana leaves were then placed on top as insulation to keep the stones hot and moisture in the food while it cooked.

Emily sat with several of the women and children plait-ing the palm fronds into primitive mats for the food and Joe waded out into the water with the others for a spot of net fishing. Part of her wished he was still wearing the translucent white shirt from yesterday as his wet clothes clung to him so she could have her very own Mr Darcy moment. At least she had first-hand experience of every solid inch of that torso to enable her imagination to by-pass that dark perv-proof fabric. She fanned herself with one of the long palm fronds as he strode from the sea, water sluicing from his body as if he'd just walked out of a dream. An erotic fantasy she'd take back to keep her warm at night in her luxurious, but empty, bed.

'You'll be feasting today,' he promised her as they brought their catch in. Soldier, medic, lumberjack, fisherman—there seemed no end to his talents, or else he never grew tired of acquiring them.

She supposed she'd managed to add mat weaver and painter to her CV over the course of a couple of days too. That was the thing about the island, a person never seemed to be pigeonholed into one area of their life. It was all about working together and sharing jobs and skills to make sure the traditions never died out. One more thing she would miss when she returned home. Little wonder Joe couldn't see himself tied to a desk somewhere, shuf-fling paperwork, after trying his hand at so many new experiences. She wasn't looking forward to it herself after roaming free in the big wide world beyond her office walls.

It took a couple of hours for the food to cook, during which time she managed to cobble together a couple of flat mats to keep their lunch sand-proof. She was starting to see why the time frame for this meal had been such an issue for Joe. It wasn't the forty-five-minute lunch break she'd been expecting either, but it was worth it when the banana leaves were lifted off to reveal the feast Joe had promised her.

As well as the *dalo* and cassava root vegetables she'd become accustomed to, today saw the addition of fresh fish and crab. It tasted all the better knowing Joe had provided it for her.

'At least I know I won't starve if we get shipwrecked here,' she said, scooping up another piece of crab meat with her fingers.

'I might not be perfect but I'll always make sure you're looked after.' He grinned and helped himself to another chunk of fish, oblivious to the thrill he'd given her with a few simple words.

A whoosh of something powerful shot through her veins, immediately revitalising her previously weary body. It was only a figure of speech but deep down she knew that promise was true. Joe was the only man other than her stepbrother she could trust not to hurt her. Her soft heart was trying to convince her she should be with him even if a few days together was all that was on offer. There was a chance she'd regret missing out on that time more than walking away from him at the end of this trip.

It didn't take long to clear away the evidence of their beach invasion and, lovely though it was, she was getting kind of antsy to return to Yasi. Once they'd checked in on their patient and made sure there was no medical emergency, she and Joe might actually get some privacy. If it took barricading the clinic door with the furniture she was willing to do it if it meant getting to explore the next level with him. Although she wasn't sure if that would make it better or worse when the time came to leave.

She and Joe made their way to the boat they'd arrived in, only to find the chief barring their way. 'I want to thank you for helping my son.'

'You already did that. This was lovely.' Every future

picnic was going to be held up to this standard. A blanket on wet grass with a basket full of cold cuts simply wasn't going to cut it any more when it would be up against an afternoon on a desert island with present company.

They tried again to step on board but the chief side-stepped in front of them again. 'We want to give you a gift. Some time alone. You can keep the boat until you're ready to return to Yasi. There is enough room in this one for all of us.'

'That's really not necessary—'

'We couldn't ask you to do that—'

They stumbled over each other's words in their hurry to get back on the boat. It was a lovely gesture that would've been very welcome in other circumstances but this gift of time didn't stop the clock elsewhere.

'It's very, very kind of you but we must see to your son.' Her heart was in her throat as she dared to refuse his generosity but she knew how anxious Joe had been about coming out here in the first place. She didn't want to prolong his agony, or have him more ticked off at her if she could help it. Their fragile relationship would splinter completely if it became the reason a patient had suffered.

The chief held his hand up. 'I insist.'

His authority dictated they comply or run the risk of upsetting the entire tribe by declining this huge privilege bestowed on them. She was going to leave the next move up to Joe since he knew them better than she did and she didn't want to be the one to make the final call.

The rest of the group were watching them anxiously and he could see Emily's silent plea for help in her wide eyes. As doctors they both wanted to do what was best for their patient but as a seasoned traveller he understood the importance of maintaining good relations with his hosts. To his knowledge, he, Peter and Emily had been the first

Westerners to ever set foot on this island owned by the Yasi-based tribe. It was a greater honour still for them to be offered use of their only transport for his and Emily's enjoyment. They were a conservative race when it came to personal relationships, especially outside marriage, but they were clearly giving them some space to be together without any interference, something he would've grabbed with both hands last night.

Now, going against everything he'd worked so hard to avoid, he was making decisions that could affect so many people. It was going to be up to him to get Emily back to Yasi in one piece, without upsetting anyone and making sure it was done in a timely fashion to prevent any further medical emergencies. He took a deep breath and girded himself for the challenge.

'We'll make sure we're back before sunset.'

He could already feel Emily's gaze burning into the back of his head so he did what any man would do and pretended not to notice. She was polite enough to wait until company was out of earshot before saying anything.

'I hope you know how to get us home. I'm putting all my faith in you,' she said, without taking her eyes off the dinghy sailing away, now full to capacity.

Dread settled in the pit of his stomach. That's what he was afraid of. It was one thing puttering out here on his own but quite another when he was responsible for Emily too. One could never plan for any unexpected catastrophes but that didn't mean you weren't left carrying the resulting guilt for the rest of your life. He was becoming too emotionally attached to these people being continually left in his charge and soon he was going to have to think about moving on.

If things weren't so complicated he would've used this time to his advantage to seduce Emily. The setting, if not the current mood, was the ideal place for them to finally consummate this attraction. Unfortunately, sex wasn't the only thing on his mind. It was having to wrestle with the dangers of the open water and the potential consequences of their absence on Yasi for prominence. For now they'd simply have to wait this out until an acceptable amount of time had passed to pacify their friends.

'Don't worry, I've done this before.' Although it was usually out of a necessity to have some space to himself rather than with enforced company.

'Oh. You mean you and the chief have some sort of understanding where he'll help you kidnap unsuspecting female tourists so you can hold them hostage here until you get your wicked way with them?' Emily folded her arms across her chest as she mocked him, stretching the light fabric of her dress taut across her bust and really not helping to take Joe's mind off the idea of seduction.

'Yeah. You got a problem with that?' They exchanged cheesy grins as their sense of humour thankfully took over from that initial urge to panic.

Emily laughed and shook her head. 'Nope. Except maybe next time you could give me some warning.'

'You're right. The timing was a little off on this one. In future I'll make sure we're better organised.' His mind flitted towards a day here together with no worries dragging them back to civilisation. They certainly wouldn't be standing here, fully dressed, counting the minutes until they could leave.

The sound of the waves lapping at their feet punctuated the sudden silence between them as what-might-have-beens stole away any further chat. It would be selfish of them to act on impulse now and get lost in each other. One taste of paradise and he knew he'd never want to leave.

With one quick movement he stripped off his shirt and his shorts to wade out into the water in nothing but his boxers. He needed to cool off.

'What are you doing?'

'Going for a swim. Come on in. The water's lovely.' He lay on his back, making small circles with his hands in the sea to keep him afloat, tempted to let the gentle current carry him away.

Emily dipped a toe in the water and stepped back again. 'Are there sharks in there?'

'I haven't seen any but they're not likely to come this close to the shore anyway.' He flicked his fingers, soaking her with spray.

She walked forward until the sea was swirling around her feet and lifting the hem of her dress. Joe held his breath as she revealed every sensual curve of her figure. It barely mattered she was wearing a pretty pink bikini beneath, she may as well have been naked the way his body was responding. She tossed the dress onto the sand and slowly waded out towards him.

Joe spluttered as water covered his face and filled his nostrils. He gulped a mouthful as he struggled to stand upright. He'd been so engrossed in the sight of her stripping off he'd forgotten he needed to work to stay afloat.

'You okay?'

He could hear the flicker of amusement in her voice even though he couldn't see her clearly as he scrubbed the water from his eyes. 'Sure. I think I just forgot to breathe there for a second.'

'How come?' Emily was a little breathy, treading water deeper out into the sea.

Joe swam out to meet her, gravitating towards her like she was his life raft in raging stormy seas. They faced each other, only their heads bobbing on the surface of the water, and he knew he couldn't lie. Either to her or himself.

'Because you're so beautiful.'

Emily immediately cast her eyes down, reluctant to

accept the truth of his compliment. If she wasn't going to listen to him then he was simply going to have to show her. He waded closer and captured her mouth with his, the salty and sweet taste of her lips a feast for his senses.

She wound her arms around his neck and he was happy to anchor her legs around his waist and take her weight. In fact, with her body pressed tightly to his, if they sank to the bottom of the sea and drowned he'd die happy. Denying themselves any longer when everyone already assumed they were together seemed futile, and by giving in to his urges he was finally able to breathe again. It seemed as though he'd been holding his breath since last night, waiting for permission to exhale, and Emily had granted him that the second she'd kissed him back.

There was a flash of light and it took a while for him to figure out it was coming from above and wasn't fireworks going off in his head. He opened his eyes to see clouds rolling in, the sky now a palette of murky greys and purples. A rumble sounded in the distance, just after a charge of electricity that seemed to reach up to the heavens.

'We need to get back to the beach and find shelter.'

'Hmm?' Emily was still nuzzling into him, oblivious to the danger around them, which was either a sign of how far she'd come or how great a kisser he was to make her overcome her natural worry state.

'There's. A. Storm. Coming.' It was difficult to get the sentence out when she insisted on kissing him between words and scrambling his brain. In the end he simply carried her ashore, still clinging to him like a limpet on the rocks. Not that he was complaining. It simply made it harder for him to care what was going on out there too.

He laid her down on the sand but she refused to release her hold, bringing him down with her. Making love to Emily here, with the waves drifting in and out between their naked bodies, was the stuff of fantasies but tropical storms came in hard and fast. That wasn't how he wanted their first sexual encounter to go just because they were in a race against the elements.

Another roar of thunder reverberated around them then the rain came down in sheets and poured cold water on their ardour. Emily shrieked and jumped to her feet.

'I did try to tell you,' he said, rolling onto his back to let the rain cool his fevered skin.

'What will we do?' Emily was already back in panic mode, grabbing up her clothes and looking to him for answers.

Joe donned his shorts and T-shirt with more urgency as the gap between the flashes of light and crashes of thunder became ever smaller. The storm was coming closer... the rain was reaching saturation point. If they didn't get struck by lightning first, their cold, wet clothes sticking to their bodies might lead to pneumonia. They needed to get somewhere that would shelter them from the elements and keep them safe and dry.

'I know somewhere.' He grabbed her hand and made a dash for higher ground. There was a recess cut into the rocks that he knew from experience would provide everything they needed until this storm passed. His secret until now.

They clambered up the boulders in the rain and Joe kept hold of Emily's hand until they made it to the rocky hidey-hole in case she slipped in her no-longer-practical sandals. It was dark inside but at least it was dry.

Emily was watching the storm from the entrance, her shoulders shaking from the cold.

'I'll start a fire to get us warmed up.' He wasn't as eager to have a ringside seat for the fireworks. Loud noises and bright lights weren't as attractive to him as they once might have been.

'How do you propose to do that?' Apparently man creating fire was more interesting than nature's fury as she turned her attention back to him.

'I could sit here half the night trying to get a spark from rubbing a couple of pieces of wood together, or we could just use these.' He was almost sorry to disappoint her with the kindling and box of matches he'd left after his last visit here instead of showing off his caveman skills. Modern fire-making methods were quicker but they weren't as manly as starting one from little more than sticks and friction.

'Wait, is this your *actual* man cave?' She said it as though it was something he should be ashamed of but this place had been his salvation at times, not merely some whimsical notion of reliving his youth.

'Sometimes a guy needs a little time out.' He shrugged it off. It was difficult to explain his need for time out now and again, away from even the small population of Yasi.

This retreat enabled him to maintain a physical and emotional distance when he was in danger of getting too close to the people he was working alongside. By bringing Emily here with him, he'd totally screwed with that idea. Now there was nothing keeping his heart out of matters. He was past the point of no return and the damage was done. There was no way he was going to walk away from this without collecting a new battle scar.

He hadn't even told Peter, his oldest friend, about this place. Peter, who, up until a few days ago, had been the closest person in his life, the only one keeping him out here. Somehow Emily had crept in and hijacked his affection. Why else would he be holed up here with her instead of doing his job back on Yasi?

He got to work setting the fire and Emily came to kneel beside him. 'You know, if this trip has taught me anything it's that it's more fun being around people than sitting moping on your own.'

'I spend plenty of time in company, have made acquaintances all around the world. I'm simply happier in my own company.' That wasn't necessarily true. *Safer* was the word he'd been searching for but he didn't want to get into that with Emily and have to explain why he didn't get involved with people. That meant sharing the most painful part of his life with her and publicly owning the part he'd played in the deaths of his friends. Something he'd never done with anyone.

'Would you prefer it if I left you alone?' Emily made a half-hearted attempt to leave but they both knew she wasn't going anywhere. Neither of them were until this storm had passed and it was safe for them to take the boat out again. Matters outside this cave were completely beyond their control.

'No.' He stood up to block her exit. 'I want you here with me.'

He meant it in every sense. He wanted her company, to share this space, and most of all to help him forget everything going on in the outside world. This was their time together when they were free to relax and be themselves, without any outside influence bursting their bubble.

Emily shivered as he reached for her.

'You know, it's going to take a while for this place to heat up. We should really get out of these wet clothes.'

He slipped one strap of Emily's dress over her shoulder, then the other, and watched the garment pool at her feet. She stood proudly before him, making no move to cover the rest of her body from view. In fact, she was already reaching up to undo her bikini top.

'I've heard the best way to fight hypothermia is to share body heat.'

'I've heard that theory.' He peeled off his T-shirt, eager to put it to the test.

Emily slowly and silently removed the last of her

clothes and time stood still for Joe. She was a goddess with a body worthy of being immortalised in marble to epitomise the beauty of woman. Her soft curves and perfect proportions deserved love sonnets written in her honour but he wasn't a sculptor or a poet. All he had to offer her was himself. So he unwrapped her gift as quickly as he could.

There was something very primitive about standing in a cave with a naked woman and his body responded accordingly. Thankfully his brain was still capable of making some of his decisions. If this was to be the only private time they were to have together, he wanted it to be truly memorable for both of them. They needed more than a frantic coupling on a cold floor.

He reached out to brush her wet hair from her shoulders and felt her tremble beneath his fingers.

'Are you still cold?' The blood pounding through his body had warmed him from the inside out so he'd assumed the same was true for her. He was relieved when she shook her head or else he really would have to start trying to get heat back into her body.

'Nervous.'

Her answer was full of her characteristic honesty. It didn't take a genius to work out he was probably the first man she'd done this with since her husband. Joe ignored all the warning signs flashing in his head about what that meant and accepted it as his privilege, not his downfall.

'There's no need. I won't do anything to hurt you.' All he wanted to do was please her, love her, make her feel as special as she deserved. He was going to be the one hurting when this fantasy ended. Emily would go home and probably find a new love, whereas he knew he'd never be this open again. She'd stolen a piece of his heart he'd never intended to give to anyone and would never, ever get it back.

It was his turn to tremble at the enormity of the revelation. They didn't have a future together when she couldn't rely on him to keep her safe when she needed him most. He would only let her down and he couldn't bear to disappoint her or, worse, face the agony of losing her because of his actions. He was in love with Emily but he couldn't tell her, couldn't do anything about it other than show her.

CHAPTER TWELVE

THERE WAS SOMETHING different about kissing a woman he was in love with. Something familiar, as if he'd found a missing part of himself, yet with an element of danger attached. He was used to living life on the edge but for once he was actually afraid of what was going to happen to him at the end of this. There was no stopping this now when the momentum was carrying him ever forward into new territory, but that didn't mean he wasn't going to get hurt somewhere along the line.

There were reasons he didn't get close to people and falling in love was probably the worst thing he could've done. It made him weak, susceptible to more heartache. Before going to the army he'd been too young to get serious with a girl, too single-minded about his career. After his retirement the layers of guilt and self-pity had been too dense for anyone to fight through them to reach his heart. Somehow Emily had found a path straight to that vulnerable spot and it was too late to plug that hole in his defences now.

He'd spent too long running from any form of affection, pre-empting the possibility when there was a chance he'd have his insides ripped apart again. The woman he loved was giving herself to him and now there was nowhere left to run. No reason to run. Any other man wouldn't think twice about letting this play out and enjoy this experience, instead of fearing it. He wanted to be that man, for himself and for Emily, and listen to his heart instead of his head for once. They both deserved a bit of honesty in their feelings for each other, even if they couldn't find the words to express it. He would deal with the consequences later. They couldn't be any more painful than ending this here and not knowing what they could've had. Even for the briefest time.

He could feel goosebumps on her skin under his fingers; the hard points of her nipples pressing against his chest. There was no denying she was as turned on as he was but she was still tense. It was his job, his pleasure to help her relax and enjoy this time with him.

He already knew how responsive she was to his touch so he cupped her breast in his hand and rolled her tight nipple between his finger and thumb. Her gasp of pleasure strengthened his resolve, and his erection. Soon they'd be so consumed with need and lust that nothing else would matter except coming together, and that's exactly how he wanted it.

He wrapped his lips around that sensitive pink nub, teased her with the tip of his tongue to claim his breathy reward. She clung to his shoulders, her nails digging further into his skin with every lap of his tongue. The sharp pain was worth it to see the ecstasy on her face and feel the tension leave her body. It was addictive.

He slid his hand down between her legs and into her wet heat. She was ready for him, her body trembling from need now with every stroke.

'What about protection?' Emily gasped as he lowered her to the floor.

Joe scrabbled for his shorts and pulled a condom from his pocket.

'I always carry one. They're an essential part of a survival kit. You can use them for carrying water and keeping tinder dry.' He didn't want her to think sex was nothing special to him, something he took for granted. Tonight it was everything.

'I think we should probably go down the traditional route and use them as they were intended.' She giggled and took the packet from him to rip it open.

Joe sheathed himself and settled himself between her thighs, slightly nervous himself now since they'd been building toward this moment for so long. Emily lifted her head and kissed him, bringing him back down to the ground with her. Sliding into her, forging their two bodies together was the most natural thing in the world. Nothing was ever going to come close to replacing this feeling of complete happiness. Part of him didn't think he deserved it, while another part never wanted it to end.

He moved slowly inside her, each second of her tight heat a gift he intended to treasure.

He loved her. He couldn't have her. The unfairness of it all drove him to find his peace, every thrust inside her bringing him closer to finding it. She was his sanctuary and he wanted to be hers too. Her body rocked against his, rising and falling in perfect time with him, climbing towards that peak. Every bite of her lip, every moan, every clench and release of her internal muscles charted her journey and Joe wanted to be the one to help her reach that final destination. He braced himself on the cold, hard floor, not caring about anything except watching that bliss play out over her features, and slammed into her again. Emily cried out, clutched him closer and he felt her break apart beneath him. Only then did he give in to his own climax, the primal roar of his release echoing around the walls.

There was a lump in his throat as he looked down at Emily, so beautifully serene beneath him. If he were a different person, in a different life, they could've had this every day. Instead, all they had was until the end of this storm. For both their sakes there was no choice but to let his love die with the embers of the fire. Forever wasn't an option.

Emily lay quietly while Joe spooned in behind her, afraid to speak in case she burst into tears and ruined the mood. This was a monumental moment for her, though she hadn't realised until just now. She had finally moved on from Greg, from her marriage, in the most spectacular fashion—by giving herself completely to someone else. She'd held nothing back here with Joe and perhaps for the first time in her life had truly been at peace, with herself, with him and with what they were doing. Hidden away here, they no longer had to be concerned about outside influences. For this snapshot in time they were able to be true to themselves and each other. When insecurities and obstacles were stripped away they were simply two people who had a very special connection. One that had sparked to life and delivered more than she'd ever dreamed of.

This had been more than sex, even though that was all it ever *could* be. It didn't matter how great they were together or how they felt about each other because it wasn't going to last. This was probably the last time she would ever feel complete happiness because when this was over she'd have to return to her world of playing it safe. It was the only way she could survive.

Joe snuggled into her neck, his warmth reminding her he was still hers for now. She closed her eyes and clung to the thick forearm wrapped around her waist. It wouldn't do any harm to let the fantasy go on a little longer. After all, she was good at this pretending lark.

Emily was jolted from a peaceful slumber by a shout and Joe thrashing on the ground beside her. He tossed and turned, mumbling incoherently as he battled some unknown force in his sleep. She couldn't see his face as it was dark outside and the fire barely more than a glow. It was chilly now they didn't have the heat of passion keeping them warm.

She pulled on her now dry clothes and knelt to add more kindling to the fire. A smile played on her lips as she hugged her knees, watching the embers catch and resurrect the flames. It was representative of what Joe had done for her—taking her dying heart and sparking it back to life. She knew he felt it too, and she'd be lying if she said she wasn't hoping they could do this again. Okay, a long-term relationship might not be viable, given his lifestyle, but he was a traveller and there was no reason he couldn't add England to his list of places to visit. Right now hooking up a couple of times a year seemed preferable to never having this again.

Another flash of lightning illuminated the cave, the crack of thunder ripping through the air after it. Joe was sitting upright, naked, panting and sweating. He was staring off into the distance almost in a trance, his face a mask of utter terror. This was more than a nightmare, he was living this horror right here and now. She moved slowly to his side and rested her hand on his arm, his skin clammy beneath her touch.

'Joe? It's all right. You're here with me.' She tried not to spook him but gently coax him back into the present.

He turned his head slowly towards her but he wasn't really focusing.

'It's me, Emily.' She took a risk by pressing her lips to his. In his current agitated state there was a possibility he'd lash out but she hoped the bond they had was special enough to bring him back to her.

It took a few seconds but he did finally respond, kissing her with a hunger that could only come from the Joe she knew.

'How come you're dressed?' he asked, apparently now wide awake and aware of his surroundings.

'It got cold and look how late it is.' She handed him his own clothes, pity though it was to have him cover up.

'I guess we're here for the night.'

The storm had struck again and Emily saw him flinch, the sight and sounds clearly part of whatever was bothering him.

'That was some bad dream you were having. I was getting worried I wouldn't be able to pull you out of it.'

'I didn't hurt you, did I?' The scowl on his face was more out of concern for her than himself and she guessed this wasn't the first time it had happened.

'No. A lot of shouting and tossing and turning but you didn't lash out.'

'Good.' That seemed enough reassurance for him but that sort of sleep disruption shouldn't be taken lightly. He could do himself serious damage in that trance state in an unfamiliar place, not to mention the exhaustion and lack of concentration that could result from lack of proper sleep—two things that could impair his judgement when it came to treating his own patients.

'Does it happen a lot?' It was in her nature to be inquisitive when it came to people's well-being and Joe was no exception, regardless of his reluctance to talk about it. Doctors often made the worst patients, refusing to accept they were human and fallible just like everyone else.

'Every now and then.' He pulled on his T-shirt so she wasn't able to read his expression. She guessed it happened more than he was prepared to admit since he'd been so quick to move into the clinic on his own.

'Afghanistan?' She took a stab in the dark. By all accounts from her parents it had taken Peter some time to readjust after everything he'd witnessed out there, along with medication, counselling and his faith. Things she was pretty sure Joe hadn't availed himself of since leaving the army. He was too stubborn and tirelessly independent to turn to anyone for help.

'There are a few things that can take me back there in a heartbeat. The senses get a little messed up after being on high alert for so long. One loud bang, a flash of light and I'm back in that tank, helpless, powerless. The mind can play cruel tricks on you when you least expect it.'

'But it's over. I know what happened must've been terrible for all of you but that life is in the past. You still have a future.' With or without her. As long as he was running away from dealing with this he was never going to have the life he deserved—in one place surrounded by people who loved him.

'Batesy and Ste don't. I was the medic, the one who was supposed to be there to save them. I failed to do the one thing I was trained to do. It's my fault they're not here today with their families. How can I expect anyone to rely on me when I can't even trust myself to do the right thing? I mean, the chief's son is lying sick back on Yasi and I'm here, carrying on as if we're on a dirty weekend away.' He wasn't looking at her any more but was staring out at somewhere beyond the ever-changing skies, caught between the past and the present.

Emily knew the rage was directed at himself, fuelled by guilt and grief, but she still took a hit. This was more to her than sex and she certainly would never have intentionally put a patient in jeopardy just to spend some time with Joe. Even if she'd had an inkling of how phenomenal it would be.

'You were injured, you couldn't help what happened to your friends. The only ones to blame are those who planted the bomb. You can't spend the rest of your life afraid of getting close to people in case you let them down. What kind of tribute is that to those who aren't here any more? Taking risks and experiencing things most of us can only imagine is one thing, but shouldn't you be embracing all aspects of life? Including love?' She swallowed hard, catching herself before she blurted out the three words guaranteed to send him running.

Joe was emotionally stripped bare before her, still reeling from his trauma. She didn't need to add more by revealing her feelings for him. He hadn't asked her to fall for him or promised her anything in return. It wasn't fair to expect anything from him now and she knew if she told him she loved him he would feel under pressure to act on it. That's the type of man he was. One who always wanted to do right by others, even if it cost him peace of mind.

There was no way she wanted to increase his burden now she knew that happy-go-lucky façade was hiding his true pain from the rest of the world. Telling him now would only be for selfish reasons, voicing that small hope he would reciprocate her feelings, while all the while knowing nothing could come of it anyway. He'd spelled out the very reasons he couldn't be with her, even if by some miracle he thought of her as more than a holiday romance.

Like her, he was damaged goods. She knew how it was to fake a smile when you were crying on the inside and it was good for him to finally be honest about what he was still going through. The day she'd revealed her birthmark to him had lifted the stress of keeping her secret from her. She hoped this breakthrough tonight would do the same for him in some way. It had taken a great deal of trust from him to confide in her as much as he had, and she was privileged she was getting to know the *real* Joe Braden.

His eyes shimmered in the darkness but he was still refusing to give in to the grief he was obviously suffering. Instead, he ended the conversation by moving in for another kiss. Emily knew he was avoiding further discussion on the subject but she was powerless to resist him when this could be their last opportunity to be together.

They lunged at each other with the urgency of two lovers soon to be separated, possibly for ever.

This time the slow burn of passion was replaced with a fierce need to block out reality and get back to that place of utter contentment as soon as possible when they were both struggling to keep it together. They tore at each other's clothes in their need for a hit of those feel-good endorphins only hot sex could provide. Clinging to each other as though they were adrift at sea, holding on to one another for survival, they joined together in one frantic thrust. For a moment that was all Emily needed, to know he wanted her, that they were together. Then he was moving inside her, turning her thoughts to more primitive needs and how quickly he could take her back to that pinnacle of utter bliss.

Her mind and body were completely consumed by the frenetic pace of their lovemaking as Joe drove into her again and again, chasing away his own demons. There was a moment when their eyes locked, that connection stronger than ever, knowing they both needed this release to free them from their inner turmoil. They came together, their combined cries drowning out the sound of thunder in the distance.

Emily had never known such pleasure and pain, knowing this was the only time they'd have this freedom together. A true passion she'd probably never experience again.

They lay in each other's arms, watching the flames dance in the corner of the cave until Joe's soft snore broke the comfortable silence as he finally seemed to find some peace.

Emily turned on her side and whispered, 'I love you,' safe in the knowledge he wouldn't hear her.

She knew it was the last time she'd ever say it.

'It's time to go.' Joe was gently shaking her awake but she didn't want to open her eyes because that meant facing the truth. The dream was over.

He tried again, a little more forcefully this time. 'We need to get moving before they send a search party out for us.'

She groaned like a truculent teenager forced to get out of bed on a school morning. 'Do we have to?'

'Yes.' He dropped a kiss on her nose.

She supposed food and a warm bed were a good incentive. Plus, if he was brave enough to get that close to her morning breath he must really want to be out of here.

Despite fighting his own demons half the night, Joe clearly hadn't put thoughts of his patient out of his mind. Now it was daylight and their return was inevitable, Emily's concern grew too over what might have occurred in their absence. A more in-depth discussion about Joe's past and his thoughts on a future with her could wait until after they'd checked in with Peter and Miriama.

There was a tad more urgency to her movements now she'd stopped thinking only of herself. She got up but there was no bed to make, no post-coital lazy breakfast together or reason to dilly-dally. Joe kicked some dirt over the fire to make sure it was out and then it was time to leave their little love nest.

They made their way back down to the beach to retrieve the boat from where it had been stashed the night before and pulled it to the edge of the water. The sea was calm today, like flat blue glass for them to slip effortlessly across to Yasi; the sky was as calm as the water. It was almost as if yesterday's drama had never happened.

That wasn't what she wanted at all. Last night with Joe had been the best night of her life. They'd connected in every way imaginable and she didn't want to lose that as soon as they stepped off the island. She still had a few days left before she went home and believed that, given time, they could make this something more than a holiday fling. He'd already started to open up to her and she was willing to risk her heart by giving this a shot.

'What's wrong? Are you sad to be leaving?' Joe didn't seem to understand her attachment to this place, which didn't bode well for a budding romance.

Sleeping with Joe had marked a new chapter in her life. It had put an end to her marriage once and for all. The divorce papers had made it official, but it hadn't been until she'd fallen in love with another man that it had become real to her. She would remember this island for ever as the place where she'd become Emily Jackson again, a single woman living her own life, making her own decisions. She kind of hoped it—she—meant as much to Joe.

He was waiting for her to answer and she thought about laughing it off, pretend last night had been nothing more than sex. But she'd spent too much of her life lying about who she was. If he couldn't handle her feelings, well, she'd simply have to live with the repercussions.

'I don't want this to end. Once we go back to Yasi we're doctors, somebody's family, somebody's friend. Here we're just Emily and Joe, with no expectations from anyone other than ourselves.' A night with Joe had exceeded any expectations she might have had and given her a taste of something special. It wasn't something she was in any hurry to abandon in favour of cool reality. Yasi now seemed like the first step back towards her actual life, where there was no hunky man to spoon with her at night and a whole lot more besides.

With his hands on his hips, his gaze cast down at the

waves washing in and out on the sand, Joe let out a heavy sigh. For a moment Emily worried he might jump in the boat and sail off into the blue without her. Instead, he splashed along the water's edge towards her and wrapped his arms around her waist.

'This won't end until we're both ready.' His words didn't bring her as much comfort as he probably intended because he was still stamping their relationship with a use-by date. It *was* going to end, albeit on a different island with more than swaying palm trees to witness her eventual heartbreak. This might be the new Emily but she still had the same old soft heart. Tears burned the back of her eyelids as Joe gave her one last castaway kiss. She doubted she'd ever be ready. No matter how much notice she had, when the end came it was going to come hard and fast. Joe had left a mark on her soul that wasn't likely to fade any time soon. She knew she'd be thinking of him every time she stepped into the sun.

Joe's head was scrambled, his troubling memories of Afghanistan mixed with those of last night and Emily comforting him. Loving him. He'd spent so long battling the nightmares on his own that he didn't know how to cope with sharing them. Nothing made sense to him any more except kissing her. In some ways he could understand her reluctance to leave. It was easier to stay here wrapped up in each other's arms and ignore everything else outside this slice of paradise. Except hiding wouldn't solve anyone's problems, his least of all.

Even if they chose to push the boat out into the ocean minus its passengers and purposefully strand themselves on this island for ever, it still wouldn't help him reconcile with his faults, or make him the right man for Emily. If something happened out here she'd be dependent on him and that was too much to contemplate for someone who couldn't be trusted with that level of responsibility. Someone who didn't want that level of responsibility again after losing two people he'd loved who were supposedly under his care. Last night, making love to Emily with complete abandon for the first time since leaving the army, had been wonderful but their status couldn't be any more permanent than his stay on this island. As much as he loved her and had probably been searching for her all his life, his wants and needs would have to come second to hers. She deserved more than him.

'Ready?' he said with a forced laugh, making a joke of his last comment before Emily read too much into it. She'd been let down too often. There was no point in leading her on with false promises into believing any of this was real. They had no chance of being together and living happily ever after. That was for heroes, strong men who'd given everything of themselves for others, not those who'd failed in their duty.

'Okay.' Her smile was as fake as his attempt at humour but at least she seemed to understand this need to stop lying to themselves. They had to go back and pick up the reins at the clinic again. It was their job, their calling, their reason for being out here, and it wouldn't do them any good to get too caught up in this fantasy when people depended on them.

As he pushed the boat into the water with Emily on board it was all he could do to jump in beside her, knowing they were sailing towards the end of this romance. The sands of time were shifting ever faster as the sea breeze carried them closer to Yasi and further away from their own personal love island—the only place they could ever truly be together.

When they came ashore on Yasi there was no singing, dancing welcome party to greet them. On the plus side, there wasn't an angry stepbrother waiting for him with a shotgun either. It was going to be pretty obvious what had happened between them left alone on that island all this time when they'd barely been able to keep their hands off each other in company. Peter had already warned him off hurting Emily and that was another promise he knew he was probably going to break when the thought of leaving was already causing him pain. Although she hadn't spoken the exact words, her every look, every touch said she loved him as much as he loved her.

They hauled the boat up onto the beach, where it could be retrieved later. Depending on what they were going back to, it might be used for another voyage soon. There was no point in dragging this out and causing more suffering. If all was well back at the clinic and the chief's house they should probably quit while they were ahead and cherish the happy memories of their night together rather than wait a week for the tears and recriminations to start.

He strode ahead on their walk back into the village in a scene reminiscent of their first meeting. A different couple would have marched along, not caring who knew what had happened or what came next. He couldn't afford that luxury and neither could Emily, though she didn't know it. It was almost inconceivable to think that a few days after their first meeting his whole world would be upside down and he'd broken every one of his relationship rules because of this woman. If Emily expected a loved-up stroll, hand in hand, making the most of their last minutes alone, she didn't say anything. At least nothing he heard.

He paused at the top of the hill to take a breath and a mental snapshot of the view he'd called home for too long. It gave his walking companion time to catch up.

'You seem in an awful hurry to get back.' She moved directly in front of him so there was no escaping the sound of disappointment in her voice.

'I'm sure it's been a long night for everyone. They'll be wondering what's keeping us with the storm long past and half the morning gone already. It's not fair to make them wait any longer than necessary.' They'd had their fun and now it was time to face the consequences.

'Joe? Is everything all right? Between us, I mean?'

This was his opportunity to tell her the truth. Everything between them was far from all right. It was crazy and messed up and scaring the hell out of him enough to consider getting the next boat off the island. Instead he slung an arm around her shoulders as if she was an old mate seeking reassurance on a trivial matter, not a lover asking him about his feelings for her.

'Sure,' he said, his confidence failing him. Going back into the community with shattered hearts suddenly seemed crueller than letting this play out until he had his bag packed.

'I guess we do need time to acclimatise again, give Peter some warning that we were together before he figures it out for himself.' She gave credence to his explanation, increasing his uneasiness by expanding on it until it became her truth. This trust in him was exactly the reason he should leave. He couldn't live up to her expectations and when the blinkers came off it would be in the most humiliating fashion.

'Right,' he said, picking up the pace and carrying the lie away with him.

'The wanderers have returned!' Peter and Miriama were every bit as exhausted and pleased to see them as he'd expected. The guilt slammed into Joe's chest harder than the group hug in which he and Emily were swamped.

'Sorry you had to hold down the fort for so long but we thought it best to wait out the storm.' He immediately felt the need to justify their long delay, even though the reason would've been obvious to anyone who'd witnessed Mother Nature's rage last night.

'I'm just glad you didn't get caught up in it. Did you find somewhere to shelter?' Peter rubbed Emily's arm as if he was trying to generate some heat for her even now. It was a reminder she still had someone to turn to, come what may. Her stepbrother was that person, not someone who was already planning to run away before they reached the first hurdle.

'Joe knew somewhere—'

'We found a place up in the rocks out of the rain.' He cut Emily off before she gave Peter the idea he'd somehow pre-planned all of it.

Besides, the cave had been his secret and it wasn't something he wanted to share with anyone but her even now. Revealing its whereabouts, leaving it open to future visitors, would defile the time they'd spent there together. He wanted them to be the last two inhabitants; the ghosts of their pasts and never-to-be-had future doomed to haunt the stony cavern for ever.

'Good. I had enough to worry about here and figured years of survival training would see you right. Although I would've thought a desert island in a tropical storm was a doddle compared to rain-soaked ditches in the English countryside.'

'You bet. I hope you didn't have too tough a night here without us.' He'd spent the night cuddled up with the most beautiful woman in the world while her stepbrother had been doing the job *he* was supposed to be doing.

'All the delights you'd expect but nothing we couldn't handle. He seems to be through the worst of it for real this time.'

'Thanks, mate. I really appreciate you stepping up to the plate for me. I'm just sorry we put you in that position in the first place.'

'I would say you shouldn't make a habit of it but I reckon we can spare you another couple of hours if you want to have a kip or get changed.'

'That would be great. Cheers.' All of a sudden Peter's generosity made Joe want that space all the more. So no one had died this time, but he had still let his friends down. He could've said no to going in the first place and saved everyone a lot of trouble. He could've insisted on leaving the island at the same time as the others or come back sooner. It had been his selfish wish to spend some alone time with Emily that had put so many people in jeopardy. Pure luck had kept them all from serious harm during his negligence.

He was distracted and unfocused, everything he'd feared would happen if he forged relationships with people. If he hung around here much longer the worst was bound to happen. There was always going to be dengue fever, diabetes, choking babies and people relying on him to save them. Without a local hospital or access to crucial medication the people he'd grown to love were someday going to need more than he could give them. He'd barely come out the other side of grief the last time and he couldn't face it again. He couldn't face these people again knowing he'd failed them. His heart wouldn't survive losing Emily if he failed her too. He'd had a lucky escape this time and it was time to check out while the going was good.

He took off out the door without a backward glance for Emily, afraid that if he looked at her he'd bottle out of this altogether.

'Hey, wait for me.' She'd really got this ninja frontal attack down pat. He didn't even know she was following him until she was there blocking his path.

'Look, Emily, I need some time on my own. Sorry.' He started walking again, unable to offer her a proper explanation when he didn't fully understand why he was throwing this away himself.

'Joe?' Another stealth move and he was faced with those doe eyes pleading with him not to do this.

He had to swallow the ball of emotion lodged in his throat. It was never easy ending a relationship and he was effectively ending two of the most important ones in his life by leaving Yasi. He didn't want to do this out here in the open. Hell, he didn't want to have to do this at all but he was supposed to be a drifter and the difficulty level of ending this was proof he'd already stayed too long.

'I never said I'd be here for ever. Last night proved to me it's time I moved on. I should never have let things get this far and I'm going now before I do any more damage. There are enough of you to carry on what I started. You don't need me any more.' They didn't need him but it was becoming clear that he was starting to lean on them too much and that was equally as dangerous. Spilling his guts to her last night in the wake of his latest nightmare had shown how weak he'd become in getting close to Emily and everyone else on the island. It was only a matter of time before someone got hurt. More hurt.

'I don't suppose the fact I *want* you to stay makes any difference?' She was killing him but this was going to take tough love to make sure she didn't end up mooning after him and ruining the rest of her trip.

'You know I can't stay still. I get bored too easily. I'm grateful for this adventure but, really, I'm ready for the next one.' He saw Emily flinch at his choice of words out of the corner of his eye.

'Joe?' Another plaintive cry for an explanation he couldn't give her.

It broke his heart to ignore it.

'I don't have much to pack so if I can get the chief to agree, I'll be taking the boat out again soon.' He didn't care how he got back to the mainland or how long it took as long as he put some distance between him and Yasi Island fast. It wouldn't take much for his resolve to weaken.

'If that's what you really want…'

'It is.' He was almost gasping for air as the lie choked him. What he wanted was a life with Emily but that was as impossible as Batesy and Ste having theirs back.

'Is that it? You got what you wanted and now you're running out on me?'

'You knew this wasn't for ever. One night together doesn't mean I've changed who I am. I was upfront from the start about my intentions. All I'm doing is putting an end to it sooner than planned. Chalk this up to part of the adventure package.'

He couldn't bear to look at her any more as he stumbled away. Ripping the sticking plaster off with a short, sharp shock was supposed to alleviate the pain more quickly but that expression of betrayal he saw welling up in her eyes was going to stay with him for a long time. He needed to get off this island. Now.

Emily couldn't breathe, the shock of Joe's words sucking the air from her lungs. After last night he knew this was more to her than a holiday fling and she'd hoped he'd felt the same. This sudden coolness and what seemed like unnecessary cruelty was difficult to get her head around when they'd shared so much, grown so close.

Frozen to the spot, all she could do was watch him go. Even the tears she needed to shed for their short-lived relationship refused to fall in her confusion. If she were a stronger person she might have given chase and demanded answers but part of her already knew the answers. He was bored with her. He'd said as much. All of that anxiety she'd felt when Greg had told her the same thing came whooshing back and left her gasping for air. This was reaffirming that idea she wasn't good enough for anyone.

The energy seemed to drain from her body as the implications of his words sank in, leaving her limp and unsteady on her feet. She reached out to brace herself against one of the palm trees that once upon a time had held so many good memories. Now she would always associate everything she loved on this island with this utterly overwhelming sense of desolation. She sank down onto the grass, her body only upright with the support of the solid trunk of the tree. This was how she was going to spend the rest of her days—alone, broken-hearted, unwanted.

Hard-hitting rejection wasn't new to her but it wasn't any less painful the third time around. If anything, it hurt even more than losing her mother or her husband when Joe had appeared so much more supportive and accepting of her for who she was. Last night she'd held him through his night terrors, made love as if they'd been embarking on the start of an exciting journey, and now he was saying it was over? It was hard for her to accept she wasn't anything more to him than any of the other women he'd spent time with on his travels when he'd come to mean so much to her. He was part of her now. He'd helped her learn to love herself again and she'd fallen head over heels for him in the process.

She couldn't imagine going back to her old life as if this had never happened. Neither could she face the rest of her stay here without him. There were memories liable to start a monsoon of tears at every turn. Even from her tragic position here on the ground she could see the hill they'd marched down laden down with her luggage and the school where they'd had so much fun with the children. Her lip began to wobble as she realised this was probably the very tree they'd sat under and shared lunch. If she was expected to forget him she was going to have to leave early too.

She struggled to her feet and resolved to make her way

back to Miriama's before she gave in to the big fat tears threatening to fall. Once she was behind closed doors she could mourn properly—cry, rage and eventually decide where to go from here. Whatever happened next was entirely down to her. From now on she was on her own.

Emily had spent more than enough time moping in her room like an angsty adolescent. Her throat was raw from sobbing, her eyes puffy and red from crying, but she knew she still had to face up to her responsibilities. Just because her life was falling apart it didn't mean she should neglect the inhabitants of Yasi. With Joe gone she was the only doctor left in residence.

She splashed her face with cold water and pulled her hair up into a ponytail. There were always going to be patients to treat and her job was the one constant in her life. At least she was always going to be in demand professionally, if not romantically. In some ways she felt sorry for Joe. The transient life he led to ensure he didn't get close to people also meant he never got to fully experience that feeling of belonging.

With her mind clearer now the initial shock of his rejection had passed, she began to analyse that last conversation. He'd given her the impression he'd tired of life here, that she'd bored him. If this had been England and she was back in her office with nothing to look forward to than a cup of tea while watching the soaps on TV she'd buy it. But not when she'd spent the last days throwing herself into local customs that ordinarily would have terrified her. She wasn't that same meek divorcee who'd set foot on the island and she was ticked off he'd made out she was. After everything he'd told her she began to wonder if it wasn't his insecurities he was running away from. He'd been so locked into his grief and guilt he'd become a martyr to it, denying himself, and her, any chance of happiness.

She found herself veering towards the clinic. If she didn't try to make sense of this now she knew she'd come to regret it. Whether he was leaving because of her or his own demons, she wanted closure before returning home so she was free to start the next chapter of her life. With or without him.

Her once weak limbs now carried with renewed strength. She'd never taken the opportunity to confront Greg about ending their relationship and had simply walked away with her tail between her legs. Not this time. Good or bad, she wanted honesty about why this was over so she wouldn't be left in limbo.

Unfortunately, by the time she reached the clinic all traces of Joe were gone. All that was left was a scribbled note on the door.

Thanks for everything.
Joe x

That was it? After everything they'd been through together all she deserved was an impersonal message that could've been directed at anyone on the island. She crumpled it in her hand in disgust. He hadn't even managed a proper goodbye to her, to Peter, or anyone else who loved him. She wasn't usually prone to violent outbursts of temper but this all seemed such a waste she wanted to punch things or scream out her frustration.

The hub of the village wasn't the place to do it and she knew she couldn't focus on work until she'd worked through this part of the grieving process. She took the path to the beach instead. The same one Joe would had to have taken to make his escape. She wondered what kind of mindset he'd been in when he'd walked this route. Sad? Relieved? Excited to be starting a new adventure?

Perhaps, instead of spending the last hours weeping

and wailing she should've been finding out. There was a small chance he might even have counted on her coming after him and begging him to stay. After all, she hadn't been honest about the strength of her feelings for him. It was too late to find out if that would have stopped him from leaving.

Her eyes were burning again with those useless tears as she reached the top of the hill. Somewhere in the distance she swore she heard a boat splutter into life. She blinked away the tears to see two figures launching the boat from shore. Joe was there, sailing away for good. This was the last time they'd probably ever see each other and she wanted to make sure there was no way back before she moved on. She raced towards the beach like a woman possessed. He didn't look back, probably because he couldn't hear her yelling over the death rattle of the diesel engine. It was up to her to make him listen.

She kicked off her shoes and didn't think twice before wading out into the water. Joe had taught her not to overthink and complicate matters but to simply jump right in and see where she ended up. Soon the boat would be too far out for her to reach. She gulped in one last breath before diving into the unknown.

Swimming out to a lover who'd jumped on a boat to escape her was either the most romantic gesture ever or the action of a desperate woman who had serious issues about letting go. It was impossible to gauge which way he'd take her action but hopefully he'd spot her soon before she drowned and became some sort of tragic folklore story. She didn't really want to spend eternity wailing for her lost love when she still had a life to get back to at the end of all this.

When she'd expelled all the oxygen in her lungs trying to reach him, she popped her head above the water and waved. The last thing she saw before she sank under the water again was Joe getting to his feet. At least she'd had one final look before she went to her watery grave. That would make the soulful songs about the lonely English-woman who drowned chasing the handsome traveller all the more poignant.

'What the hell are you doing?' Joe was reaching down through the water to grab hold of her. A hero truly worthy of becoming part of Yasi folklore.

She climbed into the boat with the help of two pairs of male hands. Excellent, she had a local to regale the rest of the island with tales of her daring escapade. Which was fine if she benefited somehow from this recklessness and didn't make a complete ass of herself. The latter seemed the more likely outcome as she was sitting between two bemused men like a bedraggled mermaid they'd accidentally caught in their fishing net.

'I. Thought. You'd. Gone.' Her teeth were chattering with the shock of what she'd just done more than from the cold.

Joe pulled a sweater from his bag and draped it around her shoulders. 'I had to wait until we could take the boat out again. It's stormy out there.'

Only now he'd pointed it out did she realise the skies had clouded over again, matching her unsettled heart.

'I want to know the real reason you're leaving now.'

'You're crazy. *This* is crazy!'

'You drove me to it so the least you can do is be honest with me.' It was true in every sense. She'd never have done anything so impulsive before meeting him, never have felt the need if she hadn't have fallen so hard for him.

He stood up, rubbed his hands over his scalp and sat down again. 'I can't believe you did something so stupid.'

'You're the one running away from this when we both know we have something special. In my book that's equally idiotic.'

His sigh came from somewhere deep inside him. Somewhere the truth was probably hiding. 'I told you what happened in Afghanistan. I don't get close, I don't get hurt. Simple.'

He wasn't saying he didn't love her, didn't want to be with her. Reading between the lines, it was because of those reasons he was leaving. Her big brave army doc was afraid to admit to his feelings because of things that might never happen. It was something she could relate to when she'd spent her whole life trying to pre-empt the negative outcome of every situation.

'That's not living. Loving someone, being loved, is part of life. You're the one playing it safe when you know sometimes the biggest risk brings the greatest rewards. What happened to going with the flow? Unless you missed it, things were flowing pretty great until you jumped into this boat and headed out to sea.' A destination that hadn't yet been corrected. If she didn't get through to him soon she'd be making the return journey with only a very tactful islander pretending not to notice her pouring her heart out.

'I don't want you to get hurt.' He took her hand and rubbed the heat back into her fingers, showing he was always tending to her needs without even thinking about it.

'You couldn't hurt me any more than you did by walking out on me without giving us a chance. I want to be with you. Beyond that we'll just see what happens.'

'Damn. You got really bossy in the space of just a few days.' He was smiling as he linked his fingers through hers but she could see the turmoil in his eyes. It was going to be down to her to convince him to take a chance on love. The knowledge he wanted to be with her was powerful enough motivation for her.

'I prefer to think of it as becoming more decisive. I'm taking charge of my life and I want you to be part of it.

I love you, Joe Braden.' Her heart was pounding like a drum as she put it all on the line for him. Joe wasn't the only one taking a risk here. After everything she'd been through, starting a new relationship was like setting foot on Yasi all over again. She had no clue what she was letting herself in for and could only cross her fingers and hope that it would all turn out good in the end.

'And I love this crazy, impulsive Emily. She sounds like the ideal travelling companion for lots of fun new adventures.'

Her heart felt as though it was beating for the first time it was so full of happiness to hear those words and know he meant them.

'So what's the plan from here?' She wanted to go with the momentum, wherever it took them.

'Well, there's a little place I know where we can reconnect and take some time out before we commit to that next step. Perhaps we could take a detour and get our captain to drop us off across the bay before the storm moves in.'

Another shiver rippled up and down Emily's spine, this time with anticipation. It was the ideal place to truly get to know each other and make plans for a future.

One thing was sure, with Joe in her life she'd never be boring again.

EPILOGUE

EMILY WOULD NEVER have believed she'd be back on Yasi Island within a year, much less for a wedding. Her wedding. She looked across at Joe, her husband-to-be, so handsome standing barefoot next to her on the beach. They were never going to have a traditional ceremony and had decided to incorporate elements from Fijian culture into their day.

'Dearly beloved, we are gathered here today to join this man and this woman in holy matrimony.' Peter give them both a smile. Having him officiate made this day truly special, as did having the rest of her family here with them. There was quite a crowd assembled on the beach, all dressed in their finery.

Her wedding dress was a simple, white, strapless gown and Joe had gone with his white shirt and linen trousers. The festive garlands the islanders had bestowed on them, including the ring of flowers in her hair, brought a bright splash of colour to proceedings. Sou, Miriama, her stepmother, and all the other women from the village wore the traditional dresses made from tapa cloth and decorated with the red clay paint that had brought her and Joe so close that special day. The men, bar her father in his Hawaiian-style shirt, were in full warrior costume—she finally got to see the grass skirts! It was all so exotic and exciting it was no wonder she'd found it so hard to settle back home.

After she and Joe had spent the second week of her trip together almost twenty-four hours a day, it hadn't taken much persuading for him to go back to England with her. They'd tried to make it work there but ultimately she'd been the one craving everything Yasi had brought into her life. The regimented schedule had suddenly become too stifling for her and she'd seen Joe's relief when she'd finally admitted it. They didn't have to box themselves into a suburban life in order to be together and he'd proposed when she'd uttered those very words to him.

It had taken a few months to get their affairs in order but they'd both agreed they wanted their new start to begin where they'd first fallen in love. She was looking forward to spending time with Peter again but they hadn't made definite plans to make the island their permanent home. There was a whole world waiting for them out there.

'I do.' Joe gave his promise to love, honour and comfort her, and Emily did the same in return. They'd been there for each other through so much already, to the point she wasn't even wearing her cover-up for her wedding day and his nightmares were becoming rarer with every passing night they spent in each other's arms.

They exchanged simple gold wedding bands as a token of their pledge of love for one another before her stepbrother pronounced them husband and wife and gave them permission to kiss in front of everyone.

'I've never kissed a married woman before,' Joe said when they finally came up for air.

'Well, make sure it's only *your* wife you're kissing,' she said with a grin to match his. 'Wife' was a title she'd worn before but it no longer defined her. She was still Emily. This ring simply meant she was privileged to be sharing the rest of her life with Joe, and vice versa.

'There's no one else I would want to do this with.' He took her hand and kissed her wedding finger, a sign he was talking about his next great adventure and not just a snog here and there. They were in this together.

As the *vakatara*—the orchestra—struck up their percussion instruments and the *matana*—dancers—assembled to begin the celebrations, Emily counted every one of her blessings. The biggest one of all she was yet to share with her new husband. She rested her hand on her slightly rounded belly. In seven months they would embark on a new chapter of their lives and all the new adventures parenthood would bring them.

* * * * *

*If you enjoyed this story, check out these
other great reads from Karin Baine*

*THE DOCTOR'S FORBIDDEN FLING
A KISS TO CHANGE HER LIFE
FRENCH FLING TO FOREVER*

All available now!

MILLS & BOON®

EXCLUSIVE EXCERPT

Could a miracle in maternity reunite paediatrician
Max Ainsley with his estranged wife, Annabelle
Brookes, in time for Christmas?

Read on for a sneak preview of
THE NURSE'S CHRISTMAS GIFT
*the first book in the heart-warming
festive Medical quartet*
CHRISTMAS MIRACLES IN MATERNITY

"It's still there, isn't it, despite everything?"

Annabelle frowned, moving under one of the street
lamps along the edge of a park. "What is?"

"That old spark."

She'd felt that spark the second she'd laid eyes on
Max all those years ago. But he wasn't talking about
way back then. He was talking about right now.

"Yes," she whispered.

She wished to hell it weren't. But she wasn't going
to pay truth back with a lie.

"Anna..." He took her hand and eased them off the
path and into the dark shadows of a nearby bench.

She sat down, before she fell down. His voice...
She would recognise that tone anywhere. He sat beside
her, still holding her hand.

"You've changed," he said.

"So have you. You seem..." She shook her head,

unable to put words to her earlier thoughts. Or maybe it was that she wasn't sure she should.

"That bad, huh?"

"No. Not at all."

He grinned, the flash of his teeth sending a shiver over her. "That good, then, huh?"

Annabelle laughed and nudged him with her shoulder. "You wish."

"I actually do."

When his fingers shifted from her hand to just beneath her chin, the shiver turned to a whoosh as all the breath left her body, her nerve endings suddenly attuned to Max's every move. And when his head came down, all she felt was anticipation.

THE NURSE'S CHRISTMAS GIFT by Tina Becket

Available November 2016

www.millsandboon.co.uk

MILLS & BOON®

Why shop at millsandboon.co.uk?

Each year, thousands of romance readers find their perfect read at millsandboon.co.uk. That's because we're passionate about bringing you the very best romantic fiction. Here are some of the advantages of shopping at www.millsandboon.co.uk:

* **Get new books first**—you'll be able to buy your favourite books one month before they hit the shops

* **Get exclusive discounts**—you'll also be able to buy our specially created monthly collections, with up to 50% off the RRP

* **Find your favourite authors**—latest news, interviews and new releases for all your favourite authors and series on our website, plus ideas for what to try next

* **Join in**—once you've bought your favourite books don't forget to register with us to rate, review and join in the discussions

Visit **www.millsandboon.co.uk**
for all this and more today!